Previous Books in the Series:

Criss Cross

Winter Memorial (a short story)

Cross Fire

Even in the darkest of times, there is always hope, flitting in and out of sight like a firefly in the night, and you need only catch it. ~C.C.~

To everyone who was there for me while I was fighting my way through hard times, for reminding me that I wasn't alone.

To my readers, whose enjoyment of this series inspires me to continue writing.

This book contains subjects and situations that might be difficult for some readers.

Psalm 142, A song of David

Look and see, there is no one at my right hand;
no one is concerned for me.
I have no refuge;
no one cares for my life.
I cry to you, LORD;
I say, "You are my refuge,
my portion in the land of the living."
Listen to my cry,
for I am in desperate need;
rescue me from those who pursue me,
for they are too strong for me.
Set me free from my prison,
that I may praise your name . . .

—(Psalm 142:4–7 NIV)

Crossed Off

A Holly Novel
By C.C. Warrens

1

*a*sh drifted down around me like snowflakes from the night sky as I watched the women's shelter smolder. It had been my safe haven for nearly a year after I fled to New York—a place for my body and spirit to heal—and now it was gone.

I knelt on the sidewalk in a state of numb disbelief as firemen scoured the rubble for bodies. I didn't want to watch them collect the tiny remains of children, but I couldn't pull my eyes away.

"Sweetheart."

The soothing Southern drawl drew me from my thoughts, and I looked at Marx as he crouched in front of me. His green eyes—the vibrant shade of grass in the early spring—shimmered with concern.

"You're hurtin' yourself."

I didn't realize my fingers were clenched into white-knuckled fists in my lap until he pried them open, revealing the bloody grooves my fingernails had made in my palms.

"This isn't your fault," he said. "I know you're blamin' yourself right now, but you didn't cause that fire."

I stared at the bloody crescents on my palms as I spoke, my voice oddly hollow. "He killed them. Because of me."

I could imagine my foster brother lighting the match that set the shelter ablaze. He would've stood by to listen to the screams and to watch a piece of my life crumble.

Collin was cold and calculating, and he had learned a long time ago that the best way to hurt me was to hurt the people who matter to me.

He targeted the shelter because I had felt safe there, and because I had grown to care about the other women. I may not have started the fire, but flames of guilt still scorched my insides.

Marx cupped my face in his hands. "That doesn't make it your fault."

My gaze slid past him to the cloud of dark smoke that clung to the night sky, and a tremor crept into my voice. "They're all dead, even the children."

Faces flashed through my mind, and I had to draw on the emotional barrier I had created as a child to wall off the rising grief. I didn't have the strength to deal with it right now.

"I know," Marx said, his tone somber. "Let's get you back to my apartment where it's safe."

He didn't wait for me to argue or agree; he gripped under my arms and lifted me up, setting me gently on my feet.

No place on this earth is safe, I thought. The shelter had been a *safe place*, until its walls became a flaming cage that trapped everyone inside.

I glanced at Jordan, who was leaning back against a parked car, his blue eyes reflecting the grief I couldn't let myself feel. He had met some of these people just a few weeks ago; he had stood outside this building with me when it was still whole.

"We have a survivor!" a distant voice called out.

Hope kindled inside me even as doubt flickered through my mind: *how could anyone survive that?* I tried to follow the rescue workers, who were rushing toward the voice, but Marx caught my arm to stop me.

"It's too dangerous, Holly."

I slipped from his grip and took off running before he could catch me again. I skirted around the ruins to the back. Over the whooshing of water hoses and shouting voices, I heard it—a child's cry.

I could feel the heat rolling off the burned remains of the shelter, and the ground beneath my feet shifted as I stepped closer. Firemen were carefully removing hot debris from where the child was trapped.

Jordan came up behind me, and I braced myself for a fight. "I'm not leaving."

He held out his hands. "Okay, but could you at least step back from the building? Please. A fire could've weakened the foundation, which means the ground you're standing on could sink or slide at any moment."

He sounded calm, but I had practiced self-defense with him long enough to recognize when he was poised to move. He was ready to grab me if the ground gave way under my feet. I took a few steps back to appease him.

Marx turned the corner, and I tensed at the anger and disapproval on his face. He had told me once that when it came to matters of my safety, he would pick me up and carry me away from danger if I decided to be difficult.

If he tried that now—

"We got her!" one of the rescue workers shouted.

Coal-black hair coated in ash identified the surviving child before the firemen had even pulled her free.

"Maya," I gasped.

I rushed forward when they finally dragged her clear of the wreckage. Someone told me to stay back, and someone else's hands caught nothing but open air as I ducked past them.

"Maya," I called again.

Little eight-year-old Maya lifted her head at the sound of my voice. She wriggled away from the stranger and stumbled the few steps toward me.

I dropped to my knees, and she flung herself into my arms, her small, trembling hands clutching at me as she sobbed. I wrapped my arms around her and held her tightly.

Thank you, Jesus.

My heart ached for everyone who was lost in the fire, but I was thankful for her—sweet Maya who loved hopscotch and fruit snacks.

"It's okay, Maya, it's gonna be okay," I said. I didn't know how it would be okay, but I would do everything I could to make it so.

"Mommy!" she cried.

Her desperate, screaming sobs threatened to break through the protective wall I had erected, and I squeezed my eyes shut, silently begging God for strength. I couldn't fall apart.

I hugged her closer, wrapping her in as much safety and security as I could. Gradually, her screams dissolved into hiccuping cries, but her small fingers still clung to me as if I were the only thing holding her to earth.

"Ma'am, we need to check her for injuries," a female paramedic said as she approached.

I looked up at Marx. "I don't wanna let her go. Will you help me up?"

He gripped under my arms and helped me to my feet once again. I cradled Maya against me. She was small for an eight-year-old, but she was still heavier than anything I was used to carrying.

"Do you want me to carry her?" Jordan offered.

"I've got her," I said, shifting her weight before following the paramedic to the ambulance.

I lowered Maya onto the edge of the vehicle and she cried harder. "Where's my mommy?"

Beth Anne, her mother, had run the women's shelter, and she had been kind to so many, especially me. I couldn't tell Maya that her mother was probably dead, but I couldn't promise she was alive either.

I knelt in front of her as I struggled to find the right words. "The firemen are looking for her."

Her lower lip trembled.

"Were you in the pantry?" I asked. The pantry had been lined by thick brick walls, and I was certain that was where the firemen had pulled her from.

She sniffed and nodded. "I was sneaking fruit snacks."

Her sneakiness was probably the reason she was alive. I smoothed my hands over her hair and forced a smile. "That's okay. I used to sneak food too."

She rubbed her dirty nose. "Really?"

"Yep. Sweet things."

That was actually how I had met her mother. I had broken into the shelter one night, trying to find a safe place to sleep, and found a shelf full of pastries. Beth Anne had walked in on me.

"Mommy says I shouldn't sneak. She says always to ask." Another hiccuping cry escaped her. "They're not gonna find my mommy, are they?"

I wanted desperately to take away her pain, but I could only reassure her she wasn't as alone as she probably felt. "I don't know, sweetie. But I'm gonna stay with you, okay?"

Her dark eyes, liquid with a pain and loss no child should ever have to know, lifted to meet mine. "Promise?"

"Cross my heart." I nodded toward the paramedic. "This nice lady needs to check and make sure you're not hurt. Can you let her do that?"

Maya shook her head before burying her face in my chest.

"Nothing that's gonna hurt. Just like a doctor checkup," I explained, but she only sniffled and shook her head again.

Jordan crouched beside me. "Hi, Miss Maya. Do you remember me?"

She peeked at him shyly and nodded. "Sheriff with the shiny badge."

He had come with me the last time I visited the shelter, and she had been fascinated by his badge.

"That's right," he said, offering her a warm smile. "There's a lot going on tonight, and I could really use a deputy. Do you know what a deputy is?"

She sat up straighter and wiped at her nose. "No."

"It's a really important job. It means you would be my backup, and you would ask people lots of questions and then tell me what they say."

"I like to ask questions."

"Good, because I need help." He pulled out his sheriff's badge and tapped her gently on the nose with it as he said, "I dub you my deputy for the evening." He handed her the badge. "Make sure you flash this badge if anybody doubts it."

Maya nodded seriously and showed the badge to the paramedic. Her chin trembled with emotion as she demanded, "What's your name?"

The woman smiled. "Julie. What's yours?"

"Maya. I'm a d . . . a dep-depity, and you have to answer my questions."

"Of course, deputy. What kind of questions?" the woman asked, taking advantage of the distraction to wrap a blood pressure cuff around Maya's arm.

"What's your favorite color?"

Maya grilled the paramedic as the woman checked her for injuries. I offered Jordan a fragile smile of gratitude. He had given her something other than her traumatic experience to focus on.

Marx stood off to the side as he spoke with one of the rescue workers, his detective's badge visible on his belt. His expression was grim.

I stood and whispered to Maya, "I'm gonna talk to Marx over here for just a minute, but you'll be able to see me, and I'll come right back."

Uncertainty darkened her eyes, but she bravely nodded before turning to the paramedic to demand what kinds of cats she had and if they all had tails.

I folded my arms and approached Marx just as the worker was departing. "Well?"

He kept his voice soft. "No other survivors."

I released a shuddering breath and looked back at the tiny girl on the ambulance. Maya was now an orphan. I knew all too well how that felt. I had been orphaned when I was just a year older than she was.

"How many?" I asked.

Marx's eyes glimmered with concern at my cool demeanor, but he answered, "They found the remains of five women and two children."

Seven. Seven lives lost in a single night.

"What caused the fire?"

"They'll need to investigate further, but they suspect arson given the degree of the damage."

I nodded. I had expected that.

"Holly—"

"What about Maya? I know her dad passed away, but do we know if she has any other family members in the city?"

"Accordin' to one of the firemen who was friends with Beth Anne's late husband, her only remainin' family is her maternal grandparents. They're in Africa on a missionary trip."

It took a moment for the implications of his words to sink in, and then my insides clenched with dread. "No."

"She has no family in the area, Holly, so until her grandparents arrive, children's services has to place her with a temporary foster family."

The thought was unbearable. I knew that there were good people willing to open their homes to children who had no one left, but there were also people who would destroy a sweet, innocent child like Maya.

"They can't do that. I won't let them do that to her."

"I realize you had some bad experiences in foster—"

"Bad?" I interrupted, astonished by his choice of words. *Bad* fell unbelievably short.

He scrubbed a hand over his face and sighed. "What do you want me to do, sweetheart? There are procedures for this for a reason."

I didn't know what I wanted him to do. I didn't want to burden him with this, especially so soon after the death of his best friend, Captain McNera, but I couldn't let Maya be placed with strangers. Her entire world had just burned down around her, and she needed stability and love.

"I'll take her home with me," I decided.

"Your apartment isn't safe," he said. "Collin broke in last month, and four months before that, you were attacked in your own kitchen. Not only that, you have no history from the time you left foster care until the time you met me. They're never gonna let her stay with you."

I had lived in hiding for the past ten and a half years, moving from place to place in the shadows, because I was afraid of this very thing. My foster brother, Collin, had tracked me down to dismantle my life.

He had a penchant for inflicting pain on others, and he had developed a fascination with me that I couldn't understand. I only knew that he terrified me more than anything on this earth, and it was only a matter of time before he came for me again.

"Then what do I do?" I asked, desperate. I needed to protect her from further pain, to preserve what was left of her innocence. "She just lost everything she knows. Her mom, her home, her friends. There has to be something I can do."

Marx looked at Maya for a long moment. "Okay. If it means that much to you, then I'll figure somethin' out."

I was so relieved that I could've hugged him, but I was afraid that if I did, I would fall apart. I straightened my shoulders and said, "Thank you."

I returned to find Maya interrogating Jordan. She must have run out of questions for Julie the Paramedic. I was glad to see that she was relatively unhurt beneath the layer of grime.

"I don't know how I feel about answering that question," Jordan said, rubbing his chin theatrically.

Maya flashed his badge and said, "You have to. I have the shiny badge."

"What question is he avoiding?" I asked, crouching in front of her.

Jordan grinned and said, "She wants to know if I'm gonna marry you someday like they do in the fairy tales."

My stomach did an uneasy little flip-flop and heat crept into my cheeks. "That's . . . you should . . . not answer that."

His grin widened. "I'm trying to *not answer*, but she's a stickler for the rules, and I don't have a lawyer. Besides, it's not my fault she thinks we'd make a nice couple."

"There will be no coupling. I don't . . . couple." It had been fifteen years since I had any kind of relationship that could be considered "coupling," and I had been thirteen at the time.

Jordan leaned toward Maya and whispered something too soft for me to hear. She looked at me and giggled.

Oh boy.

"What did you just say?" I asked suspiciously.

"That's between me and my deputy," he said, but a mischievous light danced in his eyes.

I narrowed my eyes at him, but before I could speak, Marx came over. "Maya, I'm Detective Marx."

She looked up at him and scrunched up her face. "You talk funny."

"I'm from Georgia. We all talk funny," he replied without a trace of humor. "How would you feel about comin' to stay with me for a few days? Just until your grandparents arrive."

She scrutinized him and then looked at me, uncertain. She had probably seen enough angry husbands and boyfriends outside the shelter to make her leery of any man she didn't know.

"I'm staying with him too," I said, then whispered, "He's not as scary as he looks."

14

Her wariness instantly evaporated, and she nodded. "Okay. I'll stay with Holly because she's my friend, but you can be there too. Do you have a cat? I like cats."

Marx blinked, probably at the way all her sentences ran together without pause. "No, but we do have a dog."

She perked up. "I like dogs. Is she a big dog or little dog? Does she have long hair? Can I braid it? What's her name?"

I gave Marx a questioning look, silently inquiring if he was certain about opening his home to her.

He looked a little overwhelmed by her personality, but he sighed. "What's one more pair of little feet on my couch?"

He was as particular about his couch as he was his car. I had put my shoes on his couch once and he had stolen the offending shoes. I still hadn't figured out where he'd hidden them.

"But you can answer her five million questions. And teach her to breathe between sentences or she's gonna pass out," he added, and I smiled. "Now come on. Let's get you girls to bed."

I extended my hand to Maya, and she placed her small hand in mine—some of her fingertips wrapped in Finding Nemo Band-Aids—and hopped down from the ambulance.

"Mr. Detective," she began as we walked toward Marx's car. When he grunted, she said, "I'm a *deppity* now. Does that mean I can use the radio?"

"You're not tall enough to use my radio." He opened the rear car door for her, and she climbed in. "Ask me again when you've grown a few more feet."

"Oh, okay." She buckled herself in with unexpected steadiness. Children were far more resilient than adults.

I climbed in after her, and Jordan leaned in the open doorway. "I'll be by to pick up my badge tomorrow and get a full report, deputy." He turned his attention to me. "I'll see you tomorrow, Holly."

He lingered in the opening as if he were longing for something more than a brief exchange of words.

"Good night, and thank you," I said.

He smiled and closed the door. Maya yawned and slumped against me in the backseat, her eyelids growing heavier with sleep. I brushed a stray hair from her forehead as she burrowed deeper against me.

Tomorrow I would have to shatter her world all over again by telling her that her mother was dead. How was I going to do that?

2

I curled beneath a blanket in the corner of Marx's leather couch with a mug of warm milk, sugar, and nutmeg. When I had a sleepless night as a little girl, my mother used to make this to help me relax. She had called it a warm milk toddy. I always thought the name sounded funny.

I took a small sip and let the sweet flavor of home trickle down my throat and ease some of my tension. I missed home and my family.

I glanced at Maya, who was sound asleep on the other end of the couch, the blanket still wrapped around her body like a little burrito. She had fallen asleep in the backseat of the car, and I didn't have the heart to wake her.

Marx had carried her upstairs and tucked her in on the couch, ash and all. I hoped it wouldn't ruin his nice leather.

Riley padded over and sat down in front of the couch, resting his muzzle on my knee. His soulful brown eyes reflected the sadness hanging in the air.

He could sense that something was wrong, and I knew he wanted to comfort me, to protect me, but there was nothing he could do to protect me from an enemy as invisible and oppressive as grief.

I reached down and scratched behind his ear. "Good boy."

He panted happily at the recognition. Riley was a German shepherd that had been retired from the police force. I had found him dying from a bullet wound in a cluttered parking lot not too long ago—though our history traveled further back than that—and we were taking care of each other until we found his owner.

I rested my head on my fist as my eyelids grew sticky with sleep. It became harder and harder to peel them back open after they fell shut.

My mind started to drift into shadows of memory, dark places I didn't want to go, when a voice whispered in my ear, "One down, four to go."

I sucked in a frightened breath and nearly leaped off the couch. I visually scanned the room, expecting to see my foster brother standing in front of me with a taunting smirk, but he wasn't there.

My eyes landed on the front door—it was still locked—and then moved to the windows. They were all secure.

He wasn't there.

Riley wouldn't be sleeping beneath my feet if he were. He had made it his canine mission to protect me from any man who made me anxious. Which was most of them. He had his work cut out for him.

I sank back against the cushions in relief and ran a hand through my hair. It was only a dream.

One down, four to go.

I didn't understand those words when Collin had Beth Anne recite them for me earlier tonight. But in the wake of the fire, their meaning haunted me.

Maya whimpered and twitched beneath the blanket. I leaned closer to hear the word she was whimpering: Mommy.

I gathered her into my arms as she began to cry, and let her rest her head in my lap. I murmured soothing words to her and stroked her hair until she cried herself back to sleep.

We spent the night dozing, watching cartoons, and naming the snowflakes that fluttered down outside the window.

With an eight-year-old's logic, Maya decided that unique snowflakes deserved unique names, and so she named half the snowflakes Jesus—because He was one of a kind—and a good portion of the rest, unsurprisingly, were named Jordan. Followed by John and Jacob.

I kept waiting for Jingleheimer and Schmidt to make an appearance, but they didn't. She was probably too young to know that song.

Marx was awake and stirring by six that morning, and he emerged from his room to find Maya sleeping on one of the stools with her face less than an inch from a bowl of unfinished Lucky Mallows.

"Well, that has disaster written all over it."

"I'm too tired to pick her up," I admitted, resting my chin on the back of the couch.

"You shouldn't be carryin' her anyway. She's nearly as big as you." He plucked the marshmallow-coated spoon from between her limp fingers and scooped her up. He carried her back to the couch and laid her down gently. "You didn't get any sleep," he observed as he tucked the blanket around her.

I blinked at him through bleary eyes. "I'm okay." I stood and stretched onto my tiptoes. A yawn crept up on me and mutated into something big enough to swallow my head.

"Go get some sleep," he insisted.

I shook my head. "I'm not leaving Maya. She'll be scared when she wakes up. And I have to tell her about her mom."

"I'll tell her. Go to bed."

I realized as I tried to think of an argument against going to bed that I was too tired to think. "Okay, but just . . ." Another yawn broke in, and the rest of my words tumbled out in disjointed syllables. I meant to say "just for a few minutes," but I was too exhausted to repeat myself.

I shuffled into the spare bedroom with Riley on my heels, locked the door, and crawled limply beneath the covers.

3

I blinked at the fuzzy red numbers on the alarm clock, trying to make sense of them. I had been dead to the world for five hours. My brain felt like pudding from too little sleep, but I needed to get up and check on Maya.

I got dressed in a daze, and paused with my hand on the doorknob when I realized I was wearing two different socks: one was hot pink and had "Tuesday" stamped on the side of it—was it Tuesday?—and the other one looked like someone had upchucked Skittles on my foot.

I decided I didn't care.

A familiar anxiety prickled beneath my skin when I opened the door and found Jordan in the living room. I wasn't used to being alone behind closed doors with him, unless we were hiding from gun-toting drug dealers, but the anxiety faded when Maya popped up on the other side of the couch.

I did a quick visual sweep of the apartment for Marx, caught sight of the nearly empty coffeepot, and realized he must have gone to work.

Maya let out a mischievous giggle as she flitted back and forth in front of the wall-mounted movie shelf like a firefly. I suddenly realized what she and Jordan were doing when he plucked a movie from what was probably the *B* section of Marx's alphabetized movie shelf, handed it to Maya, and she flitted to the end of the shelf to wiggle it into the *Z* section.

I felt a smile curl the corners of my lips. Marx was extremely organized. He had explained his immaculate apartment to me with one sentence: "I don't like chaos."

I had tipped the pictures on his hallway wall a few times just to drive him crazy, and then I had destroyed his kitchen, but the kitchen was an accident.

"You know he's gonna blame me for that," I said. I had no doubt I would be his prime suspect. And rightfully so.

Jordan gave another movie to Maya as he glanced over his shoulder at me. "Hey, Sleeping Beauty."

I blinked, startled, then replied inadequately, "Hi."

Jordan had a way of knocking me off balance with just his words. He handed out compliments like candy, and they probably had no more significance to him than that.

Abruptly self-conscious of my appearance, I tried to ignore my sleep-rumpled hair as I tucked it behind my ears, and didn't dare look down at my mismatched socks. I cleared my throat and turned my attention to Maya. "Bath time."

I would have to see if I had anything that might fit her once she was clean. She looked like a little ash-monster with an afro.

She pouted. "Do I have to?"

"Most definitely." I opened the bathroom door for her, and she gave Jordan a put-upon look before trudging into the bathroom to meet her terrible fate of soap and shampoo. I listened for the sound of water before walking into the kitchen.

"You're such an authoritarian," Jordan said, sitting down at the peninsula.

"I had plenty of practice with other kids in my foster homes." I stood on my toes to peer into the cupboard above the stove. I didn't see the box of cereal. Ooh, but there were Pop Tarts. Really far away Pop Tarts.

Hmm.

"Need a hand?" Jordan asked.

"Nope." I grabbed a spatula from the utensil drawer and stretched up as far as I could to bat at the box. It scooted sideways instead of forward.

Ugh.

"Holly—"

"I don't need help." I tried again and knocked the box backward. Oh my gosh, I hated being short. I gave the cupboard a hateful glare.

"Okay, I'm just gonna get it for you before you start climbing on the counter." Jordan came around the peninsula into the kitchen.

I was five-two—well, almost, but it sounded better than five-one-and-a-quarter—and Jordan was ten inches taller than me. He could reach things I could only gaze at longingly.

He paused at the invisible four-foot border that extended around me like a bubble. It made me feel safer, and he made an effort to respect it.

I raised my eyebrows at him, and he laughed. "You're not gonna give me permission to cross over, are you?"

"Nope."

"What if I just move really quickly?"

I pointed the spatula at him. "I'm armed."

He grinned and propped a shoulder against the refrigerator, clearly not frightened. "Border patrol usually have better weapons than pancake flippers."

When my stomach grumbled, I glanced up at the elusive box of Pop Tarts, then at one of the stools. I could drag one over and—

"Pick a number between one and ten," Jordan suggested.

My eyes skipped from the stools to him. "Why?"

"If I guess your number, you let me get the Pop Tarts down."

I folded my arms in disbelief. "That's your prize? Getting the Pop Tarts down? What if you lose?"

"I won't lose."

Well, somebody was confident in his mind-reading abilities. "Okay, fine." I was going to go with three. "Go ahead and guess."

"Three."

My jaw dropped. "How . . ."

He smiled mysteriously as he stepped forward and plucked the box from the cupboard. "Three was your favorite number when we were kids. You liked it because it rhymes with tree."

I didn't even remember that. I just always picked the number three. "My favorite number could've changed."

"It was a risk I was willing to take." He handed me the box of Pop Tarts. "You know you could just accept help the first time someone offers."

I crinkled my nose at him as I walked away with my edible loot. "Don't lecture." I unwrapped one of the packages as I asked, "How did Maya handle the news about her mom?"

He puffed out a heavy breath. "She cried . . . a lot, called Marx a liar, and then clung to me for an hour or so until she finally stopped crying. Marx told her that her grandparents would be here in a few days."

A few days. That was how many days I had left then. I had promised Maya I wouldn't leave her, and I would stay until she was safely in the hands of her grandparents.

But then I would have to find a way to sneak away from Marx and Jordan. If I stayed, I would only endanger the lives of the people I cared about. They might be willing to risk it, but I wasn't.

"Thank you for comforting her. And"—I held up my frosted strawberry pastry—"for getting the Pop Tarts down for me."

Amusement sparkled in his eyes. "You know, if you're dead set on getting them yourself next time, you could sit on my shoulders for a boost."

The mere mental image made me choke on the bite I had just taken.

He laughed. "Is that a no?"

I swallowed the disagreeable chunk of pastry and clarified, "That's a never." I did have *some* dignity.

I heard the scrape of a key in the lock, and the front door opened a second later. Marx came in and moved through his usual routine: tossing his keys on the side table, stripping out of his coat and hanging it on the hook by the door, and tucking his shoes against the wall beside the front door.

A sneaky idea took shape in my mind as my eyes lingered on his shoes. I still hadn't been able to find my sneakers, which he'd hidden, so I was going to return the favor. Those shoes would do.

His gaze skimmed over Jordan before finding me. "Hey, sweet pea. You get some sleep?"

I nodded. "You're back early."

He sighed as he strode to the peninsula and dropped a folder onto the counter. "I need to talk to Maya."

I glanced at the folder with concern. "She's in the shower. Why do you need to talk to her?"

I knew the answer even as I asked the question. Maya was the only survivor of a crime, both a victim and a potential witness.

"I need to know if she saw or heard anythin'. She was too distressed this mornin' to answer any questions."

"Have you found anything out yet? About the fire?"

"It was definitely arson. It looks like somebody added accelerant to the perimeter of the buildin' and then threw cocktails through the windows. There was no way for the people inside to safely exit."

My bite of Pop Tart slid uncomfortably down my throat as I thought about those poor women and children trapped in that inferno. I set the rest on the counter, no longer hungry.

"Who all was in the building?" Jordan asked.

"Unfortunately, we don't know that yet. If Beth Anne kept a record of who was stayin' there, it was lost in the fire. The coroner has only managed to identify the remains of two of the seven bodies so far."

"Can I see who?" I asked.

He slid the folder to me, and after a second of hesitation, I opened it. My stomach cramped with pain at the sight of Beth Anne's picture. She had been kind to me when the world had been nothing but cruel. Without her generosity, I might have lived on the streets until I disappeared like so many other young women.

I forced myself to turn to the next sheet, surprised to find that I recognized the woman. "Angie."

"Angela Mayberry," Marx confirmed. "She had a metal implant in her leg with a number on it that helped us identify her."

"She was in and out of the shelter while I was there. Always talking about fixing her relationship with her husband, but she was always back a month after leaving."

"Unfortunately, that's not unusual," Marx said, his tone resigned.

"Rachel struggled with that too. She was in and out probably three times during the year I was there."

"Do you remember her last name?"

"Glass, maybe?" I was terrible with names. I could probably fill the pages of a book with the names I got wrong. "Why?"

"If she had a similar pattern to Angela, there's a chance she might have been there last night," he explained.

Oh no.

I closed the folder and dropped on to one of the stools. I hadn't even thought about Rachel until now, but I should've realized she might still be there. "When Jordan and I stopped by the shelter last month, Maya said Rachel's husband kept coming around, banging on the door, angry that she wouldn't come out."

"Did she ever tell you anythin' about her husband?" Marx asked.

I thought back on conversations I had overheard between Rachel and the other women. "I don't remember much. Just that she said no one would ever believe a hero could be such a monster."

A concerned crease formed between Jordan's eyebrows. "Maybe her husband was in the military, or he's a cop."

Marx grimaced. Their precinct had undergone a massive upheaval after they discovered corruption stemming from the police captain that had trickled all the way down through the ranks.

I hoped, for Marx's sake, that Rachel's husband wasn't a member of the police force.

"I'll call Sully and see what he can find out about Rachel and her charmin' husband," Marx said.

Sully was the computer genius who worked for Marx's precinct. I had never met him, but I had overheard Marx talking to him on more than one occasion.

I decided to search my room for something that Maya could wear. I didn't have much more in the way of clothes than she did. Hers had all burned, and most of mine had been stolen. A long T-shirt would have to do until we could get to the store.

I knocked on the bathroom door and then pressed my ear against it. Maya was singing in the shower, some off-key tune about "let it go." Those were apparently the only words to the song, or at least the only words she knew.

I smiled as I cracked the door open and set the T-shirt and towel on the counter for her. Marx was just ending his call when I walked back into the kitchen, and the expression on his face was grim.

"Rachel's husband is a fireman."

I absorbed that revelation as I sat back down. Rachel's abusive husband was a firefighter, and the shelter she may have been hiding in had burned to the ground?

Jordan was thinking along the same suspicious lines. "Either that's a very unlikely coincidence, or—"

"Mr. Glass likes to start fires as much as he likes to put them out?" Marx offered. "I'm not jumpin' to any conclusions just yet, but he's definitely at the top of my suspect list."

"Do you think Collin's involved?" Jordan asked.

My instincts told me Collin had to be involved. He had been at the shelter just minutes before it caught fire, and he had sent me a text from an unknown number asking if I smelled smoke.

At least, I thought the text had been from him. There was no way to be completely certain.

Marx tapped his phone against his palm. "Collin's involved. I just haven't figured out how yet."

"What about the message he had Beth Anne deliver? What do you think he meant by that?"

One down, four to go. I could practically hear Collin's voice whispering those words, every syllable a taunting whisper filled with a frightening promise.

I could count the people I truly cared about in this city on the fingers of one hand: Marx, Jordan, Jace, Sam . . . and Maya, who Collin had tried and failed to kill. I had cared about Beth Anne too, but maybe he counted her and Maya as one. Or maybe he hadn't counted her at all. I had proven that I cared for Maya when I ran two blocks to the shelter to make sure she was safe after he sent me a picture of her playing hopscotch.

The meaning behind his message was clear to me, if no one else.

"I haven't figured that out yet either," Marx admitted.

Maya came bounding out of the bathroom in my purple T-shirt, bringing an end to the conversation. She had something blue wrapped around her waist like a belt.

Marx narrowed his eyes. "Is that my tie?"

Yep, that was his tie.

"It's a sash, and I found it," Maya declared, as if that simple fact made it hers. "And it matches my dress."

"That's a T-shirt," Marx said.

Maya's entire face morphed into a dramatic frown, and she planted her hands on her hips. "You grown-ups have no imagination."

Jordan laughed. "And she hasn't even met Sam yet. I can hardly wait."

Sam was intensely logical, and sometimes trying to have a conversation with him was like talking to a robot.

Marx gestured to the couch. "Why don't you come have a seat, Maya. I'd like to talk to you for a minute."

The lighthearted glow faded from Maya's face, and she gravitated toward me, taking my hand. "No. You're gonna tell me bad things again."

"No more bad news, I promise."

She looked up at me for confirmation, and I tried to give her a reassuring smile. "Okay," she agreed. "But only if Holly can come too."

"Yes, Holly can come too."

I led Maya to the couch and sat down. Judging by how she molded her small body against mine, she had some inkling about what was coming.

Marx asked her about the women at the shelter. Angie and Rachel had both been there last night, as well as a woman named Becky that I had met briefly, but I didn't recognize the names of the other women and children she mentioned.

Something didn't add up, though. There had been seven bodies recovered: five women and two children. Maya had listed off seven names, but she didn't include herself or her mother.

Marx leaned forward on the coffee table, his brow puckered with the same confusion I felt. "You're sure all those women were there last night?"

Maya nodded. "We had dinner, and I got to have Kool-Aid because I was good and did extra chores."

If all those people had been there last night, there should've been eight bodies. Either someone's body hadn't been recovered yet, or someone was missing.

"What happened after dinner?" Marx asked, keeping his tone light.

Maya toyed with the ends of her "sash" as she stared at her lap. "A man came. Mommy . . ." She trailed off, her eyes flooding with tears. "Mommy said for him to go away or she would call the p'lice."

"Did you see this man?"

Maya shook her head. "But Rachel was scared, so I held her hand."

Marx smiled. "That was very nice of you. Why do you think Rachel was so scared?"

One tiny shoulder lifted in a shrug. "She's scared a lot. Her husband is a meanie, and sometimes he comes over and bangs on the door and yells. Mommy says he has a potty mouth, and some potties don't smell very good, so he prob'ly has really bad breath."

I bit back a smile.

"Probably," Marx agreed. "Did your mom say anythin' else to the man?"

Maya nodded. "She said for him to leave her alone, and that she doesn't want nothing to do with him."

Marx looked thoughtful. "When your mom said that, did she say 'leave *me* alone' or 'leave *her* alone'?"

Maya thought about it. "Her."

"Did she mention a name?"

She shook her head and her bottom lip started to tremble. "Did that man hurt my mommy?"

Marx hesitated. "I don't know, sweetheart, but I'll find out."

Maya buried her face against me and whimpered, "I miss my mommy. I want her to come back."

I hugged her tightly and met Marx's eyes. She was too fragile for any more questions. He nodded in silent agreement and stood.

"I'll pay a visit to Mr. Glass in the mornin' and see what he has to say for himself. Right now, I need to meet with Shannon."

I perked up. "Really?"

Shannon was his ex-wife, but he still loved her. If she offered to take him back, I had no doubt he would accept. Unfortunately, they had only managed cool civility since their divorce.

He smiled at my excitement. "Just a business meetin'."

"It's gotta start somewhere."

"I appreciate the optimism. I'll see you tonight."

I looked over my shoulder at Jordan. "We need to find Maya some clothes this afternoon. Mine are too big for her."

I caught the flicker of male dread in his eyes before he masked it with a smile. "Looks like we're going shopping."

"You said you wanted to be just like one of the girls," I reminded him. He had told me once that he would go shopping if that was what it would take to spend time with me. I intended to hold him to that.

He grinned and said, "Yeah, let's not call me *one of the girls* in public."

4

I tugged the sparkly pink hat down over Maya's wealth of hair and sat back on my heels to look at her.

"Pink and sparkly like a princess," I told her, nudging her in front of the department store mirror. The colorful hat did nothing to lift the cloud of grief that hung over her.

I wished I could take it from her. I leaned in and whispered a suggestion that I hoped might bring a smile to her face.

A tiny flame of mischief lit her eyes.

She reached out and tugged on Jordan's shirt, pulling his watchful gaze down to her level. "Your turn." She plucked the hat from her head and held it out to him.

He arched an eyebrow as he took it. "Sparkles aren't really my thing." Then he shrugged, plopped the too-small hat on his head, and inquired, "Well? How do I look?"

Maya squinted and tapped a finger against her lips in a manner that was adorably adult, then shook her head and gave a grunt of disapproval. "Hm-mm."

"Maybe I just need the matching scarf and mittens." He pulled them from the rack and wound the hot pink scarf around his neck before trying to put the mittens on. They were too small for his huge hands.

Maya cupped a hand over her mouth and erupted into giggles. "You're silly."

"You look . . . very pretty," I informed him.

He flashed me a charming grin. "Of course I do."

Maya giggled herself breathless, and I wrapped my arms around her in a hug as she slumped against me.

"Holly." She tipped her head down to look at me. "Can I look like you?"

"Um . . ." I was pretty sure I was about ten shades too pale for that to work out. Not to mention she had midnight black hair and mine was as red as a carrot. "I think God wants you to look like you."

She frowned and toyed with the black beanie on my head, and I understood what she meant.

"Oh, you want an outfit like mine." Skinny jeans, layered tops, and hats it was. It was quite a contrast to the skirts and leggings she usually wore, but there was nothing wrong with change. "Then let's find you some skinny jeans." We set off to find her a couple of mini-me outfits.

We bought matching sparkly blue hats and boots, a few tops and pairs of jeans, and then went to find a restroom to change in after we purchased the clothes.

"Hold on," Jordan said, intercepting us before we could go into the bathroom. He knocked on the door frame and called out, "Anyone in here?"

When no one answered, he motioned for us to follow him inside. He pushed open every stall door to make sure no one was inside. Did he really think Collin might be hiding in a women's restroom?

He must have read the question on my face, because he said, "I'm not taking any chances."

I swallowed and nodded. I had been so focused on Maya that I had forgotten, if only for a moment, how determined Collin was to get to me.

Of course following me to a department store and waiting in the restroom to catch me alone wouldn't be beneath him. Nothing was beneath him.

"Looks clear," Jordan said. "I'm gonna use the restroom real quick while you girls change, and then I'll wait outside the door." He walked back to the door and pushed up the kickstand propping it open. He tapped the dead bolt on the inside. "Lock it."

I flipped the dead bolt after he left. He tested the door once from the outside, but the lock held.

Maya scampered into one of the stalls to put on her new outfit, while I looked between them uneasily. I despised small spaces. I considered changing in the main bathroom just to avoid those narrow, suffocating walls, but I didn't want Maya coming out and seeing the numerous scars I couldn't explain to an eight-year-old. And I had agreed to wear my matching outfit, so . . .

I puffed out a breath and went into the handicap stall, which afforded me a bit more space.

"Holly, do you think I'll be as tall as you one day?" Maya asked, grunting as she pulled on her clothes.

Good grief. I hoped she would be taller. The world was not made for short people. Most people could reach things in their cupboards simply by standing. I had to climb on crap.

And when I saw a kid in a high chair with their feet dangling in the air, I could empathize. It was hideously embarrassing to sit down in a chair only to realize my feet didn't touch the floor.

And then there were the pants . . .

Oh, the pants.

Because who didn't love pants that were so long they dragged behind you like a wedding gown train?

And those weren't even the long ones. Sometimes I could just buy normal-people capris and wear them as pants.

"Um, I think you'll be taller," I decided. "But whatever size you turn out to be, it's how God meant you to be." Sometimes I wondered if He was up there laughing at me: *How's it going* all the way *down there, child? You seem to be having a* little *problem today.*

"Are you all grown-up?"

That was an odd question. "Yeah, why?"

"Because everyone is taller than you."

I frowned as I tugged on my new boots. "Not *everyone.*"

"Yes-huh. Jordan and Marx, and the man with the funny blue hair at the register, and the lady with the—"

33

"Okay," I interrupted. That was about enough of that. She would list every person she had seen in her entire life if I let her continue. "I'm taller than you."

"I'm eight."

Okay, so that wasn't my best argument. "Well, I might only be five-two-ish, but my attitude is definitely six-three, so it all balances out."

Maya giggled. "That's silly."

I finished tugging my tank top down over my stomach when a strange squeaking sound drew my eyes up toward the ceiling. What was that? And where was it coming from?

A quiet grunt too deep to have come from a child set off alarm bells in the back of my mind. There wasn't anyone else in the restroom with us. Jordan had checked.

The quiet thump of feet hitting the floor sent my pulse skittering. I climbed up on top of the toilet seat and peered over the stall divider. My eyes locked on a blacked-out window none of us had noticed in the last stall, and fear slid through my veins like ice. It was open.

Before I could figure out what to do next, the lights went out. For a moment, I couldn't move. Someone was in the bathroom with us, and the realization that it might be Collin made my body shut down in terror.

"Holly, I'm scared," Maya cried, the fear in her voice giving me the strength to move.

"It's okay," I finally managed to squeeze out. "I'm coming over."

I hopped down from the toilet seat and cracked open the stall door. A small strip of light beneath the closed door Jordan was guarding and the faded glow of street lights outside the window were all that penetrated the blackness.

I couldn't see anything.

I opened my mouth to call out for Jordan, when I heard a metallic thump from somewhere to my left, followed by the slap of a body hitting the floor.

"Maya?"

I rushed toward the last place I had heard her voice, my fist clenched tight around the strap of my shoulder bag, but a hand much too large to be Maya's reached out of the darkness and shoved me backward. I stumbled into the counter and fell onto the tile floor.

"Stay down," a quiet voice hissed.

I heard another grunt, and a tall, dark shape appeared in front of the window with an odd lump slung over one shoulder. Maya. It had to be. He was going to shove her out the window and climb out after her.

I couldn't let that happen.

"Jordan!" I screamed, scrambling to my feet. I lunged at the dark shape and crashed into a solid body. Maya's added weight overbalanced him and the three of us hit the floor.

I heard Jordan's frantic voice as he pounded on the outside of the door. "Holly!" He tried to shove through it, but it didn't budge.

I crawled quickly toward the door to unlock it, but the man sank his hands into my clothing and wrenched me back across the floor. I yelped in surprise.

"Holly!" Jordan shouted. He slammed against the outside of the door again. "Someone get me a key for this door! Now!"

I swung out at the darkness, and my attacker grunted when my fist connected with his face. Something crunched, and the sickening mental image of a nose folding like a soda can flashed through my mind.

The man reeled back, but I could still feel him hovering over me. I twisted to plant my foot against him and then shoved with all my strength.

He fell back, and I heard a satisfying thump as he smacked into one of the stalls. I scrambled across the floor to Maya's still form.

Our attacker groaned and staggered to his feet. My heart thundered in my temples as the nearly six-foot man swayed and then started forward.

"Move," he commanded on a whisper.

I blinked in confusion as I gathered my shaking legs beneath me. I had assumed the attacker was a grown man given his size—possibly Collin—but the strained, gravely tone of his voice sounded more like a young boy.

Our attacker was a teenage boy. But what could he possibly want with Maya?

"Why are you doing this?" I demanded, watching him closely. Although he was little more than a vague shape, I could hear the nervous shifting of his feet and the unsteadiness of his breathing. He was as scared as I was. "Is someone making you do this?"

I could hear Jordan yelling at people outside the door. If I could just hold the boy off until he could make it through, Maya would be safe.

"Get out of the way," he growled again, sounding like a petulant child.

"I won't let you take her," I informed him as calmly as I could.

Something scraped against the lock, and the boy jerked toward the sound in alarm. The door flung inward and the light came on a breath before Jordan swept into the room with his gun drawn.

The boy sprinted toward the last stall. I knelt on the floor beside Maya and watched him squeeze back through the narrow window.

Jordan wrapped a hand around his ankle and tried to pull him back inside. The boy twisted and kicked, knocking Jordan back into the side of the stall. His legs disappeared through the window, and he vanished into the darkening evening.

I shifted Maya's limp form into my lap and checked her for injuries. I smoothed the hair away from her forehead to reveal a small knot on the side of her head.

36

Jordan holstered his gun and crouched beside me. "Is she okay?"

"I think he must have hit her or slammed the door into her."

"Are *you* okay?" he asked, his blue eyes flickering over me with concern.

"Fine." I shifted uncomfortably under his attention. All I had on was a tank top and jeans, and I felt much too exposed. I hadn't had a chance to finish getting dressed.

He seemed to notice my discomfort, because he stripped off his jacket and handed it to me. "Here. We'll get your clothes together after CSU processes the room." He purposefully kept his focus elsewhere while I slipped it on and zipped it up.

Ordinarily, I would baulk at the idea of accepting his jacket, but his nearness and the spectators crowded around the doorway robbed me of any objections.

"The police are on their way. Are you sure you're okay?" he asked.

My back hurt from being shoved into the counter, and the knuckles on my right hand were throbbing—I guess that's what happens when you punch someone in the face—but neither were worth complaining about. "I'm sure."

"Can you describe the person at all?"

"I can tell you it wasn't Collin."

That seemed to surprise him.

"He sounded like a thirteen-year-old boy. But he was at least five ten, maybe even six feet. Sort of . . . gawky. And he was scared," I explained.

Jordan's brow wrinkled in confusion. "What would a kid want with you?"

"Nothing." I looked down at the unconscious girl whose head rested in my lap. "He wanted Maya."

"Maya? Why?"

I was wondering that myself. Had that boy simply decided he wanted this beautiful little girl, or had Collin sent him to take her just so he could use her to hurt me?

Both possibilities terrified me, and I hugged her tighter. I wouldn't let anyone hurt her.

5

"Get out of my way," Marx growled, pushing aside bystanders as he forced his way into the bathroom.

I had tried to convince him not to storm the department store after he learned about the attack, but the argument was over before it even began.

The worry in his eyes gave way to relief when he realized we were all in one piece. The EMT had managed to wake Maya with smelling salts, and she was bopping about the bathroom as if nothing had happened, telling her spooky story about the bathroom going dark to anyone who would listen.

She had no memory of the boy who tried to take her, and I wanted to keep it that way. She had been through enough without visions of men in black trying to snatch her from a bathroom.

Marx looked me over. "You sure you're all right?"

"I'm fine." When he looked at Jordan for confirmation, I rolled my eyes. "I said I'm *fine*."

"Mmm hmm. You also believe chocolate is a food group and that *eggplant* is a color. Your perspective is a bit skewed."

"It *is* a color."

"It's also a fruit masqueradin' as a vegetable."

Jordan smiled. "Aside from a sore hand from punching the guy in the face, Holly actually is fine. And Maya has a knot on her head, but the EMT said she doesn't have a concussion."

"Good. Any progress on the attacker?"

Jordan glanced at the detective we had spoken with and shook his head. "No. Holly couldn't get a visual, and he slipped out the window. He was gone before backup even got here."

Maya barged between us unexpectedly and struck a pose with her arms outstretched. "How do I look?"

I had finally been allowed to finish getting dressed, and Maya and I were back to matching outfits.

The corner of Marx's mouth quirked up in amusement. "Except for the fact that Holly's as white as a snowball, you could be twins."

"I know!" She dropped her arms back to her sides dramatically. "I told her she should get a tan, but she says it won't work."

"I don't think it would," he agreed.

"Oh well." She sighed and popped the sucker she'd been holding back into her mouth. "At least I got lots of pretty new clothes. And the nice doctor man gave me a sucker after the bathroom went dark and I bumped my head. It tastes like cotton candy. I love cotton candy."

Marx raised his eyebrows. "Sounds like you had a rough afternoon. I think you deserve some ice cream. Jordan, why don't you take Maya out for some ice cream?"

Maya gasped and clapped her hands together. "I love ice cream!"

Jordan's eyes narrowed. "Why?"

"Shannon's waitin' at my place, and we have a few things to discuss with Holly that Maya doesn't need to hear."

Jordan looked at me, uncertain.

"It's fine. Just . . . please be careful." The idea of Maya being out in the open where someone could make another grab for her worried me.

"We will."

I followed Marx out of the department store to his car and gave him a more detailed account of the events in the bathroom as we drove.

"Someone comin' for Maya the day after she survived the shelter fire isn't a coincidence," he said. "It could be someone tryin'

40

to clean up loose ends, but I expect he would've killed her rather than tryin' to take her. So why take her?" He looked thoughtful. "And you said he had no interest in you whatsoever?"

I shook my head. "Just Maya. He just wanted me to stay out of the way."

Marx fell into contemplative silence, and judging by the look of concentration on his face, he was working through every possible theory. I wanted to ask him what he was thinking, but I didn't want to interrupt his detective-y process.

When we arrived at his apartment, I opened the door to find Shannon seated on the couch. She was in her late forties with black hair and eyes the color of dark, wet stones.

She stood when she saw me, smoothing the wrinkles from her skirt, and offered me her hand. "It's good to see you again, Holly."

I looked between her and Marx as I set down my shopping bags, then noticed Sam leaning against the counter in the kitchen. Marx had invited reinforcements.

And I wasn't talking about the fact that Sam was five foot eight and built like a bulldozer, or that he was a cop who could restrain me with one hand. More than likely Marx had invited him here because he had an intensely logical perspective on everything that made him hard to disagree with.

Hesitant, I asked, "Is this . . . some kind of intervention or something? Because I don't think my marshmallow addiction is that bad."

Marx smiled. "No, this is about Collin."

Anxiety rippled across my nerve endings, as it always did at the mention of my former foster brother, and I had to swallow before managing, "Oh." I would've preferred a marshmallow intervention.

"This should be relatively painless," Shannon assured me. "As I'm sure Rick has told you, I'm the District Attorney, which is why he came to me for advice about your situation. I just need to gather a few details from you before we can move forward."

41

"Move forward with what?"

"An order of protection against Collin Wells."

"A piece of paper that says do not disturb?" I almost laughed at the absurdity of it. "Collin's violated every boundary I've ever had, and you think a piece of paper is gonna keep him from coming after me?"

"It's more complex than that."

"Yes, it is, and a piece of stationary isn't gonna protect me." *Or the people I care about.*

Shannon pressed her lips together and looked at Marx, as if silently pleading with him to intervene.

"You're right," Marx said. "An order of protection won't keep you safe. But it gives us legal grounds to arrest Collin when he violates it, and he *will* violate it."

Yes, he would. I looked at Shannon. "And how long would he be in jail?"

She settled on the edge of the couch. "He could be out within hours of his bail hearing, which, depending on the day, could take place within twenty-four hours."

"Twenty-four hours." I rubbed my face with my hands. How far away from the city could I get in a day? Halfway to California?

"It's the first step in a long process," she continued. "But you'll be moving in the right direction. If this man is truly a threat to you, then I do recommend taking legal action against him."

I couldn't exactly tell them this discussion was pointless because I didn't plan to be here next week, so I relented with a sigh. "What do you need from me?"

"We just need to be able to convince a judge that Collin Wells poses a physical or psychological threat to you."

"How?"

"By establishing a pattern of behavior. Unfortunately, the text messages and phone calls he placed to your phone came from an untraceable, prepaid device, so there's no way to confirm that he was the sender or the caller."

"How do you know what number he called me from? I never told anyone the . . ."

Oh.

I looked at Sam. He had come into the precinct break room minutes after Collin contacted me, and I had asked him if he could block the number.

"What did you do, memorize the number?" I asked.

Sam didn't even blink at my tone, which had come across a bit more accusing than I intended. "A sadistic psychopath is stalking a friend of mine, so yes, I memorized the number."

While the words themselves weren't inherently negative, his deep, flat voice had a way of making everything sound angry. Then his words actually registered.

Friend?

At his small smile, I realized I had voiced that thought aloud. I flushed with embarrassment and looked away.

"I have witness statements from Samuel and Rick that Collin Wells was the caller on your birthday this past January, and that the conversation suggested he was watching you from nearby."

I nodded. "He was watching me from outside my apartment. He knew I hadn't blown out the candles on my cake."

Shannon placed a voice recorder on the coffee table and hit a button. "How long had it been since you heard from him?"

"A little over two years."

"Tell me about the first time he made an appearance in New York City."

"He was leaning against my apartment door when Marx brought me home."

"Did he threaten you?"

"Not directly, no. He's very . . . careful with his words. But I knew what he meant."

Shannon nodded in understanding. "Tell me about the calls and texts you received from him at the precinct."

"He called five times that day. I picked up the second time and . . . he asked why I hadn't come home the past few nights."

I had moved in with Marx after Collin made his first appearance.

"You were pretty shaken up when I came in," Sam pointed out when I paused for too long. He had described me as looking paler than water and on the verge of fainting. "He said more than that."

I squirmed uncomfortably. I didn't want to talk about this. "He said I was too scared to speak. And he asked if . . . if his voice made me shiver in anticipation of pain. And if it made me think about all the times . . ."

"All the times what?" Shannon prompted.

I forced the remainder of the words out. "All the times he held me down and . . . and then I hung up."

A mixture of sadness and frustration flickered across Marx's expression. "That's why you refused to answer when I asked you what he said. Because of what he meant."

I had been afraid he would think I was weak.

"Is somebody going to fill me in on what's not being said here?" Shannon asked, her attention swiveling between us.

I tightened my arms over my stomach, trying to swallow back the sudden nausea. "Can we just move on?"

Shannon looked back at Marx, who pursed his lips in silence. "All right," she said reluctantly. "The text message you received at the precinct implied that he was watching you in the break room, correct?"

I nodded.

"And he also showed up at the ice arena?"

"Yes."

"I heard secondhand from Rick what happened that day. Can you tell me in your own words what transpired?"

I reluctantly described the things Collin had said, and the way he had baited Jordan. The memories sent a tiny shiver down my spine.

44

"And Jordan didn't shoot him?" Sam asked from the kitchen, sounding surprised.

Jordan had thought about it. I had seen a side to him I had never seen before that day—not simply protectiveness, but bottled fury. I had been certain it would burst out of him in a show of violence, but somehow he managed to contain it.

Shannon folded one hand over the other in her lap as she regarded me with keen eyes. "Some of those comments suggest a history of physical violence."

I swallowed uncomfortably and looked down at my shoes.

"Holly," she pressed gently, her voice coaxing rather than demanding. "Is there a history of physical violence?"

If I said yes, she was going to want details. "Maybe."

"Has it ever been documented?"

I closed my eyes and tried to push away the memories that clawed their way to the surface. It had been two years—more than two years—and the terror and shame ingrained in those memories was still fresh.

"Would this be easier for you if Samuel and Rick stepped out?" Shannon asked, but her voice sounded distant.

I could still feel the cold pavement beneath my bare feet as I ran, hear the whoosh of the automatic doors, the voices asking questions and demanding answers.

I opened my eyes and stared at the tips of my new boots as they blurred in and out of focus through the tears. The words that left my lips were barely more than a whisper.

"Mercy Hospital. Darby, Pennsylvania. September 18, 2014. I was admitted at four a.m. as a Jane Doe."

When I brushed off a bad day with the excuse *I've had worse days*, that was the day—the one that overshadowed every other.

"And what was the nature of your injuries?" Shannon continued, her voice clinical.

My heart gave a nervous flutter at the mere thought of sharing those details, and I could feel the anxiety pressing on my chest.

"Can you find the record without her havin' to describe it?" Marx asked.

I shot him a grateful look. He knew how difficult it was for me to talk about my history with Collin, and he was trying to spare me from having to recount those details. Or he just didn't want me to upchuck on the floor.

Shannon's careful expression fractured with surprise. "You want me to track down the medical records for a Jane Doe admitted to the ER of a crime-riddled city on a busy Friday night two years ago with no details to go on?"

"Is the hospital record really necessary?" Sam chimed in. "He's clearly harassing her."

Shannon made a frustrated sound. "This situation is anything but *clear*, Samuel. All I have right now is proof that he happened to be in several of the same locations as Holly, which could be nothing more than coincidence, and two unsettling phone calls, during which he issued no overt threats."

"He attacked her in Pennsylvania," Marx snapped. "He as much as admitted it outside her apartment, and he was more than happy to rub my face in the fact that I can't touch him for it because it took place outside my jurisdiction!"

"That's not an admission of guilt, Rick, and you know it. He was baiting you. I need something substantial to go on. A medical report, regardless of what state it comes from, will back up Holly's claims."

I flexed my fingers that still ached sometimes in colder weather. Maybe if I shared a few specific details, she would be able to find the record. Of course, then she would review it and realize how much I hadn't shared with her.

"He broke into her apartment last month and stole her clothes," Sam said.

"And even if he did, there were no witnesses and no evidence," Shannon countered. "That's not going to help me procure a—"

"I had three broken fingers," I said quietly. "And a . . . fractured rib."

Shannon paused before asking, "Anything else?"

I shook my head and noticed Sam and Marx exchange a glance. They knew I was withholding information.

"Did they photograph the injuries?" she asked. At my nod, she continued, "Did you give a statement to the police?"

"I asked the nurse not to call them."

Shannon arched a delicate eyebrow. "Why?"

Bitter defensiveness rose up inside me at the disapproval in her tone. "Because I didn't believe the cops *could* or *would* protect me from Collin."

They hadn't protected me when I was a child, when I needed them to. Why would the next time I needed them be any different?

"I see," she said, but I didn't think she did.

"Holly didn't trust cops," Marx clarified, and I appreciated his use of past tense. There was no question that I trusted him. "She went to a cop for help when she was younger, and he dismissed her."

Shannon ran her tongue along the inside of her lip, clearly still irritated, then exhaled. "Okay. Can you tell me anything more about what happened that night?"

"Collin tracked me to the hospital. When I heard his voice in the hallway, I snuck out and got on a bus. That's it."

She stopped the recorder and looked at Marx. "Can we talk privately?"

He gestured toward his bedroom. Shannon stood, smoothed her skirt, and followed him into the room before closing the door.

"She's gonna find out you didn't tell her everything," Sam said.

I knew she would, assuming the hospital kept those records. Some part of me hoped they didn't, that I could leave the details of that night buried in Pennsylvania.

Shannon's irritated voice rose behind the door, fading in and out of earshot. "A complete mess. How do you expect me to . . . nothing to work with . . ."

I could hear Marx's placating tones, but his words were too soft. After another moment, the door opened, and Shannon stepped out with her professional mask firmly in place.

She gathered up her recorder and briefcase from the coffee table. "I'll set up a meeting with the judge to request an order of protection, and I'll have my assistant track down that medical file. Any evidence of past violence will help us procure the order."

"Thank you," Marx replied.

She shot him a look just a few degrees shy of frosty. "I'll be in touch." She swept out of the apartment.

"Is everything okay?" I asked.

Marx sighed. "She's a smart woman; she knows we're not tellin' her the whole story, and she's very unhappy about it."

Sam pushed off the kitchen counter and joined us in the living room. "I expected that to go better."

"So did I, but if anybody can convince a judge to sign off on nothin' but bread crumbs, it's Shannon."

They both fell quiet, their expressions pensive. I tucked my hair behind my ears and, determined to move the subject far away from Collin, asked, "Did you ever check into that address I gave you a few weeks ago?"

Marx shook his head. "Amidst everythin' else, it slipped my mind."

"What address?" Sam asked, looking back and forth between us.

I had avoided mentioning Danny, Sam's former partner, who had given me the address to pass along to Marx. His betrayal was still an open wound for Sam, and his death at Marx's hands—however

48

justified—was still raw for Marx as well. He had been forced to shoot two fellow cops that day, one of whom had been his best friend.

Awesome conversation detour, Holly.

Marx cleared his throat. "Daniel gave Holly an address to give to me. I meant to call him for the details later that night, but . . ." he trailed off. "I haven't had a chance to check it out yet."

Sam's dark eyes turned granite. "Considering he was trying to use Holly to manipulate your investigation, it's probably a trap."

"Maybe, maybe not. He didn't make the best decisions, but when he chose to do his job, he did it well."

"You mean in between drug dealing and murdering suspects in their holding cells."

"He said it was about someone Marx was looking for, so maybe he was actually trying to—"

"Help?" Sam snapped, cutting me off. "He tried to kidnap you, Holly. And you think he passed that address along out of the goodness of his heart?"

My hand automatically went to the fading scar on my forehead, my souvenir from that night of betrayal and bloodshed.

"There are several people I'm lookin' for in connection to my cases, all of whom you and Daniel were aware of," Marx explained. "I need to check it out just to be sure."

"What about Riley's owner?" I asked. "You put word out for him. It could be him, right?"

Riley trotted over at the sound of his name and bumped against my leg. If not for the door against my back, he would've knocked me flat.

"Possibly," Marx conceded.

"Can I come with you?"

"No. I have no idea who might be there. And Sam's right. It could be a trap."

"But it could just be Riley's owner, and I really wanna talk to him." And convince him to let me keep Riley.

"I'd rather you didn't."

49

"Please," I pleaded, clasping my hands together and bouncing on my toes.

His lips twitched and he shook his head. "That expression on your face should be illegal. It's an unfair advantage."

Was that a yes? I bit my lip, hopeful.

Marx exhaled in surrender. "Put your bags away before we go. I don't like clutter."

I dashed into the spare room to drop off the shopping bags, and overheard Sam say, "You're too soft with her."

"Really," Marx said evenly. "When was the last time you told her no when she asked you for somethin'?"

Sam opened his mouth, then shut it without speaking, and I caught the subtle smugness in Marx's expression as I stepped back into the living room.

"Um, Sam . . ."

He offered me a slightly perturbed look that made me reconsider asking. "What?"

I fidgeted with the envelope in my hand. "Could you, um . . . if you don't mind . . . drop my rent money off to Mr. Whittaker when you stop by to see Jace?"

Mr. Whittaker was my new landlord, and even though my apartment sat vacant while I was staying with Marx, I still needed to pay my rent if I wanted to keep it. Sam was at my apartment building nearly every day to see Jace.

He stared at the envelope I held out, seemingly unsure whether or not to take it, and then snatched it from my hand. "You have really bad timing."

Marx arched an eyebrow.

"The landlord is a creep," Sam explained defensively. "He hits on his female tenants. It has nothing to do with me being soft."

"Mmm hmm." Marx opened the front door with a small smile. He ushered me out first, and they followed me down the steps to the parking lot.

6

*I*t was nightfall by the time we pulled up next to the building. I glanced at the address on the scrap of paper and then at the ten-story brick building that might have been an apartment complex.

Yep, this was the right place.

Marx took in the shady building surrounded by rundown vehicles as we climbed out of the car. "Why do I get the feelin' my car's gonna be missin' pieces when I get back?"

That would be his luck.

He stepped into the sidewalk beside me. "You stay close to me, you hear?"

"I will stick to you like duct tape."

I couldn't see his smile—someone had broken the bulbs in the street lamps—but I could hear it in his voice. "At least you didn't say rubber cement this time."

"I didn't feel like re-explaining what rubber cement is." I followed along at his heels as we walked up to the building.

He snorted softly. "I'm only forty-seven, Holly. I don't have dementia. I do remember that conversation, as well as you describin' it as 'cool, sticky stuff.'"

I grinned. It *was* cool, sticky stuff.

He opened the door to the building and the stale scent of cigarette smoke and marijuana wafted from the opening. People lingered in the hallway, some of them smoking and others making sleight-of-hand exchanges that looked suspiciously illegal.

Marx shut the door on a flat "No."

"No, what?"

"I am not takin' you into some drug-dealer–infested slum that looks more like a prison cell block than an apartment."

I frowned at the suggestion that I was incapable of taking care of myself. "I'm a big girl."

"Compared to who?"

I scowled at him. "We're here now, so we may as well go inside." I wrenched open the door and stepped into the smoggy hallway before he could stop me.

"Holly," he gritted out in that exasperated tone I always seemed to inspire.

I was surprised at how crowded the hallway was. It was like stepping into a rave rather than an apartment building, with heavy music thrumming through the tile beneath my feet.

I spotted a flyer on a space of wall and leaned in to read it. Most of it was written in street code, but the gist of it was that Little T was having a party in room 56. Well, apparently, Little T overestimated the size of his apartment, because not everybody fit.

A woman reached out and grabbed a handful of my hair as I passed by, letting it slide through her fingers as she said, "Silky. Can I have it?"

There was a faraway glazed look to her eyes, and I noticed the fresh needle marks in her arm as I carefully removed my hair from her fingers. "You know, I think your hair suits you perfectly."

I moved away before she could grab it again. I heard her drowsy voice say something to someone behind me, and I glanced back to see her stretching out a hand toward Marx's face.

"Pretty eyes. Like shiny marbles. Can I touch 'em?"

He caught her wrist gently but firmly and pushed her hand away. "I'd rather you didn't."

I maneuvered my way through the crowded hallway toward the steps at the other end. According to the address, we were looking for an apartment on the second level.

I gasped when an arm reached out of nowhere, wrapped around my waist, and snatched me sideways. I collided with a man's wiry frame, and breath that stank of garlic washed over the side of my face.

"Wanna dance?" he asked.

I squirmed frantically, trying to break away.

Marx pried me loose and planted a hand against the man's chest, slamming him back into the wall when he moved to follow. "Hands to yourself."

A blissful grin spread across the man's gaunt, pale face. "I just wanna dance with the pretty girl."

"The pretty girl doesn't wanna dance with you. Don't touch her." Marx leveled a glare at the man and then took my arm as he moved us away from him.

"Maybe this wasn't such a good idea," I conceded, my heart still racing.

"You think?"

We had a more difficult time maneuvering through the narrow space together, but he kept a hold of my arm as he forced his way toward the steps.

"I should be arrestin' half these people right now. Degenerates."

"De-what?"

"Immoral, corrupt people."

"Oh." That sounded about right given what some of them were doing in the hallway. "You should just say that next time."

"Yo, five-o," a man shouted, and he stepped away from the wall to block our path. "I think you in the wrong neighborhood."

Marx stopped abruptly, and I stumbled into him. I peered around him at the tall man with pierced eyebrows and a sleeve of creepy skeleton tattoos.

"Bishop," Marx greeted, his tone dripping with distaste. "Who screwed up and let you out early?"

The man sneered. "You locked me in the joint for five years, ole man."

53

"No, I handcuffed you and delivered you to a jury of your peers, who then decided to have you locked up. Just between the two of us, you should still be there."

The man stepped closer to Marx as if he were hoping to intimidate him, but Marx's expression and posture remained neutral.

"You got a lotta guts coming down here, ole man. I could end you right now and ain't nobody gonna see nuttin."

"You've been out of prison how long, and you're already threatenin' a cop? If I didn't know better, I'd think you were eager to go back."

Bishop scowled, his eyebrows drawing together. "You better watch—" He blinked when the flash from my phone momentarily blinded him. "What the . . ."

I attached his photo and a tidbit of useful information to a message and sent it to Sam and Jordan. If anything happened, the NYPD would descend on this building like a flock of angry birds.

"Whatchu think you doin'?" he demanded. "Did you just take my pitcha?"

I tucked my phone into my side pocket with slightly shaky fingers. "It was a good picture, but I think you might look better if you smiled."

He sputtered. "Whatchu takin' my pitcha fo'?"

"I have a few friends who are cops. I just wanted to let them know we ran into you, you know . . . in case . . . the evening doesn't go as planned."

He stared at me and then turned in a whirlwind of curses to storm back into one of the apartments. The violent slam of the door was nearly muted by the pulsing music.

Marx lifted a brow at me, and I shrugged. "You weren't getting anywhere."

He glanced behind us before we moved forward, and I caught the "why me" expression that flashed across his face. I turned to see the skinny man who had wanted to dance with me trailing along behind us like a puppy seeking affection.

"Don't make me shoot you," Marx said. He stared at the man until he meekly retreated.

"Boy, you sure draw out the weirdos," I teased.

He placed a gentle hand on my head and smiled. "Up the steps before you cause more trouble."

We climbed the steps toward the second floor, dodging empty beer bottles and food wrappers along the way. I reached the top and scanned the doors, looking for apartment eighty-seven.

One of the nearby doors opened and a man stepped out. He glanced at me, his dark eyes sweeping over me and then away with disinterest before landing on Marx. I caught the abrupt shift in his body language—from calm and casual to coiled for a fight.

I glanced at Marx.

He looked equally tense, and he kept his eyes on the man as he said, "Holly, I need you to go over there to that corner and call Sam."

While Bishop had seemed like a minor irritation, the way Marx was gripping the butt of his gun as he watched this man told me he was worried.

"Now, Holly." The urgency in his voice had me fumbling for my phone in my side pocket. I punched in Sam's number as I backed away.

"Well, if it isn't the detective who ruined my life," the man greeted with a sneer. "I've been waiting a long time for this day."

He put two fingers in his mouth and let out a shrill whistle that had me covering my ears. I watched with dismay as the people loitering in the hall skittered back into their apartments like cockroaches fleeing the light.

Sam's voice came over the line, sounding annoyed. "I haven't had a chance to deliver your rent money yet, Holly."

"I think we need help."

Sam didn't miss a beat as his focus shifted. "What's going on?"

I described the situation for him to the best of my knowledge, which was, unfortunately, very little. All I knew was that the tension in the hallway was steadily rising.

"I'm calling it in, and I'm on my way," Sam said. "Try to stay out of the way. Marx knows what he's doing."

"I didn't expect to see you again, Leo," Marx replied as I snapped my phone shut. "I heard you had an unfortunate accident in prison."

The man's lips twisted into a bitter smile. "An accident." He lifted up his shirt to reveal a jagged scar that bisected his torso. "They tried to gut me like a pig."

"I'm sorry to hear that," Marx said, but his voice was devoid of sympathy.

Leo let his shirt drop back over his stomach. "You and I have some unfinished business."

Marx held his ground as the man stepped forward. "We have nothin' to discuss."

"Nothing? Is that what my little brother was to you? Nothing?" Anger sharpened his voice, and I felt my heart rate pick up in response.

Leo was paying no attention to me, but the way he was looking at Marx—he was a breath away from violence.

"What happened to your brother was unfortunate," Marx said calmly.

"Unfortunate. You cops and your excuses. It was *unfortunate*; it was a tragedy; it was unavoidable; it was justified. There is no justification for what you did. You killed my baby brother."

"Your brother pulled a gun on me. He didn't give me a choice."

"He was fifteen!"

"And I'm sorry for that, but I did my job." I could hear the pain in Marx's voice, the regret that he'd been forced to take the life of a child.

"He was just the lookout. He didn't deserve a bullet," Leo continued. "I didn't even get to go to his funeral. You shot my brother in cold blood, and I promised you I would return the favor someday."

He stepped toward Marx, and even though I didn't see a weapon, he was too confident to be unarmed.

Marx held up a hand. "That's close enough. You need to keep your distance." His tone was bland, like he was just going through the motions even though he didn't expect the man to obey.

Leo's eyes shifted from Marx to me, but this time they held interest. "Is this your woman?"

A muscle in Marx's jaw flexed. "She had nothin' to do with what happened to your brother. Leave her out of it."

Leo grinned, and I could see the calculation glittering in his eyes. I reached into my coat pocket and squeezed the canister of pepper spray for reassurance.

"Maybe I'll introduce myself to her when I'm done with you." With that, he swung a thick fist at Marx's head.

Marx ducked back, and the blow caught him on the shoulder. Before he could recover, Leo plowed into him, slamming him into the wall hard enough to dent the plaster.

I winced.

Leo drew a switchblade from his back pocket and flipped it open. "This is for my brother."

I sucked in a terrified breath.

Marx elbowed him in the face and grabbed his wrist before he could sink the knife in. Leo drove two vicious punches into his side.

"Stop!" I shouted. I didn't know what else to do. If I tried to spray the man with my pepper spray, it would hit both of them.

Leo grabbed for Marx's gun with his free hand, and Marx tried to block him while keeping a hold of his wrist.

I stepped forward, hesitated with indecision, and then took another uncertain step. There had to be something I could do.

I grabbed the nearest large object I could find—which, oddly, was a George Foreman grill someone had tossed out with the trash—and clubbed the man over the back of the head. Twice.

I felt the vibrating thump of the impacts all the way up to my shoulders, but the man barely grunted. He threw out an arm that missed me by less than an inch as I scrambled out of the way.

"Holly, get back!" Marx shouted.

I retreated back against the wall. Marx bent Leo's wrist back at an odd angle, and the knife dropped from his slack fingers.

He let out a howl that might have been from pain, but it could just as easily have been from rage. Marx kicked him in the side of the knee, then twisted his arm behind his back as the man's legs buckled.

He shoved him facedown on the filthy floor and knelt, pressing one knee into his back.

"This isn't over," Leo protested.

"Oh, it's over," Marx replied breathlessly. He snapped a cuff around one restrained wrist and then wrenched Leo's other arm behind his back to repeat the procedure. "You're under arrest for the attempted murder of a police officer."

Leo's cold eyes locked on me, and I swallowed uneasily. "Maybe I'll go after your woman first next time. Her life for my brother's. How does that sound, *Detective*?"

"Sounds like a good way to get yourself killed, because if you ever try it, I will shoot you. And then it will be *very* over."

I stepped away from the wall. "Are you okay?"

Marx glanced at me. "I'm fine. What did you hit him with?"

I held up the broken George Foreman grill by the cord. "I grilled him."

Marx choked back a laugh and continued searching pockets for any more weapons. He found a second knife jammed into Leo's boot. "Did you know I was gonna be here tonight?"

"If I'd known, I would've had a gun, and you never would've made it to the top of the steps."

"Who lives in apartment eighty-seven?"

58

Leo growled as he tried to twist free, then surrendered, panting. "I'm not telling you nothin'."

"That's your right."

Marx glanced at the apartment in question, and I could see his mind working. I wondered if his thoughts were following the same track as mine—something was wrong with this situation.

I knew he had enemies, bitter people who blamed him for their time behind bars, but it couldn't be normal for him to run into two of those people on the same night, let alone in the same building.

Sam came up the steps a few minutes later in his street clothes, one hand resting on his gun. He took in the situation with one sweep of his eyes, and some of the intensity drained from his expression. "Looks like you didn't need me after all."

"Give me a hand with him," Marx said.

They each took an arm and hauled Leo to his feet.

Sam's brow furrowed. "Isn't this the guy who screamed all the way out of the courtroom that he was gonna kill you?"

Marx tipped his head toward the open blade lying against the wall. "He tried."

Uniformed officers sprinted up the steps, saw Marx and Sam holding a handcuffed man, and came to a stop. I recognized the male officer as the one I had dubbed the Keebler elf—because of his pointy elf ears—when I first met him six months ago.

He had been the first officer on scene at the park when two men tried to attack me. He recognized me too, because he looked directly at me when he said, "We got a call about a possible assault in progress."

Really?

"It wasn't me this time." I pointed to Marx. "He's your victim."

Marx tried to contain a smile as he handed the man off to the officers. "Book him for attempted murder."

Keebler read the man his rights as they led him away. Leo's protests were eventually drowned out by the bass of the music

59

downstairs, but he let loose a creative string of curses and threats before he was out of range.

Sam folded his arms with a fierce scowl. "I told you this was probably a trap."

Marx released a frustrated sigh. "Yes, I remember."

"What are the chances you would run into an ex-con bent on revenge at the address Danny gave you?"

"Slim. But Daniel wasn't lookin' to have me killed, so if this was a set-up, I don't think it was his doin'. If anythin', he was probably just the messenger."

"You think he honestly didn't know? That someone used him to set you up?"

I followed Marx's and Sam's eyes to the apartment. If this was a trap, what or who was waiting behind that door? I seriously doubted it was Riley's owner.

"I want you to take Holly home," Marx said.

Indignation bubbled up, but before I could tell him I wasn't about to be dismissed, Sam said, "I think it would be better if I stayed."

Marx grimaced, but he didn't argue. "Well, let's find out what's behind door number eighty-seven, shall we?"

He took up position to the left of the door, and Sam mirrored him on the right, gun drawn.

Marx knocked and called out, "NYPD." There was no answer. He knocked again and said more loudly, "This is Detective Marx with the NYPD. I'd like a minute of your time!"

Silence. He exchanged a look with Sam and then gripped the doorknob. He turned it carefully and the door clicked open. He nudged it with his fingertips before stepping back.

A scream caught in my throat when a small body dropped into the open doorway with a noose around her neck.

7

I couldn't pull my eyes away from the small body that swayed in the doorway, her flowery dress rustling with the movement. Black hair framed walnut-tinted features, and her small feet were bare.

It took me a moment longer than Sam and Marx to realize that it wasn't a little girl, but an eerily realistic doll.

Marx lowered his gun that he had snapped up the moment the doll dropped from above, and looked at Sam, who looked equally puzzled.

"I don't even know what to say to that," Sam admitted.

"Neither do I." Marx leaned through the doorway to peer into the apartment.

"There's a note." Sam reached up and grabbed a folded sheet of paper that was taped to the inside of the doll's hand. He read it to himself, then handed it to Marx.

The creases in Marx's forehead deepened with each sweep of his eyes across the page. "It says, 'In case your memories were hanging by a thread,'"—he glanced at the rope the doll was hanging from and grimaced— "'here's a reminder.'"

I didn't *need* a reminder of the long-ago scene that inspired this one. Every haunting detail was carved into my memory.

It had been a tree rather than a doorway, and it hadn't been a doll hanging from the end of the rope.

I wrapped my arms around my nauseous stomach and backed away, needing to put as much distance as possible between me and the dangling memory.

"Not gonna cut this one down?"

I whirled toward the voice that had just purred in my ear, and came face-to-face with ice-blue eyes.

I froze as my mind tried to process the fact that my living, breathing nightmare was a single step away from me.

He smiled. "Hello, gorgeous."

I fumbled over my own feet as I scrambled back from him, then turned and darted toward the emergency exit at the other end of the hall.

I yelped when Marx caught me around the waist and snatched me off my feet before I could get there.

"Holly," he grunted, struggling to hold onto me as I wriggled and twisted, determined to reach the exit.

Collin was right there. He had only been inches away, so close that I could feel his breath on the back of my neck. Close enough to touch me.

Marx murmured something in my ear as he fought to keep a hold of me, but I couldn't focus on anything more than my own internal voice screaming, *Run*.

Marx pulled me against his side and wrapped both arms around me in a secure hug that left me barely able to twitch. He rested his chin on top of my head and whispered, "You're safe, sweetheart. Just breathe."

I felt him draw in a deep breath and exhale slowly, the rhythm of his breathing inviting me to follow along.

Collin's lips curled into a smile as he calmly ascended the last step onto the second floor, and my insides shivered. "My, my, everyone is so tense." His gaze flickered over each person in the hallway, finally landing on Marx. "This is a tough neighborhood, Detective. I sure hope you didn't run into any trouble. A man like you must have quite a few enemies in this part of town."

"Since you designed this entire situation, you already know the answer to that," Marx replied. "And I assume you forwarded the tip that someone I was lookin' for was livin' here."

"That would be clever," Collin agreed, without confirming it. "One could assume the tip would eventually reach you."

"I get the feelin' you didn't intend for me to leave this buildin' alive."

"Then who would Holly cling to? She would practically be alone. We all know the sheriff is only interested in her . . ."—he paused to consider his words—"assets, and Sam here has failed to watch over her so many times that it's obvious he doesn't care."

I glanced at Sam. He tried to protect me, but circumstances always seemed to be against him.

"I'm surprised you would bring Holly to this part of town, Detective. It's full of unsavory people, and she's so . . ."—Collin gave me a thorough once-over—"savory."

My trembling fingers clenched a fistful of Marx's shirt, and he hugged me tighter, reminding me that he wouldn't let Collin touch me.

"You should really be more careful with her," Collin suggested. "It's so easy for her to get hurt. In fact, someone should really take her home. I'll gladly give her a—" He stepped forward and collided with a wall of Sam. He staggered back a step in surprise.

"Walk away," Sam demanded.

Collin brushed at his shirt as if it were somehow contaminated by coming into contact with Sam. "If I don't, are we going to have a Mexican standoff?"

I couldn't see Sam's face, but I could imagine his stony expression.

"No?" Collin asked. "Then why don't you step aside. This is my apartment, and I have a right to be here."

"Can't say I'm surprised to discover that you play with dolls." Marx nodded toward the doorway.

"I prefer to play with people. They're much more interesting. Isn't that right, Holly?"

Marx tightened his arms around me protectively. I knew he could feel me shaking, but I couldn't seem to make myself stop.

"Is that why you torture women and children?" Marx asked with audible disgust.

Collin's expression morphed into a convincing mask of wounded indignation. "I would never hurt women and children. What kind of man do you think I am?"

"A coward," Sam offered, his tone matter-of-fact.

Collin offered Sam a dismissive look. "The Americans are having a conversation here."

Sam ignored the racist remark. "You didn't even have the guts to come after Marx yourself. Instead, you play games and hope someone else does it for you. A little research into the recently paroled, and then all you had to do was rent an apartment, send word through the grapevine that someone Marx was looking for was here, and wait. You're pathetic."

I caught the slight twitch at the corners of Collin's eyes, a subtle sign that I had come to recognize meant he was irritated.

"And the things you did to Holly," Sam continued. "Does it make you feel powerful to hurt a girl?"

Collin smirked. "Are you trying to elicit a confession? Because I think I deserve a better effort than that. At least employ a little strategy."

He tried to step around Sam again, and to my surprise, Sam shoved him hard enough to lift his feet off the floor and send him sprawling back by the top of the steps. Another few inches and he would've fallen down them.

"In case I didn't make myself clear the first time, I'm not letting you near her," Sam said.

The landing might not have hurt, but Collin looked momentarily stunned. He staggered back to his feet and straightened his clothes. "I think you're my least favorite of the three amigos. No intelligence at all; just brute force. You do realize you just assaulted me."

"Have fun proving it without witnesses."

Collin looked between him and Marx. "Ah. I see how it is. Cops band together."

"It has nothin' to do with us bein' cops and everythin' to do with you bein' a sexual predator who preys on women and children," Marx explained.

"I think your facts are little confused, Detective. I've never touched a child that way."

"Really," Marx replied. "Because my understandin' is that the first time you forced yourself on Holly, you were eighteen. Holly was fourteen."

Sam's gaze flickered to me, as if seeking confirmation, and then back to Collin. He must have thought Pennsylvania was the only time Collin had crossed that line.

Sam's usually bland tone dripped with disgust. "You molested a child?"

Collin rolled his eyes. "Relationships between an eighteen-year-old and a fourteen-year-old are legal in the state of Maine."

"A consensual relationship, maybe," Marx said. "But everybody in this hallway knows Holly didn't consent. *That* makes you a child molester."

I tried to swallow the bile that crept up my throat. My history was unraveling all over the floor for everyone to see.

"Someone should inform his neighbors that there's a child predator in the building," Sam suggested.

Collin's eyes narrowed. "You wouldn't. You're peacekeepers by trade, and that could cause a riot."

"I'm not feelin' terribly peaceful tonight," Marx admitted. "So I would recommend you be on your way before he makes an announcement and your neighbors decide to tear you to pieces. Even drug dealers and junkies have children."

Collin grimaced. He had just been outmaneuvered, and he knew it. "Interesting move, Detective." His gaze raked over me one last time, and he smiled to himself. "I'm looking forward to our time together, Holly. It's going to be long and memorable."

Sam shoved him back another step. "Stop talking and walk."

Collin's smile spread into a taunting grin. "Very memorable." He turned and trotted down the steps, humming a jaunty tune to himself.

Nerves, memories, and fear congealed into a nauseous ball in my stomach. I tried to hold it down, but it pushed back violently. I shoved away from Marx and rushed to the nearest corner to throw up.

8

I curled into the passenger seat of Marx's car with his coat wrapped around me. It was warm, and with my knees drawn to my chest, it swallowed me from chin to toe like an impenetrable cloak. I felt oddly safer inside of it.

I stared through the windshield at the dark, snow-dusted street and thought about how easy it would be to disappear. I could just melt away into the shadows.

I had learned how to be invisible, and I could hide until Marx gave up searching for me. Abandoned warehouses provided shelter, and I could scavenge for food and necessities.

If I disappeared, Collin would leave the people I cared about alone and try to track me down. And I wouldn't make the same mistake in the next city; I wouldn't allow myself to form attachments.

An image of Maya's tear-stained face materialized in my mind, and all thoughts of running fled. I had promised her I wouldn't leave her. Regardless of my fears, I needed to stay with her until she was safely delivered into the loving hands of her grandparents.

I burrowed deeper into Marx's coat, burying my nose in the collar. It smelled like his cologne. Collin hadn't touched me tonight, but I could smell him on my skin—like a toxic memory seeping from my pores—and Marx's cologne smothered his nauseating scent.

"I probably should've followed Collin to find out where he's staying," Sam said. He was leaning against the hood of the car, talking with Marx. "He can't have gotten far. I could probably track him down if I go now."

Marx rubbed the back of his neck as he considered it. "No. We have no idea who else he might have enlisted to help him. I'm not so much concerned that somebody else might come after me once you leave as I am with the possibility that it might go badly. That would leave Holly completely unprotected."

Sam folded his arms and glanced at me through the window. "And then he would double back for her."

"Precisely."

My stomach dropped at the thought.

"Okay. I'll follow you guys back to your place to make sure no one tails you." Sam scanned the faces of the people loitering near the rundown apartment building. "If there's anyone else here with a grudge against you, we don't need them following you home."

Marx nodded and they parted ways. Cold air rushed into the car as he opened the driver's door and slid behind the wheel.

He smiled at me. "You're like a little Eskimo over there."

All he could see were my eyes peeking out from between the collar of his coat and my hat.

Headlights glinted off the rearview mirror, signaling that Sam was behind us. Without a word, Marx stretched an arm across me to grab the loose seatbelt, wrapped it around me, legs and all, and buckled it as if I were a dazed and confused child. He placed a gentle hand on my head. "It's gonna be okay, sweetheart."

The sadness and worry in his eyes made my throat tighten. If I didn't know better, I would think we had run into his nightmare rather than mine.

"I need you to trust that."

I dropped my eyes to the floorboard. I *didn't* trust that everything would be okay; I didn't trust that at all.

He drew his hand back with a quiet, regretful sigh and buckled his own seatbelt. He started the car and pulled out onto the street.

"I know you don't feel much like talkin' right now," he began with a careful glance my way. "But we need to."

He could never just let things go; he had to *talk* about everything. "You wear cologne," I said, hoping to distract him.

The right side of his mouth quirked up. "Yes I do, but that's not what I wanna talk about."

"Was it expensive?"

"It was a gift from Shannon for our tenth anniversary. Stop tryin' to distract me."

"I can smell it on your coat. It smells . . ." *Good* wasn't the right word. It wasn't a scent I would ordinarily like, but it wasn't terrible either. It made me think of him. "Safe," I finally decided on.

Marx blinked and then looked at me a little longer than he should've while driving. He cleared his throat, but I could hear emotion clinging to his voice as he grunted, "Good. I'll buy you a bottle for Christmas next year."

I smiled a little at that. What would I do with a bottle of cologne?

We turned the corner onto another dark street. "I need you to tell me about the doll."

I sighed and squirmed in my seat. "It's . . . complicated."

"Things revolvin' around Collin usually are." He tapped his fingers on the steering wheel and waited patiently while I tried to pull my thoughts together.

"You asked me once if Collin had ever tried to kill someone." I drew in a fortifying breath and looked out the passenger window. "Her name was Cassie, and she was six."

"Six?" He blanched. "He tried to kill a six-year-old girl?"

After everything that Collin had done, that surprised him? The man didn't have a conscience, and no one—regardless of age or gender—was anything more than something to play with for his amusement.

He exhale a slow breath and asked, "What happened?"

"The Wells family had a lot of property, and there was a tree a few acres from the house. I was looking for Cassie, and I found them just as he was setting up his . . . his *playground*. I tried to stop him. I remember screaming at him and hitting him, trying to take the rope, but . . ."

I closed my eyes as a wave of anger crested over me. Collin had simply tossed me aside.

"I couldn't," I finally bit out. "He told me that if I wanted to save her so badly, I could walk over to the tree and cut her down."

I saw the reflection of Marx's fingers in the window as they tightened on the steering wheel. Anger radiated off him like heat.

"So he just let you cut her down?" he finally asked.

"Something like that." He had made sure doing so would be excruciating. Even thinking about that day made the scars on the bottoms of my feet itch.

"What happened after you got her down?" At my slight flinch, he cast me a compassionate look. "We don't have to talk about that part if you don't want to. What happened after that?"

I rested my head against the window, and my breath of relief sent steam stretching across the cold glass. He wasn't asking me to describe what Collin had done to me. I couldn't—I wouldn't—put those awful experiences into words.

"He went back to the house, and I told Cassie to run and never come back."

"Did she?"

It had taken some convincing for her to leave me behind, but I'd been so afraid that Collin would come back to finish what he'd started with her if she didn't go. "She did."

I had promised her that I would find her when it was safe—a promise I had yet to fulfill—and she had agreed to go. I had watched her disappear into the distance before I curled into a ball in the middle of the field and cried.

I pulled back from the memories. "I don't know what happened to her after that, but I hope wherever she ended up was safer than that house."

Marx flexed his fingers on the wheel as he silently absorbed the story. "So he left the doll to remind you of that day. Why that day in particular?"

That day represented the moment he realized he could do more than control me by hurting the people who mattered to me; he could make me suffer. And now he was targeting my friends.

Lights flickered behind us, and Marx's attention shifted to the rearview mirror. Sam was fifty feet behind us, and another vehicle was behind him.

"Why is he flickering his lights?" I asked.

Marx's relaxed posture didn't change, but his eyes were alert and watchful. "Because we're bein' followed."

My heart thumped faster in alarm. How could he be so calm about that after one man had already tried to kill him tonight?

I twisted in my seat to look behind us, but all I could make out of the distant vehicle were twin beams of light.

"Why flash his lights? Why not call?"

"Because a phone call is a distraction. He's keepin' both hands on the wheel and all of his attention on the vehicle behind him."

Marx's eyes flickered between the mirrors as we turned down another side street. The mysterious vehicle hesitated before gliding around the corner after Sam.

"Not exactly discreet, are they?" I asked.

"I would guess they haven't realized that the car they're tryin' to hide behind belongs to a cop."

"Do you think this is because of Collin?"

He tilted his head. "I'm havin' a hard time believin' it's a coincidence. He definitely wants me out of the picture."

The car rocked as we drove over a bump and into an alley in the opposite direction of home. I shot Marx a questioning look when we slowed to a stop, but his attention was fixed on the side mirror.

It seemed to me that if we were being followed, we should probably drive *faster*, not come to a dead stop.

Sam's car rolled into a vacant space along the curb of the main street, and his lights winked out.

There were a dozen questions buzzing around inside my head, but I settled on one for the moment. "Why did Sam park on the street?"

"When the car passes him, he can get the plate. If the person pulls into the alley behind us, he'll back up and close him in," he explained.

The mysterious car—a red vehicle with rounded edges—slowed to a stop on the street just outside the alley. It idled, and my fingers dug into the headrest of my seat as I waited for something to happen.

Marx's fingers tapped an impatient rhythm, and he muttered, "Come on. Make a decision."

The vehicle lingered for another breath-stealing moment before it crept forward down the quiet street and disappeared from view. Relieved, I slumped down in my seat.

I caught the red glow of Sam's taillights in the rearview mirror, and then he pulled into the alley behind us.

"He's not gonna follow them?"

"No," Marx said. "He's gonna make sure we get you home safe. That's more important at the moment."

Except for the fact that the crazy people were out to get him rather than me, sure, that made sense. Thankfully, Sam was the only person who followed us back to the apartment.

I fumbled out of my boots, stripped off Marx's jacket and mine, and headed for the shower the moment we stepped inside, determined to expunge the memories from my skin.

9

I stared up at the dark ceiling of the spare bedroom as thoughts tumbled through my exhausted mind. I wanted to sleep, but every time I closed my eyes, I was back in that field, watching Cassie struggle to survive.

A verse floated to the surface of my thoughts: *The Lord will strengthen you and protect you from the evil one.*

From . . . the Collin?

I almost laughed. The evil one might refer to Satan, but it suited Collin quite nicely. I knew he was only a man, but so much darkness surrounded him that it made me shiver all the way to my soul.

I turned my head to look at the still form sleeping peacefully beside me. She was nothing but light—a tiny light that Collin had tried to snuff out.

I stretched out a hand and brushed a few wiry hairs back from Maya's face. I had oiled and braided her hair last night so it wouldn't look like a puff ball in the morning, and she'd asked if she could stay with me. After everything she had been through, I couldn't deny her that small comfort.

She was snuggled under the covers on one half of the bed, her small hands still dangling over the edge where they had been resting on Riley's head when she fell asleep.

Being with me seemed to ease her fear when she woke up in the middle of the night and suddenly remembered that her mother was gone.

Thankfully, the nightmares that had woken me hadn't disturbed her.

A warm nose pressed against my left hand. Riley was standing by the bed, his big, warm eyes peering at me with canine concern. I rubbed behind his ears as I sat up and slipped soundlessly from beneath the covers.

I patted the mattress gently, giving him permission to come aboard, and he happily hopped up. He lay down flush against Maya's back.

"Stay," I whispered, and he rested his muzzle on his paws.

I tugged on a sweater over my tank top and long-sleeve T-shirt before sliding my feet into my slippers. Clothing couldn't protect me, but in moments like this, I wrapped it around myself like armor and let myself believe that it could.

It was a little after five in the morning when I stepped out of the spare bedroom and closed the door behind me. I shuffled into the dimly lit kitchen to make something warm to drink, and found Sam sitting at the peninsula, sipping coffee and reading a newspaper.

"I'm surprised you're still here," I said, flipping on the overhead light.

He didn't lift his head, but his dark eyes flicked to me for the briefest instant before returning to the newspaper. "I figured it couldn't hurt to have backup after everything that's happened lately."

"But shouldn't you be working?" He usually worked the night shift, but he wasn't in his uniform.

He turned the page. "I'm still on paid leave, courtesy of the lieutenant."

"I thought they cleared you."

After it came to light that Sam's partner was deeply involved in a drug ring, he'd fallen under suspicion by association. The department had suspended him with pay and investigated him down to his sleep patterns and last dental appointment. Sam was squeaky clean, which didn't surprise me.

He sighed and set down his cup of coffee. "When your partner of five months turns out to be crooked and then is shot by another cop, they force you to take some time off. They're also *suggesting* I talk to a counselor."

I turned on the stove light and rummaged through the nearby cupboard for the ingredients to make marshmallow hot chocolate. Marshmallows always made me feel better. "You're avoiding the shrink?"

He grimaced and ignored the question. "On the subject of *shrinks*, you should consider visiting one for your post-traumatic stress disorder."

I shot him a dark look. Marx had already tried to persuade me to talk with someone, and I wasn't interested. "I do not have PTSD."

He arched an eyebrow, unintimidated by my glare. "You threw up in the hallway last night."

"Maybe I ate something that didn't agree with me."

"You tried to scrub your skin off when we got back." He stared at me, and I tried very hard not to squirm. "Even though every inch of skin Collin touched is long gone."

He made it sound so illogical. Whether the skin my foster brother touched was gone or not, I still felt him. "You don't know what you're talking about."

"You have screaming nightmares, you're jumpy, you don't like to be touched by men, and you get sick to your stomach when you confront Collin or your memories of being r—"

I slammed my mug down on the counter. "Don't . . . say it."

Sam paused for a moment before continuing. "The word fits, Holly. To destroy something of value, to take by force, and sometimes to damage irreparably."

I resisted the urge to hurl my mug at his head as a fiery anger scorched through me. "I'm intimately familiar with the definitions of that word, Sam."

Damage irreparably. That one singed most of all, because it touched on the fear that I would never truly be whole again. No matter how much God mended me, some part of me would always feel . . . damaged.

Sam inhaled and opened his mouth, but I didn't want to hear anything more he had to say.

"I don't need a therapist, I don't have PTSD, and I'm done talking about this."

I popped my mug of chocolate mix into the microwave and leveled a warning glare at him in case he had any more thoughts about speaking. His lips pinched into a frown, but he stayed silent. Good. I liked him better that way.

I exhaled a long, slow breath and tried to rein in my temper. I needed space, but there was no place to go in this small apartment with four people and a dog. A distraction was my only hope of not losing my temper and chucking something at Sam's head.

My wandering gaze glossed over the tidy apartment and landed on the pair of shoes beside the door. Ah, perfect.

I piled a mountain of marshmallows on top of my hot chocolate and took it with me into the living room. I started to switch on the lamp beside the couch when I noticed Sam watching me with a curious expression.

"What?" I asked defensively.

"You're turning on all the lights."

"Not *all* the lights." I looked around the apartment for a bulb that wasn't lit. "The hallway light's not on."

"You realize lights don't actually keep you safe."

I lifted my chin. "You realize grimacing doesn't actually intimidate people."

He smiled, barely, and returned his attention to his newspaper. I switched on the lamp. I needed lights as much as I needed my layers right now.

I gathered up Marx's shoes—he had big feet—and chewed on my bottom lip as I turned in a slow circle, searching for the best place to hide them. I was getting my sneakers back one way or another, even if I had to hold his shoes for ransom.

I stashed one shoe behind the television and stuffed the other beneath one of the couch cushions before plopping down on top of it.

Ha! They were my shoes now.

I turned on the television and tried very hard to pretend that Sam wasn't sitting a few feet behind me. I stumbled across a bizarre show called *The Twilight Zone*, but I got irritated and flipped the channel when Sam started commenting on how things "weren't logical" and how certain elements of the show weren't "realistic." Well, what did he expect from science *fiction*?

I settled on a cooking show and cast him a warning glare over my shoulder. If he started pointing out how they diced their onions illogically, I was going to hit him in the face with a pillow.

"That wasn't sanitary," he said when the cook dipped a finger into the frosting she had just made.

"Really, Sam?" I knew he was a germophobe, but good grief.

Marx's alarm went off—that dreadful rhythmic sound that reminded me of a stuttering bee—and I knew it must be six o'clock.

A moment later his bedroom door jerked inward, and he lurched into the hallway in his sweatpants and T-shirt. He rubbed a hand through his hair as he yawned, and his hair stuck up at odd angles.

He disappeared into the bathroom.

I had about twenty minutes to get ready, but I had to be careful not to wake Maya. She needed her rest.

I tiptoed back into the spare bedroom to change. I was running a brush through my hair when someone knocked on the front door. There was a second of silence before I heard Jordan's voice.

"Um, did I get the day wrong? Because I could swear Marx told me last night he was following a lead this morning, and I was gonna hang out with the girls."

"He wasn't expecting me to stay," Sam replied. The dead bolt clicked as he closed and bolted the door.

"Oh. Why *did* you stay?"

"It was a bit of a rough night last night."

I leaned against the door, listening. Apparently, when Jordan brought Maya back while I was in the shower, no one had bothered to tell him what had happened at the address Danny gave us.

"Why am I always the last to know?"

"It's not like we have a meeting and collectively decide not to tell you things," Sam said.

"Is Holly okay?"

"Physically."

"What is that supposed to mean?"

"It means she doesn't have any physical injuries."

"Sam," Jordan snapped impatiently.

Sam sighed. "Someone tried to kill Marx and we ran into Collin."

I stepped back from the door and continued getting ready. I could still hear the anger that laced Jordan's voice, even if I couldn't understand his words.

I wrapped my new scarf around my neck, then snuck back out of the room on tiptoe.

"Hey," Jordan greeted, his usual lighthearted warmth returning to his voice.

I tucked my hands into the back pockets of my jeans and smiled. "Hi."

"Sam was telling me about what happened with Collin last night. Are you okay?"

"I'm fine. Sam stepped between us." I glanced at Sam, whom I was still very much annoyed with, and forced myself to say, "Thank you for that, by the way."

He inclined his head.

The bathroom door opened, and the aroma of shampoo flooded the apartment. Marx came down the hallway, rubbing a towel against his damp hair, and grumbling something about soap.

He paused at the threshold of the kitchen when he noticed me. "Hey, sweet pea."

"About the soap thing," I began a little reluctantly. "I sort of used it all last night."

His gaze swept over me from head to toe. "On what? You don't exactly have a lot of surface area."

I shrugged a shoulder. "I have my ways." There had been a quarter of a bottle of generic body wash in there, and I had used every last drop to clean myself—repeatedly.

"Why is every light in my apartment on?"

I shifted self-consciously and struggled to come up with an explanation that didn't sound pathetic.

I was surprised when Sam cleared his throat and said, "I needed light to read the paper."

"Every light?" Marx demanded.

"I didn't realize it would bother you." Sam deliberately turned the page and focused his attention back on the sports section.

Marx sighed and muttered sarcastically, "Why would it bother me that I'm payin' to light up the entire neighborhood at seven in the mornin'?"

Sam pulled out his wallet and set a five-dollar bill on the counter. "That should cover it."

"Put that away." Marx stepped around me to pour himself a cup of coffee.

I shot Sam an appreciative look while Marx's back was turned, and he gave me a small smile before saying, "Marx isn't much of a morning person before his coffee."

"I'm perfectly fine in the mornin'," Marx grouched.

I choked back a laugh.

"Don't you laugh at me," he chided. He suddenly noticed my jeans, boots, and purple sweater, and his eyebrows knitted with disapproval. "No."

I blinked. "No what?"

"You know very well what. I'm goin' to see Mr. Glass this mornin' to talk to him about the fire at the shelter, and you're not comin' with me."

I scowled at him. How did he always know what I was planning before I even said anything?

His eyebrows lifted at my expression. "Are we gonna have an argument?"

"Yes," I bit out.

He sighed and set down his coffee, then grabbed the last vacant stool and set it in front of me.

Okay . . .

"What's that for?"

"For you to stand on so we can argue face-to-face," he said simply.

"I am not that short!"

"You are kind of on the small side," Sam commented. "You're what, five foot one?"

Why was he always so irritatingly accurate? "You're the last person who should be calling me short, Sam. You're only five . . . something."

"I'm average."

Jordan coughed into his fist, "For a woman."

Sam pressed his lips together and glowered at him. I folded my arms and tried to give Marx the same intimidating look, but my face just didn't do what Sam's did.

"Glare at me all you want, Holly, but I am not takin' you to the house of a man who abuses women, especially when he's likely conspirin' with Collin."

When he put it that way, it did sound like a bad idea. "I'm not afraid of Rachel's husband, and I wanna help."

"I know you wanna help, but it's not worth the risk."

"Shouldn't that be my decision?"

"No, that's the decision of the people tryin' to protect you."

"I—"

He held up a hand and cut me off with a single, clipped sentence, "You're not comin' with me and that's the end of it."

I resisted the urge to stomp my feet in outrage. I understood that he wanted to keep me safe, but he was the one who needed to be protected.

Collin was targeting the people I cared about, and nothing would stop him until he managed to cross every one of them off his list. I didn't intend to hide out like a chicken while that happened.

I looked at Jordan for support.

Hesitation was written all over his face. "I don't know, Holly. You and Maya were attacked in a public bathroom yesterday, and then Collin made an appearance. Maybe you should give yourself some time to—"

"I'm fine."

He exhaled and scratched the back of his head as he looked between Sam and Marx. "Sam, you wanna weigh in here?"

Sam took another calm sip of coffee before answering. "Negotiate or cave. Those are your only choices."

"Seriously?"

"Seriously."

Jordan considered that for a moment. "Why don't we go back downtown and show Collin's picture around? See if anyone can place him at the scene of the fire, and we'll meet Marx at the house after he interviews Glass."

It wasn't ideal, but at least I would be doing something to further the investigation into Collin. I wanted him off the street before he hurt anyone else I cared about.

"Okay," I agreed.

The pinched set to Marx's mouth said he wasn't pleased with that option either. "If Collin comes anywhere near her—"

"You'll be my first call," Jordan assured him.

"Good." Marx walked to the front door to grab his shoes and paused with a frown. He turned, searching for them. "Where in the . . ."

81

I slapped a hand over my mouth to stifle my laugh, but that just made it sound more like a squeaky snort.

Marx's eyes narrowed in on me. "Where are my shoes, young lady?"

I cleared my throat and lowered my hand from my mouth to suggest innocently, "Maybe if you put things in the same place every time, you wouldn't lose them."

"I've put my shoes in that same spot for two years," he said, pointing to the vacant spot. "I didn't *lose* them."

I tried not to smile, but I couldn't help it.

"That mischievous little smirk on your face tells me you know exactly where they are."

Sam arched an eyebrow at me—he had watched me hide them—and I gave a slight shake of my head. Marx caught our silent exchange.

"Sam, where are my shoes?"

Sam looked pointedly into his mug. "I think I need a refill." He stood and strode into the kitchen.

I lifted my chin triumphantly. "Maybe your shoes disappeared to the same place my sneakers did."

Understanding registered on his face and his lips twitched. He had just realized *why* his shoes magically disappeared. "Mmm hmm. I somehow doubt they're in the same place."

He strolled into the kitchen and reached on top of the cabinets over the refrigerator. My sneakers appeared in his hand.

My mouth fell open. "How was I ever supposed to get those all the way up there?" I hadn't even thought to look there. When I tried to take them, he held them out of my reach. "Hey!" I protested. I stretched onto my toes, and he moved them over his head. "Stop that!"

Jordan laughed and Sam mumbled into his coffee cup, "I don't see this ending well."

"If we're doin' an exchange, I need to see my shoes," Marx bargained.

I had a feeling if I left the room to get his shoes, he would hide mine again while I wasn't looking. I glanced at the stool and thought about climbing on top of it to grab them. Then I thought of a sneakier plan that wouldn't involve me falling off a stool onto my face.

I tickled him.

"Holly!" he said, his voice caught somewhere between a reprimand and a laugh as he jerked his arms down to protect his ribs. I snatched my shoes from his hands and darted into the living room. "That was completely unfair."

"Why? Because you didn't see it coming?" I asked, hugging my shoes to my chest.

"Nobody saw that coming," Sam said evenly. "You never touch people."

I seldom touched people by choice, but I wouldn't say never. It was just . . . unusual.

"It's unfair because we both know I can't use the same tactic," Marx explained.

That was true. He wasn't allowed to tickle me. "Well . . . I can't hold things above your head and make you jump for them, so you don't need to tickle me."

"She has a point," Sam said.

Marx sighed. "Okay, fine. You win. Now, where are my shoes?"

I quickly collected his shoes and carried them over to him.

"You need to work on your hidin' places. I would've found them within ten minutes," he pointed out as he put them on.

"Is that an invitation to practice? Because I'm sure I can find better places to stash your shoes."

"No, it is not an invitation."

I put my sneakers away and returned to the kitchen. "Time to go." I headed for the front door with Jordan on my heels.

Marx's warning drifted down the hallway after us. "Be careful with her, Jordan!"

10

"*H*ave you noticed how Marx warns me to be careful with you every time I take you someplace?" Jordan asked. "He acts like I'm gonna take you bar hopping or let you play in traffic."

"No, you just take me to creepy alleys to knock on stranger's doors." I tapped my knuckles on the faded, paint-chipped door of the squat building and leaned back against the archway to wait. "And I haven't played in traffic since I was like six."

"Yeah, I'm pretty sure it was just last month that you ran out into traffic. Twice, actually."

Oh. Right. I did do that. But I had good reasons.

I knocked again, trying to put more force behind it. We had visited every occupied building in the area and had spoken to some of the people on the street, but no one had much to say.

We had worked our way through an apartment building before this place, but we had skipped the last apartment. The door had been wide open, and the tenant—a man who was probably in his forties—had been dancing around the living room in little more than his skin and an eye patch, serenading a stuffed parrot.

"You're smirking," Jordan observed, and I pressed my lips between my teeth sheepishly. "You're thinking about the parrot pirate, aren't you?"

I grinned. "He had a pretty good singing voice."

"I didn't notice. I was a little distracted by the amount of clothes he *wasn't* wearing."

He banged on the door with the side of his fist, but no sound came from inside. He sighed and glanced around the cramped alley. "Well, I guess no one's home."

We had spent an entire morning and afternoon searching for witnesses, and this was our last stop. The time felt wasted.

"I'm gonna let Marx know we're on the way over to Glass's house," Jordan said, pulling out his phone.

I caught a flicker of light behind him as sunlight glinted off the windshield of a car pulling into the alley. Maybe it was the person who lived here and the trip wouldn't be wasted after all.

"All right, let's head back to the car," Jordan suggested, returning his phone to his jacket pocket.

The moment he stepped out of the archway into the alley, the red car let out a growl of acceleration and launched forward.

"Jordan!"

I grabbed his arm and yanked him back. The car scraped the side of the building where Jordan had been only a second before, and flecks of paint and metal peppered the ground.

The vehicle skidded to a stop halfway down the alley. My heart pounded violently as I stared at it, stunned. Jordan had nearly been hit.

"Are you okay?" I tried to look up at him, but all I could see was the underside of his chin.

"Yeah," he exhaled, but he sounded as rattled as I felt. "I'm gonna check on the driver."

He released me and stepped back into the alley. He started toward the stopped vehicle with his hand on his gun.

A flash of taillights was our only warning before the car slammed into reverse. Jordan was too far from the archway to duck back into safety, and whoever was behind the wheel of the car was intent on backing over him.

He dashed toward the nearest possible safety—the dumpster—and, with a kick jump off the wall that would've landed me on my back, scaled the dumpster. He barely had time to find his footing before the back of the car rammed the dumpster and knocked him off balance and into the side of the building.

He recovered just as the driver of the car made a second attempt. Metal screeched and glass shattered as the taillights collided with the dumpster.

Jordan braced for it and managed to keep his balance. When the car pulled forward, he drew his gun and took aim.

I clamped my hands over my ears as he fired at the vehicle. The two rear tires popped, but the car shot forward down the alley as the driver stomped on the gas.

I tried to catch the plate number, but the driver was speeding and swerving so wildly that I couldn't read more than GUE. The car whipped around the corner at the end of the alley and disappeared.

Jordan tucked his gun back into the holster and slid down from the dumpster, glass crunching beneath his shoes. He pressed the back of his hand to a cut above his eyebrow and glared in the direction the car had fled.

"Are you okay?" I asked.

"I'm a little peeved that someone just tried to turn me into roadkill, but yeah, otherwise I'm good."

I folded my arms and frowned disapprovingly. "You don't *look* good." There was blood running down his temple.

"First time I've had a woman tell me that."

Heat crept into my face. "I mean . . . you're bleeding and you should . . . go to a hospital."

He flashed me a teasing smile. "I know what you meant." He pulled out his phone and called to report the incident.

A patrol car arrived within minutes, and a female officer, probably in her midthirties, came to take our statements. Her name tag read N. Miffton.

She was about my height with sharp green eyes and wisps of blonde hair escaping from beneath her hat. She looked familiar.

"Nance?" I asked.

"Hey, Red." She bumped me on the shoulder with her fist, and I staggered back a step. "See you still haven't learned to plant your feet."

"You two know each other?" Jordan asked.

I rubbed my shoulder—she hit like a guy—and explained, "We met at the officer's memorial banquet in January. She helped me up after—"

"Some guy plowed her over," Nance cut in. She had one of the thickest New York accents I had ever heard. "Big lug of a guy too." She looked up at Jordan. "So, who is it messed up your handsome face?"

Nance's partner, who barely looked old enough to be out of high school, wrote furiously in a notebook in between glances around the scene, but said very little.

Nance pursed her lips after Jordan gave her the abridged version of events. "Either of you got any enemies who might wanna see you dead or seriously injured?"

I felt Jordan's attention shift to me. I had an enemy who wanted me seriously injured, but he wouldn't do it with a car. And I hadn't been the target.

Jordan cleared his throat. "I don't know anyone with a burning desire to run me over, no."

I waited with dread for him to tell her about Collin, but he didn't say anything more. He wasn't going to put me in the situation of having to explain my painful past to two more strangers.

"What about the vehicle?" Nance pressed on. "Can you describe it?"

"Red," I said.

"Make and model?"

I shifted self-consciously. "Um . . . bright red . . . with doors. Four of them." I didn't recognize the make or model of vehicles. My automobile dictionary consisted of truck, car, van, and a variety of colors.

She blinked at me a few times before turning back to Jordan, who was making an effort not to smile. "Same question."

"It was a Honda Accord sedan. Looked brand new, maybe a 2016. But it's in pretty rough shape now."

"Plate?"

"GU . . . something."

"E," I added, finally able to contribute something. "The third character was an E. I don't remember the numbers after it."

And I had a feeling it was the red car that had followed us last night. I couldn't be a hundred percent certain, but it was the same color and shape.

"And neither of you saw the driver?" Nance asked.

"The sun was glaring off the windshield," I explained. "I couldn't see anyone."

When Jordan shook his head, she sighed. "Okay. Just one more question. Are you two . . . together?"

Jordan and I exchanged a look before he said, "No, we're just friends."

Nance grunted thoughtfully. "We'll look into the vehicle and let you know if we uncover any information. Call if you remember anything else." She scribbled something at the bottom of her notepad, tore it off, and folded it before handing it to Jordan.

He opened the sheet of paper as Nance and her partner pulled out of the alley, and an odd expression crossed his face.

"What is it?" I stretched up on my tiptoes to see what she wrote.

He handed it to me. There was a phone number on it with a brief message: *Call me sometime. —Nance.*

Oh. That was why she had asked if we were together. "She thinks you're cute."

He grinned. "Men aren't cute, Holly."

"Pretty?" I offered. He was definitely pretty.

He lifted an eyebrow. "It's just one insult after another. Any more punches you wanna deliver to my ego?"

I bit my lip and smiled before returning my attention to the phone number on the strip of paper. I felt an unexpected twinge of sadness at the thought of him dating someone, but I kept it from my voice as I asked, "Are you gonna call her?"

"I wasn't planning on it."

I couldn't help but wonder if he was ignoring her offer because of me. As much as I wanted him to be a part of my life, I didn't want to hold him back.

I drew in a breath and said, "She's pretty. You should think about it." I handed the phone number back to him and started off in the direction of the car.

11

I stared out the passenger window, watching the city pass by without really seeing it. My mind was whirling with awful possibilities.

The tapping of Jordan's fingers on the steering wheel drew me from my thoughts. I caught his reflection in the window, glancing at me for the hundredth time.

"Something's bothering you," he finally said. "You haven't said a word since we got in the car, and you're hugging that door like I'm gonna bite you."

I hadn't even realized how far I had withdrawn from him. My shoulder was pressed against the side of the car and I was curled toward the door.

"Did I do something?" he asked, and I could hear the concern in his voice.

"No."

He was quiet for a moment. "I'm sorry I violated your space back there in the alley. I didn't mean to. It was just instinct to try to protect you."

Somehow, even though I had pulled him out of the path of the oncoming car, I had been the one up against the door with his arms wrapped around me.

"I know, and I'm not upset with you," I said almost absently, my mind slipping back to my previous thoughts.

His fingers tapped louder. "Is this because Officer Miffton gave me her phone number?"

I blinked in confusion. "What?"

He looked at me again before saying, "Because if it is, I'm not interested."

His disinterest sounded genuine, but I had seen the woman. Her uniform had masked her curves, but she was striking, and clearly attracted to him. I had a hard time believing any man wouldn't feel the same.

"Really?" I asked, my skepticism obvious in my tone. "She's curvy and pretty."

"That doesn't mean I wanna date her. There are plenty of pretty women in the world, and some of them have about as much depth as a mud puddle."

Curious, I shifted my body toward him in the seat. "Am I a mud puddle?"

His dimples appeared as he grinned. "Hardly. You're more like . . . an ocean. There's an entire world of beauty and depth beneath the surface, but there's also mysterious things lurking down deep that make a man afraid to stick his toe in the water."

Hmm. I wondered what it was about me that made him so afraid for his toes.

"And if a man tries to traverse this ocean without guidance or a map, he runs the risk of doing—or saying—something stupid and sinking. So how about you toss me a life jacket and explain what I did wrong before I start drowning."

"I promise, you didn't do anything wrong. I'm just . . . I have a lot on my mind."

I couldn't shake the memory of the car speeding toward him or the sound of glass shattering as the driver repeatedly tried to back over him. I had been so afraid the moment the driver slammed the car in reverse that he wouldn't be able to get out of the way.

First the shelter, then the attempt on Marx's life, and now someone had just tried to run Jordan down in the street.

How was I going to protect them?

We pulled up in front of Rachel Glass's house, and I frowned at the sight of squad cars parked on the street. Marx was just supposed to speak with her husband, but something must have gone wrong.

I flung off the seatbelt and hopped out of the car. I started up the walkway toward the front steps and nearly collided with a police officer.

I took a startled step back. "Mer. Hi."

Mer had been one of the officers on my protection detail last autumn. He looked just as unpleasant as I remembered: pale, blank-faced, and so gaunt that he could've just popped out of a grave.

Crinkles of dissatisfaction formed around his mouth. "Officer Meredith, if you don't mind."

"Right, sorry."

Officer Meredith's head rotated toward Jordan in that owlish way that left his body perfectly still—giving me the creeps—and scrutinized him. "I don't know you."

Jordan held out his hand. "Jordan Radcliffe. I worked with Marx when he brought Holly to Kansas."

Meredith ignored the offered hand and returned his attention to me. "You can't be here. No civilians allowed at an active crime scene."

Active crime scene?

My heartbeat picked up. Had Collin sent someone else after Marx? Had Rachel's husband attacked him when he came to the door? "Where's Marx? I wanna see him."

I tried to rush around Meredith to the front door, but he blocked me. "He's busy."

"But he's okay? He's not hurt?"

"He's fine. He's out back. Now remove yourself from the premises, Ms. Cross, or I'll have to *escort* you from the premises."

"You're not *escorting* her anywhere," Jordan said, stepping up beside me and folding his arms.

Meredith's beady eyes narrowed. "This is an active—"

"Active crime scene. Yeah, we heard you the first time," Jordan cut in. "We're here to see Marx. He's expecting us."

Meredith looked doubtful, but he grabbed his radio to confirm that we were expected. A garbled voice responded, and he scowled. "It would seem that living with Detective Marx affords you certain privileges, Ms. Cross."

I didn't miss the innuendo in his words, and I shot him a frigid glare. Half the precinct seemed to think there was more than friendship between me and Marx, and denying it didn't change anything.

Meredith stepped aside. "Don't contaminate the crime scene."

"Thanks, *Mer*," I replied, not bothering to hide my annoyance. I strode past him with Jordan on my heels.

I heard his irritable grumble—"It's Officer Meredith"—as I bounded up the steps into the house.

A stench strong enough to offend a skunk wafted from the open doorway, and the hot dog I had eaten earlier performed a few nauseating backflips in my stomach.

"Wow," Jordan said, pressing the back of a wrist to his nose. "I haven't smelled anything this rank since college."

I lifted my eyebrows at him.

"No, not me," he clarified. "Gamer across the hall. I think the only time he left his dorm room was when he ran out of beer. Keep in mind that the bathroom was down the hall."

Ew.

We waded through the house cluttered with empty beer bottles, pizza boxes, cigarette butts, and half-empty take-out containers that were sprouting patches of fuzz. Apparently, without Rachel, cleaning didn't happen. Or laundry, for that matter.

I stepped over a pile of dirty clothes and paused in the hallway when a picture drew my attention. Disfigured by cracked glass was a wedding photo of a much younger Rachel—her auburn hair draped over one shoulder in shimmering waves and her smile radiant—with her new husband beside her. It was a picture of hope, love, and new beginnings.

And it was a lie.

I was there the day Rachel sought refuge at the shelter. I saw the bruises and the fear in her eyes.

The man in the picture, Darin Glass, was dark-skinned and tall, with broad shoulders and hands the size of my face. I remembered those hands, curled into fists, hammering violently on the shelter door.

I had been taking out the garbage one night, when I noticed him peering through the windows, looking for a way inside. I had stopped for just an instant when our eyes met.

Then I dropped the garbage on the pavement and darted back inside, slamming and bolting the door a second before he smashed the sides of his massive fists against it in a drunken rage.

He had come for Rachel, and it was frightening to imagine what he might have done if he'd managed to get inside that night. There was no one there to protect any of us—just Beth Anne, children, and a handful of frightened, traumatized women.

I slept with a knife under my pillow that night, afraid that the next monster at the door would be mine. I never told Rachel how close her husband had come to getting in because I knew it would terrify her.

I had seen the depth of her fear shortly after she arrived. We were paired for clean-up duty after dinner on her third night when one of the plates slipped from her soapy fingers and shattered on the floor.

She flinched, as if she expected someone to hit her, and retreated into the corner. She apologized through her tears for her clumsiness until the words were barely more than unintelligible whimpers.

Remembering it now made me wish I had hugged and comforted her. It also made me wish I had slammed her husband's fingers in the door hard enough to break them the night he tried to get in—it was hard to beat someone when you had splinted fingers. Unfortunately, I hadn't done either.

I hadn't spoken much since Collin attacked me in Pennsylvania, and I wouldn't have known what to say to console her anyway, so I had grabbed a plate and purposefully dropped it on the floor.

When it didn't shatter to my satisfaction, I stomped on it with my boots. Rachel had gaped at me in shock from the corner. I put my hands on my hips and made a show of looking around for any bully who dared reprimand me for breaking a plate.

When no one came to knock me off my feet and scream at me, I broke another one.

Rachel's frightened eyes flitted around the room. Still, nothing happened. I let her come to the realization on her own that the only consequence of a broken plate in the shelter was a broken plate.

After a couple of minutes, she wiped her face and crept out of the corner, and together we silently cleaned up the mess. As I was leaving the kitchen, I spotted Beth Anne leaning against the wall around the corner. She didn't say a word that evening; she merely smiled at me with a glimmer of interest in her eyes.

I did feel a little bad that I had intentionally broken two plates, but it had been for a good reason. I simply shrugged and muttered, "Therapy," before going to my room.

"Somehow I didn't expect a wife abuser to look like such a nice guy," Jordan said from behind me, and I glanced back to see him studying the same photo.

"Pictures lie." I walked away toward the back of the house, pushed open the screen door, and stepped onto the back stoop.

Rachel and Darin had a small rectangle of fenced-in yard, most of which was occupied by a blue car. There was a large, open gate at the far end with tire tracks that led out onto the street.

Marx looked up from the trunk of the car when I hopped down the steps to join him. "You know, for such a tiny person, you make a lot of noise when you walk. You're like a baby hippo."

I grinned. "At least you always know I'm coming."

"So does half the neighborhood."

Jordan followed me down the wooden steps, his footsteps remarkably quiet by comparison. "I thought you were just coming over to talk to the guy. What happened?"

Marx stripped off the rubber gloves he was wearing. "He didn't answer the door, so I came around back to see if he was in the yard. And this is what I found."

He gestured to the bottles and containers the crime scene techs were bagging and labeling.

"CSU is collectin' chemicals along with bottles possibly used for the flamin' cocktails that were thrown through the shelter's windows. They're gonna compare them with the trace chemicals recovered from the scene. But that's not what concerns me."

He pointed to a few reddish-brown stains that dripped from the edge of the car's trunk onto the bumper.

My stomach clenched with fear. "Is that . . ."

"Blood," he confirmed. He hesitated before adding, "There's more in the trunk along with a few strands of brown hair."

I swallowed. "Rachel's?"

"We won't be sure until we get the DNA results back. But considerin' she wasn't present in the shelter durin' the fire, it's likely he grabbed her and stuffed her in the trunk before startin' it."

"Why? If he was angry enough with her to start a fire that killed seven people, why not just burn the shelter down with her inside?" Jordan asked.

"If I had to guess, I would say it's because a fire wasn't personal enough for him. Men like him enjoy the feelin' of control and power they wield over others. He likely wanted to teach her a lesson for leavin' him. We just don't know what he did with her body afterward," Marx explained.

Her body. Those two words hit me like a punch to the stomach. If Darin Glass could justify beating his wife over a broken plate, what other cruelties could he justify?

Was he so angry that he could burn his wife's safe haven to the ground with seven innocent people inside? So angry that he had stuffed her in a trunk and . . .

"Maybe she's not dead," I said. "Maybe . . . he's just holding her somewhere or . . . or maybe she got away. That's possible, right?"

Marx's eyes shimmered with sympathy when he looked at me. "Maybe. We're not gonna stop searchin' for her. And we have units out lookin' for Darin Glass now."

I hadn't known Rachel well, but I could empathize with her situation, and I was afraid for her, for what her husband might do to her. Or, if Marx's instincts were right, what he might have already done.

"Any luck on witnesses to the fire?" Marx asked.

"Unfortunately no," Jordan replied. "We spoke with everyone in the area, but no one had much to say."

"I'm not surprised." Marx rubbed the back of his neck, a sign that he was both tired and out of ideas. "What happened to your head?"

"Someone almost ran me over."

"Intentionally?"

"Well, when they put the car in reverse and tried again, I assumed it was intentional."

Marx's attention shifted from Jordan to me.

"I'm fine," I assured him. "Whoever it was wasn't interested in me."

He grunted thoughtfully. "I doubt that very much. Did either of you get a look at the driver?"

"No," Jordan said. "But I think we all know who's responsible, even if he wasn't behind the wheel."

Marx nodded. "We're all gonna need to be more cautious. Especially you, sweet pea." He gave me a firm look.

"I'm always cautious."

"Your idea of cautious is not bein' seen when you sneak off and do things you know you shouldn't. *My* idea of cautious involves you stayin' off the street and behind locked doors."

"I don't like your version."

"Yes, I know. So just don't do anythin' or go anywhere alone, includin' department store bathrooms."

I folded my arms. "Whatever you say, *sugar.*"

He narrowed his eyes at the teasing nickname I seldom used, but I could see the glint of humor in them. "Don't you sugar me, *peanut.*"

"Peanut?" I repeated hotly.

"Mmm hmm."

"I am not a peanut."

"You're about the size of one."

I bristled and tried to look taller, but it was pointless with Jordan standing beside me. I gave him a frustrated look. "You're making me look bad."

He cocked an eyebrow at me. "Am I supposed to shrink?"

"You could try to look shorter."

"The offer to sit on my shoulders is still up for grabs. That'll give you a few extra feet."

I deflated with a huff. It was too hard pretending I was taller; it was making my calves hurt, and I was not going to sit on his shoulders.

"We should get back to the apartment," Jordan said. "Sam's probably going crazy with Maya."

As irrational as it was, I was reluctant to leave. I knew that my presence would do nothing to keep Marx safe, but after the attempt on his life last night and Jordan's near-death experience a couple of hours ago, I was worried. What if something happened on the way home?

Heavenly Father, please watch over the people I care about.

Marx nodded. "Let me know when you're safely—"

I stepped forward and wrapped my arms around him without warning, startling him to silence. I felt his surprised stiffness for a bare instant, and then he relaxed.

"Please be careful," I mumbled into his chest; then I ducked out quickly before he could fold his arms around me.

He gave me a puzzled look as I retreated back to my spot beside Jordan. I wasn't much of a hugger, but I'd had the urge to let him know how much I cared. That didn't mean I wanted to be hugged back.

He dropped his empty arms back to his sides and smiled. "I will."

I fidgeted self-consciously. "Okay. Bye." I scampered back up the steps into the house and Jordan followed.

12

I sat on a stool at the peninsula, tapping the eraser of my pencil against my lips and rubbing my toes into Riley's coarse fur as I considered my journal entry.

I had learned at a young age that life could take even the brightest light and snuff it out—my sister Gin had been the brightest of them all—and the only way to keep those lights from vanishing completely was to remember and acknowledge them.

Nightmares, riddled with terror and indignities I would rather forget, left me drained and clinging to those tiny flickers of light at four thirty in the morning.

I jotted them down in my notebook, hoping they might pull my mind away from those murky memories.

Dear Jesus,

Thank you for the people You've placed in my life. I used to think I would always be alone, but then You brought Marx and Jordan into my world. Marx makes me feel safer than I ever thought possible, and I'm thankful for him even though he hides my shoes.

Thank you for Jordan, who makes me laugh and reminds me of home. When I'm with him, sometimes I feel like a kid again, like that little girl who was stolen all those years ago. Maybe he was right and she does still exist inside me. Maybe she isn't gone.

I'm thankful for Maya's life, for Sam's friendship, and for Jace—

Quiet water drop noises scattered my thoughts, which were hard enough to hang on to given the tired, sludgy consistency of my brain, and I blinked at my phone.

100

Who could possibly be calling me at this abominable hour?

Jace's name flashed across the screen, and I frowned. My best friend didn't do mornings, especially before the sun woke up. She should've been hibernating for about five or six more hours.

Worry had me dropping my pencil and snatching up my phone before the next ring.

"Jace?"

A sob crackled over the line, and my chest constricted. Jace was prone to fits of emotional tears, but this sounded different.

"What's wrong?" I asked.

"It's Scott," she managed.

Scott was her older brother. He had been mugged a couple of years ago and left for dead. He'd been in a coma since that day, and Jace and I visited him every week in the hospital. Her family should've gone with her, but they had given up on Scott a long time ago.

They weren't exactly the huggable, cozy type of family, which had surprised me the first time I met them. Jace was a tackle-you-to-the-floor kind of hugger.

"Is he okay?" I asked when she continued to cry. I had the sudden fear that his condition had taken a turn for the worse.

If he died, it would devastate her.

She was still sobbing, and I could only pick out a few words here and there. "The hospital and . . . kill him."

I couldn't make sense of what she was saying, but one thing was clear: my best friend needed me at the hospital.

"I'm coming. I'll be there as soon as I can." I hung up and dashed into the spare room to change, managing not to wake Maya in my clumsy haste.

When I was dressed and standing by the front door, my desperate desire to protect and comfort Jace receded just enough for fear to creep in.

I couldn't go outside alone.

101

I stared at the door as I wrestled with my options. Sam would likely be at the hospital with Jace, Jordan would be asleep at five in the morning, and Marx . . .

I looked down the hall at his closed bedroom door. He hadn't gotten home until after eleven, and I knew he was exhausted. He was working the shelter fire, Rachel's missing persons case, and who knew how many other cases.

I didn't want to wake him for this. I asked so much of him already—of all my friends—and I didn't want to push their kindness and generosity to the breaking point.

I could call a cab, but then I would have to wait for it to arrive. The hospital was only a few blocks away. I could run that in minutes.

I felt a flutter of anxiety in my chest at the thought of going out alone, especially after dark. I glanced at Riley.

Maybe I didn't have to go alone. I reached for the leash hanging on the coat rack, and Riley was at my side in an instant, tail wagging excitedly.

I exchanged my boots for sneakers, jammed some cash, my cell phone, keys, and pepper spray into my jacket pockets, and then hurried out the door with Riley.

The first gulp of icy air made my lungs burn, and the shadowy street brought the anxiety rushing back full force. Collin could be anywhere.

My fingers spasmed on the leash as I visually scanned the sidewalks. "You're not gonna let him get me, right?" I asked, looking down at Riley.

He gazed up at me intently, as if he could sense my distress. No, he wouldn't let Collin get me.

We broke into a run in the direction of the hospital. I wished there were more street lamps to break up the darkness, but as Sam had so casually informed me yesterday, lights wouldn't keep me safe.

I ignored the whistles and unwanted attention from people loitering on the street corners, and Riley let out a few warning growls whenever he thought a man was too close to me.

I was winded by the time we shot through the front doors and into the lobby of the hospital. We ducked into an empty elevator, and I slumped against the wall, trying to catch my breath.

I made it.

Of course, if Collin had been watching Marx's apartment, he could've followed me. It wouldn't be the first time he came after me in a hospital.

I slapped the close button a few dozen times just to be on the safe side, and saw a flash of Kermit the Frog scrubs as a nurse shouted, "Miss, you can't bring that dog in here!"

Oops. We would just have to pretend he was a therapy dog or something.

I held my breath when the doors sealed. I hated elevators—suffocating cans dangling from a string—and I watched the floor number climb with agonizing slowness. The moment the doors dinged open, I shot out onto Scott's floor, dragging Riley with me.

Jace's voice, reaching a shrill, hysterical pitch, cut through the otherwise quiet hallway. "Please don't do this!"

"Stop whimpering, Jacelyn. You're acting like a child."

The crisp, refined voice made me want to groan. I deeply disliked Jace's mother, not only for the way she treated me the few times our paths crossed but also because of the cold, critical way she treated her daughter.

I reminded myself to be civil as I stepped through the doorway into Scott's room. Jace's tear-streaked face lifted when she saw me, and she released Sam's hand to roll her wheelchair into me and throw her arms around my waist.

"Oh, Holly," she cried, her voice thick with despair.

Sam glanced at Riley, looked behind me—probably for Jordan or Marx—and frowned when no one else appeared.

"Honestly, Jacelyn," Mrs. Walker said with obvious disapproval. "We couldn't handle this as a family? You needed to invite *her?*"

She said *her* like I was something distasteful she had to scrape off the bottom of her shoe. Not that she did that herself. She probably had professional shoe scrapers considering how many people she stepped on to get her way.

"Pleasure to see you as always, Mrs. Walker," I said. God forgive me for lying.

"I'm afraid I can't say the same," she replied with an upward tilt of her nose.

Apart from the Asian curve of their eyes and their slender frame, Jace had nothing in common with her mother. Mrs. Walker was closer to my height, and she carried herself like royalty. Although they were ridiculously well-off due to their family business, something to do with supplying essential parts for automated machines around the globe, that didn't give her the right to treat everyone else like lowly paupers.

I ignored her rudeness and turned my attention to her husband. Jace had gotten her height and quirky smile from him.

"Hi, Mr. Walker."

He offered me a nod and a smile that failed to hide his sadness. "Holly. It's nice to see you. I appreciate you being here for our daughter."

Mrs. Walker shot him an irritated look, and he cleared his throat before dropping his eyes. He reminded me of a turtle. One sharp glare or curt word from his wife, and he ducked for cover in his shell.

"Our *daughter* would do well to choose better friends. Someone educated and influential or, at the very least, someone with drive and style. Not this . . ."—her eyes raked over my appearance with disapproval—"girl who does nothing to enhance her reputation."

I tried not to react to the insult. I was *educated*. It might only be a high school freshman education, but it wasn't like I couldn't read or write.

Jace pulled away from me but kept a desperate grip on my hand as she leveled a furious look at her mother. "Don't be rude, Mother."

"I'm simply speaking the truth. I advised you many times to associate with better people."

"I'm so sorry my choices embarrass you," Jace replied venomously. "Ever since my car accident you've been embarrassed by me."

"That isn't true. Yes, your condition as a result of the accident is . . . unfortunate. And I do regret that you didn't marry while you were physically able. I expect your condition will make marriage more difficult now, but I'm sure if we offer the right incentive, any man would—"

"Are you kidding me?" I couldn't keep the outrage from my voice. How dare she make Jace feel bad for being in a wheelchair. It wasn't a life she chose, but it was a life she thrived at. "Jace is an amazing person, and you have no right to—"

"I am her mother."

"So that means your love is dependent on whether or not she can fulfill the plans *you* had for her life? Maybe nobody told you, but it's her life, and you don't get to control it."

Mrs. Walker smiled coldly. "I've noticed a lot of poor decisions on her part this past year, and I see where they're coming from."

I glared at her. "Hard to believe you've noticed poor decisions since you've only come to visit her twice this year."

I tried to be polite with this woman, but the way she treated people got under my skin, and inevitably I lost my temper.

"Since she's met you, she's chosen to work at a library like some college dropout, live in a rundown neighborhood full of crime, and now she's dating a civil servant she met while he was protecting you from a man who was no doubt one of your mentally unstable *clients*," Mrs. Walker replied.

"Mother!"

"Holly isn't a prostitute," Sam interjected, and I blinked. I had assumed she meant photography clients, not . . . that. But that made more sense considering who it was coming from. Last time she called me a "disreputable transient."

"I don't care what she does to pay her bills. She brings unhealthy influences into my daughter's life."

"Jace worked at the library and lived in her current apartment before Holly even moved to town," Sam countered. "And Holly was never in any kind of relationship with the man who stalked her. She's no more responsible for Jace's decisions than you are, but maybe she has more influence than you because she chooses to be a part of her life."

Mrs. Walker's lips pressed together so tightly that they turned white.

"As for her civil servant boyfriend, I care very much for your daughter, and I think the feeling is mutual."

Jace reached back and took the hand Sam had resting on her shoulder. She flashed him a tender smile that elicited a disapproving sigh from her mother.

"Well," Mrs. Walker said crisply to Jace. "One day you'll grow up and come to regret the life choices you've made."

"One day you'll grow old and regret the days you chose not to love and cherish your daughter," I informed her matter-of-factly. Jesus forgive me, but I couldn't seem to control my tongue.

Mrs. Walker sent a blistering look my way, and I stared right back. I had come face-to-face with evil; wealth and status didn't even begin to intimidate me.

"I think we're done here," Mrs. Walker decided with a glance at her husband. "Come along, Bert."

Her husband's eyes shimmered with sorrow as he looked between his children. He lowered his head and muttered, "Yes, dear."

"No," Jace objected, blocking the door with her wheelchair. "We're not done. You can't do this!"

"The decision is made," her mother said. "Now control yourself. You're making a scene."

"I won't let you!" Jace shouted.

"Jacelyn Annabelle Walker," her mother scolded. "You will mind your tone when you speak to me. I'm not one of your dysfunctional friends. I'm your mother."

"You're his mother too!" Jace gestured at the still body of her brother, kept alive by whirring machines. "But that doesn't stop you from wanting to kill him!"

Her words shocked me, and I slid my gaze from her, to Scott, and finally to her mother. They wanted to remove him from life support?

Mrs. Walker drew in a deep breath and clasped her manicured hands together. "I understand that you were close with your brother, but this . . ."—she nodded to Scott—"isn't your brother anymore. My son is dead. This is just a hollow shell, and a painful reminder of a tragedy. It's time we put it behind us and move forward."

"I love him, Mom. Do you even know what that word means? Or is it all just about appearances to you?"

"You're just a child. You couldn't possibly understand."

"I'm not a child. I'll be thirty-one next week."

"Nevertheless. This is our decision."

Anger brightened Jace's cheeks, and she squeezed my hand in a death grip.

Ow . . .

"Why is it your decision? You haven't been to see him in over a year. I visit him every week. Holly, who isn't even his family, visits him more than you do."

"Legally it is my decision."

"I will fight you on this. I will sue you for emotional damages. I will drag your precious reputation through the mud."

Mrs. Walker lifted her chin. "You wouldn't."

"I would, and I will . . . if you take my brother from me."

Mrs. Walker's face took on an odd expression—a mixture of irritation, worry, and a hint of pride that seemed oddly out of place. "We'll discuss the matter at length after the company dinner in August. Perhaps by then you'll be over this irrational attachment, and you'll be able to think clearly. I expect you to dress for the occasion and bring a respectable date." She strode out of the room, her heels clicking on the tile, and her husband followed.

Jace covered her face with her hands and started to sob. I rubbed her back as I gazed at Scott, a deep sadness growing in my chest. Jace and I rarely talked about his condition when we came to visit, but one day stuck out in my memory when she asked, "Do you think he's gone?"

I hadn't known what to say then any more than I did now. Some people woke up and some didn't. And some were never the same. I didn't know if Scott was still in there, imprisoned by his own body, but I hoped that if he was, he hadn't heard his mother's cold, heartless words.

Jace drew in a shaky breath and sat up. "I think I want some time alone with my brother."

"We'll be in the hall," Sam said. He nodded for me to follow him, and we left the room. I was starting to wonder where we were going when he finally stopped and turned to face me in front of the vending machines. "How did you get here?"

"The elevators." I pointed in their direction.

He frowned and crossed his arms, staring at me with such intensity that I fidgeted. "To the hospital, Holly."

"Um . . . a couple of left turns, a right . . ." I pretended to think about it. "I'm really bad with street names, so . . . that's all I can really tell you."

"You walked here, didn't you?"

"No," I said honestly.

He narrowed his eyes. "You try not to lie, which means it's a semantics issue. You *ran* here. That's why you were so breathless when you arrived."

Silence hung between us when I refused to answer, and I tried to gauge how he was handling it, but his expression, which was permanently angry, didn't change.

"I would've given you a ride," he said.

"I didn't want you to leave her. She was upset and—"

"She would've been more upset if her best friend had been abducted on her way to the hospital."

That was a valid point.

"I was careful," I said. "I even brought Riley."

Sam gave me a frustrated look as he pulled his phone from his pocket. I didn't hear the vibration until it was in the palm of his hand.

"Yeah," he answered. He listened for a moment, and I could hear a frantic voice on the other end of the line. He looked pointedly at me as he said, "She's at the hospital." He pulled the phone away from his ear as the voice shouted something in response. "No, she's fine. She's visiting Jace." A pause. "How did she get here? I'll let her tell you that. I'm bringing her back now."

I didn't bother arguing as he walked me to his car. I hunkered down in the passenger seat and stared out the window at the passing streetlights. There really was no way to brace myself for the conversation with Marx.

He was going to be furious and possibly combustible. I checked my cell phone, which I had avoided looking at up until now. I had several missed calls from Marx and Jordan, as well as text messages. He must have called Jordan when he realized I was gone. Great, now Jordan would be worried too.

We pulled into the parking lot and climbed out of the car. I trudged silently up the steps into the apartment with Riley beside me and found Marx seated on the arm of the couch with a stony expression.

Sam popped his head in to say, "I'm gonna head back to the hospital."

Marx gave him a brisk nod. "Thanks for bringin' her back."

Sam pulled the door shut and left me alone with the angry Southerner. I swallowed and mumbled, "I'm sorry if I worried you."

One eyebrow crept up. "If?"

That one word conveyed every drop of the anger he was holding inside. It made him look stiff and uncomfortable.

"There's no *if* about it, Holly," he said, voice tight. "You disappeared in the middle of the night. No note, no message, nothin'. I woke up to find you gone, your journal entry lyin' open on the counter unfinished, and no response to my phone calls."

"I'm sorry. I had my phone on silent, and I didn't think to leave a note." I wasn't used to being accountable to another person.

He crossed his arms. "And how did you get to the hospital?"

Oh boy. There was no point in avoiding that one; he would circle back to it as many times as necessary until he got his answer. "I ran there."

"I see." He was quiet for a beat. "By yourself. In the middle of the night. Fully aware that there is a crazy man lookin' for any opportunity to grab you. After I specifically asked you to be more cautious."

I didn't know what to say to that, so I decided saying nothing was probably better.

"What were you thinkin', Holly!" he shouted, all pretense of calm gone.

I flinched and snapped, "Don't yell at me."

He visibly struggled to control his anger. "I'm sorry," he bit out. "I don't mean to yell."

I held tight to Riley's leash so he didn't attack, and watched Marx warily. He wanted very much to explode, but he had done that once before and it had damaged the fragile trust between us. I knew without a doubt he would never hurt me, a confidence I hadn't had then, but I still didn't appreciate being yelled at.

"I took Riley with me," I said. "He protected me before. In the park."

"This is different and you know it. There is next to nothin' he can do against somebody who can't feel pain."

"I thought it was the best option at the time."

"Don't give me that. You knew it wasn't the best option. You could've called Sam or Jordan or woken me up." He stood. "You just didn't wanna *inconvenience* anybody."

"I—"

"I know you, Holly, so there's no point in arguin'. Did you even stop to consider how scared and worried I might be when I woke up to find you gone?"

Guilt clogged my throat. I hadn't actually thought about that.

"Or how it might affect me or Jordan if Collin snatched you on the way to the hospital? You would've simply disappeared without a trace. No one knew you were goin' alone or which route you were takin'."

I shifted uneasily at the thought.

"I know how terrified you are of Collin, and the only reason you went was because Jace needed you. The fact that you went alone despite that fear tells me you still don't understand how much we care."

"I know you care."

But *caring* was a fleeting and conditional thing in this world. People cared so long as it was convenient or beneficial. The moment you became a burden, or you couldn't fulfill some need or desire they had, they pushed you off on someone else.

I had twelve foster families as proof of that. Most of them had *cared* for a while, so long as they were receiving a check from the state, but inevitably they passed the trouble of regular therapy sessions and doctor visits onto the next family.

"I'm not sure we define carin' the same way," Marx said. "So let me make a few things perfectly clear." He cupped my face in his hands, and I looked up at him. "We're not gonna stop carin' just because you ask us for a favor that's inconvenient or because you can't be self-sufficient all the time."

How had he known what I was thinking?

"We're not those foster families who rejected you, sweetheart."

Tears blurred my vision. Was the pain that visible?

"We're not gonna abandon you because you can't make it *worth our while* by givin' somethin' back."

Most of the foster families had wanted some kind of compensation for putting up with me. I had offered Marx money and help around the apartment when he invited me to stay, but he had refused both.

If I didn't already know he wasn't interested in my body, I would've been terrified he was angling for that offer. But he only seemed interested in keeping me safe.

He brushed the tears from my cheeks with his thumbs. "We care about you, Holly. No conditions. You understand me?"

I tried to nod, which was really hard to do with him holding onto my head.

"Good. I will tell you that every day for the rest of your life if that's what it takes to get it through that thick little head of yours."

I choked on a laugh. "My head's not little."

"It's perfectly proportional to your body, I remember," he said, releasing me. "Of course, you realize that only supports my previous statement given that you're . . ."—he held his thumb and forefinger an inch apart—"this big."

I rolled my eyes and unhooked Riley's leash from his collar.

"I expect you to wake me up and ask me for a ride next time," he said. "I don't care what time it is. I don't care if I have pneumonia. You wake me up. Don't you ever risk your safety that way again, you hear me?"

I nodded again and glanced at my journal lying open on the counter. "So . . . you read my journal?" There were far more private things in there than just my daily words of gratitude to God, and I hoped he hadn't flipped through it.

He leaned down and kissed the top of my head. "I'm thankful for you too."

Well, I knew he had read the unfinished entry. I walked into the kitchen and closed my journal, setting it aside on a stool.

I poured myself some chocolate milk and sprinkled in a few marshmallows.

"I will never understand that," Marx admitted.

I took a sip and chewed on my marshmallows. It tasted like comfort. "I like it. You should try it."

"Chunks and milk don't go together." He leaned against the counter beside me. "And we need to find you a better copin' skill that doesn't involve puffed sugar."

"Why?"

He took the bag of marshmallows and wound it shut. "Because you're barely sleepin', and all this sugar isn't helpin'." At my surprised look, he said, "I hear you up at all hours of the night, and you look exhausted."

I *was* exhausted, but it had nothing to do with marshmallows.

"You're still havin' nightmares," he said.

I lifted one shoulder in a shrug.

"Is that what woke you up this mornin'?"

I tapped my fingers on the countertop. I didn't want to talk about this. "If I say yes, can I have my marshmallows back?"

"No, I'm cuttin' you off. And then I'm gonna make you some real food."

"I can make my own food."

"Not in my kitchen you can't. I don't want it burstin' into flames. Last time, you set off every smoke alarm in the apartment."

He disappeared down the hall with my marshmallows, and I heard his bedroom door open a moment later.

I rummaged through his lower cupboard until I found the old toaster he never used. I pulled out one of the Ziploc bags of marshmallows I had stuffed into the toast slot for safekeeping.

Try to keep my marshmallows from me . . . ha! I had Swiss rolls in a Tupperware container behind the TV, and the Cheetos were everywhere.

I moved into the living room to curl up on the couch and watch a movie while I drank my chocolate milk, periodically tossing in a few more little marshmallows.

Marx shook his head and smiled at the bag of marshmallows I tried to hide under the pillow when he came over. He handed me a glass of orange juice and a bowl of fruit.

"Thanks," I smiled.

A few minutes later he handed me a plate of what looked like a mountain of scrambled eggs with cheese and two slices of toast with jam.

I blinked. "Um . . . I can't eat all this."

"Try," he suggested, before going back into the kitchen. I sighed, thanked God for the insurmountable pile of food, and then stabbed a bite of egg with my fork.

I managed to eat about a third of it, then set down my fork in defeat. If I ate another bite, I would explode.

Halfway through my movie, Maya shuffled into the living room with fresh tears on her face. I opened an arm to her, and she crawled onto the couch and curled up with her head in my lap. I covered her with a blanket and stroked her hair as we watched the rest of the movie together.

I needed to do something to ease her grief. Being cooped up in the apartment wasn't going to help her. The snowflakes falling outside caught my eye, and an idea came to me. We were going to build a snowman.

13

Maya grunted with exaggeration as we tried to lift what would soon be the snowman's overly round belly onto his bottom, which was the circumference of an extra-large pizza.

"There's an easier way to do this," Jordan pointed out as he stepped away from his guard duty to come over and help us.

I surrendered and sagged overtop of the ball, out of breath. "Yeah, call Sam. I'm pretty sure he can lift a truck, so a fat snowman's no problem."

Jordan scoffed. "What am I? Weak?"

Maya squeezed his arm and then shook her head solemnly. "You don't have very big muscles."

I bit down on my lips to keep from laughing at the expression on his face. His masculinity had just been insulted by an eight-year-old girl.

"Really?" he replied with mock indignation. "Well, I'm still strong enough to do this." He scooped her up under her arms and swung her in dizzying circles. She giggled and squealed. When he set her down, she stumbled dizzily and fell over into the snow.

He looked at me. "Your turn."

My eyes widened, and I took a step back from him. "Don't you dare." He took a small, teasing step closer, and I retreated around the half-made snowman. "Jordan!" I pointed a mitten-covered hand at him. "Don't . . . make me hit you in the face with a snowball."

He grabbed a massive handful of wet snow. "Let's see what you've got."

I hesitated, then scooped up a mitten full of snow and armed myself. Before I could finish shaping it into a ball, he tossed the handful of loose powder at me. I ducked and flung my snowball on reflex.

A deep, irritated sigh drew my attention to the corner of the building, where Sam stood with globs of snow falling from his jacket.

I sucked in a breath through my teeth. "Sorry, Sam."

He looked from me to Jordan as he brushed the snow from his jacket. "Picking on the girls?"

"Just the cute ones."

Heat pooled in my cheeks. Why did he have to say things like that? I fixed my attention on Sam. "Shouldn't you be sleeping?"

"If I slept as much as you seem to think I do, I would never get out of bed."

I couldn't quite figure out when he slept or if he slept. The last time I asked him about it, he accused me of making him sound like a sloth.

Maya tugged on my wrist. "We have to make his head. He looks silly without a head."

"We have to dress him first," I told her. I plucked the hideous knitted sweater from our small box of items and wiggled and tugged it down over his belly. "There. That'll keep him warm."

"I think you're missing the point of a *snow*man, Holly," Sam commented. "Warm is a death sentence."

I waved off his cynical comment and helped Maya pack fist-sized snowballs together until we had a misshapen blob the size of a basketball. We hefted our snowman's head carefully on top of the other two snowballs.

The moment we let go, it rolled off the back and splattered into little Frosty brains all over the ground.

Maya and I broke out in a fit of laughter.

We managed to plop head number two squarely onto his nonexistent neck, and then shoved two bottle caps into his face for eyes. He didn't have a nose because someone had eaten all the carrots.

116

We stepped back to take a look at our masterpiece. He was a little lopsided and extremely plump.

Maya pointed and said, "He has a big belly."

"It's from all the snow cones he eats," I said seriously. "What should we name him?"

"I think we should name him Jordan."

"Okay, now I'm offended," Jordan said from behind us. "First I have no muscles, and now I'm fat."

"At least you're not bald," Sam offered.

"Is that my sweater?"

We all turned toward the Southern voice that hadn't been there a moment ago. Marx lifted an inquiring eyebrow at me as he descended the steps to join us.

"He was naked," I explained. "He needed something to wear."

"Well, at least I know how I'm gonna look in it if I eat too many doughnuts."

Jordan grabbed a handful of snow, pounded it into a small snowball, and lobbed it at Sam. It smacked him in the chest and he blinked down at himself before shooting a glare at Jordan.

Jordan pointed to me.

Wait a minute, how was I now involved in this? Sam turned his attention to me, and I held up my hands innocently.

"Yeah," he grunted. "We all know Holly can't aim."

"She hit you the first time."

"By accident," Sam clarified. "I doubt she could manage it again to save her life."

Now that was just rude. Just because it was true didn't mean I appreciated having my nose rubbed in it.

"I have to go to the bathroom," Maya announced.

"Well, come on then," Marx said, offering his hand for her to take. "I need a cup of coffee anyway." Maya plopped her hand in his, and they went inside.

I blinked when a snowball breezed past me and smacked Jordan in the face. I winced in sympathy. That had to hurt.

"Oh, brain freeze." Jordan wiped the snow from his cheeks. "You had to go for the face? Really?"

Sam shrugged. "I guess you should've ducked."

"You realize this means war."

Uh-oh. I backed out of the way and flattened myself against the building before the snowballs started to fly. Jordan nailed Sam in the face just to return the favor.

He dodged Sam's returning snowball, and it smacked the snowman, leaving a giant knot on the side of his head.

I threw a few sneaky snowballs at Jordan's back.

"What is this?" he laughed, when one of my snowballs nailed him between the shoulders just as Sam's hit him in the stomach.

When Jordan aimed one at me, I squeaked and ducked behind the snowman.

"Chicken," he teased.

Sam's phone rang, and he held up a finger to halt the snowballs. "Yeah. Okay, hold on." He trudged away through the snow to continue his phone call in private.

Jordan dropped to the ground and flopped back in the snow with a contented sigh. He blinked up at the snow flurries drifting down before looking at me.

"You wanna join me?"

I looked at the snow-laden ground and wrinkled my nose. "The ground is cold and wet."

He sat up, unzipped his jacket, and stripped out of it. He spread it out on the snow and patted it. "Have a seat."

"Jordan," I said in exasperation. "Put your jacket back on."

He flopped back into the snow a few feet from where he'd placed his jacket and just gazed at me expectantly. I sighed and sat down on his jacket. It was warm and cozy, and I felt instantly guilty because he had nothing on but a long-sleeve T-shirt.

He angled his face toward me. "Can I ask you a question?"

I rubbed my mitten-covered hands together in an effort to keep warm. "You know I don't really do questions."

"I know, but I really wanna ask this one." He propped himself up on his elbows. "Will you come over to my place and let me make you dinner tonight?"

My surprise quickly gave way to unease as I considered the invitation. "Um, I don't think . . ."

"It's just dinner. No strings attached."

Just the two of us at his place for dinner sounded like a date, and that was a dangerous line to cross. "What about Maya? I can't just leave her alone."

The look on his face suggested he hadn't considered that. None of us were used to having a little one around. "I think I have an idea about that. So if I can find her a safe, reliable babysitter that she likes, will you consider dinner?"

I struggled for a response. "I'm not sure it's a good idea."

"Inviting you over to my apartment isn't code for something else, Holly. It's just two friends having dinner."

Except I would be alone in an apartment with him, a situation I had deliberately avoided for a reason. The last time I was alone in an apartment with a man who was attracted to me . . .

I shivered at the memory.

Even thinking about putting myself in that situation again made my heart trip with anxiety. It would be foolish and—

"Hey," Jordan said, tilting his head to study my face. "What's going on in there?"

I swallowed and looked at him. I knew he was nothing like Collin, but a part of me was still scared to put myself in that vulnerable position.

But the only way to grow was to step out of my comfort zone, and I was tired of always being afraid. "Okay, but . . . can we have pizza?"

His eyebrows lifted. "You want me to make homemade pizza?"

"If you think you can."

He grinned at the challenge. "Oma made me an apron and started teaching me to bake when I was three. Trust me, I can handle a pizza." He stood up and brushed the snow from his clothes. "But we will need to make a grocery run."

He started to offer his hand to me, thought better of it, and then waited for me to stand. I shook out his jacket and handed it back to him.

"Let's go do some shopping, shall we?" he suggested.

14

"I can't believe you roped Marx into a movie and popcorn night with Maya," I said.

Jordan grinned. "Yeah well he had it coming."

He had used the same tactic Marx had used the other day, only instead of suggesting Marx take Maya out for ice cream, he had suggested a night in with popcorn, pizza, and lots of movies. The moment Maya turned her big brown eyes on Marx, begging for princess movies and popcorn, he was doomed.

I still felt a little guilty, even though it hadn't been my idea, but Marx had nudged me out the door with strict orders to "have fun."

Jordan shifted the bag of groceries to one arm and unlocked his apartment door. "After you, fair lady."

"Are you calling me pale?"

"Well, you did almost blend in with the snow. If you weren't wearing that black jacket, you'd be practically invisible."

I rolled my eyes and stepped into the unfamiliar apartment. There was a milky glow pouring through the far windows, brightening the unfurnished space. I thought my apartment was sparse, but all he had was a couch, a television, a boxing bag, and a lamp sitting on a side table.

"So," I began, stopping in the middle of what was probably the dining room, "the less furniture you have, the less you break when you're angry?"

Jordan set the groceries on the kitchen counter. "I broke something *once*."

"Only if you're not counting the wall."

"Okay, twice."

Jordan was usually very laid-back, but when Marx broke the news to him about my history with Collin, he hadn't taken it well. He had thrown a table into Marx's wall, which reduced the side table to kindling and left a pretty sizeable hole in the living room wall. It was still there.

"Besides, I have other ways to take out my anger," he said, with a nod toward the boxing bag that hung from the ceiling by a thick chain. "I'll have to get a pair of gloves your size for the next time you visit. Then we can train."

"Maybe some chairs and a table first," I suggested, tapping the bag with a fist. He was in desperate need of some furniture.

"Furniture's overrated," he said with a small smile. "I would rather teach you to kickbox. I'm working with Sam right now. He might have some force behind his swings, but the guy's not limber at all."

"Sam comes over to practice with you?"

"Most mornings. He and his sister Evey live down the hall. He's the one who told me this place was for rent. It's a nice apartment for the price, and it beats a motel room."

"Sam lives with his sister?"

Jordan joined me by the punching bag, hitting it just hard enough to make it creak and sway on its chain. "Technically *she* lives with *him*. Her husband is a control freak, and he tried to force her to stay when she wanted to leave, so she's staying with Sam for a while."

Evey's nervousness at the bowling alley the first time I met her made sense now. She had been afraid her husband would show up.

"You should talk to her sometime," Jordan suggested, walking back to the front door to close it. "I think you two might get along."

I heard the dead bolt click, but it was the sound of a chain sliding into place that made my stomach cramp with unexpected terror.

It echoed back through my memories to that night I tried to forget—the chain sliding into place again and again, locking in the horror of what I knew was coming.

"Take it off," I said urgently.

Jordan blinked in confusion. "Take what off?"

"Take it off." I rushed to the door and tried to unhook the chain. My fingers were shaking so badly that I couldn't slide it free from the slot. "Get it off," I pleaded, yanking on it desperately. "Please get it off."

"Okay, okay," Jordan said soothingly. He gently pried my fingers off the chain and slid it free. "It's off. Okay? It's off."

I backed away until I hit the far wall, and sank down, burying my face in my knees.

They're just memories, I told myself, trying to will away the images and feelings of that awful night. *Just . . . memories.*

I'm not sure how long I sat there, counting my breaths and trying to separate the past from the present, but I looked up when I heard the telltale snap and fizz of a soda can opening.

Jordan was crouched in front of me with a cold can of cherry coke. "Here. Sugar helps steady the nerves."

I stared at the offering for a long time, uncomprehending, before voicing the only lucid thought that popped into my head. "You hate cherry."

He lifted up a can of regular coke that I hadn't noticed beside him. "Yep, but my best friend loves it, so I keep some in the icebox."

I took the can with shaky fingers and said with as much lightness as I could scrounge up, "You know, most people just call it a refrigerator."

He smiled, but it didn't ease the concern in his eyes. "Yeah, well, Oma always called it an icebox and it just stuck with me."

I wiped the tears from my face and looked down at the can of soda in my hands, embarrassed. "I'm sorry I freaked out on you."

He sat down on the floor across from me. "I should've realized that locking the door was a bad idea, especially since this is your first time alone in an apartment with me."

I lifted the can with both hands, trying to hold it steady, and took a sip, focusing on the taste of cherry bubbles on my tongue.

"I did some research after Marx told me what Collin did to you. I wanted to understand and to be able to help you, so I spent a lot of my free time reading books, articles, and testimonials."

I didn't know what to say to that.

"There are a lot of overlapping themes," he continued. "The idea of triggers was a predominant one—sights, smells, feelings, *sounds*. Things that can trigger a flashback or a panic attack because they remind the person of what happened. It's pretty common in trauma survivors."

I swallowed and looked away. "I've figured out what most of my panic triggers are." The list was embarrassingly long. "But I never realized the sound of a chain lock would be one of them."

He sat quietly, not pressing me for details.

"I wasn't home when Collin broke into my apartment in Darby. I worked open to close that day at the restaurant because one of the morning servers was sick. I was so tired by the time I got home. Maybe if I hadn't been so tired, I would've noticed something was wrong."

I focused on my can of coke, drawing a finger through the condensation in mindless patterns.

"My bedroom door had a chain lock on the inside, and I can still hear the sound of it sliding into place while I was getting ready for bed. I knew—the moment I heard that sound—that I was trapped, and he . . . he was gonna . . ." I couldn't bring myself to finish the sentence.

"You're never trapped with me, Holly," Jordan said. "If you wanna leave at any point tonight, I can take you back to Marx's apartment or you can go hang out with Sam and Evey down the hall. Okay?"

"Okay."

"So how about we leave the door unlocked and make some pizza," he suggested.

We stood, and I hung my coat on a hook in the hallway before following him into the kitchen. He kept a conscious four feet of space between us while I unpacked the grocery bag.

"The dough's gonna take some time to rise, but it only takes a few minutes to put together," he explained.

"Can I do it?" I had never made pizza before.

"I'm supposed to be making *you* dinner."

"But I wanna help. You can do the hard part since I tend to burn things a little."

He grinned and pushed a large bowl toward me. "A little?"

I scrunched my nose at his playful jab, then focused on my task. "Okay, so what first?"

"According to Oma, if you're gonna bake, you need to be properly attired." He opened a drawer and pulled out two folded pieces of cloth. He snapped the first one open, and I laughed.

It was a small apron with "Jordy" stitched across it with tiny pockets embroidered with baseballs. "Courtesy of Oma when I was ten, but I think it'll fit you better than it does me now."

He offered it to me, and I pulled his childhood apron over my head. I looked down at myself and then shot him a cautious look. "I know that sometimes girls wear their boyfriend's clothes, but just because this has your name on it doesn't mean—"

"No, it doesn't mean that." He smiled as he tied his own apron around his waist. "But you do look cute in my apron."

I crinkled my nose at his comment.

"Keep scrunching that button nose at me, and I'm gonna kiss it," he warned.

I blinked, grabbed the bowl, and moved another foot down the counter. I lifted my chin and called his bluff with a deliberate scrunch of my nose. He snorted a laugh. I knew he wouldn't follow through with his threat.

"Now what?" I asked, staring into my empty bowl.

He passed the measuring cup and sack of flour. "Now we see how good of a pizza maker you are."

He listed off the ingredients and their proportions, and I tossed everything into the bowl for mixing. I dug my fingers into the dough with determination. This stuff was fantastic. It was like edible Play-Doh.

"Is it done?" I asked.

"Yep. And you have flour all over your face."

I rubbed at my face with my sleeve before I realized there was flour all over the sleeve of my shirt, and I had just made things worse. The inside of my nose tickled, and I sneezed.

"God bless you."

I tried to wipe the flour away with a towel, then sneezed again. Good grief. "Did I get it all?" I asked, looking up at him.

His lips quirked up at the corners. "Not quite. Can I give you a hand?"

I gave him a wary look before silently reminding myself that I was tiptoeing out of my comfort zone today. "Okay."

He closed the distance between us, and I stiffened against the instinctive urge to retreat. His touch was warm and surprisingly soft as he smoothed his thumb over the tip of my nose and along my hairline.

I wasn't attracted to him in the traditional, physical sense, but I felt drawn to him in a way I couldn't explain.

"Jordan." I gazed up into his blue eyes as I fought not to cave to the panic trying to gnaw its way through my nerves.

He swallowed hard as his thumb swept away the flour on my cheek, and there was a glimmer of some deep emotion in his eyes, but then he blinked, cleared his throat, and backed away from me.

He pressed his palms to the counter, staring hard at the laminate. "I'll be back in a minute." He pushed away from the counter and disappeared into one of the rooms down the hall.

I stared after him in confusion. Had I done something to upset him? I hadn't even freaked out on him again, despite the pressing urge to put space between us.

As I tried to figure out what I had done wrong, I poked the ball of pizza dough with a finger and smiled at its squishiness. I wasn't sure what to do with it at this point, so I left it sitting on the counter while I started off down the hall in search of a bathroom.

I paused when I heard Jordan's voice coming from the room to my right. "Well, what was I supposed to do? If I didn't walk away, I was gonna kiss her and we both know that wouldn't go over well."

Fear spread its wings in my stomach, and I pressed a hand against it to try to calm its frantic fluttering. He had left the kitchen because he was tempted to kiss me?

"I know that," he said in exasperation. He must have been on the phone because I hadn't heard anyone else speak. "No, Sam, I'd rather you not list all the reasons why it's a bad idea to kiss her."

I took an uneasy step back and glanced at his front door, my mind instinctively planning an escape.

Nothing's changed, I reminded myself. I had already known he was attracted to me. The fact that he wanted to kiss me and had chosen to leave the room instead should've been a comfort. Right?

Still, worry lingered in the back of my mind as I went into the bathroom to wash my hands and face. Jordan was doing his best to respect my wishes, but I knew he wanted more than friendship even if he didn't say it. I was the one unable to budge.

Just because he wanted more didn't mean he would force the issue. I knew Jordan would never hurt me, but . . .

No, no buts. He wouldn't hurt me.

The men in my life now weren't like the men in my life before: they weren't abusive alcoholics or sadists who spent their free time dreaming up new ways to hurt me. They were my friends.

I finished washing away the flour from . . . everywhere—how had I even gotten it in my hair?—and then left the bathroom. Jordan was still in the bedroom on the phone, so I wandered into the living room.

I crouched down and perused the book titles on the shelf of his side table: *Boundaries: Establishing a Safe Zone; Fighting Back: Regaining Your Sense of Self and Safety; Loving a Woman Who's Afraid to Be Loved; Fear in the Shadows: Recognizing the Signs and Symptoms of PTSD after Sexual Trauma.*

Emotions clogged my throat as I realized just how desperately Jordan was trying to understand what I'd been through and the ways those experiences had impacted my life. There were more books tucked into the corner between the table and wall.

"Checking out the library?"

I looked up at the sound of his voice. He was leaning against the wall with his arms crossed.

I cleared my throat. "I figured you for more of a westerns kind of guy. Maybe some *Kung Fu Panda* . . . or something."

His lips curved slightly at the corners. "Good movie, but I doubt it's a very interesting read."

I looked back at the stack of books with post-it notes sticking out in random places. I couldn't even begin to imagine how long it had taken him to read through these books, and he'd said he read articles and testimonials as well.

"You weren't kidding about the research," I said, because I didn't know what else to say.

"I don't ever wanna hurt you, Holly," he admitted quietly. "I'll read a thousand more books if it helps me to understand."

He meant it. I could see it in his eyes.

"Does it help?" I asked. "Reading the stories about what others have gone through?"

"Knowing that you went through most of those horrors, that you probably feel the way a lot of those women feel . . ." His fingers tightened around his arms, and he shifted against the wall. "Some of it's pretty hard to get through. But yeah, I think the knowledge is helpful."

I didn't think I could read about another person enduring what I had. I narrowed my gaze at the book sitting on the top of the pile against the wall: *Sexual Abuse and Eating Disorders*. I plucked the book off the pile and stood up.

"I do not have an eating disorder." I tossed the book at him, and he caught it with a small grin.

"You have a don't-eat-enough disorder."

"I do not."

He stepped around me and returned the book to the pile. "Yeah? It's almost five p.m. What have you eaten today?"

I folded my arms and lifted my chin. I didn't have to answer that question. "I'm about to have pizza. So . . . stop nosing in my eating habits."

"I'll stop nosing when you actually eat the pizza."

The dough took two hours to rise, and then we spread the sauce and cheese before piling on the toppings. Jordan's half was a deluxe, which apparently meant everything, and I strategically placed mushrooms and pineapple on my half.

"Holly," he said, watching me as I pinched a piece of pineapple between my thumb and forefinger and moved it through the air over the pizza, trying to decide on the best place to put it.

"What?"

"It's a pizza, not a puzzle. Just plop it on there."

"Hey, you did your half. I'll do mine." I pressed it between two mushroom halves and smiled. "Done!"

He shook his head as he placed the pizza in the oven. He turned on the timer and opened his mouth to say something when his phone rang.

He pulled it from his pocket. His brow furrowed. "Dad. Great. I'm gonna take this in the bedroom, but come get me if you need me, okay?" He stripped off his apron and laid it across the counter before answering the phone. "Hey, Dad."

He didn't sound thrilled to hear from him.

"Yeah, I know I haven't been home in a while," he said before closing the bedroom door. Maybe his dad was upset that he was here spending so much time with me.

I lingered awkwardly in the kitchen as I tried to figure out what to do with myself. I certainly wasn't going to be reading any of the books. Firsthand experience was enough for me.

A man's voice rose in the hallway outside Jordan's apartment, and my eyes darted to the unlocked door.

My heartbeat picked up as I listened, but when the voice spoke again, I realized I didn't recognize it. It wasn't Collin. I crossed the room and peered through the peephole as I rested my fingers on the dead bolt.

I didn't see anyone.

Curious, I cracked the door open and peered down the hallway toward the stairs. A man was crouched in front of a door, doing something that suspiciously resembled lock picking.

I frowned, trying to decide whether to say something or to go and get Jordan. I knew which one *he* would prefer. I drew in a hesitant breath and said, "If you knocked and they didn't let you in, it probably means you're not welcome."

The man froze, tools still jammed in the door handle, and looked at me. He was an average man with sandy-blond hair and a scar that made his left eyebrow zigzag.

I expected him to either bolt down the steps or launch himself in my direction to keep me from calling the police, but he did neither.

He lowered his tools and stood slowly, his crouched body unfolding into a taller-than-me frame that had me gripping the edge of the door and preparing to slam it.

"I could use a hand," he said.

I blinked in surprise. "I'm not really into breaking and entering." *Anymore.*

"It's not breaking and entering if it's your apartment."

Okay, I didn't see that coming. I glanced at the apartment in question. "Landlords usually give tenants a key. They're considerate that way."

"My keys are still inside. My wife and I had an argument, and she locked me out." He stepped forward. "Look, it's—" He stopped when I shifted away from him. "It's complicated. She has a mood disorder and she's having an episode. I tried to convince her to take her meds, and she accused me of conspiring against her. I just need to make sure she's okay."

Either he was a phenomenal liar or he was telling the truth, because his expression was pained and there was a desperate look in his eyes.

"Please, would you try knocking?" he asked. "She won't open the door for me, but she might for you."

I shifted with uncertainty.

"What harm could it do to try? If she won't open the door for you either, then I'll call the police. Please."

This wouldn't be a difficult decision for Marx or Jordan—they wouldn't hesitate to check on someone who might need help—so I scrounged up some courage. "Okay."

"Thank you."

I stepped cautiously into the hall and stuck close to the wall as I approached. The man backed away to give me space, but having him behind me still sent my anxiety levels spiking.

"W-what's your wife's name?" I asked.

"Evelyn, but everybody calls her Evey."

I hesitated as I absorbed the familiar name. Jordan had said Sam's sister, Evey, was staying with him in an apartment just a few doors down, because she was afraid of her husband.

I uncurled my fist and pressed my palm flat against the door. How did I get myself into these situations? I just wanted to make a pizza.

"Well?" the man prompted, impatience and irritation seeping into his voice. "Are you gonna knock?"

I had a feeling he would explode if I told him no, so I decided to try to slip away instead. I barely made it three steps before he slammed a hand against the wall directly in front of my face, cutting me off from Jordan's apartment.

I cringed and looked up at him.

Anger tightened his features, erasing any pretense of the caring and worried husband. "It's rude to walk away when someone's talking to you."

I glanced at Jordan's open doorway and considered screaming. I loathed the idea of crying out for help. I had gotten myself into this mess; I could get myself out of it.

"You need to leave or . . . or I'm gonna call the police," I said.

He stepped toward me, and I pressed myself flat against the wall to keep him from touching me. "Are you threatening me?"

"No." It came out as a frightened squeak, and I hated my cowardice.

"Let me tell you how this situation's gonna go. You're gonna get her to open that door for me, and then you're gonna go home, and you're gonna keep your mouth shut."

It wasn't an "or else" statement, but the look in his eyes clearly communicated what would happen if I refused.

15

I stiffened my spine and tried to make my voice firm. "I'm not knocking on that door so you can hurt Evey."

I didn't know the exact details of Evey's situation with her husband, but this man had anger issues. I could see it building behind his eyes.

"Why would I hurt my wife?"

Because you're an unstable nut. I clamped down on the thought before it could travel to my mouth and escape.

"I love my wife."

"If you love her, then leave her alone."

The muscles in his jaw flexed. "I just wanna talk to her. All I need you to do is knock on the door and convince her to open it. Then you can go back to doing your nails or whatever you do in your spare time."

"No."

He slammed a hand on the wall again, and it was sheer force of will that kept me from cringing this time. "It's a simple request, lady. It's not like I'm asking you to break the law."

I swallowed and stared up at him, unsure how to diffuse his anger.

"Is it money? You want money to knock on the door? Fine." He reached back to pull out his wallet. "All you women care about is money."

I took advantage of his distraction and ducked under his arm, but he caught me and jerked me back, his grip so tight on my forearm that it made my fingers tingle with the beginnings of numbness.

"You got a real listening problem, sweetheart."

The endearment Marx used sounded cold and patronizing coming from this man's lips.

"Don't touch me!" I wrenched my arm free the way Sam and Jordan had taught me, and drove my knee into him as hard as I could.

I darted for Jordan's open door and yelped when I smacked right into a body and bounced off like a pinball. Gentle hands caught me and steadied me before I could hit the floor.

"Are you okay?" Jordan demanded. "What's wrong?"

Evey's husband straightened, his face crimson with rage. He didn't seem nearly as intimidating with Jordan standing beside me. He was nothing but a bully, and I could handle a bully.

I scrounged up every bit of anger, irritation, and fear the man had inspired, and forced it into my voice. "You need to leave."

"You mouthy little—"

"Hey!" Jordan shouted, cutting him off before he could finish the insult. He angled himself between us. "Don't talk to her that way."

Evey's husband hesitated when Jordan stepped in front of me, but he recovered quickly. "Mind your own business."

"Holly is my business."

The man shifted his weight with a small wince of pain. I was pretty sure I had bruised more than his ego. "Maybe you should teach your woman how to behave then. Before someone else does it for you."

I wanted to run back over there and knee him again for that comment, but I knew Jordan would intervene.

"I think you should leave before I teach *you* how to behave," Jordan suggested.

The man's fingers clenched into white-knuckled fists at his sides, and Jordan's eyes narrowed.

"Try it. See what happens."

The intensity between them swelled to the point that I feared one of them was going to take a swing at the other. I would bet on Jordan in a heartbeat.

As quickly as the tension had swelled, it deflated when Evey's husband blinked and dropped his eyes first. His shoulders slouched, and he uncurled his fingers with obvious reluctance. He rolled his lips as if he wanted to say something, but then limped toward the stairwell door without another word.

"Who was that guy?" Jordan asked.

"Evey's husband."

I gave him a brief overview of the events in the hallway—minus a few arm-tingling details—and he ushered me back into the apartment. "I'll call Sam and let him know Drew was here." He closed the door behind us but left it unlocked.

I ducked into the bathroom and pushed the door shut while he filled Sam in. I rolled up my left shirt sleeve to check my arm. There was a large red mark in the vague shape of a hand encircling my arm.

Crap.

That was going to bruise.

I tugged my sleeve back down and adjusted my bracelet before opening the door. Jordan was just hanging up the phone when I stepped out.

"Hey, everything okay?" he asked.

I nodded.

His eyes narrowed, and he leaned back against the wall. "You remember when I told you your lips do this little twitching thing when you try to be deceptive?"

I pinched my traitorous lips together.

"Did Drew hurt you?"

If I said anything to suggest that he had, I was afraid he would hunt him down and throw him through a wall. "He . . . freaked me out a little."

Regret flashed through his eyes. "I'm sorry. I wanted you to feel safe here, not get accosted in the hallway."

135

I shrugged. "It could've been worse." It could've been Collin in the hallway instead of Evey's husband. That thought lent a shivery edge to the breath I let out.

"Yeah." I knew by the way Jordan was looking at me that he was thinking the same. "I'm gonna invite Evey over for dinner. Sam doesn't want her alone right now. I'll be right back, but maybe don't go wandering down the hall and talking to strangers this time, okay?"

That made me smile. "No promises."

I walked into the kitchen to check on the pizza after he left. Pockets of cheese were turning brown and bubbly. I grabbed an oven mitt and pulled the pizza from the oven. It smelled amazing.

"Mmm," I said as I placed the tray of deliciousness on the counter. "Hello, tasty."

I hunted through the drawers for a pizza cutter or a really sharp knife. I opened the furthest drawer to find Jordan's gun, badge, and wallet. I hadn't even realized he wasn't wearing his gun. Marx took his off when he got home too.

I glanced at the door as I picked up his wallet and opened it. A small photo—worn and yellowing with age—slipped from the folds and fluttered to the floor.

I picked it up carefully, half afraid it would crumble in my fingers, and paused at the barely visible letters written across the back of it in faded purple ink. I squinted to make them out, filling in the gaps that were worn away: *Best Friends 4-ever.*

It was my handwriting.

I flipped over the picture to find nine-year-old Jordan and eight-year-old me sitting together on the steps of my childhood home. He had his arm around my shoulders with that familiar mischievous grin on his face.

I leaned on the counter as I tried to remember that day. My leggings—formerly white with pink polka dots—were covered in mud and grass stains, and I had a twig sticking out of my unruly red hair. Jordan had a smudge of dirt across his forehead. That was the day we had gone on a treasure hunt through the woods, and I had hit him in the face with a mud pie.

The forest floor was riddled with treasures, sometimes from people passing through and sometimes from animals swiping things out of people's yards and garbage.

Jordan had found several lighters and a pocket knife that day, and I had found a bracelet with part of a name engraved on it. I knew most people would see something broken and worthless, but I thought it was beautiful. Jordan took the money he earned from doing yard work during the summer and had one made for me that Christmas.

I looked down at the tarnished silver bracelet on my left wrist that still had a shadow of my name engraved on it, and smiled. It had survived twelve foster homes and nineteen years, and I still cherished it.

I heard footsteps in the hallway, and I closed Jordan's wallet and shoved it back into the drawer.

A tall, slender woman with flawless almond skin and raven hair came through the door first, her ink-black eyes sweeping over the apartment with caution.

Jordan followed her in and closed the door. "Evey, you remember Holly."

She spared me a glance, and I didn't miss the flash of resentment in her eyes. "How could I forget?"

Yeah . . . I was the reason her brother had been roofied by a serial killer and left lying unconscious in the grass this past October. She wasn't my biggest fan.

Jordan cleared his throat at the obvious discomfort in the room. "We were just about to have some pizza. You're welcome to join us."

Evey gravitated toward the windows and peered down at the busy street. "When will Sammy be here?"

"About ten minutes."

Jordan joined me in the kitchen, and I retreated when he reached for the drawer I was standing in front of. His hand paused by the slightly open drawer, and I realized I hadn't shut it all the way.

He pulled it open, paused again, and then moved his wallet off his gun and back to its original spot. He cast me an interested look, and I bit down on my bottom lip.

"I was looking for a knife," I hurried to explain. "To cut the pizza with. I wasn't trying to snoop."

He smiled as he clipped his gun to his belt and closed the drawer. "You know, if you have questions, you can just ask. I won't keep anything from you."

"Okay. Where are the knives?"

He stepped around me to open a drawer I hadn't gotten to. He plucked out a knife, but when I tried to take it from him, he held it beyond my reach.

"No threatening to stab me with it?" he teased.

I rolled my eyes. "I only threatened to stab you once, and that was only if you tried to pick me up and carry me back into the diner against my will."

"She threatened to stab you?" Evey asked in surprise.

"Yep. She also tried to stab Marx with a kitchen knife, and what was it you threatened to stab Sam with? A fork?"

I scowled at him. "Marx was an accident. He snuck up on me in a parking lot after dark, and I thought he was a serial killer."

"And Sam?"

"He said his family tradition was to give a hug or a gift on a birthday, and I made it clear that a hug would be bad for his health."

Evey's lips curved into a reluctant smile. "You're . . . quite the interesting person."

Jordan started slicing the pizza. "She also stole my car and managed to wreck it without ever leaving the parking lot."

Evey arched an eyebrow.

Why was it everyone could do the one eyebrow thing except me? I tried it a few times in front of the mirror, but without Scotch tape holding one eyebrow up, it was impossible.

"You don't know how to drive?" she asked.

"Of course I do," I replied defensively. "Just . . . not legally. Yet. Marx is teaching me."

I scowled at the smirk on her face and turned to search the cupboards for plates. I glared up at the top shelf. Of course they would be all the way up there.

I stood on my tiptoes and reached for them, but I may as well have been reaching for the moon. I dropped my heels back to the floor with a huff of frustration. Fine. I was going to have to do this the hard way. I opened the bottom drawer and used it as a step stool to climb onto the counter.

"Uh, Holly, what are you doing?" Jordan asked. I heard him set down the knife and come up behind me.

"What does it look like I'm doing?"

"Leaving shoe prints all over my counter."

I looked down at my ankle boots. In hindsight, I probably should've taken my shoes off before traipsing all over his countertop. Too late now.

"Why don't you let me get the plates," he said.

"I'm already up here. Besides, this is personal now." I was not admitting defeat just because the odds—and my five-foot-two-ish inches—were against me. I grabbed four plates just in case Sam was hungry too.

"No one can say she isn't determined," Evey commented.

She should see me when I'm thirsty and my drink has a screw cap.

When I turned around on the counter, Jordan was less than a foot away and his head was level with my stomach. I almost dropped the plates on his head.

"Jordan . . ."

"Yeah?" His eyes were fixed on mine, and he seemed completely unaware of just how far into my personal space he had stepped.

"Could you, um . . ."—I swallowed and tried to press myself as close to the cupboards as I could—". . . get away from me?"

He blinked at my blunt request, then seemed to realize the uncomfortable position he was putting me in. "Sorry." He stepped back.

I released a long, slow breath through my nose and tried to force myself to relax. I wanted to spend time with my friend without being a twisted bundle of nerves.

I felt a little shaky as I set the plates down and scooted off the counter, but I didn't have another panic attack. Maybe I was getting better at this.

I moved the plates to the island counter where the pizza was and breathed, "Success. And sorry I walked all over your counter with my shoes on."

Jordan smiled wryly. "You could just ask me to get them down next time."

"I believe we've had this discussion, lecturer." Only the last time it had been about Pop Tarts. "Besides, I was always better at climbing than you, so I knew I could do it."

He laughed. "That's because you always cheated. You would throw leaves and twigs at me. I think you threw one of Oma's apples at me once too."

I raised my eyebrows. "*I* cheated? You would tickle my feet to try to slow me down."

"I told you not to climb in your bare feet," he said, giving me one of those charming grins that brought out his dimples. "How many pieces of pizza do you want?"

I reached across the counter and pointed. "I want that one." It had more pineapple.

Jordan scooped it onto a plate for me and piled a few onto his plate. There were no chairs, so I hopped onto his island counter.

140

I said a quick prayer of thanks for my food before taking a nibble of my pizza. Oh my goodness, it was delicious. I pointed at another slice of pizza in the pan. "Can I have that one too?"

Jordan plopped it on my waiting plate. "I'll be amazed if you eat both of those."

Between Marx's breakfasts and Jordan's pizzas, I was going to have to go up a size in my jeans pretty soon.

I looked over at Evey to find her staring down into the street again. She rubbed absently at her arms, her expression pinched. I wondered if I looked like that when I was scanning the streets for the one person who terrified me.

"Do you think Drew might get violent if he comes back?" Jordan asked, broaching the uncomfortable subject.

Evey drew in a breath, paused, then admitted, "I honestly don't know. I didn't think he would even come near Sammy's apartment. He's afraid of him."

If Sam was angry with me, I might be a little afraid of him too, especially after seeing him toss a grown man down a hallway.

Evey turned her back to the window and leaned against it. "Drew and Sammy never did get along."

"I'm guessing that had something to do with Drew's controlling personality," Jordan said.

"I thought it was romantic when we were dating and he always insisted on picking me up and paying for dinner. He planned every date. I didn't realize until after we were married that the motivation behind his actions wasn't romance. He intended to control not only our marriage but every aspect of my life."

Her eyes and voice grew distant, as if she had been carried away by the memories.

"The restrictions started out slowly—giving me a curfew, limiting my time with friends and family, dictating my schedule. I refused to give up my job, and a few weeks later I was fired. Customers had called in anonymously to complain about me, and the real estate company let me go. Before I even knew it was happening . . ."

"He had you trapped," I said softly.

There were tears in her eyes when she looked at me, and my stomach clenched. I hated to see people cry.

"He said it was because he loved me and he wanted me safe. But I never felt safe with him. Not really."

"Did he ever hurt you?" Jordan asked.

"He didn't hit me, if that's what you're asking. He didn't have to. He had a gun, and he told me that if I ever tried to leave, he would kill Sammy and then me. So I stayed."

He had practically kept her prisoner in her own home. Walls and bars constructed by fear.

My own memories of being imprisoned by fear pulled at me, but I forced them away. "Why aren't you with him now? What happened?"

"Sammy," she said, love and respect flowing off her tongue with the nickname. "He and I used to talk on the phone several times a week, but Drew didn't want him interfering in our marriage. He monitored the phone calls to make sure I didn't say anything about what was going on, and he made sure I spoke to Sammy less and less. Once a week, then every two weeks, once a month, and then not at all. He knew that if he just cut off my communication with Sammy abruptly, Sammy would know something was wrong, and he didn't want him searching for me."

Jordan grimaced. "I can't imagine Sam just sitting back and letting that happen."

"I didn't," a deep, tense voice broke in, and we all turned to see Sam stepping through the door. Sam shot Jordan a look of disapproval. "You should really lock your door."

Jordan tapped his gun. "I'm good."

Sam strode across the apartment and pulled his sister into a hug. Sam never struck me as the affectionate type, but the relief on his face as he squeezed Evey to him made me reconsider.

"Are you okay?" he breathed into her hair.

She nodded. "I'm okay."

They were the same height. Evey was just the skinnier, prettier version of Sam. I should tell him that sometime just to see his face. I bet he would scowl even more than usual.

Sam nodded his chin at Jordan. "Thank you for stepping in."

"Holly's actually the one who caught him picking the lock and told him to leave."

Small frown lines formed between Sam's eyebrows, and his dark eyes studied me from across the room. "I'm surprised he listened. Usually he gets angry when a woman tells him what to do."

Oh, he'd gotten angry. "Does his face always turn that radishy shade of red when he doesn't get his way?"

A hint of a smile touched Sam's lips. "Pretty much. Thank you for looking out for my sister."

It would feel awkward to say "oh, you're welcome" to something like that, so I took another bite of my pizza and grunted.

Jordan slid a plate of pizza to Sam. "So Evey was just about to tell us how you rescued her from Drew."

Sam glanced at Evey before saying, "He tried to cut me off from my sister. He took her phone and gave her one of those basic phones with coded parental locks so she could only call him. I had no way to reach her. And they weren't living in the apartment where they were initially, so I had to put an unofficial BOLO out on my own sister."

I raised my hand. "A what?"

"Be on the lookout," he clarified.

Oh. I thought they only did that for cars.

"Drew took Ev to the grocery store for their weekly shopping trip, and an off-duty cop recognized her. He tailed them back to their house and called me to give me the details. I went over to get her when Drew left for work. It took me an hour to convince her that he wouldn't be able to hurt either of us, and it was safe to leave with me." Sam tightened his arm protectively around his sister. "I'm surprised he had the nerve to come to the apartment. I'll have to figure out a few more security measures."

"I'll keep an eye out when I'm home. You can always come knock on my door if you feel uneasy or threatened, Evey," Jordan informed her. "And Sam can give you my number."

"Thanks," she replied, flashing him a smile. She looked at her brother. "I think I'd like to go home and take a bath before bed. Try to relax a little."

"Guess we're taking the pizza to go." Sam grabbed the plate Jordan had prepared for him and nodded his thanks. "Good night, Holly, and thanks again."

I waited for the door to close before saying, "They seem close."

"They are. Their mom passed away when Evey was born, and their dad died in the line of duty when Sam was eighteen, so he took care of Evey since she was younger. As protective as he is of her, I'm honestly surprised her husband's still breathing."

"Yeah," I murmured thoughtfully. "Me too." I had seen a glimpse of Sam's protective anger when he stepped between me and Collin. I couldn't even imagine how he would react if he was stepping between his sister and her controlling husband.

I nibbled my first piece of pizza down to the crust and started on the second.

"Seriously? You still don't eat the crust?" Jordan asked. When I shook my head, he reached over, snatched it from my plate, and popped it into his mouth.

"Hey!" I protested. "Boundaries."

He assessed where he was standing. "I'm four feet away. That was just a flyby. Doesn't count."

I rolled my eyes and ate the rest of my second slice of pizza. Jordan walked into the living room, pulled a dartboard from behind the couch, and propped it up on the cushions.

I gave him a wary look as he came back into the kitchen. "You're not really gonna give me pointy things to throw, are you?"

He snorted. "No." He pulled a handful of rubber bands from a drawer and sat down along the wall opposite the dartboard. "Come on over."

Curious, I hopped down and went to sit against the wall with him. "Now what?"

"Hit the bull's-eye and you get to ask a question that the other person has to answer." He held out a handful of rubber bands, but I didn't take them.

"What is it with you and questions?"

"I wanna know everything there is to know about you."

I folded my arms over my stomach and looked away. "No you don't."

He lowered his hand back to his lap. "There's nothing you've done and nothing that's been done to you that I'm afraid to know, Holly."

I wasn't so sure about that, and I would not be playing a game of questions.

"Okay." He paused to think of an alternative. "Instead of a question, name three facts about the other person and they'll tell you if they're true or false."

That sounded nearly as dangerous, but if it became uncomfortable, I could always refuse to play. When he offered the rubber bands again, I took them.

"You know I can't aim, right?" I reminded him. It occurred to me then that maybe that was the point. He would probably be able to hit the dartboard every time and keep asking questions.

"Try a few practice shots."

I wrapped the rubber band around my fingers to mimic his, held it up, and let it fly. I laughed when it flopped limply on the floor two feet in front of me.

"Yeah, let's try that again," he suggested.

The second one launched across the room, but nowhere near the target. When I tried a few more times and failed miserably, he laughed, "Forget the bull's-eye. How about we just hit the board?"

145

I smiled and tried again. By the time I managed to hit the board, there were rubber bands all over his living room floor and a few in the hallway. My last one grazed the board and I threw up my hands. "Ha! I got one!"

"And it only took your entire ball of rubber bands and half of mine," he said with a grunt of amusement. "List your facts."

I looked around, trying to come up with a fact, and then my gaze fell on my bracelet. "You gave me this when we were kids because we were best friends."

He hissed in a breath through his teeth. "False. I . . . may have had a crush on you."

"You did not."

"Yep. How can a boy resist a pretty girl who beats him up?"

I laughed at the ridiculousness of that. "Your favorite color is blue." He didn't contradict me, so I continued. "And . . . you . . . like westerns."

"True and true."

He snapped a rubber band across the room and hit the bull's-eye on the first try.

I threw him a suspicious look. "You've done this before."

"Yep. Fact one—you are incredibly beautiful." When I flushed at the compliment, he grinned. "Fact two—it's completely adorable that you're blushing."

I covered my face in embarrassment. "Don't say that."

He laughed. "I'm gonna enjoy this moment, because the first time I called you beautiful, you went completely white."

The first time he called me beautiful, I hadn't known anything about him, and it had felt like a threat. It still caused a flutter in my stomach, but not an entirely unpleasant one. Maybe because now I knew he wouldn't force his desires on me.

I cleared my throat and looked up at him. "And three?"

"You really wanna hug me."

I raised my eyebrows at him.

He shrugged with a wry grin. "A guy can hope."

146

I smirked and picked up a rubber band from the floor to try again. He was not getting a hug, no matter how much he hoped for one.

We played the silly game well into the night. He took three turns for every one of mine, because I couldn't seem to hit the dartboard. We worked our way through favorite movies, foods, and activities.

By the time he took me back to Marx's apartment, my sides ached from hours of laughter.

16

I sat at the peninsula and sipped my warm peppermint tea as I gazed out the window at the sunrise. Bright pinks and oranges splashed across the snow-laden buildings and trees in the distance. It was early—too early—but my sleep had been restless as usual.

A creak of floorboards drew my attention to the hallway. Marx paused at the edge of the kitchen when he saw me, his hair tousled and his eyes rimmed with tiredness.

Guilt threaded through me. My presence in his home was wrecking his ability to sleep. "I'm sorry."

"You have no business apologizin' for havin' nightmares."

It had been more of a memory than a nightmare, and the images were still playing through the back of my mind like a horrifying film reel.

Apparently my raw, terrified screams had spilled over from my nightmarish memories into Marx's guest room last night, frightening Maya and waking everyone in the building . . . except me.

I woke to find a distinctly male silhouette seated beside me on the bed, and scrambled up against the headboard in a panic. Unable to reach my knife in the nightstand, I tried to fend him off with my bare feet and fists.

I wasn't sure how long it took for his voice to pierce the haze of terror, but when I realized it wasn't Collin in my bed, that I didn't have to fight to protect myself, I folded over, limp with relief, and sobbed into the blankets.

"I'm sorry for waking you up and then . . . beating you up," I said reluctantly, my cheeks burning with humiliation. I despised feeling that vulnerable. "And, um . . . for the cops coming."

His lips turned down at the corners.

One of his neighbors, probably the elderly woman across the hall, who seemed to think I was Marx's live-in housekeeper, had probably called the police.

Two officers had shown up at the door to investigate reports of screams coming from his apartment. I had been tucking Maya back in when I overheard them interrogating him and demanding to take a look around.

"Well, it could've been worse," Marx sighed. "But I did learn a couple things. One, wear body armor when wakin' a woman from a night terror, and two, we need to work on your fightin' skills." He rubbed a spot on his jaw. "Though you certainly left your mark."

I winced. "Sorry."

"Stop apologizin'."

I started to apologize for apologizing, then realized how utterly ridiculous that was, and closed my mouth.

I sighed and took a sip of my tea, wishing it would settle my stomach and calm my nerves. I was always restless after a nightmare.

Marx leaned back against the refrigerator, his expression creased with concern. "When was the last time you slept through a night?"

I shrugged a shoulder. "I don't know."

I had never been able to sleep for long stretches of time, but since the shelter burned down, I was lucky if I managed a total of three or four hours a night. The lack of sleep left me feeling vaguely nauseous, and a slowly thickening fog clung to my mind, making it difficult to think straight.

"And the last time you slept without nightmares?"

I pressed my lips together. I honestly couldn't remember.

"Holly—"

"Please don't tell me I need to see a therapist," I interrupted curtly. "I'm not interested in having that conversation with you again. And Sam already tried this week."

"You need to sleep. You're makin' yourself sick."

I tried to bite back my irritation. "I'm fine."

"If you're not willin' to talk with somebody who can help you work through your anxieties, then maybe we should look into some kind of sleep aid."

"No drugs."

"There's nothin' wrong with—"

"No drugs," I repeated more firmly. If I took something that made me sleep, I might not hear Collin coming, or I might be too disoriented to run. It wasn't worth the risk.

He blew out a breath before opening the cupboard to grab a coffee mug, and paused with his hand in midair.

I held my cup of hot tea in front of my mouth to hide the smile creeping across my lips. I had removed every coffee cup and stashed them so he had no choice but to use the one remaining cup I had placed there.

At least I had done something productive while awake all night.

He lifted the giant tea cup from the shelf and read the hot pink words written across the front of it in delicate flourishes and swirls: "I am a hot Southern mess."

A muffled snort of laughter escaped my lips before I managed to cut it off.

He considered the cup for a long moment before saying seriously, "Yes, yes I am."

I burst out laughing. He set the tea cup on the counter and started the coffee as if everything were perfectly normal.

He turned around and reclined back against the counter as he waited for the coffee to brew. There was a barely perceptible curve of amusement to his lips as he folded his arms. "How odd that all the other mugs disappeared."

I tried to arrange my face into something resembling serious and replied, "The strangest things happen in your apartment." I tapped my fingers on my mug of tea as I fought to hold back another laugh.

"And it all started when the first tiny person moved in. What a strange coincidence."

I took a long, slow, innocent sip of my tea. Marx lifted the filled pot of coffee and poured some into his giant tea cup. I couldn't help but smile when he lifted it to his lips and took a drink.

He swallowed and asked, "And just how long are you fixin' to hide my coffee mugs?"

"You know there's a *g* at the end of that word, right? Fix-*ing*."

"There's no *g* in fixin'." He took another casual sip of coffee from his hot Southern tea cup. "How did things go with you and Jordan last night?"

"Fine."

The silent way he studied me told me "fine" wasn't the answer he was expecting, and he wasn't fooled. He knew being alone with Jordan was a challenge for me, and he knew why. "No panic attacks?"

I tapped my fingers on my mug and looked into my tea. "One, but it passed pretty quickly." But it had followed me into my dreams last night. "I think I'm gonna take a shower."

Marx's brows drew together, but all he said was, "Okay. I'm here if you wanna talk about it."

I forced a smile and fled into the bathroom. I didn't want to start my day talking about that awful night. I didn't even want to think about it.

After climbing into the shower, I remembered that I had used all the soap last time. I would just have to use shampoo. Marx had bought me coconut shampoo on his last trip to the store, and the soothing aroma filled the bathroom.

I dressed in a pair of cargo khakis and a few long-sleeved T-shirts when I was finished, then started on my hair. I was working out the tangles when I heard Marx's frustrated voice snap, "Maya. Do you have a box for your toys?"

"Yes, Mr. Marx."

"Then use it."

Jordan and I had stopped by Walmart last night to pick up some toys for Maya since all of hers had perished in the fire. We had left them for her to find this morning.

"Mr. Marx."

"Yes, Maya," he said with strained patience.

Maya hesitated before saying, "I think somebody hurt Holly."

I set the comb down on the counter and listened with concern. I had been very careful not to talk about Collin while she was around.

"What makes you say that?" Marx asked. He had been cautious too; neither of us wanted to expose her to any more fear and violence.

"Holly's scared when she sleeps. Sometimes she says things, and sometimes she cries," she informed him, and my heart clenched like a fist in my chest.

I heard Marx exhale slowly before responding. "Well, a bad man did hurt Holly, but it's been a while. She's safe now."

"Then why does she have bruises?"

Oh boy.

"I saw them last night when she was sleeping, and Mama always says if I see bruises, I should tell, because maybe someone is hurting that person, and I don't want anyone to hurt Holly. Because she's my friend."

Marx's eyes locked on me the moment I opened the bathroom door, and I braced myself for another lecture. I seemed to be getting a lot of those lately.

"Thank you, Maya," he said. "I appreciate you tellin' me. Now go watch some cartoons."

"Okay." She scampered into the living room and belly-flopped onto the couch. It would probably hit her in a minute that she had spoken about her mother in the present tense.

Marx's expression was stern when he asked, "What kind of bruises?"

I shrugged a shoulder.

"Don't you shrug at me. Let me see."

I resisted the urge to drop my head back and groan. He wasn't going to let this go, and there was no hiding it from him now. I rolled up my left shirt sleeve. The handprint had darkened to a hideous shade of plum, and it spanned two-thirds of my forearm. Perfect.

I saw his lips tighten in anger, but he didn't raise his voice when he demanded, "Who grabbed you?" He took my fingers gently and turned my arm so he could see the bruise from all angles. When I didn't answer, his eyes snapped back to my face. "Who, Holly?"

I pulled my arm back and tugged my sleeve back down. "It doesn't matter."

"It matters to me. And considerin' you didn't have this bruise before you were alone with Jordan last night, you better start talkin' before I pay him a visit."

Alarmed, I said, "He didn't do it."

The last thing any of us needed was those two getting into a fight over a misunderstanding. That would be a disaster, and I wasn't really sure who would win.

"Then who?"

I hesitated before saying, "Evey's husband."

Judging by his expression, he hadn't expected that answer; no one had told him about Drew's impromptu visit yesterday evening. I gave him the long, detailed version in hopes of avoiding questions.

My reasoning that Drew hadn't meant to grab me so hard did nothing to alleviate the anger in his eyes. "He had no business puttin' his hands on you at all." He walked into the kitchen, pulled an ice pack from the freezer, and wrapped it in a towel. "Have a seat."

I shuffled to a stool and plopped down. "I don't need an ice pack," I protested, even as I rolled up my sleeve at his silent gesture to do so. I doubted it would do any good at this point.

"There's no way your arm isn't hurtin'."

I had a much higher threshold for pain than he probably realized. He wrapped the ice pack around my arm, and I fidgeted, unaccustomed to being coddled.

"You ice it every twenty minutes durin' the first twenty-four hours to help with pain and healin'," he explained. The coolness from the ice pack felt surprisingly good. "Now explain to me why you didn't scream your head off the moment you realized he was a threat."

His tone made me want to squirm. "Because . . . I had it handled."

"Exactly which part did you have handled? The part where he had you trapped against the wall, or when he grabbed you and left a bruise the size of your forearm?"

I glared at him.

"You should've asked for help, Holly."

"You didn't ask for help when Leo had you trapped against the wall the other night. He hit you and tried to stab you, but you—"

"Don't try to turn this around on me, young lady."

"Why not?" I demanded. "I know your cracked ribs from being shot aren't healed, and you got beat up in the hallway two nights ago. So why—"

"That's different."

I slapped my hand on the counter in frustration. "Stop interrupting me!" He had a bad habit of doing that. "You're making a big deal out of nothing."

He leaned on the counter and lowered his voice. "How would you feel if somebody left bruises on Maya?"

I glanced at her over my shoulder. Even the idea of someone hurting Maya made me instantly angry. She was innocent and sweet, and I wanted to protect her.

Marx must have been able to read the thoughts on my face, because he said, "Now you know how I feel."

A knock on the door drew him away, and I stared after him in bewilderment. I understood—in theory—that he cared about me, but I couldn't quite grasp why or how much, or for how long . . .

"Jordan!" Maya squealed when Marx opened the door. She flung herself in his direction and hugged his waist.

Jordan scooped her up and propped her on his hip. "Hey there, Miss Maya."

She giggled and ducked her face into his shoulder. "I missed you. You took Holly and left, and then it was just me and Mr. Marx and"—she threw a cautious look at Marx before whispering—"he's like a grumpy bear."

"I'm standin' right here, Maya," Marx reminded her. He was still holding onto the door. "I can hear you."

She blinked her big, innocent brown eyes at him. "I know."

"I'm not grumpy."

"Have you told your face?" Jordan asked. "Because it seems to disagree with you."

Marx shot him an irritated look. "Why are you here?"

"To see my two favorite girls."

Maya giggled again as he let her slide slowly back to the floor. I couldn't help but smile at how absurdly cute she was. She bounded back to the couch to watch cartoons.

"Where exactly were you when Holly was in the hallway with Drew last night?" Marx demanded.

Jordan blinked, blindsided by the question, and I came to his defense. "It wasn't his fault. I'm the one who left the apartment while he was on the phone. That was my choice."

"And if it had been Collin waitin' in the hallway instead of Drew?"

I couldn't even put into words how much that possibility terrified me.

"We'll be more careful," Jordan said.

"See that you are." Marx stepped aside to let him enter. "Because if she comes back here with any more marks on her, you and I are gonna have a serious talk."

Jordan's eyes bounced between us with concern. "What are you talking about? What marks?"

"Holly has a bruise!" Maya shouted helpfully.

I dropped my head on the counter with a groan. Why did she have to announce it to the world?

"Drew got physical with her before you stepped in," Marx explained, closing the door and bolting it.

Jordan's gaze snapped to me as I lifted my head. "You told me he didn't hurt you."

I bit down on my lip before replying, "I didn't exactly say that."

"I asked you if he hurt you and you said . . ." His eyes turned thoughtful as he recalled the conversation, and then frustration flashed across his face. "You said he freaked you out a little. You never actually answered my question."

"Mmm hmm, she's sneaky that way."

I shot Marx an annoyed look.

"She didn't tell me either. I had to hear it from Maya." He strode back into the kitchen and leaned against the counter.

Jordan dropped onto the stool at the other end of the peninsula. "How bad is it? Can I see?"

"Promise you won't throw anything?"

He pursed his lips and waited. Apparently he was unwilling to make that promise. I rolled up my shirt sleeve.

Something shifted behind his eyes, and I thought he might snap, but his voice was calm. "Why didn't you say something yesterday?"

"Because . . . I didn't want you to put him through a wall."

The expression on his face told me he would've done exactly that. "He hurt you."

156

I tugged my sleeve back down and tucked my arm back beneath the counter. "It's just a bruise. It's not like he hit me or . . . you know. He just grabbed my arm. It's not that big of a deal."

Jordan's brow furrowed. "Holly—"

"It's fine," I said, abruptly uncomfortable. I really wanted to be done with this conversation.

"It is not fine and you're pressin' charges," Marx informed me, like it was a fact rather than a suggestion.

"No I'm not."

"Yes you are."

Irritated with his pushy attitude, I snapped, "You can't make me." I intended the words to sound determined, but they sounded petulant, like a pouting child, which irritated me even more. I folded my arms and scowled at him.

"Explain to me why you won't press charges." He folded his arms on the countertop and fixed his intense gaze on me. "I have a feelin' I already know why, so you may as well just say it."

I lifted my chin. "I won't be a victim again. Ever."

Jordan rubbed a hand over his hair and blew out a breath.

Marx didn't even blink. "Because you think bein' a victim makes you weak and vulnerable."

I lifted one shoulder noncommittally. "Maybe."

"Anybody can be a victim, Holly—from an innocent child to the most hardened soldier who doesn't know the definition of the word 'weak.' Bein' a victim means a wrong has been done to you; it doesn't mean you're weak or helpless . . . or broken."

I tightened my arms around myself and looked away. Collin had tried more than once to break me, and sometimes I wondered if he succeeded. He had broken . . . something.

I glanced at Jordan, wondering what it might be like to be a normal woman, to be able to hop one stool over, within inches of him, and feel something other than anxiety. Maybe something warm and tingly—like soda bubbles on my tongue—but all over.

Jace said Sam gave her butterflies in her stomach. The only time I felt butterflies in my stomach was when I tripped and fell over something.

"You hear me, sweet pea?"

I nodded stiffly and muttered, "I heard you."

"It's important to speak up when somebody hurts you." When I opened my mouth to argue, he held up a hand to cut me off. "Now, I know you're gonna refuse to press charges for yourself, because for somebody who's been through what you have, this feels as insignificant as a paper cut—a misperception I intend to remedy later—but do it for Evey."

That caught me off guard and diffused the last of my argument. "What do you mean?"

"If Drew was tryin' to break into Sam's apartment to get to Evey, then she's not safe, and she won't be until he's off the streets. For that to happen, somebody needs to press charges and make a statement."

I hadn't considered that. I knew what it was like to be afraid of a man who wanted to hurt me. I couldn't do anything about Collin right now, but I could do something to help Evey.

"Okay," I agreed reluctantly.

Jordan's eyes widened a little in surprise. "Okay?" His gaze shifted to Marx. "She just agreed with you."

"Miracles have been known to happen." Marx grabbed a notepad and pen and set it in front of him. "Now tell me again what happened, every detail, and then we'll take a photo of your arm."

I sighed and explained the entire situation. Again. I signed the statement after reading through it for accuracy, subjected myself to the humiliation of pictures, and then asked, "Are we done? Can we please be done?"

Marx smiled. "We're done. I need to drop this off at the precinct to be filed, and then a warrant will be issued for Drew Carson's arrest. Then I need to go shoppin'. Somebody used all the soap, and I'm out of eggs."

I hopped off the stool. "Do you mind if I come?" I needed to replace his soap, but I also had a serious craving for some Froot Loops.

"Can I come too?" Maya asked excitedly, bouncing on the couch.

He sighed. "Yes." He looked at me and muttered, "She's like a miniature you—a tiny ball of energy who manages to be both adorable and frustratin' at the same time."

I grinned. "Getting tired of us?"

"Not even a little bit." He glanced at the side table near the door and frowned. "Where's my wallet?"

"It's in your jacket pocket. I thought it would be safer there than lying around where someone could, um . . . play with it."

"So am I riding with you?" Jordan asked.

"Only if you wanna be pushed out of the car in the middle of the street," Marx replied evenly. "I am not sharin' a car with you."

I took Maya to change out of her pajamas, and thirty minutes later we piled into Marx's car. Jordan met us at the grocery store after we stopped by the precinct.

Maya, naturally, wanted to ride on the end of the cart while Marx pushed it down the aisles. Every now and then he would speed up just to make her squeal with delight. He might prefer his gruff detective image, but he was all soft and huggable inside.

"Ooh, chocolate marshmallows," I said, grabbing the bag from the shelf. It smelled amazing, like fluffy s'mores.

Marx plucked it from my hands and put it back. "No. No more marshmallows."

I rolled my eyes and continued down the aisle, drawing in the aroma of the sugary treats. I may have had a slight sugar obsession, but I didn't really do vegetables. Who wanted to eat green things?

I mean, unless it was pistachio pudding, which was amazing.

"You realize you're enablin' her addiction," Marx said, and I glanced behind me to see Jordan tossing the bag of chocolate marshmallows up and down in his hand.

"There are worse things to be addicted to. Besides, if she stops eating marshmallows, she'll probably starve."

"He doesn't want me to have marshmallows because he thinks I'm chunky," I commented casually. "He pretty much said so ten days after we met."

Jordan blinked, then looked at Marx. "You called her chunky? Seriously? Is there something wrong with your eyesight?"

"I did not call her *chunky*. I would never say that to a woman, even if it was true, because I don't have a death wish. What I *said* was she was out of her weight class."

He had meant that I was outmatched, but I had been almost certain he was calling me fat at the time. I enjoyed teasing him about it, because it never failed to fluster him.

I stayed closed to the cart as we moved into the bread aisle. Marx was partial to whole grain breads, and I looked for his brand with all the weird little seeds in it.

I spotted the twelve-grain bread at the end of the aisle and walked down to grab two loaves. I hesitated when I heard the very faint click of a camera. I looked around and saw a woman with a camera trained on us.

She was taking pictures of us. I opened my mouth to ask her what she thought she was doing, but then she disappeared behind a shelf.

I waited to see if she would pop back out, but she didn't. Maybe I was just being paranoid.

I grabbed the bread and walked back to drop it in the cart while keeping an eye on the spot where she had disappeared. I didn't recognize her, but something didn't feel right.

I gathered a few ingredients to bake Jace a cake for her birthday and found a present that I knew would make her grin from ear to ear.

Marx and I had a minor disagreement at the register when I insisted on paying for the soap, and he insisted that I was being stubborn. Like he had room to talk. It took a bulldozer to make the man move an inch on an issue he disagreed with.

The poor cashier was at a complete loss and eventually just dropped his arm while he waited for us to sort out who would be handing him the money.

Marx reached into his pocket to pull out his wallet, and a thoughtful crease appeared between his eyebrows. I glanced at Maya, who had both hands clasped over her smile.

He pulled his wallet from his pocket and blinked at it before slanting an accusing look my way.

The brown leather of his wallet was smothered by pretty purple and pink beads. Maya had picked the colors, and I had bedazzled it last night after putting her back to bed.

The cashier's eyes widened as his gaze shifted from the shimmering wallet to the gruff detective.

"What?" Marx asked him in a tone that dared him to comment. "You've never seen a grown man with a shiny wallet before?"

He handed the money to the cashier, who finally managed, "It's totally cool, dude. It's a free country."

"It goes with your sparkling personality," Jordan commented, and I choked back a laugh.

Marx collected his change and grumbled under his breath about beads. "At least it wasn't bags of heroin this time."

I smirked. I had bedazzled those before too.

I was exiting the store with Maya when a short, bald man in a polo stepped around the corner and directly into my path.

"Holly, can you tell me about your experiences with known serial killer Edward Moss Billings?"

He shoved a handheld recorder in my face, and I jerked back in surprise. I smacked into Jordan, who smoothly tucked me and Maya behind him.

"You need to step back," he told the man, who was wearing a journalist badge, and I heard the authority of law enforcement in his voice.

The journalist must have detected it too, because he fixed his sights on Jordan with new interest. "Are you the detective who was involved in breaking the case?" He squinted at the notepad in his other hand. "Detective Richard Marx?"

I shot a frantic look at Marx. How did he know who we were? Someone must have told him. Who had told him?

Marx leveled a suspicious look at the man. "Where are you gettin' your information from?"

The man looked excited to have yet another person to pester for information. "I spoke with the former sheriff of the town where the crime took place: Jedidiah Radcliffe."

Shocked, I looked up at Jordan. "Your dad talked to the press?"

He looked as dumbstruck as I felt. The journalist heard my question and turned his attention back to Jordan. "You're the sheriff of Stony Brooke? Jordan Radcliffe?"

Jordan said nothing, and I had a feeling he was struggling to come to terms with his father's actions.

"How does it feel to be reunited with your childhood love? Rumor has it you never stopped looking for her."

Jordan had searched for me in one form or another for eighteen years, and the same serial killer who caused our separation had led to us finding each other again.

"Can you confirm that you nearly died trying to save her life?" When Jordan didn't answer the journalist, the man returned his attention to me. "Holly, what was going through your head when you realized that the man who abducted you was the same man who murdered your family?"

I swallowed the knot that expanded in my throat.

"What kind of ignorant question is that?" Marx demanded tersely. He squeezed through the doorway and wrapped an arm around my shoulders. "Come on, sweetheart."

He led Maya and me toward his car. Jordan cast me an apologetic look before blocking the nosey journalist to keep him from following us.

"Are you the detective who accompanied Holly back to Kansas?" the bald journalist shouted after us. "Is it true the killer abducted you so he could kill you as a couple? Are you a couple? Janny, get a picture of them!"

I caught a glimpse of the woman with the camera as she came around the building, snapping more pictures of us.

What was wrong with these people? What gave them the right to take pictures and shove recorders in our faces, demanding details about our lives?

Marx unlocked the passenger door first, and Maya and I ducked inside to hide from the camera. He walked around the car, climbed in, and we squealed out of the parking lot.

17

Maya sat cross-legged on the bed in front of me in her pajamas after her bubble bath. She smelled like strawberries. I had lightly oiled her thick black hair, and I was carefully working it into small cornrows.

"Holly," she said, my name hitching on a yawn. "How's come you're so good at my hair?"

"Practice."

"But you have white people hair."

I smiled. "White people hair, huh?"

She nodded, almost making me lose my grip on her slippery strands. "Skinny and flat."

I grunted softly in amusement. Some might say that described more than my hair. "When I was fourteen, I shared a room with a little girl named Cassie, who had hair just like yours. I helped her with it almost every night."

"Was she your sister?"

My fingers stilled for an instant. How did I explain foster care to a little girl who had always lived with her mother? "Mmm, not exactly. We lived in the same house, but . . . we came from different families."

"Like the shelter? Lots of kids and women lived with us, but we were like a family. Did you live in a shelter for kids because someone hurt you?"

She was eerily insightful for an eight-year-old. "My parents . . . passed away when I was nine, so I got a new home."

Maya's mood sobered, and she twisted around to look at me, her big eyes liquefying with tears. "Am I gonna go with foster people too? I don't have a home anymore and my mama . . ."

I brushed the tears from her face and shook my head. "No. Your grandparents are coming to get you. It's just taking them a while to get here."

Her bottom lip quivered. "What if they don't want me? Mama always says I'm a handful, and they're really old."

She had suffered more than her fair share in these past several days. If her grandparents decided not to keep her, it would break her heart.

"They're gonna love you," I assured her, and I prayed I wasn't lying.

She threw herself into my arms and cried harder, grief and fear making her small body tremble. I rubbed her back and held her until her sobs faded to whimpers and finally, to yawns.

"I think it's time for bed." I nudged her back toward the pillows and tucked her beneath the blankets.

She yawned and protested halfheartedly, "But I'm not even tired."

I smiled. Sure she wasn't. "How about I read for a little bit. I have the perfect book." I leaned back against the pillows on my side of the bed and grabbed the book resting on the side table.

The Wizard of Oz was one of two possessions I had that had belonged to my twin sister, Gin, and I cherished not only the book itself but the memories of hours spent reading it together in our father's bookstore.

I never had the chance to finish the story with Gin, and I was reading it to the end for both of us now. She would be ecstatic to know it was bringing another little girl comfort, even if only for a few days.

I barely finished the first chapter before Maya drifted to sleep. I closed the book and watched her. I would never be able to adequately express how thankful I was that she had survived the fire. I grabbed my journal and jotted down the things that I was especially thankful for today, and she was at the top of my list.

Shannon's voice snapping through the apartment drew my attention from my nearly finished entry. "Did you know?"

Curious, I set my journal aside and climbed silently from the bed. I cracked open the bedroom door and peered into the kitchen just in time to see her pull a manila folder from her briefcase and slap it onto the countertop.

Marx set his drink down. "Did I know what?"

Shannon's mouth compressed into a thin line. "That her injuries were far more severe than a few broken fingers and a fractured rib."

My stomach twisted at the sight of the folder. She had found the hospital records from Darby.

"Either she has the worst luck of any human being imaginable, or this man has hurt her more than once. Scar tissue and X-rays show signs of previous abuse."

Marx flipped open the folder, and I wanted to rush into the kitchen and rip it away from him. He turned slowly through a few of the pictures.

"Oh, Holly," he breathed. He picked up one of the photos and stared at it, his expression pained.

"She didn't tell you either," Shannon realized.

"She didn't tell me it was this bad." He seemed to have difficulty flipping through the rest of the photos. Finally, he slapped the folder shut and shoved it across the counter. "I'm gonna shoot that man."

"Collin Wells isn't just some overly attached stalker with a temper like she let me believe, Rick. He's a sexual predator."

"I know."

Shannon's eyes narrowed. "You knew this man sexually assaulted her and you didn't tell me when I was here gathering information for the court order?"

"She told you what she was comfortable tellin' you, and I had no intention of betrayin' her confidence."

"I see."

166

"If it makes you feel any better, she only ever told me the basics. Most of what I know I pieced together from her mannerisms, anxieties, and the occasional comment she makes. It didn't take me long to realize that when she says 'he hurt me,' she's not talkin' about cuts and bruises. She just can't bring herself to say the word."

"That's not uncommon for victims of sexual assault. Euphemisms like 'he hurt me' or 'what he did to me' make it seem less devastating and easier to manage." Shannon pulled another file from her briefcase. "On that subject, we have more to discuss. They recovered DNA from . . ."

The floorboards beneath my feet let out a quiet creak under my shifting weight, and Shannon's attention moved to the doorway of the spare bedroom. All emotion disappeared from her face behind a mask of professionalism.

"Good evening, Holly."

"Hi." I shifted my attention to Marx, who had turned to see me eavesdropping in the doorway—although I wasn't really sure it could be considered eavesdropping when I was the topic of conversation.

Compassion shimmered in his eyes, and he cleared the remnants of anger from his throat before speaking. "Hey, peanut."

I smiled thinly at the ridiculous nickname. I would have to find a way to repay him for all his "sweet peas" and "peanuts." I had lots of sneaky tricks up my sleeves.

My gaze skipped to my medical file on the counter and then to Shannon. "My exam photos—"

"No," she said, understanding my concern before I could even voice it. "The photos you're concerned about aren't in there."

That gave me a small measure of relief. I didn't want anyone to ever see those, especially Marx and Jordan.

"You should've told me, Holly," she said, but there was no bite to the reprimand.

I hugged my stomach and looked at my toes. I had never told anyone; I didn't think I could physically force the words from my throat.

I heard her sigh and draw another folder from her briefcase. I looked up to see her hand it to Marx. "Take a look at this when you have time, and then call me. Things are more complicated than we previously thought."

What did that mean—more complicated? My gaze lingered on the new folder as I pondered the awful possibilities.

She tucked my medical file back into her briefcase and turned her attention to me. "I have a meeting with the judge tomorrow afternoon. With your medical file and your word that Collin Wells is responsible for your injuries, I don't anticipate any resistance in the granting of your protection order." She studied me for a moment, then asked, "Is there anything else you're not telling me about your history with him?"

"Yes."

She lifted an eyebrow when I didn't elaborate. "Are you going to tell me?"

"No."

I didn't miss the frustration that flashed through her eyes, and she looked at Marx. He gave a barely perceptible shrug of one shoulder.

She pursed her lips. "Well then, I'll talk to the two of you tomorrow evening." With that, she swept out of the apartment and closed the door behind her.

Marx rubbed a hand over his face, and I could practically see his mind cycling through the pictures he'd seen.

"It wasn't always that bad," I said, climbing onto one of the kitchen stools.

Things had gotten progressively worse in my foster home during my eleven-month stay, but Collin had always been . . . careful. If he left bruises or cuts, they were usually in places no one would see. And he explained everything away with such ease, spinning stories of clumsiness that none of us dared dispute for fear of what he would do next.

I had hoped my words would soothe Marx, but they only seemed to spark his anger. "Meanin' he hurt you, but he didn't leave you hospitalized."

"Yeah," I said beneath my breath. I tucked my hands between my knees and stared at my jeans. I had never realized how much Collin had held back until that night. I swallowed the emotions trying to push their way up my throat and decided to change the subject. "Any sign of Rachel?"

"Unfortunately no," he said, letting my abrupt change of subject pass despite the questions I knew he must have. "But we did confirm that the blood and hair in the trunk of the car belong to her."

My heart constricted. "Oh."

"The bloodstains were partially dry, which means her body was in that trunk no more than a few days ago, which coincides with the fire."

"So she's . . ."

"I'm sorry, sweetheart. I wanted to find her for you."

I nodded because I didn't know what else to say. "Um, what about her husband? Did you find him?"

"We did. A fellow fireman gave us his location while you were with Jordan, and a patrol car picked him up."

"Do you think he did it?"

"Given the accelerant found at his house, the blood in his trunk, and the fact that he frequently visited the shelter to try to force Rachel to leave with him, it's very possible. But he says he has an alibi for the night of the fire and that he never touched Rachel."

Never touched her?

"I was there the day she came to the shelter. He knocked one of her teeth out."

"I know. I read the report from when Rachel pressed charges. She later dropped them, which is unfortunately a common occurrence in these types of situations."

169

He opened the second folder Shannon had given him and angled it away from me as he skimmed the contents. His expression became unreadable, but his tone of voice didn't change.

"He also vehemently denies any connection with the shelter. He says he didn't even know where it was until he saw it on the news."

"Then he's a liar," I shot back. "I saw him there, and so did Maya." And besides, what kind of fireman wouldn't know that their old fire station had been turned into a shelter, or at least turned into something?

He lifted his eyes to me as he closed the folder. "You know for certain it was him you saw?"

"Yes. He was trying to break into the building one night while I was taking out the trash."

He frowned. "If he wanted in that badly, he could've grabbed you and used you to leverage his way inside. And why on earth were you takin' the trash out by yourself? Given the situation most of those women were in, I'd think you would've been more cautious."

I gave him an incredulous look. "Really? You're scolding me for taking the trash out alone *two years ago*?"

"Point taken. Why didn't he use you to get inside?"

"Because I ran inside and bolted the door before he could follow me in."

He pulled out his cell phone and punched out a quick text before saying, "Well, I'm afraid your word that you saw him at the shelter two years ago will do little to benefit us now. Proof of a lie is not proof of guilt."

I tapped my fingers on the counter. "What about Collin? Did you find any connection between Darin Glass and Collin?"

"Not yet."

"If Darin wanted Rachel that badly, and Collin managed to get his hands on her, he could've made a bargain with him."

Marx's expression turned thoughtful as he set his phone down. "A fireman would know best how to set a fire. Glass would

170

get his wife and revenge on the woman who kept her from him, and Collin could send his message without actually gettin' his hands dirty."

It was exactly something Collin would do, which would make it all the harder to link him to the crime.

"Glass says he's never seen Collin before, and at the moment, we have no evidence to the contrary," Marx said, a line of thought still visible between his eyebrows.

"Well, he hasn't exactly been truthful so far."

"We know Collin's involved somehow. We just have to find hard proof or someone willin' to roll on him."

I didn't foresee that happening.

"What about the car? The one that nearly hit Jordan?" I asked, clutching at the last available straw.

"Reported stolen the mornin' after the fire. Looks like it was taken some time durin' the night. It's also a match to the car that followed us home from the apartment downtown."

"What about the driver?"

"The owner of the car has an alibi, and she has no idea who might have stolen it. Until we recover the vehicle and dust it for prints, or somebody steps forward—"

"We have nothing." I slumped lower on my stool.

"It's not *nothin'*, Holly. It's just gonna take time."

"We don't have time!" I shouted before I could stop myself. I bit down on my lips and tried to rein in my fear.

Collin wasn't simply trying to clear a path to me by hurting the people I cared about; he was trying to kill them. He never intended for Marx to survive the altercation in the apartment any more than he intended for Maya to survive the fire, or for Jordan to walk out of that alley.

I was running out of time to help the people I cared about, and I didn't know what to do. What if he killed one of them before Maya's grandparents arrived? What if by not running now I was condemning one of them to death?

171

"I promise it's gonna be okay, Holly."

"You can't promise that," I said on a sigh as I slid off the stool. I folded my arms and paced along the wall.

"You're right. I can't promise that," he said, following my anxious movements with his eyes. "But so long as you're safe, we're headin' in the right direction."

He didn't understand. My life wasn't in danger. "Collin wants me alive."

"I'm aware of that. I'm also aware that he wants you alive because he intends to hurt you." At my slight wince, he clarified gently, "I mean *hurt* in general terms. Not just the way you usually mean it." He watched my endless pacing. "Holly—"

"I know, I'm gonna get dizzy if I keep pacing."

"Who cares if you're dizzy. You're makin' *me* dizzy."

I offered a fragile smile in response to his pitiful attempt at levity. "What's in the folder? You went all blank-faced when you were flipping through it."

He glanced down at it. "Nothin' you need to worry about."

That sounded suspiciously evasive. "Does it have anything to do with Collin?"

His pursed lips were answer enough.

I walked around the peninsula and held out my hand. "I wanna see it."

"No."

I narrowed my eyes at him. "He's here because of me. I have a right to see what's in there."

He moved it beyond my reach when I stepped toward him. "Don't make me hold this above your head."

"If you do, then you apparently haven't learned your lesson."

"And what lesson might that be?"

"That I will tickle you without remorse to get what I want." He moved the folder even further beyond my reach when I made a grab for it. Why did everyone have to be taller than me? It wasn't fair.

"Vicious, aren't you?" he teased. "Threatenin' to tickle people. But fair warnin'—if you tickle me, I will return the favor this time."

I had just stretched out my hand when his threat made me hesitate. "You wouldn't."

"Are you sure you wanna take that chance?"

I was pretty sure he was bluffing, but the twinkle in his eyes made me less certain than I wanted to be. I drew my arm back and wrapped it around my stomach. "I think you're bluffing."

"Possibly. Or I might tickle you until you cry tears of forfeit."

A sharp rap of knuckles on the front door distracted me from the folder and the threat of tickling. I glanced curiously at the clock on the wall, then at the door, and saw Riley do the same out of the corner of my vision. I wasn't the only one who thought it was a bit late for visitors.

"It's us," Sam announced through the door.

Knowing it was just Sam on the other side of the door and not some crazed lunatic, Marx didn't object when I walked to the front door to open it.

I couldn't remember the last time I had opened a door when someone knocked. Small pleasures.

I expected to find just Sam in the hallway, but Jordan was standing beside him. Well, he *had* said "us."

"Hey," Jordan greeted with a smile as he entered.

His smile sent a small flicker of warmth through me. He always seemed genuinely happy to see me, whereas Sam acknowledged me with a tight nod and a brusque "Holly" before walking inside.

18

I closed the front door and locked it before leaning back against it. My eyes danced over the three men now gathered in the living room. Sam's expression was blank as he turned through the file I had been trying to wrest from Marx's fingers only moments ago.

"What's going on? Why are you guys here this late at night?"

"Why don't you give us a few minutes to talk, Holly," Marx suggested.

Irritated at his attempt to dismiss me, I opened my mouth to object, but Sam beat me to it. "If this folder means what I think it means, I think she should stay."

"You know exactly what it means," Marx replied tersely. "And the effect it will have."

"She might have some insight for us."

Jordan studied the contents of the folder over Sam's shoulder, and the expression on his face made my stomach cramp. What was in there?

"I wanna know what's going on," I demanded. When no one made a move to explain, I folded my arms resolutely. "You may as well just tell me, because I'm not leaving."

Marx expelled a defeated breath. "This is gonna be an uncomfortable discussion, so if you change your mind or you need a break—"

"I'll be fine." I joined him in front of the couch.

"Do we need Shannon for this?" Sam asked. At Marx's nod, he called her and put his phone on speaker before setting it on the coffee table. He had one of those smartphones with all the nifty gadgets.

"This is Shannon," a female voice announced from the phone.

"Hey, Shannon. It's Sam. Jordan and I are here with Marx, and we have the folder."

"Did you have a chance to review it?"

"Briefly," Marx replied. "You mind fillin' us in on the details? Keepin' in mind that Holly's here too."

I frowned, wondering what difference my presence made.

There was a brief pause over the line before Shannon spoke again, and she seemed to be choosing her words carefully. "The doctors collected DNA from Holly when they conducted her exam in Pennsylvania."

My spine stiffened. I had assumed this discussion would be about Collin, not me. Not about . . . that.

"The DNA was a match to sixteen other unsolved sexual assault cases."

My breath left me in a rush, and I felt suddenly light-headed. Sixteen? Collin had attacked sixteen other women?

I felt the warmth of Marx's hand on my back as he said, "Why don't you sit down, sweetheart."

I blinked at him as he settled me onto the couch, and heard myself ask disconnectedly, "Sixteen?"

"All of the women were single and in their midtwenties to early thirties," Shannon's disembodied voice continued.

I stared at the floor as my mind tried to wrap itself around the fact that Collin had tortured sixteen other women. I had known he was a monster, but . . .

My voice sounded strangled as I asked, "Are you sure?"

"The DNA's conclusive," Shannon confirmed.

"W-where? When?"

"Spread out between Maine and Pennsylvania over the past ten years," she answered.

The women had been attacked along the path I traveled while trying to stay ahead of Collin.

"Considering sex crimes are the most underreported crimes in the country, there's probably more than sixteen," Sam reasoned.

Horrified, I looked up at him. "More?"

"There's a possible case in New York, but the victim refused a sexual assault kit, so we can't link it to the others with DNA," Shannon continued.

"What makes you think her case is connected to the others?" Marx asked.

"She denies any sexual assault took place, but everything else fits. All of the women were held captive in their homes for twelve to forty-eight hours, during which time they were repeatedly assaulted, beaten, and strangled by the same man who attacked Holly."

Nausea rolled over me, and I fought to keep the contents of my stomach where they belonged. I buried my face in my knees, trying to control my body's urge to purge the memories all over the floorboards.

I was not going to throw up Froot Loops in front of everyone.

I felt Marx's hand come to rest gently on my head as he asked, "And the condition of the women?"

"He left them alive."

There was something she wasn't saying; I could hear it in her voice. I looked up at the phone just as Marx asked the question ricocheting around in my head.

"But they're not all alive now?"

There was a second of hesitation before she answered. "Unfortunately no. But none of them died by suspicious means."

My stomach lurched again. Some of the women were dead. Maybe not by Collin's hand, but I had no doubt he had driven some of them to take their own lives.

"So strangulation was never intended to kill the women," Marx said, his tone equal parts thoughtful and disgusted.

"Sounds to me like he's just a sadist who enjoys the rush of power he feels by controlling whether or not they can breathe," Sam offered. "He probably thrives on the fact that his victims are alive, terrified, and broken when he leaves."

I flinched at the matter-of-fact nature of his voice, like he wasn't talking about something awful that had happened to me too.

Jordan shot him a blistering look. "Maybe you could try not being insensitive for once."

Sam blinked in confusion. "I'm just stating facts. Collin might be a sadist, but he's not a killer."

"There are things worse than death," I murmured. Far, far worse. I held out my hand. "I wanna see what's in the folder now."

Sam still had it in his hands, and he stepped forward to offer it to me despite Marx's look of disapproval. I opened it to find it filled with photographs of women. There was a note attached to each photo that listed the woman's name, age, and location.

I studied the red-haired woman with brown eyes and porcelain pale skin. There was a light dusting of freckles across her cheeks and nose. I flipped to the next image: another red-haired woman, this one with hazel eyes and an impish smile. As I leafed through the photos, a growing sense of dread filled me.

I looked up at Marx, a sick feeling creeping up the walls of my stomach. "Why do they all look like me?"

His conflicted expression confirmed my fears without words.

The pictures in my hands blurred behind a flood of tears. "He hurt these women because of me? This . . . it's my fault?"

"It isn't."

"But he—"

Marx took the folder from my hands, setting it aside, and sat down on the coffee table in front of me. "I understand why you might think it's your fault, sweetheart, but it's not. Collin is a predator, like Edward, and he was gonna hurt somebody no matter what. Edward became obsessed with young married couples who reminded him of his parents. Collin targets petite redheads."

"Because they remind him of me," I said, my voice trembling. "I'm the reason he picked them, the reason he—"

"Just because he chooses women who look like you in order to fulfill some sick fantasy doesn't make it your fault. Even if he'd never met you, he still would've hurt people. If not these women, he would've chosen others."

"If I'd told someone when I was fourteen, maybe—"

"Don't do that. You tried to tell somebody, remember? He didn't listen. You're in no way responsible for what Collin's done. You understand me?"

I sniffled and nodded.

A noise came through the phone—like someone clearing their throat—and Shannon said, "We can't do anything about the cases in Pennsylvania or Maine, but Wells can be arrested and tried here if the woman who was attacked in New York is willing to identify him."

"Then we're gonna wanna talk to her," Marx said.

"Her name is Melanie Bordeaux. She's thirty-one years old and she lives in New Hope. I'm sending her photo and information to Samuel's phone."

"New Hope?" Marx asked as he stood, concern in his voice.

Sam's phone chirped, and I looked up just as he was lifting it from the table. He clicked something and then offered the phone to Marx.

"Son of a . . ." Marx bit off the last word, but fury and something that might have been guilt shone in his eyes. "This is the woman I saw Collin havin' dinner with when I first tracked him down." His grip on the phone was so tight that I thought he might snap it in two. "I should've arrested him then. Instead I walked away and this poor woman suffered for it."

Sam fumbled to catch his phone when Marx shoved it toward him. "You couldn't have known what was gonna happen."

Jordan glanced at me with concern. "What he did to those women—that's what he's planning to do to Holly?"

I could feel all of their attention on me, and it made me want to crawl beneath the couch cushions.

"He kept those women for two days at the most," Sam said. "He said he intends for his time with Holly to be long and memorable. I expect he has more than two days of torment planned."

Jordan's eyes flashed with anger. "Someone needs to put him down."

"I'm not busy." Sam folded his broad arms. "But I'll need an alibi."

"Pizza and beer at my place?"

Shannon heaved an exasperated breath. "You realize you're joking about committing murder and falsifying an alibi with the district attorney listening in."

"Who says we're joking?" Sam deadpanned, and I couldn't tell if he was serious or not.

"I would rather you just get a positive ID from the victim and arrest him."

Marx glanced at his watch. "It'll take me two hours to get there. I'll have to go first thing in the mornin'. See if she's willin' to talk to me."

I stood slowly and tucked my hair behind my ears, trying to appear steadier than I felt. "I wanna go with you."

"No."

No? That was it? Just . . . no? "Why *no*?"

"Because I want you right here with Sam or Jordan—possibly both—where we can guarantee your safety."

"But I wanna talk to her."

He stared at me, unmoved by my argument. Apparently, I needed to be more persuasive.

I folded my arms and scowled up at him. "I'm going and you can't stop me." See? I could be persuasive.

He lifted an eyebrow. Oh my goodness, he was so frustrating.

"She's not gonna talk to you. You're a man, and if he . . ." I tried to use the appropriate word, but it stuck to my tongue like glue, and I couldn't spit it out. I settled for one of the easier euphemisms

Shannon had mentioned. "If he did to her what he did to me, she's not gonna want anything to do with you."

"I know how to talk to a victim, Holly."

"But I can help her through this. I didn't have anyone to help me back then, and I felt alone and scared and desperate. I don't want her to feel that way. Please. Just let me come with you."

I caught the flicker of uncertainty in his eyes as he considered my request—if anyone in this room could connect with her and help her, it was me—but then his jaw firmed and he shook his head. "I'm sorry, but no. You're not comin' with me."

Fine, if he wanted to be difficult, I could be too. I excelled at difficult. I marched over to the door and plucked his car keys off the side table.

I shoved them into the front pocket of my jeans, folded my arms, and shot him a challenging glare. "You're not going *without* me."

19

*I*t took us just over two hours to arrive at Melanie Bordeaux's house the next morning. I tried to convince Marx to let me drive—he was teaching me so I could get my license—but he squashed that hope with a flat "no."

Just because I hit a few trash cans that *happened* to be on the sidewalk the last time I drove didn't mean I was a bad driver. Besides, they were really ugly trash cans, and the owners probably wouldn't even notice a few extra dents.

Jordan followed behind us in his own car, leaving Maya and Riley with Sam, just in case the mysterious red Honda decided to make another appearance.

They hung back on the sidewalk, giving me a chance to talk to Melanie first. I knocked on the teal door and folded my arms against the cold breeze that whipped around the corner of the house as I waited on the porch.

The blinds were closed over the windows, which was to be expected, and I could see a dim glow coming from inside the house. Someone was home.

I tried ringing the doorbell.

"If she doesn't answer, we'll head home," Marx decided.

I knocked again and listened for the sound of a voice or approaching footsteps, but there was nothing. I wasn't sure why, but I had an uneasy feeling.

On impulse, I wrapped my fingers around the doorknob and turned it. The door clicked open.

Something was definitely wrong.

No woman who had been attacked the way she had would ever leave her door unlocked. She probably checked compulsively to make sure the windows and doors were secured, just to reassure herself that she was safe.

I pushed the door inward and slipped inside, ignoring the quiet snap of my name that sounded distinctly irritated . . . and Southern.

The house was dark but for a single lightbulb burning in the hallway. I gripped my pepper spray in one hand as I stepped nervously into the living room. "Melanie?"

My voice echoed in the tidy space. My gaze skipped over the family photographs on the mantle above the fireplace and the cute matching furniture. If I had to judge by her home alone, I would say Melanie had a very peaceful, well-put-together life.

Until Collin turned it upside down.

Marx and Jordan stepped into the foyer behind me.

"Holly, you can't just walk into somebody's house," Marx whispered sharply.

"She wouldn't leave the door unlocked," I explained. "Something's not right."

"All the more reason not to go bargin' inside." He drew his gun and Jordan did the same. "Ms. Bordeaux! I'm a detective with the New York City Police Department. We're just here to ask you a few questions."

Silence met his announcement.

I strode past the kitchen table and snapped back to the sheet of paper resting at the center of it. I squinted to read the words in the fading light.

Dear Elsie,

I've thought a lot lately about how inseparable we were as kids. I miss the laughter and all the precious moments we shared. I guess a disagreement as adults managed to do what physical fights and bickering as kids never could: it drove us apart.

I wish that we could've spent more time together, but I want you to know that I forgive you for what happened with Tom. He chose you, and you both followed your hearts. Know that I love you with all of mine. If only I could see your smile one last time, but it hurts too much and I'm not strong enough.

    I wish you every happiness, and I hope that you know this isn't your fault. Give my beautiful niece a hug and kiss from me. I wish I had embraced her sooner. I know that she'll grow into an amazing woman, just like my sister.
All my love,
Melanie.

A few phrases from her letter stuck out: *I wish that we could've spent more time together, if only I could see your smile one last time*—things that would soon be impossible—and *this isn't your fault . . .*

"No" escaped beneath my breath. She was going to kill herself. I pushed away from the table and rushed through the small house. I had a feeling I would find her in the bathroom or the bedroom. "Melanie!"

"Holly, stop," Marx called after me.

I flung open the first door and my eyes skipped frantically over the white porcelain bathroom. I pushed back the ocean-themed shower curtain, but she wasn't in the bathtub.

I backed out of the bathroom and ran to the next room. A guest bedroom. Blue bedding with a lamp made of seashells on a driftwood nightstand. Melanie loved the ocean.

I abandoned the empty room and threw open the last door. I froze in the doorway as my eyes fastened on the red-haired woman huddled in the far corner of the room, brandishing a bloody knife.

Even though she was a shadow of the smiling woman in the photograph, I recognized her. "Melanie," I called softly.

Haunted brown eyes met mine.

She stared at me, no doubt startled by the resemblance between us, then pointed the knife at me when I stepped into the room.

"Don't come any closer." Her voice was deeper than mine, almost husky, and it shook with terror.

"I just wanna help you." My attention lingered on the tip of the knife, which was slick with blood, as I took another small step into the room.

"I mean it, I'll stab you if you come any closer," she warned, and she shook the knife for emphasis.

"Okay." I pressed back against the wall and slid along it until the bed was no longer obstructing my view of her. I noticed two things in that moment: the hesitant slice up her left forearm and the swell of her stomach.

She was pregnant.

I felt a wave of sickness sweep over me as I realized the unborn child was probably Collin's.

Marx appeared in the doorway with Jordan behind his shoulder, and Melanie turned white with fear. "Stay away from me!"

Marx had his gun drawn, and he angled it toward her as he instructed gently, "Put down the knife please, Ms. Bordeaux. We're not here to hurt you."

If I weren't standing in the room, I don't think he would've pointed his gun at her.

"Who are you people?" she demanded. "Get out of my house. Leave me alone."

Marx showed her his badge and explained, "I'm Detective Marx, and I need you to put down the knife. Holly, come out of the room."

"No. I wanna talk to her."

He flicked an impatient look my way. "That's not an option right now. I'm not leavin' you unprotected in this room when she has a knife."

"Holly, he's right," Jordan said from behind him. "Just step out of the room and let us take care of this."

"I'm not leaving her alone, and you're just gonna make it worse." If they wanted me out of this room, they would have to forcibly remove me, and I doubted either of them would.

Jordan glanced at Marx, uncertain.

"I'll be careful. Just give us some space," I pleaded. "Please. Trust me."

Marx glanced at the knife again, reluctant, then warned me softly, "You keep your distance." He waited for my nod before saying, "I'll be right outside the door."

He kept his gun in his hand as he stepped out of sight and took a very reluctant Jordan with him. I pushed the door three-quarters of the way shut to give us a modicum of privacy.

Moving as slowly as I could so I didn't set her off, I sat down against the dresser five feet away. "My name's Holly."

"I don't care who you are. Just get out. Leave me alone."

"I saw the letter on the table to your sister."

She visibly swallowed. "That's none of your business."

"I had a sister once. Her name was Gin. She was murdered when we were nine, and she probably died thinking that I didn't love her enough to stay with her, that I abandoned her. I would give anything for just one more day with her . . . even an hour. Just to hug her and tell her that I love her. I lost my whole family that day, but losing my sister breaks my heart the most." I missed Gin so much that sometimes it made my chest ache.

She was quiet for a beat before finally saying, "My sister isn't dead."

"No, but if you follow through with this, Elsie's will be."

Fresh tears spilled over onto her cheeks, and I fought not to cry with her. My words seemed to make her think for a moment about how her decision might devastate her sister. "I . . . I can't . . . live like this."

She pressed the blade to her forearm and a bead of fresh blood welled. *Oh God*, I thought, pleading for guidance I didn't even know how to shape into thoughts.

185

I couldn't watch her give up and die the way I watched McNera die. I needed her to make it through this. I needed to know that she could survive what Collin had done to her, that we could both survive.

I did the only thing I could think of: I scooted toward her. As I hoped, she snapped the knife up toward me and away from her wrist to ward me off.

"Stay back," she snarled, but the thick, choked sound of tears in her voice made her sound more desperate than threatening.

"I know that right now everything feels hopeless, and you can't see a light in this darkness, but it's there. It's just . . . smothered by pain and fear."

She sneered at me. "Losing your family when you were nine doesn't give you the right to pretend you understand what I'm going through."

"I do understand, Melanie."

"That man," she said, shaking the knife at me. "He . . . held me captive in my own home. He . . . he did things, and I can't . . . I c-can't . . ."

I drew in a strengthening breath before speaking again. "I know you're scared. He made you afraid to be in your own skin. He stepped into your life and ripped it to pieces. It feels like he stripped away parts of you that you can never have back, like you're just a shadow of the person you used to be. There are no words to make that okay."

The knife wavered in her hand as I spoke.

"I know that you probably haven't slept a solid night since the attack, because the nightmares are so vivid that it's like reliving every awful moment. You see his face, you feel his hands, and nobody comes to save you when you're screaming."

Melanie started to sob.

"I know that you can't even imagine ever having a life again, and that dying sounds peaceful compared to the pain and the constant memories, but you can have a life, Melanie. It doesn't have

186

to end in this room." I held out my hand slowly. "Please give me the knife."

"Holly," Marx muttered in warning from the hallway. He had told me to keep my distance, but I really wanted the knife.

Melanie's eyes flicked to the door, and she gripped the knife tighter, fear etched across her face.

"Ignore them. They're not coming in. It's just you and me," I said.

Her eyes flickered between me and the door a few more times before she finally dismissed the men. "How do you know so much?"

"The man who hurt you . . . hurt me too."

She blinked and the knife dropped an inch. "What? When?"

I swallowed as my throat tried to rebel against the effort of speech. "It started when I was fourteen and I was placed with his family as a foster child. He . . . hurt me . . . a lot, and . . ." I glanced at the cracked doorway as I thought about Marx and Jordan listening in. "I've been where you are, Melanie, but it wasn't a knife. It was a bottle of pills."

I heard a quiet intake of breath from the hallway, but I wasn't sure who it came from. Neither of the men knew I had tried to take my own life when I was still just a girl.

That was why I was removed from the Wells household, and why I spent a year of my life in a therapy center for children before returning to foster care.

"But you're alive," she said.

"By the grace of God," I told her, lowering my hand back to my lap. "I shouldn't be, after the number of pills I took that night, but I'm grateful that I am."

Nat, the youngest of the children, had found me dying on the bathroom floor, and he ran to get Ms. Wells, who then—much to her inconvenience—called for an ambulance.

The knife fell a few more inches as Melanie choked out, "How many women has he hurt?"

"Too many."

She started to sob again. "Why is he doing this to us? He took . . . everything from me. I lost my job because I'm too scared to leave the house. When I can sleep, I sleep with the lights on." She looked down at her stomach, and I saw the pain ripple across her face. "I don't know what to do anymore."

"I know. He's taken so much from you, but don't let him have your life too. He doesn't deserve it, Melanie." I offered my hand again. "Let me help you."

She looked at the knife shaking in her hand and then down at her wrist. I didn't know what I would do if she chose death. Would I even be fast enough to stop her before she slit her wrist open the rest of the way? Would she stab me if I tried to stop her?

God, please help her choose life. Please . . .

I held my breath as she wrestled with relinquishing the only object that gave her some semblance of safety and control.

I could've fainted with relief when she scooted forward and placed the knife in my hand. I closed my fingers over it before she could change her mind and snatch it back.

"What now?" she asked.

"You just took the first step—deciding to live." I tucked the knife behind me so it was out of sight.

She gave me a tremulous smile. "What's step two?"

It wasn't like I had a twelve-step program for this. I was just fumbling my way through it like I did the rest of my life. I wanted step two to be calling an ambulance, but somehow I doubted she would go for that.

"Step two . . . is realizing that while what he did to you might be a dividing line in your life, it doesn't have to control your life." I doubted he would come back to hurt her again; she would be able to pick up the pieces of her life and heal. "Everything will be a world of firsts again—your first step out of the house without a panic attack, your first night of sleep free of nightmares, your first laugh, your first date. Maybe you'll have ice cream in February."

I'd had my first February ice-cream cone with Jordan, and while he had tried to convince me it wasn't a date, I still wasn't so sure.

"It doesn't sound so bad when you put it that way," she admitted.

"I won't lie to you. It's hard, and you have to fight for every one of those moments. But it's worth it." I told her about Pennsylvania, about my time hiding in the shelter, and how I fought to pull my life back together. "I never would've made it as far as I did without God. He kept me on my feet, and then He brought someone into my life who could help me when I'm feeling overwhelmed or scared."

Melanie wiped at her face and sniffed, "I don't have anyone like that."

"You have a sister. Does she know?" When she shook her head, I said, "I can't imagine she wouldn't drop everything, even a disagreement or grudge, to be here for you."

"Maybe."

"And you have me now. You can call me anytime." I would've said we could get together, but I didn't plan to be in the city much longer. I stood and offered her my hand. "But can we get your arm cleaned up before we do anything else? It's kind of distracting me."

She accepted my hand, and I helped her up. She was shaky and unsteady on her feet, but I suspected it was more nerves than blood loss, because she hadn't cut very deeply. I bent down to scoop up the knife before announcing, "We're coming out."

I heard the shuffle of feet as they backed away from the door to give us space. I escorted Melanie out of the room. She stiffened when she saw the men, but I nudged her in the opposite direction toward the bathroom.

"I'll be there in just a second, okay?"

My gaze caught Jordan's as I turned around, and I was surprised to see the pain in his eyes. "Please tell me you're never gonna try to hurt yourself again."

I stared up at him, unsure what to say. I had no plans to try to take my life, but I knew one thing for certain: I would rather die than be at Collin's mercy again.

"Holly," Marx said, worry deepening his voice when I didn't answer. "Promise me you'll talk to me if that thought ever even crosses your mind."

If that thought ever crossed my mind, it would be because there was no more hope. And I doubted he would be there to talk to. I handed Marx the knife. "I'm gonna check on Melanie."

"Holly," Jordan called after me, but I ignored him and went into the bathroom.

I helped Melanie bandage her arm and watched her very carefully as she took some Tylenol for the pain. We settled in her kitchen to talk, and I prepared some coffee for everyone.

She had a different kind of coffeepot; it wasn't really a pot, but a fish-tank-looking thing that made one tiny cup of coffee at a time—what was the point?—and it took me a while to figure it out.

I handed Jordan a mug full of "Mocha Caffe Latte," according to the tiny cartridge I wrestled into the machine, and repeated the process for the others.

"Ms. Bordeaux," Marx began, taking a seat opposite Melanie. I sat down between them as a buffer. "Can you describe the man who assaulted you?"

Her muscles tightened. "I'll never forget him. He was about your height, black hair, pale skin, chilling eyes the color of an aquamarine stone."

That sounded like Collin. Marx pulled a picture from his wallet and showed it to her. "Is this the man?"

She flinched and averted her eyes. "Get that away from me."

Marx flipped the picture over and glanced at me. My reaction had been similar the first time he showed me a picture of Collin.

"Ms. Bordeaux, I need you to confirm or deny that this is the man who assaulted you," Marx said.

"He said that if I tried to have him arrested, he would come back and it would be worse. He went after *her* more than once." She gestured to me. "I won't do anything to make him angry."

"If you identify him, we can arrest him."

"Really?" she asked skeptically. "Do you know where he is at this very moment?" When Marx pursed his lips, she said, "I didn't think so. I'm not an idiot, Detective. Police are first responders, which means they respond *after* the crime has been committed."

"We can place you in protective custody until after the trial."

She shook her head. "If he finds out I talked to you at all . . . I have to protect myself. I'm sorry, Detective, but I can't help you."

"Ms. Bordeaux—"

"Please. See yourselves out and don't come back."

Marx glanced at me and then sighed. He didn't have the best luck negotiating with redheads. I didn't blame her one bit for her fear or reluctance.

"Okay." He slid a card across the table toward her. "Thank you for your time. Please give me a call if you change your mind or think of anythin' else."

I snatched the card and wrote my name and number on the back of it before pushing it the rest of the way toward her. "In case you wanna talk."

She gave me a fragile smile. "Thank you, Holly. I might take you up on that sometime."

We left the house no better off than when we'd come.

20

Marx unlocked the apartment and pushed open the door. He caught my arm before I could step inside, and I stiffened.

"Did you turn the light off before we left?" he asked, but his tone caused a spark of anxiety in the pit of my stomach.

I peered into the dark apartment in the direction of the lamp. "No. Are you sure you left it on?"

"I'm sure," he said, drawing his sidearm.

"Maybe the bulb just blew out. You leave it on a lot when you work at night, and sometimes you fall asleep with it on."

"Maybe, but I don't intend to take any chances. Stay with me."

I stayed on his heels as he crept into his apartment. He didn't need a light to maneuver around the furniture, and neither did I. I had every inch of it memorized.

My foot bumped against something soft on the floor: a pillow. It should've been on the couch. The apartment had been immaculate when we left. It could've simply fallen off the couch. Maybe.

Marx reached the lamp he'd left on, and I heard a quiet click as he pulled the string. Nothing happened.

For a brief moment, I thought maybe the bulb *had* blown out, but that fragment of relief fled when Marx whispered, "The bulb is loose. Somebody unscrewed it."

The unease I had felt when we entered the apartment gave way to fear. Someone had been inside, could still be inside.

Marx looked back at me, and I straightened my spine, trying not to look as frightened as I felt. He grabbed my right wrist and tugged my hand gently away from my stomach, placing it on his shoulder.

I shot him a questioning look I wasn't sure he could see in the darkness.

"It's dark and you have a tendency to wander. I don't wanna confuse you with an intruder. If I don't feel you, I'm gonna assume somethin's wrong."

"Why can't we just turn on a light or open the drapes?" Had we closed the drapes before leaving this morning? They were all pulled shut.

"Because if somebody's here, chances are I know my apartment better than they do in the dark. And there's no tellin' what they touched or what they did, so we're gonna touch as little as possible for now."

I swallowed and nodded. I knew he couldn't very well leave me in the hallway with Collin in the area.

He pushed forward through the inky blackness, and I moved stiffly on his heels, my hand pressed between his shoulder blades. He scanned the kitchen and then proceeded down the hall as smoothly as if he had done this a thousand times.

He paused in front of the guest bedroom, and my heart pounded in my throat. He wrapped a hand around the knob and pushed the door inward.

My shoe bumped something that sounded small and metallic as I followed him into the room, and it skidded across the floor.

Something else out of place.

Marx checked each side of the bed and then searched the closet. The room appeared to be just as I had left it.

We made our way across the hall into the bathroom, and I nearly jumped out of my skin when I caught sight of my own reflection in the mirror.

I exhaled a long breath through my nose and tried to remind myself to be calm. Marx brushed aside the shower curtain, but no one was hiding in the bath tub.

We searched the last room of the small apartment: his room. I had never been in his room before, but given the orderly nature of its contents, nothing seemed to have been touched.

A sharp creak of floorboards from the living room made me freeze. I looked at Marx with wide, worried eyes, and he pressed a finger to his lips.

I tiptoed after him as we left his bedroom, my nerves buzzing.

We were rounding the corner into the kitchen when a figure materialized to our right. I barely swallowed my scream as the intruder mirrored Marx's movements and snapped his gun up.

A beat of silence passed before Marx sighed and lowered his weapon, "You're lucky I didn't shoot you."

Confused, my gaze moved between Marx and the shadowy figure. I couldn't make out more than an intimidating blob.

"Sorry," a familiar voice said as the man lowered his gun. Jordan.

Relief flooded me, and I dropped my forehead against Marx's back with a groan. I felt him laugh before asking, "You okay back there?"

"I think we broke my adrenaline button," I muttered into his coat. "And can I let go of you now?"

"Yes, you can let go."

I slouched back against the refrigerator just as Jordan switched on the light over the sink.

"What are you doin' here?" Marx asked.

"I meant to ask if we were doing self-defense training in the morning, but I forgot. I figured since I was still in the parking lot, I would just come up and ask. Your door was open. You never leave your door open."

"Somebody was in here. We must have just missed them. They unscrewed the lightbulb in my lamp, but it was still warm."

Jordan's brows drew together. "Did they take or damage anything?"

"Not that I've noticed so far. I'm gonna have CSU inspect everythin'. Call Sam and let him know to keep Maya at his place a little longer. I don't want this situation to scare her. Holly, why don't you go check your room with the light on. Make sure nothin's missin'."

I walked back into the spare room and flipped on the light. My gaze drifted over the bed and nightstand. Nothing seemed out of place, and yet . . . something didn't feel right.

As I stepped further into the room, I bumped something with the toe of my shoe—the same small, metallic something I had kicked in the darkness—and bent down to pick it up.

It was a nail.

When I kicked it the first time, it had been just inside the door. Curious, I gripped the edge of the door and pulled it away from the wall so I could look behind it.

The nail dropped from my slack fingers as I sucked in a shuddering breath. Nails had been pounded into the bedroom door from the inside, spelling two chilling words: Sweet Dreams.

21

$\mathcal{M}$ arx tapped a knuckle lightly against the outside of the bathroom door. "Sweetheart, please open the door." I buried my face in my knees beside the bathtub and tried to ignore his voice. I just wanted to be left alone.

"Holly."

"Please go away."

I heard his fingers tapping on the outside of the door frame. "I'm not goin' anywhere. I'll wait out here all day and night if that's what it takes for you to open this door, even if I have to sleep in the hallway."

He had sat out there once before, waiting for me to come out, and I didn't doubt he would sit out there all night just to make a point.

I glared at the door in frustration. "Fine. You can come in. But just you, and just for a minute."

He whispered something too soft for me to hear, then said more loudly, "Okay. Jordan's gonna stay out here and handle CSU when they come."

I crossed the bathroom to unlock the door, then retreated to my spot against the wall.

The door cracked open, and light from the hallway pooled across the dark floor. Marx stepped in and shut the door behind him. He gestured to the space along the wall beside me. "May I?"

I scooted over to give him room. He sat down beside me and stretched out his legs, crossing them at the ankles. Silence hung between us, and I knew he was trying to work out how to comfort me, but there was nothing he could say.

"I'm never gonna be safe, am I?" I asked, and I could hear the resignation in my own voice.

"You're safe with me."

I longed for that to be true, but Collin had broken into Marx's apartment. He had been in my room, and he had lingered long enough to hammer a message into my door. Sweet dreams. That was what he had said to me before leaving the ice rink.

"No. No place is safe from him." Even my own body wasn't safe. I drew my knees tight to my chest and wrapped my arms around them. "He's gonna hurt me again." The thought sent numbness creeping through me as my mind tried to brace itself for the inevitable. "I can't go through that again."

Marx let out a long breath and leaned his head back against the wall. "There are some evils in this world I will never understand—the desire to hurt children and the desire to take from a woman what she's not willin' to give." He was quiet for a beat. "I may not understand Collin's desires, but I do understand *him*. He might break into my apartment while nobody's home, but he's too much of a coward to try it with a man here. And one of us is gonna be with you at all times. He's not gonna get to you again."

He would find a way. He always found a way. "I wish he'd died when I stabbed him."

In my desperate attempt to escape him in Pennsylvania, I had stabbed Collin in the shoulder with a pair of scissors before pushing him down a flight of stairs. If he had died, Melanie would never have been hurt, the people I cared about would be safe. I would be safe.

"Holly, you are one of the most beautiful people I know." When I gave him a skeptical look, he clarified, "I don't mean physically."

Oh, so now he was calling me hideous.

"And no, I'm not sayin' you're ugly," he continued, as if he'd plucked the passing thought from my mind. "I know that thought's bouncin' around in that little head of yours. My point is, you cherish human life, even if that life isn't one you agree with. If you'd succeeded in killin' Collin, I don't know that you could've ever forgiven yourself."

I never wanted to take a life, but if there was one person in this world who could drive me to do it, it was Collin. I had nearly taken my own life because of him.

Life was supposed to be a gift, but there were people on this earth who took it and twisted it until it was an unbearable curse. He was one of those people.

I knew he wouldn't kill me, at least not right away, but the suffering he would cause would make me long for death all over again.

"Please talk to me." Marx waited for me to fill the silence, but I had nothing to say. "Okay, I'll talk." He interlocked his fingers and tapped his thumbs together. "When I was a boy, my dad drank, and he had a temper. He thought physical discipline was the cure for any ill. No matter what I did wrong—stayed out too late, looked at him wrong, failed to meet his expectations—he used his belt."

Stunned, I looked up at him. "He beat you?"

"He called it discipline. But it left me an angry, hurt kid, and I couldn't talk to anybody about it. He made me feel helpless, which only made me angrier."

"So what did you do?"

"I needed to find a healthy outlet before I exploded, so I learned to shoot, and then, as you know, I joined the army. I worked hard and learned how to defend myself. But I carried that secret pain until I fell in love with Shannon. I told her everythin'. You two are the only people I've ever told."

I never imagined he would share such a deep secret with me. I appreciated that he trusted me with it. "What happened with your dad?"

"We don't talk much. I love my dad, but he's a stubborn man. Not that you would know anythin' about stubbornness . . ."

I smiled faintly. *Me, stubborn? Never.*

198

"But my point is, if you don't find a way to express your pain and your anger, or deal with the shame that you feel, then it just festers and starts to corrode your insides slowly until you give up or until you implode and have an emotional meltdown."

I looked down at the floor.

"I know you had to hide your feelin's when you were trapped in that house with Collin. He hurt you and he forced you to keep silent. And you've suffered in silence for so long, I'm not sure you even know how to express how you're feelin'. The most I've seen you do is shed a few tears and lock yourself in a bathroom."

I did seem to always end up in a bathroom when I was upset. My bathroom, his bathroom, the bathroom at the precinct. I have no idea why.

"I know you're angry," he said.

I was, but I didn't know what to do with my anger. It just burned in my chest with no hope of escape.

"Collin took away your choices and your power, and he made you feel helpless. He forced you to live in fear every moment of every day, and you've never let yourself deal with it. So we're gonna try somethin'."

He stood up, grabbed a twenty-four pack of toilet paper from the cupboard by the door, and tore it open as he sat back down beside me.

"It's okay to yell, to scream, to cry until you can't breathe, and sometimes it's even okay to throw things." He offered me a roll of toilet paper.

"You want me to throw toilet paper?"

"I do."

"Why?"

He shrugged. "Why not?"

Puzzled, I took it from him. I turned it over in my hands as I pondered the point of this exercise, and then tossed it lazily across the room. It landed on the floor and rolled to a stop against the door. "Now it's dirty."

He laughed and dropped another roll into my lap. "Try usin' a little bit of that anger you're bottlin' up."

I sighed and flung the next one a little harder. It smacked off the door and rolled back to me.

"That was irritation, not anger. Try again."

"This feels silly."

"Just humor me. Think about the reasons behind your anger. If it makes you sick to your stomach, you're in the right place." He gestured to the toilet.

"Do I have to tell you the reasons?"

"No, but just know that you can."

I bit my lip and considered the roll of toilet paper in my hand. I looked at the strip of light below the door that reminded me of all the times Collin had snuck into my room in the middle of the night.

I funneled my anger into my throw and hurled the roll at the bottom of the door.

"Again." Marx dropped another roll in my lap.

All the times Collin made me feel helpless and vulnerable sent the next roll bouncing off the ceiling. I launched several at the vanity, remembering every moment I stood before a mirror hating the bruised and broken girl staring back at me.

I pelted the shower curtain in remembrance of every shower I rushed through out of fear, for every time I tried to scrub him away.

For each roll I threw, I put the force of another source of anger or fear . . . or shame behind it. Marx collected the closest ones and stacked them up between us like a triple-ply arsenal.

He joined in, and we took turns rapid-firing the toilet paper across the bathroom. My last roll unraveled in midair and turned into a streamer that somehow managed to get tangled over the shower rod before plopping into the toilet.

"Ew," I said, crinkling my nose.

Marx laughed. "It was bound to happen eventually."

I leaned against his shoulder, and he wrapped an arm around me.

"So we're clear, that little voice inside your head, the one sayin' you should be ashamed of what Collin did to you—it's lyin'. You have nothin' to be ashamed about."

The tears I had been holding back for the past hour welled up into my eyes.

Marx rubbed my arm as if he might be able to soothe away my pain. "You did nothin' wrong, and you certainly didn't do anythin' to deserve what he did to you." He let those words hang in the air for a few minutes before he spoke again. "I need you to tell me about the nails."

I closed my eyes as I tried not to be swept under by the riptide of emotion the memories triggered, and my voice came out as barely more than a whisper. "They hurt to walk on."

He had asked me about the scars on the bottoms of my feet once, but I hadn't answered.

"He made you walk on nails?"

"He didn't make me," I corrected. "He gave me a choice between two unbearable things. I chose the nails."

He hesitated before asking, "What was the other unbearable thing?"

"The death of a six-year-old girl."

"The little girl he hung from a tree? Cassie?"

I nodded and leaned harder against his side as my many sleepless nights crashed into me like a tsunami. I felt completely and abruptly drained. "Walking across a board of nails in my bare feet was the price I had to pay to cut her down."

He didn't say anything to that, but I could feel the tension in his body. He was angry. Instead of swearing or shouting, which seemed to be his default response to anger, he rested his chin on top of my head and squeezed me just a little bit tighter.

It made me feel strangely warm and secure, like being wrapped in a heated blanket in a bomb shelter that only I had the key to. Nobody could hurt me right now. "Thank you."

"For what?"

I tried to speak, but my words were nearly engulfed by the yawn that crept up on me. "For making me feel safe when I have no reason to feel safe."

"I'm always here if you need me," he said with a hint of a smile in his voice, then added, "About the bags of Cheetos I noticed stuffed behind the toilet paper . . ."

A tired laugh bubbled out of me.

"You know there's room in the kitchen cupboard." The silence that followed his words was peaceful. "Holly."

"Hm?" My eyes felt so heavy, and I just needed . . .

"You're fallin' asleep."

That was ridiculous. I couldn't sleep in a bathroom . . . on the floor. I licked my lips and muttered, "No I'm not. I'm just . . . resting my . . . my . . ." What was I saying?

A black curtain slowly descended over the already darkened room, blocking out the pale strip of light beneath the door. I was dimly aware of a gentle but distant voice calling "sweetheart," but that, too, faded away.

22

Something disturbed the quiet, steady rhythm beating in my ears, and I opened my eyes to stare into the darkness of the spare bedroom.

Awareness returned sharply when I realized I was propped up against a warm body rather than my pillows, and the rhythm in my ears was a heartbeat.

I snapped straight, my pulse skipping in terror.

"Easy," a familiar, gentle voice said. "You're safe."

"Marx?"

I could hear the smile in his voice when he replied, "How many Southern men do you know?"

The stiffness in my spine eased, and my muscles relaxed. I scooted away from him slowly, bumping into something cold and ceramic. A toilet. I was in the bathroom.

Why was I in the bathroom?

My gaze flicked around the room in confusion, and as my eyes adjusted to the darkness, I noticed the graveyard of toilet paper on the floor. In the absence of fear, the memories came trickling back.

Stunned, I asked, "I fell asleep on you?"

"Mmm hmm."

"For how long?"

His shape slowly became visible, and I saw him leaning against the wall. He had drawn his knees up and draped his arms over them, gripping one wrist. Light reflected off his face as he checked his watch. "A little over four hours."

"Four hours?" I couldn't believe I had fallen asleep against him to begin with, let alone for four hours.

"You were exhausted."

"Why didn't you wake me? You had to be uncomfortable."

"Well, my left side went numb after the first ten minutes, so only my right side was uncomfortable, but it was worth it knowin' you felt safe enough to sleep."

I dragged my fingers through my hair and pushed it back from my face. "I'm sorry. I didn't mean to fall asleep on you."

"You have nothin' to apologize for. I would've carried you to your room, but I didn't wanna risk wakin' you or scarin' you."

A quiet knock drew my eyes to the door. Jordan's voice followed a second later. "Sam and Maya are back."

I stared at the door, suddenly reluctant to leave the seclusion and safety of the bathroom.

I forced myself to my feet, tucked my hair behind my ears, and offered Marx my hand. He was in the process of getting up when he paused and looked at my hand.

"Are you tryin' to say I'm old and I need help off the floor?" At my quiet snicker, he snapped, "Put your hand down."

The door opened and Jordan filled the doorway. He took in the rolls of toilet paper littering the floor. "Do I even wanna know?"

"You don't need to know," Marx replied.

Maya poked her head around the door frame, and her eyes widened. "Mr. Marx, your bathroom is messy. You're supposed to clean up when you're done playing."

"You're right, I probably should, but I think I might pay somebody to do it for me. Five dollars ought to do. I don't suppose you know anybody who might be able to help me out."

Maya sucked in an excited breath and raised her hand. "I'll do it!"

Marx gave her a considering look. "Do you have any references?"

She scrunched up her face in confusion and looked at Jordan. "What's a *references*?"

Jordan smirked and leaned down to whisper, "He means do you know anyone who can say you're a good worker."

"Oh! Holly can say that."

Everyone looked at me. I pretended to struggle with the decision. "She is a good worker, but I don't know. I think this might be a better job for Jordan."

"No, no, no!" Maya protested, and she tried to push Jordan out of the doorway and out of sight. "Pick me."

Marx laughed and handed her the five dollars. "I suppose you're hired. But if you don't do a good job and earn that five dollars, I'll be back to collect it."

"I will!" She darted into the bathroom and started picking up the toilet paper rolls.

I stepped into the hall with Jordan and felt a chill snake down my spine as my eyes landed on the spare bedroom. I didn't want to go back into that room. I couldn't sleep in there.

Marx stepped between me and Jordan and pulled the spare room door shut. "Why don't you and Maya take my room tonight?"

"We can't take your—"

"You can and you are."

"But where will you sleep?"

"Good question," Jordan said. "Since I'm taking the couch."

Marx frowned. "You're not stayin'."

"That psychopath broke into your apartment to taunt Holly. There's no way I'm *not* staying. If he's got the . . ."—Jordan glanced at me and seemed to reconsider his words—"guts to break into the home of a cop and hang around long enough to pound a message into Holly's bedroom door, who's to say he won't come back, and that he won't bring someone with him? You need backup."

Marx looked past Jordan at Sam, who still had Riley on a leash. "I think it would be safer if someone stayed," Sam agreed. "If I wasn't worried about leaving Evey alone for too long, I would."

"It's okay to admit when you need help," Jordan said, his tone a mixture of smugness and determination.

Marx glared at him and opened his mouth to snap something in response, but his phone rang. He looked at the caller ID, then grumbled under his breath as he left the room, "Arrogant pain in my . . ." He slammed his bedroom door before answering the call.

The conversation must have been brief because Marx reappeared a minute later while I was checking the locks on each of the windows. "Maya's grandparents will be here tomorrow evenin' to pick her up."

One more day.

I gazed out the window into the snowy street. I was scared to leave everything and everyone who mattered to me, but it was the only way to keep them safe.

I needed to figure everything out tonight. I would go south toward Ohio or Kentucky and then find a shelter . . . no, not a shelter.

He would look there, and I didn't want to endanger any more innocents. I had money saved in an old pink Hubba Bubba bubble gum container in my bag. It wasn't much, but if I slept in an unoccupied house or closed factory and ate sparingly, I could make it stretch for a while.

The trick to survival on the street was trusting no one—kindness generally came with unseen strings attached—and always having an escape plan.

I needed a way to make money without identification or drawing attention to myself so I could afford a safer place to stay, but those were dangerous waters to navigate.

Not all job offers were genuine. I had learned that the hard way when I lived in Darby. Sometimes girls disappeared when they accepted under-the-table job offers.

The memory brought goose bumps to my arms.

Maybe I could find another restaurant that needed help and was willing to let me work strictly for tips. That was safer than dealing with strangers offering odd jobs. It would take me a while to establish any kind of clientele for my photography, but I would have time to figure that out.

I could use the taxi passes Sam had given me for my birthday to get to the bus station, and then ride it as far as I could without ID. I would have to travel on foot or hitchhike across state lines.

Hitchhiking was a terrifying gamble. It wasn't the safest method of travel, especially for a woman, but it was the most efficient when you didn't have a car or money. I was careful about the offers I accepted. I would rather walk than get in a vehicle with a man I didn't know. Elderly people were usually a safe bet.

I smiled as I remembered Sam's passionate lecture about the dangers of hitchhiking. He would flip his lid if he knew I was even considering it.

It would be hard going back to trusting no one again after I had finally started to trust these men and Jace. Back to living on the streets after having a warm bed, to being vulnerable and unprotected after having locked windows and doors to hide behind. Back to being alone.

I didn't want to be alone again—to be that woman with no name, no home, and no one to turn to. I didn't want to be a ghost.

Lord, I feel like I'm losing everything.

I rested my head against the glass and closed my eyes. Running was my life; it had been my life since I was girl, and these beautiful months of being someone who mattered would become a cherished memory.

"Hey."

I stiffened and wiped my damp eyes as discreetly as possible before turning to see Jordan. He kept his distance, but he was watching me with concern.

"You okay?" he asked.

I shrugged with a nonchalance I didn't feel. "Why wouldn't I be okay?"

"Oh, I don't know. Maybe because a psychopath with a thing for you broke into the apartment and left you a creepy message made of nails." He mirrored my shrug as he sat down on the arm of the couch. "That wouldn't bother me at all."

A reluctant smile crossed my lips. I closed the drapes against the world and dropped wearily onto the opposite side of the couch.

"It's gonna be okay, Holly."

People kept saying that. *It will be okay. Everything will be fine.* But everything wasn't okay, and I couldn't imagine how it ever would be. I wanted to have faith that everything would work out, that God had a master plan to make things right, but if He did, I had no idea what it was.

I was stumbling through the darkness blind, one step at a time, just like always.

"Are you staying the night?" I asked, deciding it was best to think about something else.

"Yeah. Marx is pretty peeved about it, but he'll deal with it if it makes you safer."

Sam unhooked Riley from his leash, and my canine companion bounded over to rest his head in my lap and wave his tail affectionately. I smiled and scratched behind his ears.

"I love you too," I told him before kissing his snout. I considered whether or not I could take him with me, but I wouldn't be able to feed him properly, and I couldn't guarantee shelter.

Nope, he would have to stay.

I leaned forward to hug his head. "You'll be just fine with Marx," I whispered even though I knew he couldn't understand me.

"So the dog gets a hug, but I don't?" Jordan teased.

I smirked. "I like him more than you."

"It's because he's fuzzy, isn't it?" He rubbed his chin with a thoughtful expression. "I could grow a beard."

I laughed, as I suspected he had meant me to, and shook my head. "You're ridiculous."

Maya came bouncing out of the bathroom, scurried between Marx and Sam, and nearly tackled Jordan off the arm of the couch in her excitement. "Look!" She pinched the five-dollar bill between her fingers and stretched it out. "I got five dollars and you didn't, because I'm a better cleaner than you! But if it makes you sad, I'll share."

Jordan grinned and set her back on her feet. "I didn't do any of the work, so I don't deserve any of the money. But it was nice of you to think of me."

"Okay," Maya agreed before shoving the money into the pocket of her skinny jeans. She twirled into the living room to music that only existed in her head.

"I thought you might wanna see this," I heard Sam say. I looked up to see him hand a newspaper to Marx.

Marx scowled at the front page. "Wonderful. Just what we need."

I stood and walked over to see what it was. It looked like a tabloid, but there was a photo of me and Marx on the front cover. He had his arm around my shoulders, tugging me close, and beside it, there was a smaller image of me gazing nervously at the photographer.

The title of the article read "From Mystery to Mistress: The Kansas Carver's Last Victim Carves Out a Relationship for Herself."

"What?" I gasped in disbelief. I snatched the newspaper away from Marx and carried it to the peninsula to read.

> Tragedy struck in the little town of Stony Brooke, Kansas, one night in 1998, when serial killer Edward Moss Billings brutally murdered a local family the night before Halloween. The only survivor of that awful night was Holly Marie Cross, the nine-year-old daughter of Cristopher and Emily Cross, twin to Ginevieve Cross.
>
> According to the former sheriff who worked the case, Jedidiah Radcliffe, Holly disappeared in the middle of the night, only to be seen again eighteen years later when the killer tracked her down. Holly returned home to Stony Brooke just this past fall in the company of one of our very own detectives, Richard Marx (pictured with Holly).
>
> Though the FBI declined comment, it's rumored that The Kansas Carver fixated on young, attractive couples. Why then did he target Holly? Because she was the only survivor? Or did she fit his

preferences because she is young, attractive, and in a relationship with a man the killer would have viewed as a dominant male?

It's no secret that Detective Richard Marx accompanied Holly well beyond his jurisdiction to her hometown in Kansas, and it's also no secret that they stayed together at the local inn. Could there be romance?

The killer must have thought so. He abducted both Detective Marx and Holly, and according to our sources, he carried out his ritual as he had only done before with couples. But there was a surprise twist this time: the Stony Brooke sheriff, Jordan Radcliffe, Holly's childhood sweetheart, stepped in to save the day.

He shot Edward as he was preparing to kill the woman he loved. Sheriff Radcliffe was speechless when asked about his feelings for Holly, but his father was very forthcoming about his son's affection for nine-year-old Holly and his lifelong devotion to tracking her down.

Is he still in love with her? Is he disappointed to find her in a relationship with another man? We'll be seeking an interview to find out just what's going on with this love triangle and who this intriguing survivor's heart truly belongs to.

I smacked the tabloid onto the counter in outrage. "Wha . . . why. . . this is ridiculous."

"What does it say?" Marx asked.

My nose wrinkled in disgust.

Sam spoke up. "That you and Holly are in a romantic relationship and Jordan is probably jealous."

I didn't even realize that Jordan was behind me, reading the article over my shoulder, until he grumbled irritably, "I need to call my dad." He stalked into the spare room and slammed the door.

I had a feeling the talk with his dad wasn't going to go well.

"Why did they do this?" I demanded.

"Because you were the sole survivor of a man who killed fifty-one people across the country. That makes you a celebrity," Sam said.

"I don't wanna be a celebrity!"

"I'm just answering your question, Holly. Don't take my head off."

"And what business is it of theirs if I'm in a relationship? Maybe I'll become a nun and never have a romantic relationship."

"I think you have to be Catholic for that."

Marx rubbed the back of his neck and sighed. "They didn't have enough details about the case, so they focused on speculatin' about your love life. Unfortunately, that was only one paper. Our names and pictures are out there now, and other papers and journals are gonna be interested in your story."

"But I don't wanna talk to them." Then a horrifying possibility surfaced in my mind. "How deep are they gonna dig? Are they gonna find out about my foster placements? About . . . Collin?"

Marx and Sam exchanged a grim look.

That looked like a yes. I sank onto a stool and dropped my head on the counter. Why was my life such a wreck?

Marx's phone rang again, and he answered, "Hi, Shannon." I looked up just in time to see relief ripple across his features. "Okay. I'll send Sam to pick it up." He covered the mouthpiece of the phone and looked at Sam. "Shannon has the order of protection from the judge."

"I'm on it." Sam left the apartment without so much as a good-bye.

"Thanks, Shannon," Marx said before hanging up.

"Now what?" I asked.

"Now we need to track him down and deliver it. And the moment he violates it, we can arrest him."

What good was an order or protection if the person could just walk right over it? Collin would never obey a piece of paper. He would just send it up in flames like the shelter.

"I'm gonna clear out my room for you girls, and then you should try to get some rest," Marx suggested.

"No, it's not okay!" Jordan's usually soft-spoken voice was laced with anger as it rose behind the closed door, and it startled me.

I was grateful that he never spoke to me in that tone of voice.

"Because, *Dad*, she has enough to deal with, and you just made things harder," he continued, his voice gradually lowering until only his agitated tone was audible.

"Is Jordan mad?" Maya asked, snuggling under my arm and watching the door with wide eyes.

"He's upset with his dad for telling secrets," I explained. "It's okay to be a little angry about that, but he's not mad at us."

She relaxed against me. "Mama always says you shouldn't yell, even if you're mad, because it can comm . . . conum . . ." Her brow wrinkled as she struggled with the word.

"Communicate?" I offered.

She nodded. "Yeah, it can comnumicate the wrong thing. And people don't really listen when you yell because they get scared or angry."

"Your mom was a smart woman."

She let out a mournful sigh. "Yeah."

My heart ached for her. She was so brave and resilient despite losing everyone and everything. She was only a child; she shouldn't have to be this strong at such a young age.

"Why don't we make a mess of Mr. Marx's kitchen while we bake Jace's birthday cake?"

We were celebrating her thirty-first birthday tomorrow at the restaurant of one of her friends, but they didn't have anything on the menu that qualified as cake.

"Okay," Maya said with a sniffle.

We went into the kitchen to prepare the cake and eat spatulas full of frosting before we had to pack her things.

23

The pizza shop where we were meeting for Jace's birthday was cozy with its green, red, and yellow walls, and the aroma of pizza sauce and garlic was mouthwatering.

I gazed up at the hand-painted pictures on the walls. There was one of a stone patio overlooking an orchard that looked peaceful enough to crawl into. Another painting had Philippians 4:13 on it.

"Warren's wife painted these," Jace said from behind me.

I turned to see her and smiled. "Hey, birthday girl. You're fifteen minutes late." I had to point that out for the simple fact that if I was ever five minutes late, she thought something tragic had happened.

She waved an airy hand, as if my point were moot. "I know, but I'm not you, so it's not like I got abducted."

I laughed. When Marx was first investigating my incident in the park—which was how we met—he had called Jace in an effort to find me, and she had been convinced I was abducted because I missed dinner.

She grinned and hugged me.

I hugged her back. "I thought you were coming with Sam."

"That was the original plan, but I decided to get my hair done at the last minute. Kinda makes me look more grown up, right?"

The tips of her black hair had been frosted with blue for as long as I had known her. Now her hair was silky black. I gave her a concerned look. "Did you change your hair because your mom accused you of being childish?"

She shrugged a shoulder. "I figure if I have to take her to court over Scott's life support, I need to look as prim and proper as she does."

I smirked. "I somehow doubt your prim and proper mother has a Cheshire Cat tattoo on the back of her neck."

She grinned broadly, mimicking the crazy cat's smile. "Hair down and he's invisible."

I snorted softly at the cheesy joke. The Cheshire Cat had a tendency to turn invisible in the movie.

"Do it! Do it!" Maya cheered, and we both looked back to see her jumping up and down on the booth seat by the far window, pumping her fists into the air.

We were on the side of the dining room that was designed like a large alcove—separated from the rest of the dining room by a half wall, with only a small opening at one end—making it a fairly private space.

Jordan and Sam were engaged in an arm wrestling match at the table, but I couldn't tell which one of them Maya was rooting for. Jordan's face was flushed, and there was a line of deep concentration between his eyebrows.

Sam looked completely relaxed. "Maybe you should just give up now."

"I don't give up," Jordan grunted.

I stopped beside Marx, who was watching the silly display of masculinity with a bored expression.

Sam sighed and slammed Jordan's arm down on the table with ridiculous ease. "Maybe you should stick to arm wrestling people you might have a chance of beating."

Jordan shook his arm. "Like who?"

Sam nodded to me. "You could probably beat Holly."

"Hey!" I objected, folding my arms indignantly. "I could win."

"Sure, if you were hopped up on PCP and he had a sprained wrist."

Jordan grinned at me. "Wanna give it a try?"

I shook my head. "No. But maybe Marx will."

"Marx will not," Marx said.

"Why? A little out of your weight class?" I gave his stomach a quick pat, and he lifted an eyebrow at me.

"Are you callin' me fat?"

I snickered. I had been waiting months for an opportunity to repay that line. He deserved it.

Warren came around the corner. He was a member of Jace's sled hockey team, and one of a few people who had stood up for me when Collin showed up at the ice rink to antagonize me.

Well . . . he didn't really *stand*.

"Look!" Maya shouted, pointing. "Look, Jace, he has wheels too!"

I covered my face and groaned, but Jace and Warren just laughed good-naturedly.

"Yep, and he wishes his wheels were as fast as mine," Jace teased.

"Yeah, you talk a big game, but I think I can outrun you in every sport," Warren retorted with a grin.

Maya gave him a funny look. "Wheelchair people can't run."

Apparently she didn't understand figures of speech.

"You know, Sam," Jordan began. "Technically I think the winner of an arm-wrestling match is supposed to challenge someone. What do you say, Warren, you up for the challenge of arm wrestling Sam?"

Warren chuckled a little to himself. "That's supposed to be a challenge?"

Sam frowned at the veiled insult, and Jace shook her head. "Don't do it, Sam."

"I'm not gonna do it. He practically walks with his arms," Sam replied sourly.

Marx gestured to me and Maya. "I'm payin' for these two and myself." I barely managed to draw in a breath to object before Marx said, "It's not up for negotiation. I'll take a large all-meat pizza, a personal size pizza with mushrooms and pineapple for Holly, and whatever Maya wants."

Maya hopped up and down. "French fries, please! With cheese! And ketchup!"

The others chimed in with their orders, and Warren left to make our food.

I picked up Jace's gift and tossed it at her. "Incoming!"

She had thrown a gift at me once, and I told her it was going to be our new tradition. I was glad she caught it, though, because I would've felt really bad if it had hit her in the face.

She was like the Tasmanian devil when she opened gifts: a whirlwind of shredded paper and bows. She popped open the box and peered inside. "So totally awesome!"

She pulled out a pair of Darth Vader earmuffs and put them on. Then she pulled on the matching gloves.

"I love Star Wars!" In the bottom of the box was a pair of Darth Vader slippers. She pulled those out and laughed. "Seriously, Holly? Slippers for someone who can't feel their feet?"

I grinned. "Those are actually for Sam. So you guys can match."

One of Sam's eyebrows crept up. The other one followed when Jace tossed the slippers to him and commanded eagerly, "Try them on."

Sam looked like he had just been told he had to drink someone else's backwash, which was no doubt a thing of nightmares for him. "Now?" When Jace nodded, he sighed and began untying his shoes. He pulled on the slippers, which fit perfectly, and grimaced.

"You should try walking in them," I suggested.

Sam stood reluctantly and took a couple steps. With each step, the slippers mimicked Darth Vader's breathing—a whispered "hole-purr." Jordan and Jace cracked up. I bit down on my bottom lip and smiled when Sam shot me an irritable look.

"You could've just said you hate me. You didn't have to waste money on slippers."

Maya and I decided that cake would be excellent appetizer, so we stuck all thirty-one candles into the cake and lit them while the rest of the group handed over their gifts to Jace.

Marx stabbed the edge of his slice of cake with his fork and frowned when he had to push harder to get through it. "Holly . . ."

I plopped down beside him at the edge of the booth. "Yeah?"

He looked at me like he wanted to say something, but then just smiled and shook his head. "Never mind."

The cake was . . . extra crispy with patches of frosting. I supposed that was what happened when you let someone in their single digits frost the cake. It was probably the ugliest cake I had ever seen. And it wasn't exactly the tastiest.

Sam poked at his piece. "Who baked this?"

"I did!" Maya chirped before shoveling a piece of frosted brick into her mouth. She chewed contentedly before asking, "Don't you like it?"

Sam looked down at the cake and seemed to wrestle with whether or not to be honest. "It's . . . very well done."

Maya brightened at the compliment, completely unaware that he hadn't *meant* it as a compliment. I covered my mouth and laughed.

"Maya?" a woman's voice called.

We all looked at the small entryway into this side of the dining room. An elderly couple stood there.

"Nana!" Maya called out excitedly, all fear of rejection forgotten. She ducked under the table instead of waiting for us to move and let her out, and ran to her grandmother. She threw her arms around her waist and hugged her.

Reluctantly, I slid out of the booth to go over and greet them. I wasn't ready to see Maya go, but as much as I wanted to keep her, I knew I couldn't.

I could see Beth Anne in her mother's face. Pain glistened in the woman's eyes, and I knew this must be a bittersweet moment for her and her husband. They were probably grateful their granddaughter was alive, but the very fact that they had to be here meant that their daughter wasn't.

Before I could introduce myself or do something stupid like apologize for getting their daughter killed, Maya snatched my hand and announced, "This is Holly. She's my friend. She used to stay at the shelter with us so the bad man who used to hurt her couldn't hurt her anymore."

Her grandmother looked at me. "You're one of the women my daughter helped?"

"Yes," I said after a moment of hesitation. "She, um . . . she helped me when no one else would. And for nearly a year, she made sure I felt safe. When I asked her why she helped me, she said, 'The Lord gives each of us a heart for something in this world, something we can change. Helping women who've been hurt is my heart, and I follow it.' She was an amazing person who changed my life."

Tears streamed down the woman's face, and she drew me into an unexpected hug. "Thank you."

Her gratitude was like a knife between my ribs. If not for me, her daughter would still be alive, and she was thanking me.

She drew back and let me go. "I'm proud of what my daughter did with her life. I'm happy she made such a difference in yours. And I will never forget that you were kind enough to take in our granddaughter when she had no one else."

I didn't know what to say.

Marx laid a gentle hand on my shoulder, but he spoke to Maya's grandparents. "Maya's things are in my car. I'll go unload them so we can move them to yours." He stepped past them and headed outside.

"Yes, we do need to be going," Maya's grandfather said. "We need to make the final arrangements for . . ."

His wife petted his shoulder and finished his sentence with a hoarse voice. "For Bethy."

"I want Holly to come," Maya announced. "Her mommy and daddy are gone too." She turned to me. "You can be my big sister, and we can read books and you can braid my hair."

My heart broke as I crouched down to her level. "I can't go with you, sweetie." For her safety, I would never be able to see her again.

Her bottom lip trembled. "But . . . I'll miss you."

I ran my fingers over her tiny braids and cheeks. "I'm gonna miss you too."

Maya threw her arms around my neck, and I squeezed her in a hug, reluctant to let her go.

When we broke apart, Jordan was standing there, waiting for his turn. He scooped her up and propped her on a hip. "Hey, munchkin."

She hugged him tightly.

He rubbed her back. "You can come see me anytime your grandparents are in town, okay? We'll build a snowman or go shopping for sparkly pink things."

She smiled through her tears. "Promise?"

"Promise." He set her down, and she stepped between her grandparents, grabbing both of their hands. She looked back at us as she walked out of our lives.

"You okay?"

I tucked my hair behind my ears and glanced at Jordan. He was watching me. "I'm gonna go to the bathroom," I said. *And cry privately.*

Jordan insisted on securing the women's room before I went in, and he checked for secret windows this time.

"Can you, um . . . not hover outside the door?" I asked. I was barely holding it together, and I didn't want anyone standing in the hall, listening while I burst into tears.

He hesitated. "It's really not a good idea for you to be alone, especially after—"

"I'm not going anywhere, and unless someone's hiding in the ceiling tiles, I'm gonna be perfectly safe in here."

He gave the ceiling tiles an interested look. "I should probably check those."

"Jordan."

He raised his hands in surrender. "Okay, I get it. You need some space. I'm not comfortable with it, but okay. I'll be just on the other side of that wall. Shout if you need me. And if you're not out in ten minutes, I'm coming back to hover in the hallway."

I forced a smile. "Deal."

I closed the door, locked it, and dropped back against it. It had been a long time since I allowed myself to get close enough to another person to mourn the loss of them in my life.

I had cried for weeks when the police ripped me away from Paul and Izzy, because they told me I could never see them again. Never was an impossible concept for a child. I cried next when I learned my first foster family only wanted one child, and they hadn't chosen me.

By my fourth foster placement, I learned to protect my heart by keeping people at a distance. I packed my travel bag with dry eyes each time another family rejected me, and climbed stoically into the back of my caseworker's car. I knew I would never see any of my foster siblings again, but I never allowed myself so much as a pang of grief.

I had been doing just fine behind my protective walls until I met Jace. She had chipped slowly away at the stones, inching her way through the cracks, but Marx had come in with a wrecking ball.

Now the walls were in ruins, and I was hiding in a public restroom because I couldn't hold back my grief any longer. I let it trickle out of me and then washed the salty tear tracks from my face.

I had about three minutes before Jordan came knocking. I pulled myself together with a long, slow breath, dried my face, and stepped out of the bathroom to try to enjoy my last night with my friends.

I barely made it two steps out the door before nearly running into someone. I opened my mouth to apologize as I looked up, but the words died in my throat as fear twisted my vocal cords into knots.

"Hey, sis."

Collin stepped forward, and I backed up so quickly that I smacked into the wall. He closed the small space between us and planted his hands on either side of me, trapping me.

"Look at you. A little bird panting in terror."

I wanted to call out for help—Jordan was just on the other side of that wall—but I couldn't seem to untangle my voice.

Say something. Scream. Do something.

Collin leaned closer, his lips almost touching mine, and a sound finally escaped my throat: a pathetic little whimper that I wished I could take back.

Dark amusement twinkled in his eyes. "I love it when you're scared," he whispered, his moist, hot breath sending a shiver through me.

Suddenly he was jerked backward, twisted around, and slammed face first into the opposite wall. Marx had a hold of him by the back of the neck like a disobedient cat.

He pinned him in place.

"I realize you struggle to grasp the meanin' of the word no, but I didn't realize you were also stupid," Marx bit out angrily. "You've got a lot of nerve comin' after her here."

"Coming after who?" Collin asked with feigned confusion. "I'm just here for a little something sweet. I hear they have delicious items on the menu today."

Marx pulled a folded paper from the inside of his coat pocket and said, "I have somethin' sweet for you." He shoved it into Collin's hand. "Have a look."

"Did you write me a love letter, Detective? Because you're not really my type."

"I'm well aware of your type. You brutalized eighteen women, includin' Holly."

221

"Eighteen? Now you're just insulting me," Collin said, sounding far too smug. "You may want to check your numbers again."

My stomach heaved. There were more? How many women had he attacked?

Marx glanced back at me. "Sweetheart, why don't you go back to the table with the others. And send Sam over."

"I'm already here," a deep voice said, and I dragged my eyes away from Collin to see Sam standing in the lobby of the restaurant with his arms crossed. He was glaring at the back of Collin's head. His gaze shifted to me, and I realized I was still plastered against the wall where Collin had cornered me. "Are you gonna faint?"

I shook my head. Did I look like I was going to faint?

His eyes narrowed. "Why don't you come out of the hallway and sit down." He grabbed a nearby chair and plopped it beside him.

I didn't move.

"Out of curiosity, how am I supposed to read this note when you're holding me against the wall?" Collin asked.

Marx kept his grip on the back of Collin's neck as he pulled him away from the wall so he could read the letter.

Collin stumbled. "You know, I'm noticing a trend with you cops and this excessive use of force."

"I haven't even come close to excessive."

"We could just discuss things like civilized men."

"You're not a man."

"He's not civilized either," Sam added.

Collin sighed and unfolded the paper. He cocked his head with interest. "An order of protection?"

"You're not allowed within five hundred feet of Holly. Do you know what that means, Mr. Wells?" Marx asked. He didn't wait for Collin to answer. "It means you're in violation of your restrainin' order and you're under arrest."

Collin smiled. "I don't think it works that way."

"I don't think I care." Marx plucked the paper from Collin's fingers, then looked expectantly at Sam.

Sam took my arm in a gentle grip and tugged me from the hallway. The moment we were both clear, Marx slammed Collin onto the floor so roughly that I winced. It would've hurt a normal person, but it only knocked Collin breathless.

"You have the right to remain silent. Anythin' you say can and will be used against you in a court of law," Marx recited, wrenching Collin's arms behind his back.

"You seem a little angry, Richard," Collin said, still trying to recapture his breath.

"You have a right to an attorney."

"From what I hear, you've been angry and bitter since your wife left you two years ago. Or maybe it started when you realized you could never have kids."

"If you cannot afford an attorney, one will be appointed to you."

"Is it my turn yet?" Sam asked.

Marx glanced up at him. "I've got him."

"Looks like he's struggling. Maybe I should help."

Collin was lying perfectly still.

"Hey, what's . . ." Jordan's voice trailed off when he crossed the restaurant lobby to see what all the commotion was about. His relaxed expression turned granite when he saw Collin.

He started toward him, his movements frighteningly intense, but Sam caught him and hauled him back. "Take it easy. He's down."

"Get off me." Jordan shrugged Sam's arms away.

Sam shifted into his path. "You need to calm down."

"Don't tell me to calm down." Jordan tried to shove him back a step, but Sam was not in the mood to be moved.

"Would the two of you knock it off?" Marx snapped, dragging Collin to his feet.

"Oh my gosh," Jace gasped as she wheeled up behind me. She parked her wheelchair and stretched out an arm, wrapping it around my waist in an awkward embrace. I wasn't sure if it was meant to comfort her or me.

Her friend Warren parked beside her. "Is everything okay? Is there anything I can do?"

Sam nodded to the cameras on the ceiling. "Do those work?"

Warren must have recognized Collin from the ice rink, because he glanced at me with a glimmer of concern and then back at Sam. "Do you need them to work?"

Sam deferred the question to Marx, who shook his head. "I don't think they'll help us."

Warren's lips thinned in thought and then he said, "Sometimes they work, sometimes they don't. I don't really know much about them, but it's possible they could be down right now."

Jace grinned at him. "Possible?"

"Probable."

"Good." Marx flicked an accusing glare between Jordan and Sam. "Can I trust the two of you to take Holly back to my place and keep her safe, or am I gonna come back to find her on her own again?"

Sam and Jordan both shifted uncomfortably under the reprimand, and I spoke up. "It's not their fault. I asked for privacy. I just . . . I wanted some space."

The anger left Marx's voice, but his tone was still firm. "I understand that you want space, sweetheart, but that's not an option right now." He returned his attention to Sam and Jordan. "Take her to my apartment and stay with her until I get back. Both of you. No matter how much she wants space, until we find his accomplice, she does not leave that apartment alone."

Collin let out a grunt of amusement, and Jordan took another step toward him, only to be barred by Sam, who said calmly, "We'll make sure she's safe."

Jace pulled me back protectively as Marx led Collin by, and I lost my balance and ended up in her lap. She took that as permission to hug me tighter. Any tighter and I wouldn't have been able to breathe.

Collin gave me a devilish smile as he passed by, and I wanted to slap it off his face, but that would require me to touch him, which I wasn't willing to do.

24

I packed the last of my things and tightened the drawstring of my travel bag. Collin was in jail, which meant tonight would be the safest time for me to leave. I just had to wait for everyone to fall asleep so I could slip away undetected.

Someone knocked on the bedroom door, and I looked between the door and my travel bag, then stuffed the bag under the bed.

I opened the door to find Marx standing in the hallway. It dawned on me that he probably needed clothes to change into for the night, and I had locked him out of his own room. "I'm sorry. You probably need clothes and—"

"I got what I needed earlier. I just wanted to make sure you're okay. You don't seem quite yourself today."

I was exactly myself: scared, desperate, and ready to run. I had been that person since I was fourteen. Marx and the others had just made me forget her for a while.

"I'm fine."

He looked over my head into his bedroom, and I glanced behind me, concerned that he might see my travel bag, but it was completely hidden beneath the bed. "Are you sure there's nothin' on your mind?"

I tucked my fingers into my back pockets. "We've had this conversation before, remember? I'm a woman."

"Which means your mind is goin' in a dozen different directions at any given time." He smiled and checked his watch. "It's late. You should probably try to get some sleep. Jordan's on the couch, and I'll be in the spare room if you need me."

I didn't want to just let him walk away, not when this was my last chance to see him. I stepped into the hall and hugged him, and I let him hug me back this time. His arms felt so warm and safe that I didn't want to leave them for the cold streets.

"I'm by no means complainin', but what happened to 'I'm not a hugger'?" he asked.

"Oh, be quiet."

He chuckled. "Good night, sweet pea."

"Good night." I hoped he couldn't hear the good-bye in my voice as I fought back tears. I was going to cry all the way to the bus station.

I forced myself to let go and step back. I sagged against the door frame and closed my eyes after he went into the spare room and shut the door. Now I just had to wait until I knew he and Jordan were both asleep.

It was nearly two hours later before the apartment fell quiet, and I peered out to find the spare room light off and Jordan snoring softly on the couch.

I slung my bag over my shoulder and looked at the closed spare room door. I wanted to hug Marx one last time and tell him good-bye, but I knew he wouldn't let me leave.

I placed the folded note I had written on the counter next to the coffeepot where I knew he would find it. He accused me of being addicted to marshmallows, but he could drink two pots of coffee on his own.

I hadn't been able to find words adequate enough to express my gratitude and affection for him, so I had simply written:

Dear Marx,

Thank you for everything, but I have to go. Please take care of Jace and Riley, and please don't look for me.
Love, Holly

I set two more notes on the coffee table in front of the couch, moving as quietly as a mouse.

Jordan,

Thank you for being my friend and for never giving up on me. I hope when I'm gone, you'll finally go home to be with your family. Please give my note to Jace and tell her that I'll be okay. Good-bye.
—Holly—

I released a long, trembling breath as I walked to the door. I unlocked it, wincing at the click that had woken Marx the last time I tried to sneak out, and glanced back at the couch. Jordan was still asleep. I took one last long look around the apartment, then stepped into the dimly lit hall.

I turned toward the stairwell and screamed when I found a man standing there. I pressed a hand to my chest as my heart slammed against my rib cage, and stepped back.

Twice in one day, someone had snuck up on me.

"What . . . what are you . . ." I sputtered. Marx was leaning against the wall on the other side of the door.

The apartment door wrenched open, and Jordan appeared, looking rumpled and worried. "I heard a scream." His eyes bounced between us and then narrowed. "Wait, what's going on?"

"Apparently, we're runnin' away," Marx replied, his voice tight with suppressed anger.

I blinked and looked down at the packed travel bag resting at his feet. "We?" was all I could manage.

"Mmm hmm. I told you that if you ever ran away, I would spend every available moment searchin' for you. I figured we would just skip the searchin' part and I'd go with you. So where are we goin'?"

My mouth dropped open. "I . . . but that . . ." I was so flustered I couldn't speak. I looked between them. "H-how did you know?"

"You mean aside from the fact that the picture of your family you always keep beside your bed wasn't there when I checked on you earlier?"

I glanced at my bag where I had packed my family photo. I should've known he would notice its absence; he was trained to recognize clues.

"'One down, four to go,'" Marx recited. "You knew from the beginnin' what it took me about two days to figure out. Collin intended for Maya to die in that fire, which would've left four people in this city that you care about: Jace, Jordan, Sam, and me."

I swallowed and said nothing.

"I figured the only thing keepin' you here was Maya. I heard you promise her that you wouldn't leave her, and you never break your word. Which meant the moment she was gone, you would be too. And then you hugged me good-bye tonight."

I hoisted my bag back up my shoulder, annoyed that I had given my plan away without meaning to. "I have to go."

Jordan opened the door the rest of the way and stepped into the hall. "Why? Why do you have to go?"

"Why?" I shot him a disbelieving look. "Collin burned down the shelter I stayed in. He tried to have Marx killed. He had someone try to kidnap Maya after she survived the fire. Someone tried to run you over. How can you ask me why?"

"We're fine."

"Right now, but for how long? You don't understand how persistent he is, Jordan."

"But if you run . . ."

"He'll follow her."

I glanced at Marx, and then away, unable to hold his gaze. "If I'm not here, he won't be either, and you'll be safe."

"But you won't be," Jordan said with growing agitation.

Marx's voice softened. "You can't run forever, sweetheart. Eventually, he will catch you. And judgin' by how bad it was last time, I don't know that you'll survive."

I stared hard at the floor, trying not to imagine all the awful possibilities. "I know, but I have to try."

"We are perfectly capable of takin' care of ourselves, and I will not stand idly by while you put yourself in danger."

"Neither will I," Jordan agreed.

I shrugged my bag back up onto my shoulder when it started to slide down again. "You're not gonna talk me out of this. Everyone will be safer if I go, and your lives can go back to normal."

"*Normal?* Do you have any idea what my *normal* life was like before I met you?" Marx asked. "I went to work in the mornin' and came home at night just to sleep and do it all over again. I couldn't even remember the last time I laughed or smiled, or did somethin' that didn't revolve around crime, death, or take-out Chinese food."

I had seen the take-out Chinese food in his refrigerator when I moved in, so I knew that was true.

"And then I met you. One of the most stubborn, hardheaded, frustratin' girls I have ever met. And I was married to a lawyer, so that's sayin' somethin'."

Jordan snorted. "Don't forget her 'I don't need help' attitude and the way she scrunches her nose and glares at people when things aren't going her way."

"That too," Marx concurred. I was starting to wonder if I had any good qualities. "But you brought light back into my life, Holly. You're so full of compassion and kindness for people and, despite what this world has done to you, a beautiful innocence. You bring me a joy I'd given up hope of ever havin' in my life. I have no desire for things to go back to *normal.*"

I blinked at the tears gathering in my eyes and glanced behind him at the stairwell.

"Please, Holly," Jordan pleaded. "I just got you back after eighteen years. Don't make me spend the rest of my life searching and wondering where you are and if you're okay."

Why did they have to make this so difficult? Why couldn't they see that I was trying to protect them? "If I stay, he's never gonna stop. This is the only way to keep you safe."

"We'll keep ourselves safe," Marx said. "Please just trust me, sweetheart." He held out his hand for my bag, and I was reminded of the moment in Melanie's bedroom when I held out my hand for the knife, begging her to trust me and to trust that everything would be okay. She had been strong enough to hand it over.

If I didn't leave, there was nothing I could do to protect them. I had brought danger into their lives, and all I would be able to do was stand by and watch the events unfold. But I didn't want to hurt them by leaving either.

Reluctantly, I let my bag slide off my shoulder to the floor with a thud. Jordan scooped it up by the strap before I could change my mind. "I'll take this back inside."

Marx stepped over his bag on the floor and bridged the gap between us, pulling me into a tight hug. "Thank you."

I burrowed into his warm embrace, letting him wrap me in safety in a way only he seemed able to do. "I don't know what to do," I admitted hopelessly.

He kissed my hair. "I know."

The door directly across the hall cracked open, and an elderly woman in a pink housecoat with tight gray curls and a pinched mouth stuck her nose into the hall.

"I'll have you know I called the police again. There's been an awful lot of screaming coming from your apartment, young man, and I've a mind to file a complaint with the landlord. Something's not right with you."

He sighed, and his exasperated breath ruffled my hair. "There's no need, Mrs. Neberkins. Everythin's fine. And I *am* the police."

Mrs. Neberkins lifted her nose and stared him down through her bifocals. "That doesn't mean you're not hurtin' some poor girl in there. I hear the stories. I watch the news. Cops are just as bad as the criminals."

"For the love of all things holy," Marx muttered. "I'm not hurtin' anybody."

"Why don't you let that child go so she can answer for herself?"

Child? Well, I supposed she was nearing eighty and she had bifocals, so I couldn't blame her for her confusion.

I pulled free of the hug to meet her eyes. "I'm fine, Mrs. Neberkins. He just startled me."

She looked me over from head to toe, her studious gaze lingering on my face. "If you need a safe place to stay, you just knock on my door. I'm always home."

I forced a smile. "Thank you."

"Thank you for your concern, Mrs. Neberkins," Marx said graciously.

She tossed a disapproving grunt his way before closing her door.

He sighed and picked up his bag. "Funny how I'm the one with a bruised jaw from bein' kicked in the face the other night, but she thinks I'm abusin' you."

"It's not my fault you hit my foot with your face."

I had done a lot more than kick him in the face when he woke me from my night terror, but that was the only bruise I could see.

"Mmm hmm. I don't recall puttin' my face anywhere near your feet. You're just freakishly limber." He wrapped an arm around me, like he was still worried I might wander off, and led me back into the apartment.

The night that followed was restless for all of us.

I was too anxious to sleep, and Marx and Jordan took shifts so that one of them was awake at all times, and I knew they were making sure I couldn't sneak away again.

Feeling like I was about to climb the walls, I decided to do a little snooping. I opened Marx's closet and surveyed his wardrobe:

suit jackets, nice jeans, every black T-shirt in existence, perfectly organized shoes on a tiny rack.

I pulled open his top dresser drawer next and grinned at the drawer full of socks. Yep. I had wondered once if he organized his socks by color, and he did. He had three separate sections: black socks, gray socks, and navy-blue socks.

I decided to do a little reorganizing. I paired each sock with a different color and then put them back in the drawer.

I noticed a picture on top of the dresser of Marx with his family. A woman I assumed was his sister, Cresceda, had the same vibrant green eyes and black hair, but she was heavier like their mother. Everyone in the picture was smiling except the older man with salt-and-pepper hair and a build strikingly similar to Marx's.

He looked cold and stern, and I remembered Marx telling me his father had beaten him with a belt. I could see that man beating his son while he recited what he'd "done wrong." I decided I didn't like him and hoped I never met him.

Marx's mother, on the other hand, looked like the grandmother I had always imagined having when I used to dream about a family: plump, cheerful, and huggable. She probably baked a lot of tasty treats too.

I closed the sock drawer and picked up the bottle of cologne next to the picture. It was a pretty bottle for guy perfume. I pressed the spray button and a familiar scent misted the air—and the bed and everything on it, including the clothes I had started to unpack. It was the anniversary cologne from Shannon that Marx wore every day. I smiled and put the little bottle back.

I opened the bedroom door and wandered out into the hallway. Jordan was asleep on the couch again, which meant Marx was awake. I could see the light glowing beneath the spare room door. I padded quietly down the hall and knocked.

"Come in," he said.

I pushed the door open and gave the room a wary once-over. I knew it was just a room, but knowing that Collin had been inside it made it feel somehow . . . tainted. I hesitated before stepping inside.

Marx was resting back against the headboard with a folder in his lap, but he closed it when I stepped into the room. "Can't sleep?"

I shook my head. "What are you reading?"

"Melanie's file." He dropped it on the bed beside him and interlaced his fingers in his lap. "I know she's not ready to come forward and she refused an exam, so we have no ID and no DNA, but I'm hopin' to find somethin' to connect Collin to the crime."

I folded my arms behind me and leaned back against the wall. "What about the picture you took of him dining at the restaurant with her? That puts him with her, right?"

"It does, but she met with a lot of people that day. She was interviewin' for a teachin' assistant, so there was a number of possible suspects."

"What about here? Did they find any evidence that he was the one who broke into your apartment?"

He sighed. "Unfortunately no. No prints, no hair, no witnesses who saw him break in, which is a wonder given Mrs. Neberkins's nosiness. And the nails he put in the door can be found at any hardware or department store."

"So . . . what? They're just gonna let him go?"

"I'm doin' everythin' I can, and so is Shannon. He has a bail hearin' set for nine a.m. tomorrow mornin', and she'll do what she can to make sure his bail is set high enough that he won't be able to buy his way out. Unfortunately, he's not short on funds. Apparently, he has stock market shares in several thrivin' businesses, so she can't make any guarantees."

"Are you gonna be there?"

"No. Shannon all but banned me from the courtroom. She's concerned I'll do somethin' . . . reckless."

I frowned. "She's worried you'll lose your temper?"

"I can understand her concern. The man opens his mouth and I have a nearly overwhelmin' urge to put my fist through his face."

I folded my arms tightly over my stomach. "What if something goes wrong? What if he lies and they just let him go? What if he breaks out? He could find a way to—"

"I know you're worried, but it's gonna be okay. We just have to let the system work."

I resisted the urge to scoff. I had very little faith in man-made systems. Children's Services—one of those systems—had left me in some very dark places as a child, and an officer, a part of the system Marx trusted so implicitly, had refused to help me when I was fourteen. And I had witnessed firsthand the corruption that could infect a police department. How could I trust the court system to be any better?

"What if he buys his way out of it?" I asked. "He could pay off guards or even the judge. What if he manipulates the system? He manipulates everyone and everything. What if he tells them he didn't know about the restraining order?"

"I have no doubt he'll bring that up at the preliminary hearin', but the bail hearin' has nothin' to do with determinin' whether or not he's guilty of a crime. It's about whether or not he can be trusted to abide by the law and appear at his scheduled court date. I'm hopin' we'll have somethin' more solid against him by then."

It all sounded so flimsy.

Marx's phone vibrated. He snatched it off the nightstand and flipped it open. It must have been a text, because he was quiet for a moment. "Drew was picked up outside a convenience store an hour ago."

I rubbed at my bruised arm. "So Evey will be safer now?"

"Much safer, yes." He set his phone back on the nightstand. "Why don't you try to rest? I'll let you know if I find anythin' new about the case."

I doubted I would be able to rest; if I didn't spend the remainder of the night pacing his bedroom in a state of anxiety about tomorrow, I would lie in bed while my mind raced through endless possibilities.

"Go get some sleep, sweet pea. And Holly . . ."

I paused near the door and looked back at him.

"I need you to promise me that no matter what happens tomorrow, you're not gonna run."

I pressed my lips together to contain the long list of excuses that wanted to escape and nodded. "I promise."

He gave me a relieved smile, and it warmed me to know that he trusted my word implicitly. I left him to his research and crawled into bed.

25

I was standing in line with Jordan the next morning, waiting to order a hot dog from a street vendor, when Marx called to update us on Collin's bail hearing. After Shannon presented my medical file and statement to the judge, he set Collin's bail at fifteen thousand dollars.

I hoped the amount would be hard for him to come up with, but I doubted it.

Marx was supposed to join us for self-defense training around noon, but he had to follow up on one of his other cases, which pushed training back to the evening. I didn't mind. There were plenty of things to do in the city.

Jordan and I passed the time by nibbling on food from various food stands and popping into small shops. We bought a huge pretzel and fed the pigeons in the park. Jordan made them work for it, teasing them left and right, then up into the air after a tiny morsel.

I spoiled the little pigeon with one leg because he looked like he needed it. He wasn't as quick to snatch the food as the others. He was so pitiful looking he was adorable, and Jordan had to talk me out of taking him home.

I supposed Marx wouldn't appreciate a pigeon in his apartment.

"What would you have named him anyway?" Jordan asked.

"Barbosa," I said decidedly.

He laughed. "After the one-legged pirate?"

"Of course."

We arrived at the gym a little before eight p.m., and I went into the locker room to change. I stuffed my belongings in a locker, braided my hair, and headed out.

I pulled open the locker-room door and found Marx leaning against the outer wall. He cocked his head and smiled.

"I was startin' to wonder if you got tangled up in all those layers you wear."

"I happen to like my layers, and you were the one who was late. Not me."

"True."

We headed toward the training room when his phone rang. He answered in his normally brusque way, and I watched with a sick feeling in my stomach as his expression darkened.

"Okay, thanks for lettin' me know, Michael." He hung up.

"He's already out, isn't he?"

"I'm sorry, sweetheart. They tried to hold him, but he posted bail an hour ago."

I felt suddenly cold, fear stealing away all my body heat. A dozen frantic thoughts raced through my head—what would he do, who would he hurt next, why hadn't I fled while he was behind bars—each thought vying for my attention.

"If you'd rather grab your things, I'll take you home," Marx offered.

I could run home and hide behind locked doors and drawn curtains. I could barricade myself in Marx's bathroom with my knife and pepper spray, or I could stand my ground.

"He can't touch me with you and Jordan here, right?"

"Right."

"Then . . . I'm going to self-defense training so I can learn how to beat him up."

He smiled, and I thought I saw a glimmer of pride in his eyes. "Well, let's go work on your fightin' skills then." He wrapped an arm around me, imparting some of his warmth, and we walked to the training room.

Jordan was already on the mat in his workout clothes, tapping his fists together as he waited.

"Are you ready yet?" Marx asked him, as if he were the reason for the delay rather than us.

Jordan's eyebrows lifted. "I'm always ready."

Marx leaned down and whispered to me, "Why don't you test that theory?"

I smirked and walked across the mat without him while he found a comfortable spot against the wall. I paused at the four-foot boundary and then made a show of stepping over it.

Jordan grinned. "Trespasser."

I padded up to him and asked, "So what are we doing today?"

When he glanced at the boxing gloves behind him, I swept his right leg out from under him like I was kicking a hockey puck across the ice. He lost his balance and fell backward, smacking the mat.

It was kind of satisfying knowing I had taken down a man almost twice my size—again—and I enjoyed the advantage as I leaned over him. "I thought you were ready."

He dropped his arms spread-eagle on the mat and laughed. "You're lucky you're a girl."

I grinned and bounced on my toes. I knew he wouldn't retaliate, so I didn't feel the need to scamper out of his reach this time.

"You know," he began as he sat up. "That's twice now. The next time you knock me flat, I'm gonna pick you up and twirl you in circles."

"I'll throw up on you."

"Well, at least they have showers here." He got his feet beneath him and tossed me my gloves.

I looked down at them, considering. What we did in training felt more like exercise than practical training, and that wasn't going to protect me from Collin.

"Show me how to fight."

"That's what we're doing."

"No, I mean . . . teach me how to fight *him* so he can never hurt me again."

He blinked in surprise. "Fighting isn't really your best option, Holly."

"Why?"

The question seemed to make him uncomfortable. He scratched the side of his head as he said, "Well . . . because . . . uh . . ." He trailed off and grumbled something under his breath that sounded like, "Where's Sam when you need him?"

"Because I'm a girl?"

"Okay, please don't hold this against me, but . . . yeah, that's part of it. Not that women can't fight, but you're not exactly Ronda Rousey."

I frowned in confusion. "Who?"

"Never mind. My point is, you're barely five feet tall, you don't have any extra weight to throw around, and . . . you're not exactly . . ."—he gestured with his hands as he groped for the right word—"strong."

I straightened my spine. "That's not true. I can be strong."

"Strong-willed," Marx muttered from behind me, and I threw a sharp scowl at him.

"You're talking about fighting a guy almost my size who can't feel pain, Holly," Jordan explained. "And you literally have zero advantage or skill."

He sounded like Sam.

"So teach me some skills."

He sighed and rubbed at his face. "A little help here, Marx."

"I'm enjoyin' this. Go ahead and fumble the rest of your way through it," Marx replied casually.

Jordan glared at him briefly before refocusing his attention on me. "Your best bet for survival is gonna be to surprise him and run."

"Why do you think I've been running for ten years?" I snapped irritably.

240

Jordan's lips compressed into a grim line.

"But what if I can't run? What if I'm . . ."—my voice faltered under the weight of painful memories—"trapped?"

Understanding registered in Jordan's eyes. "Like in your room in Pennsylvania?"

I averted my gaze and nodded. I hadn't known how to defend myself that night, and even when I finally managed to stab Collin, I missed everything important.

Jordan blew out a breath. "Okay. If you're trapped or injured and all you can do is fend him off, you'll have to disable him." He rubbed his hands together as he thought. "If it were any other guy, I would say kneeing him in the groin is a good start, but I don't suppose that works on him."

I shook my head. I had tried that before.

"Okay. Since he can't feel pain, your best bet is gonna be to focus on the weaknesses of every living being: brain, eyes, oxygen, and blood. If you can get a hold of something heavy, aim for the head. You can still knock him out and, if you still can't run, tie him up or . . ." He trailed off, but I knew he wanted to say *keep hitting him until he's dead.*

I squirmed at the idea of taking a life.

"Go for the eyes with your fingers. If he can't see, you have a better chance of escape. There's also the option of cutting off his air. If you can wrap something around his neck, you might be able to choke him unconscious or kill him. I wouldn't recommend using your hands because you have short fingers. You can try using an arm, but you're light enough that he could probably just toss you off."

This whole petite thing was really inconvenient.

"A rope, wire, even a shoelace would be a better option," he continued. "If that's *not* an option, use your fists. It may not hurt him when you hit him, but he still needs to breathe, so aim for the throat. That'll leave him sputtering for a bit."

I listened, absorbing every word.

"And lastly, blood. How familiar are you with anatomy?"

241

I tried to remember the last time I had learned anything about anatomy. I had been two years behind in school because of the years I spent with Izzy and Paul, so I only had a high school freshman education.

"Basic," I said with uncertainty. As long as he didn't quiz me on where all the organs were, I was good. Heart, lungs, stomach, uterus, intestines, bladder—check. Everything in between—mystery.

"Well, the carotid artery in the neck will cause massive blood loss if severed. If you can't hit that one, aim for the femoral artery that travels through the thigh and groin." He ran his fingers along his body to demonstrate the best spots. "He'll bleed out in minutes. Got it?"

I swallowed and nodded.

A phone rang, and we both looked at Marx. He pulled his cell from his coat pocket. "Hey, Mama," he said, walking to the doorway for more privacy. I saw his shoulders tighten and then he asked, "Is he gonna be okay?"

He left the room, and we waited in concerned silence for him to return. When he came back into the room a few minutes later, his eyes were clouded with conflicting emotions.

His voice sounded shocked as he said, "My dad had a heart attack. He's in the hospital."

I thought about the stern-looking man from the photo on Marx's dresser. He might not be a kind person, but he was still Marx's dad, and he loved him.

"You have to go," I told him.

"Holly, I can't just—"

"Yes, you can. You have to go be with your family. Your mom's gonna need you. I'm sure your boss will understand."

"It's not my boss I'm worried about."

I glanced at Jordan and said, "I'll be okay."

"She's right. If it were my dad, I would go," Jordan agreed.

Marx gave him a stern look. "If I leave—"

"I won't let her out of my sight."

242

Marx walked over and pulled me into a hug I wasn't prepared for, but after the moment of surprise passed, I hugged him back. "Please be careful, sweetheart. Don't take any chances, okay?"

"I won't."

He let me go and looked at Jordan. "He's out." With those two words, Jordan's demeanor changed, and I saw the hard, protective cop move closer to the surface. "Call me if you need me."

I said a silent prayer for Marx's family as I watched him go. Despite my assurances that I would be okay without him here, I already felt less safe. It was disconcerting how much I'd come to rely on him.

"So do you wanna go home or finish our lesson?" Jordan asked.

If we continued, this would be my first time training alone with him. "You're gonna respect the boundaries, right?" I asked, only half teasing.

"Promise. And nothing intense without Marx here. We can just work on that punch of yours."

Oh good. At least he wouldn't be wrapping his arms around my throat for this lesson. "There's nothing wrong with my punches. I punched someone just last week."

And my hand was still a bit tender.

"Well, come and get me then," he said, taking a couple steps back.

"How am I supposed to hit you when you're moving?"

"Bad guys don't stand still."

I sighed and stalked after him. I tried to hit him three or four . . . or five dozen times. I lost count. But I couldn't seem to get any closer than an inch. By the end of the lesson, I managed to hit him in the chest, but I had a feeling he let me so I wouldn't feel completely discouraged.

"We're definitely gonna have to work on your hand-eye coordination," he said as we walked out of the building.

I rolled my eyes. "I'm not that—"

I turned the corner into the parking lot and screamed. Jordan pulled me behind him so quickly that it left me fumbling for footing on the icy blacktop.

"Mmm, I do miss that sound," Collin said with a theatrical shudder. He was leaning against the side of the building, hands tucked in his pockets.

The parking lot lights illuminated his features, highlighting the blood and swelling that disfigured his face. He looked like he'd been in a bar fight.

Jordan stepped toward him, his fingers curling into fists, but I grabbed his wrist. "Jordan, don't. Please."

The sound of my voice seemed to freeze him in place.

"Aw, how sweet. She has you wrapped around her pretty little fingers," Collin taunted. "Did she ever tell you I broke some of those fingers?"

I tightened my grip on Jordan's wrist when I felt his tendons flex, silently begging him not to let Collin bait him. "He's just . . . trying to make you mad."

Jordan let out a long, slow breath before uncurling his fists. "You're violating your restraining order."

"How was the workout?" Collin asked, ignoring the comment. "It has to be a challenge for you, being around so much temptation. Does it get your heart pumping? Your hormones racing?"

The way he looked at me made my stomach flip over, and I squeezed Jordan's wrist tighter out of fear.

"I'm curious, when it's just the two of you in that room, do you ever have the urge to just . . . slam her down on the mat?" Collin continued, his lips curling into a wicked smile. "You should try it sometime. She's incredibly cute when she tries to fight back."

I yelped and cupped my hands over my mouth when Jordan pulled free of my grip and punched Collin in the face, knocking him back into the side of the building.

"If you ever touch her, I'll kill you," he growled.

Collin spat blood on the pavement and smiled, his teeth glistening in the lamplight. "You're a little late with that threat, Wyatt. I've touched her many, many times."

Jordan shoved Collin off his feet. If not for the flashing lights that pulled into the parking lot, he might not have stopped. Two officers spilled from the squad car.

"Hands where we can see them. Everyone," the driver demanded.

Jordan stepped back from Collin and lifted his hands. I huddled against his back, watching the approaching cops with uncertainty.

I could make out little more than their silhouettes in the glare of the car's headlights. One was shorter and more confident—probably more experienced—and he reached us first. I winced when the bright beam of a flashlight swept across my face.

"Miss, step away from him and put your hands where I can see them."

I hesitated but, realizing I didn't have much choice, took two steps back from Jordan and held my hands in front of me.

"My name's Jordan Radcliffe. I'm a Kansas sheriff and I am armed."

Jordan's announcement sent a barely perceptible ripple of tension through the officers, and their attention immediately shifted to him.

The one with the flashlight nodded to his partner—who was clearly the younger of the two—and the man carefully disarmed Jordan, then guided him up against the wall of the building.

He ran his hands over Jordan's clothing and then felt inside his pockets. My heart started to pound harder. Were they going to do that to all of us? The officer plucked the badge from Jordan's belt, pulled his wallet from his pocket, and said, "I'll call it in."

"Are you all right, sir?" the officer with the flashlight asked, turning his attention to Collin. "We received a call about an assault in progress."

Collin gave a convincing grimace of pain as he climbed back to his feet. I supposed he had tortured enough people to know how to imitate suffering.

"I will be," he said, pressing a hand to his chest. "Thank you so much. I think you might have saved my life. He attacked me for no reason and I think he intended to kill me."

"You're a liar!" I shouted.

Collin's lips curved just enough that I could see the menace. "You know, I think she has a knife on her."

The flashlight beam snapped back to me, and I stiffened.

"Miss, do you have any weapons on you?"

"No, I . . . I don't."

The light traveled the length of me. "You seem awfully nervous for someone with nothing to hide. I'd like you to put both hands on the hood of the cruiser and spread your feet shoulder width apart."

Fear flashed through me. Collin knew I was afraid to be touched by men because he had instilled that fear, and this was just another way for him to humiliate and torment me.

"Please, I don't . . ."

"Hands on the hood. Don't make me tell you again."

When I took a step back instead, he started toward me. "I don't have anything, I promise."

Jordan, keeping his hands in the air, stepped between me and the approaching officer. "She doesn't have a weapon. There's no reason to frisk her."

The officer's hand dropped to his weapon and he snapped, "Back against the wall!"

I tried to swallow the lump of dread that lodged in my throat as I hid behind Jordan. This was going wrong very quickly.

"She's not hiding anything. She's just scared," Jordan tried to explain.

The officer grabbed Jordan and shoved him back up against the building. He pointed a finger at me and barked, "You don't move."

"Rogan," the younger officer called out as he returned.

The older officer paused with one handcuff around Jordan's wrist and looked back at his partner. "What?"

"He checks out. He's a sheriff from Kansas."

Rogan sighed. "Never simple. Check the girl's ID. Make sure she's not a known troublemaker."

I shifted anxiously as the younger cop drew close enough for me to read his name tag: R. Clayton. He gestured with his fingers and said, "ID."

I tossed my shoulder bag on the ground at his feet, and he scowled as he bent down to pick it up.

Rogan released Jordan. "I'm gonna give you the benefit of the doubt. As a sorta courtesy. You got ten seconds to convince me not to arrest you and your noncompliant girlfriend over here."

He shot me a suspicious look.

Jordan lowered his hands as he turned around. "Your supposed assault in progress is Collin Wells. Holly has an order of protection against him, which he's aware of." He nodded toward Collin, who was watching the situation with interest. "He was waiting outside for her."

Rogan glanced at me, then at Collin. "You roughed him up an awful lot."

"I hit him once."

"Well, somebody did a number on him."

"I don't know what's wrong with his face. I didn't do that."

"She's got no priors or outstanding warrants," Clayton announced, dropping my ID back into my bag and offering the bag to me. He tossed Jordan's badge and wallet back to him, but he held onto Jordan's gun for the time being.

Rogan sent Clayton to check Collin's identification next with a simple nod of his head before asking, "What are your reasons for being here tonight, Mr. Wells?"

Collin groaned as he shifted his weight. "I've had a gym membership here for months. I just came to work out. I had no idea either of them would be here."

"So this meeting was a coincidence?" Rogan asked.

"Yes, sir."

"What's your connection with this young woman?"

"Holly and I used to have a pretty intense relationship."

I tried not to flinch.

"We broke things off, but her boyfriend's the angry, jealous type, and he talked her into a restraining order when I moved to town."

Rogan glanced between us, clearly uncertain. Collin was a chameleon, and he was blending into his role as the wounded, wronged party seamlessly.

"He's her foster brother from Maine," Jordan explained. "He followed her across several state lines."

Rogan's eyes widened a fraction. "Stalking?" He eyed Collin with renewed interest. "Are you stalking this young woman, Mr. Wells?"

"Of course not. He's got some kind of jealousy issue, and he attacked me completely unprovoked. I'm pressing charges for assault."

"Are you kidding me?" Jordan snapped indignantly. "After what you did to Holly in Pennsylvania, you're the one who should be arrested for assault!"

The officers exchanged a conflicted glance, and then Rogan cleared his throat. "We did receive a call about an assault in progress, and when we arrived, we did see you shove Mr. Wells to the ground. Also, by your own admission, you hit him. I'm sorry, but my partner here is gonna have to place you under arrest."

Jordan's fingers clenched into angry fists, but he placed his hands behind his back when Clayton instructed him to. He glared at Collin as the officer snapped the handcuffs around his wrists.

"I expect the two of you to meet us at the station for a full statement," Rogan said.

It took a moment for his words to sink in, and then a fresh wave of fear washed over me. "I can't go with Jordan?"

"Afraid not. We can't put you in the back with him," Rogan explained.

"But . . ." I looked at Collin, and he smirked. They were just going to leave me here with him.

Jordan planted his feet when Clayton tried to lead him toward the squad car. "You can't leave her alone with him."

Rogan hesitated. Maybe some part of him could sense that something was off about Collin. "Mr. Wells, why don't you go and get yourself checked out at the hospital before coming to the station?"

Collin's eyes twitched slightly, the first sign that he was bothered by the way things were unfolding. He must have expected them to leave me behind with him.

"Good idea," he agreed, betraying none of his frustration. He looked pointedly at me. "I'm sorry if I scared you, Holly. That was never my intention." He looked at the officers. "Thanks again for your help, officers."

With that, he ducked his head against the cold wind and walked away. I watched his retreating figure until it melted into the darkness.

"Okay, now let's go," Clayton urged.

Jordan resisted yet again. "He's just gonna double back and grab her as soon as we leave the parking lot."

Annoyance flashed across Rogan's face. "Look, I'm inclined to extend you some leniency and respect because you're a member of law enforcement, but we're not a taxi service for your girlfriend."

"He's hurt her before. Please, we can't just leave her here unprotected," Jordan pleaded. "Call Sam Barrera from the twenty-fifth precinct. The detective handling Holly's case left on a personal matter, but Sam knows the details."

Rogan's jaw shifted in irritation. "Fine. But then you get in the car or I'm gonna add resisting arrest to your list of offenses." He pulled out his cell phone and stepped away from the car to place his call.

I walked over to Jordan. "He set this entire thing up. He probably beat himself up, called the police, and then provoked you to make you look violent and irrational."

"Yeah," he agreed. "He's trying to get me out of the way so he can get to you."

"I'm so sorry. This is—"

"Not your fault."

Rogan must have been able to reach Sam, because the look he shot me across the dimly lit parking lot was slightly horrified. I had a feeling he had just learned about the seventeen women Collin had attacked.

He twisted to look in the direction Collin had gone, and I noticed his fingers flexing on his gun. Yep, he knew. When he ended the call, he joined us by the car.

He looked at me with a mixture of interest and pity before turning his attention to Jordan. "That phone call was very enlightening." He tapped his phone against his palm. "We'll stay until Barrera gets here."

"He told you about the victims and what Collin did to them," Jordan assumed.

Rogan nodded once, his gaze shifting to capture my face, and I averted my eyes uncomfortably. "He mentioned that DNA was recovered from Ms. Cross's sexual assault kit in Pennsylvania, but that you don't have a sample of his DNA to compare it to."

"Yeah, so he gets to walk around free to torment her."

"You struck Mr. Wells." When a light went on in Jordan's eyes, Rogan smiled. "What do you say we take a look at those knuckles for DNA?"

When they removed the handcuffs, there was blood on Jordan's right hand from where he had struck Collin. They collected the evidence and then let him sit in the back of the cruiser without the restraints. I plopped next to him on the seat.

"I'm sorry we had to tell them," he said. "I know how much you hate people knowing."

"Rogan looked at me like a victim."

"I know, and I'm sorry. If it makes you feel any better, I don't see a victim when I look at you."

"What *do* you see?"

"If I tell you, you'll blush and get all adorably awkward."

Heat crept into my cheeks, and I fidgeted. "No I won't."

He laughed. "You already are."

I rolled my eyes, and silence fell between us. I glanced at his hand resting on his leg and considered something. I had never held a man's hand before, and if I ever had any intention of trying to, this would be a good place to start. I stretched out my hand but hesitated. I was afraid to cross that line.

Don't be a chicken.

"Can you, um . . ." I drew in a strengthening breath and exhaled determination. "Put your hand right here?"

He lifted an eyebrow when I pointed to the open seat between us and moved his hand from his thigh to the seat.

"Can I try something?" I asked.

"So long as you're not gonna try to stab a knife back and forth between my fingers as fast as you can. We both know you have terrible aim, and I'm not in the mood to lose a finger."

I smiled. "Just don't move, okay?" His expression turned wary, and I laughed. In hindsight, it really did sound like I was about to try something that would cost him a finger.

I set my hand tentatively on top of his, palm to palm, and glanced at his face. He smiled but otherwise remained perfectly still.

His skin felt warm and a little rough against mine. My heart thumped faster in my chest, and I slid my hand up his large palm to align my fingertips with his.

He had big hands.

A whisper of fear brushed across my mind: *those big hands can hurt you easily.* I snatched my hand from his and clenched my fingers into a fist.

He would never hurt me.

I met Jordan's warm, patient gaze. He held perfectly still, letting me work through this moment of anxiety. My fingers shook a little as I uncurled them and placed them back on top of his.

I slipped them between his fingers and folded them. It felt . . . frightening, nice, and unfamiliar all at once. "You can, um . . . you know." It wasn't my most articulate sentence, but he seemed to understand.

Slowly, he folded his fingers over mine and our hands locked. Anxiety churned through me, and I was tempted to pull away, but I forced myself to remain still.

This was the most intimate thing I had ever done with a man. Well . . . willingly. Intimacies had been taken from me, but I had never given them of my own free will.

I was terrified that by doing this I was inviting more. I didn't want more. I just wanted this. I met Jordan's eyes and thought about telling him so, but nerves made the words stick in my throat.

He was watching me.

I swallowed. "What are you thinking?"

The small smile on his lips spread into a grin. "That you have very small, cute hands."

"Maybe your hands are just gigantic."

"Why don't we ask Sam? He's blatantly honest and irritatingly logical."

252

I had been so wrapped up in my own feelings that I hadn't noticed the car that just pulled into the lot. Sam exchanged a few words with the officers before coming over to the cruiser.

He crouched down in my open doorway, arched an eyebrow at our connected hands, and then looked past me at Jordan.

"You punched Collin in the face."

Jordan's shoulders tightened defensively. "You didn't hear the things he was saying, Sam. He—"

"It's not a criticism. I'm actually a little jealous. Though, as a sheriff, I figured you would know how not to get arrested."

Jordan dropped his head back against the seat with a sigh.

"We'll figure it out. I'll call Shannon and see if she can recommend a good lawyer. It's Friday night, so at best we can have you out by Monday morning. Until then, Holly, you're gonna stay with me and Evey," Sam said. "We should get going before they get in trouble for stalling any longer." He nodded toward the officers a few feet away.

I unwound my fingers from Jordan's and released him. My hand felt warm from the body heat I had stolen.

"Thanks for, um . . . not moving," I mumbled, flashing him a small, nervous smile.

He grinned and his dimples reappeared. "Any time you want me to not move, I'm good with that."

I laughed softly and slid out of the backseat. "Be safe." Jail could be a dangerous place, or so I had heard.

His face turned serious. "You too."

We watched Rogan and Clayton drive away with Jordan, and I had an uneasy feeling that things were only going to get worse from here.

26

I studied a photo in Sam's living room. He must have been about thirteen, and the broad smile on his face looked like genuine happiness. I had never seen him smile like that.

Now he looked like his father, the man standing between him and Evey in the picture—all softness chiseled into sharp, serious edges. It made me wonder what had stolen that innocent smile from Sam's face. Maybe it was just the life of a cop.

"This is my home too, and you should've asked me!" Evey stormed out of a room down the hall and stomped toward the living room.

She hadn't been happy to see me follow Sam into the apartment, and I couldn't blame her. I did have a crazy man after me, one who wouldn't think twice about attacking her and her brother.

She stopped when she saw me standing there with a picture in my hand. "Congratulations. I guess you have a place to stay for the night. But that doesn't mean you can make yourself at home."

She plucked the picture from my hand and returned it to its spot on the shelf.

"Sorry," I said. "I just . . . I've never seen Sam look that happy."

"Yeah, well, he was a happy kid. He was always logic this and logic that, but he used to smile."

"What happened to make him so . . ."

"Grim?" she offered. "Life, I suppose." She walked to the couch and dropped onto it with a quiet sigh. "Dad was busy a lot when we were growing up, and we were always afraid we would get that visit or call to tell us he wasn't coming home, but when he *was* home, life was . . . great. Cookouts, fishing trips, decorating the tree."

She folded her long, slender legs beneath her on the cushions, somehow managing to look elegant in her jeans and sweater.

I wondered what it would be like to be tall, stunning, and full of presence. I felt . . . stumpy and clumsy by comparison.

"Sammy had a full ride to OSU for football, but when Dad died, he gave up his dream of professional ball to take care of me. He worked nights in a factory and days in a restaurant kitchen just trying to keep us from losing the house. He didn't want me to lose our home too, but we lost it anyway."

My heart ached for the boy my friend had once been. I understood now why he was so hard.

"I realize Sammy's a cop, and he's accustomed to danger, but he's all I have. And you're putting him in danger again." She fixed me with a hard look that could rival Sam's. "I will not lose him like we lost our dad, so whatever your problems are, whoever you're hiding from, don't you dare get my brother—"

"That's enough, Ev," Sam said, coming down the hall. "If you push her out the door, I'm just gonna have to go look for her."

Evey crossed her arms and rolled her eyes. "Why?"

"Because without Marx and Jordan, I'm the only person standing between her and a serial rapist, and I'm not gonna step aside to make you more comfortable."

Evey sat forward on the couch. "Please tell me you're not serious. You brought her here knowing there's a rapist looking for her? Did you even think about the danger you could be putting *me* in?"

"Of course I considered the danger. You're not his type. So the only thing you're at risk of is feeling put out."

Evey stood and stomped her foot. "I can't believe you're doing this."

"You're being a brat, Ev."

"And you're being an idiot!" She stormed out of the living room and down the hall. Riley trotted along at her heels, no doubt sensing her distress, and a door slammed.

255

Sam stared after her with regret. "She doesn't mean the things she says. She's just upset."

I lifted my eyebrows.

"Okay, she means everything she says in the moment that she says it, but she usually regrets it and apologizes later," he amended. "She doesn't cope well with stress."

I walked over and plopped on the far cushion next to my travel bag. Everything I had unpacked last night had gone right back into the bag this evening. "I overheard you tell Marx that I remind you of her."

"You overhear a lot of things you're not supposed to hear." I didn't think he was going to continue, but then he said, "You're both emotionally impulsive, quick to anger, and hardheaded. You're just nicer than she is."

"I'm not hardheaded."

He offered me a look that said, "Are you kidding me?" then sighed. "I'm gonna go talk to her."

I tapped my fingers on my thighs and looked around the apartment. A faint scraping sound drew my attention to the front door. It took me a moment too long to identify it, and the dead bolt clicked.

"Sam!"

Sam came back down the hall. "What's the—" The door flew open before he could finish his question, and I saw his eyes dart toward his gun on the kitchen counter, but he didn't have time to reach it.

A gunshot reverberated through the apartment, and I dropped to a crouch behind the coffee table with my hands over my ears.

I shifted my weight, ready to run, as I watched a man stride into the apartment, the gun still raised in his hand. I recognized him: sandy-blond hair, pinched lips, and a scar that zigzagged through his left eyebrow. Drew, Evey's husband. But he was supposed to be in jail.

Evey's screams as she raced to the end of the hall mingled with Drew's shouts, and their voices melded into indistinguishable noise.

I followed Evey's panicked gaze to the body sagging against the wall. There was a trail of red where Sam had slid, and blood blossomed across his chest and down his stomach.

I started to crawl toward him, but Drew's voice froze me in place. "Stay put!"

A loud whine, accompanied by the scrabbling of claws on wood, drew my eyes back to the hallway. Riley. If we could get to him and let him out of Evey's room, we might have a chance. I tried to get Evey's attention, but she couldn't pull her eyes away from her brother.

"You," Drew growled, spittle flying from his lips, as he returned his attention to Sam. "You tried to keep my wife from me."

Sam's arms lay limply at his sides, but his glassy eyes blinked slowly. They shifted to his sister, whose screams had died to muffled gasps. "Ev," he struggled out. "Run."

"The only place she's going is with me." Drew snatched Evey's arm, and she let out a fresh wail of fear as he jerked her to his side. "Husband and wife are meant to be together. We're meant to be *one* under God. You don't get to be a part of her life any longer."

My heart thudded in my ears as I watched the situation unfold. Sam was bleeding to death, Riley was trapped in Evey's room, and Drew was going to take Evey with him.

I needed to do something.

"Say good-bye to your brother." Drew pointed the gun at Sam's head, and Evey started screaming again.

Sam would probably have told me I was illogical for what I did next, but I had to seize the opportunity while I had it. I climbed onto the coffee table and monkey jumped onto Drew's back.

My sudden weight threw him off balance, and he staggered. The bullet he'd intended to put in Sam's head erupted from the gun with a loud crack and hit the wall.

"Ev . . . go," Sam said, his voice nearly strangled by his desperate attempts to breathe.

Evey squeezed his hand, hesitating, and then fled from the apartment.

"Evey!" Drew bellowed. He tried to shrug me off, but I wrapped my arms tight around his neck and clung on. I might not be able to take him down, but I could sure be a pest.

I was not going to let him shoot my friend again.

He slammed me back into the wall and pain lanced up my spine. He drove me into the wall again, sending a wave of dizziness through me that had me clutching tighter in desperation. I didn't really see a good ending to this.

If he kept slamming me into the wall I was going to pass out, and then he would shoot me. If I fell off, he would shoot me. At best, the police would arrive and he would hold me hostage . . . until he decided to shoot me.

Crap.

Way to think it through, Holly.

Drew was cursing and spitting foul names in a fit of rage. He tossed the gun on the couch and gripped my arms with both large hands. He dug into the bruise on my forearm, and I gasped in pain.

He ducked sharply and flipped me off his back. I landed, dazed and breathless, on the floor. He snatched up the gun and pointed it at my face.

"You worthless little piece of trash. You should've minded your own business."

My heart staggered with fear.

Well, it wasn't like you didn't see this coming, my mind offered up as I braced myself for the bullet that would end my life. Dozens of thoughts raced through my mind in that moment—fragments of memories, hopes, regrets—and then one final thought settled: *it could be worse.*

"I have plans for that one," a terrifyingly familiar voice said, a split second before a bat cut through the air and cracked against the back of Drew's head.

His eyes rolled up and he wilted to the floor. My breath left me as I stared up at the man towering over me with a bat.

It was worse.

Collin plucked the gun off the floor before I could even think about scrambling for it. "Hello, gorgeous."

I didn't even have time to think beyond the heart-stopping terror that gripped my entire body before he drew back the bat and swung.

27

*P*ain splintered through my skull, and I groaned quietly as I lifted a hand to press it to my head. Why did my head hurt so badly? The last thing I remembered was . . .

Oh, God, please no.

The last thing I remembered was a bat arcing toward me and a brief moment of blinding pain before everything went dark. My eyelids fluttered open to see ice-blue eyes peering down at me.

"Look who's finally awake," Collin purred.

I lay there, momentarily frozen, then flipped and scrambled across the floor. He grabbed a hold of the leather belt on my jeans and dragged me back.

I screamed and clawed desperately at the cement floor, but there was nothing to grab hold of. I kicked at him frantically, but no matter how many times my feet slammed into him, it didn't faze him.

He forced me onto my back and grasped my wrists, pinning them in one large hand above my head.

A scream that was as much fury as it was terror ripped from me.

He laughed, the cold sound echoing through the empty room. "You're beautiful when you're scared. I've never seen anything make your eyes sparkle quite like fear. Well, except maybe anger."

"Get . . . off me," I demanded, and I hated the terrified quiver in my voice.

"Why would I want to do that?" He brushed a thumb lightly across my lips.

I turned my head and pulled my lips between my teeth when he leaned down, pressing his face mere inches from mine.

"What, no hello kiss?"

My memories bridged the finite gap between our bodies, and my heart felt like it was going to pound through my rib cage.

His fingers traced my collarbone and then came to rest on my neck. "I can feel your pulse racing." His thumb caressed my throat tenderly, and his touch made my skin want to crawl away. "You're practically shaking, and I haven't even touched you yet."

Desperation tempted me to beg him not to hurt me, but I knew that would only heighten his enjoyment.

His fingers tightened fractionally, sending another wave of panic through me, and I tried to twist free.

He laughed, shifting his weight to compensate. "Always the little fighter."

His fingers squeezed harder, and my airway constricted. My body struggled to come to terms with what my mind already knew was coming: no more air.

His hot breath splashed over my face as he whispered, "I've missed this." And then he pressed his lips to mine in a bruising kiss.

I wanted to hit him, to push him off me, but all I could do was scream inside my head.

Make it stop, please make it stop!

He broke the kiss after what felt like an eternity and said in a bored voice, "I suppose I should let you breathe now."

He released my wrists and throat just as patches of darkness began to appear in my vision. I coughed and dry heaved as I rolled onto my side, my body torn between throwing up in revulsion and gasping for air.

"Breathe, Holly."

I dragged myself away from him until my back smacked the cement-block wall across the room, and coughed between ragged gulps of air.

"That's going to leave a bruise," he said as he stood, a small smile curling the corners of his lips. "How does it feel? Does it hurt to breathe?"

I staggered to my feet—one hand hovering protectively over my throat—and huddled in the corner. I had to keep him from touching me. Somehow, I had to protect myself.

"It took me a while to figure you out. Did I ever tell you that?" he asked. "Most of those kids cried from a splinter. But not you. Your tears were so hard to come by."

He thrived on the suffering of others, finding pleasure in their pain and desperate cries for mercy. He was a monster. No one had made him this way; no abuse had driven him to inflict suffering on others. He chose to do it because he enjoyed it.

"I remember the first time you cried for me," he said, sounding nostalgic.

I remembered it too. It was a night I would never forget. He had taken something from me that I could never have back, something that should've been mine to give. That cruelty had transcended physical pain and fractured pieces of my spirit.

"That was the night I figured you out," he continued. "It wasn't just the physical pain for you."

I slid along the wall as he stepped closer.

"Do you remember that night? You were asleep when I came in, curled on your side with both hands tucked under the pillow. You were wearing your pink 'Different is Beautiful' shirt with your black leggings."

I had loved that shirt. It made me feel good about myself during a time when I felt especially different and unaccepted. But I hadn't been able to look at it again after that night.

"Your pinky finger was in one of those little homemade splints." He wiggled the finger in question and smiled, no doubt remembering what he had done to break that finger. "I learned that night that your heart and spirit are far more fragile than your body. Physical pain just wasn't enough."

I tried to tune him out as he reminisced about that night. I needed to escape before he tried a repeat performance. My eyes darted frantically over the room, taking in the thick gray stone of the walls, the lone bulb caged by wire on the ceiling, the single closed door.

There were no windows.

My eyes landed on the wooden box against the far wall, and the room seemed to suddenly shrink around me, closing in from all directions. It was the box he'd said he was building for me, the one that resembled the gun chest he used to lock me in.

"And then there were the others," he said, his slow steps devouring the space between us. "What were their names? Michael, Cassandra, and . . ." He snapped his fingers as he tried to recall the last name. "The littlest one you nicknamed after an insect."

Nat.

He dismissed the name with a wave of his hand when he couldn't grasp it. "It nearly killed you when I made you watch them suffer. That compassionate little heart of yours has to be such an inconvenience."

Sometimes he had hurt them just to make me suffer. "You tortured children. You're sick," I said, and the effort of pushing words through my throat hurt.

"Mostly children," he corrected. "You were hardly a child, but I have to admit that I like what the past thirteen years have done to you."

The way his eyes slithered over me sent goose bumps of terror cascading across my skin, and I braced myself for a fight.

He stepped within reaching distance, and I drew on my self-defense training, if only to hold him off a little bit longer.

"The weight gives you some—"

I punched him in the throat, choking off the rest of his words. He might not feel the pain, but he still needed to breathe.

I kicked the side of his knee, forcing the joint to buckle, and swept his legs out from under him the way Marx and Sam had taught me.

He landed on the floor with a hard smack, and I leaped around his coughing, sputtering form as I darted for the door. I tried to jerk it open, but it only rattled. Then I noticed the padlock over the latch.

"No!" I smacked the door.

Collin would have the key on him somewhere. I whirled to see him picking himself up off the floor.

"Well, that was new," he wheezed, sounding vaguely amused. He coughed and massaged his throat. "You've become quite the feral little creature. I'm guessing that was the sheriff's doing. Teaching you to fight back so you don't get *victimized*. How's that working out for you?"

I searched the room again for anything I might be able to use to defend myself. My gaze landed on a short stool I hadn't noticed before. It must have been behind Collin. A video camera sat on top of it, and a blinking red light indicated that it was recording.

I didn't have time to ponder the fact that Collin intended to record his torture session. He had never done anything like that before.

"There's nowhere to go, Holly. It's just you and me in this little room with plenty of time to play."

He stepped forward, and I shrank away, keeping as much distance between us as possible.

"Just like old times," he said. "Except now there are no parents or caseworkers to get in the way, and no neighbors to hear you scream."

I bumped into the box as I backed away from him, and nearly fell on top of it. Something shifted inside, knocking against the sides.

I cracked the lid with shaking fingers and blinked when I saw a baseball bat lying in the bottom of the box. It looked like the same one Collin had hit me with at Sam's apartment.

I could still feel the deep throbbing reminder all the way from my cheekbone to the back of my skull. I snatched the bat on impulse and took up a defensive stance along the wall.

"You can't hurt me, Holly. But just to be fair, I'll give you three chances to hit me. If you strike out, I'm going to take the bat from you and beat you with it." He paused and added with a shrug, "To be honest, I was going to beat you with it anyway, but at least you feel like you have a chance."

My hands grew slippery with sweat as I gripped the bat. "What do you want from me? Why can't you just leave me alone?"

"Oh, I enjoy you far too much for that. Besides, I've tried others, and they're just . . . not the same. You were always my favorite."

He spoke so casually that he could've been talking about ice cream flavors rather than the seventeen or more women he'd assaulted.

"I knew the moment your caseworker dropped you off that you were the piece I'd been searching for over the years, the elusive spark that I just couldn't find. And I tried repeatedly to find it. But you, Holly, you were my first real thrill."

The bat began to tremble in my hands.

"I think I'll keep you this time. Kind of like my own little pet. I haven't decided just how *long* I'll keep you—weeks, months, maybe a year. I suppose until you bore me."

A year.

My knees felt suddenly weak. He wanted to lock me up like an animal to play with at his leisure . . . for a year.

"I'm curious how far I can push you before you break. No matter what I do to you, you have a tendency to just . . . bounce back. It's fascinating."

"I won't let you break me."

His eyes glittered with eagerness. "Everyone breaks eventually. Most, unfortunately, within hours. You're just a little more resilient, but I've had two years to come up with new ideas."

"You c-can't keep me here," I said, and I couldn't keep the tremor from my voice. "They're gonna look for me and—"

"No one's looking for you. The orphan, the runaway, the woman who lives under the radar so she can disappear at a moment's notice. No one even knows I have you. You're completely alone."

I shook my head. "That's not true."

"Drew, if he survived the blow to the head, which would be unfortunate for the human race given his level of stupidity and cowardice, won't say a word because it would incriminate him. Evelyn scampered away before I stepped inside. And your bag, which was conveniently packed and sitting on the couch, is now in my possession. Do you know what that means, Holly?" He paused before explaining, "Everyone will think you just ran away. Again."

Doubt and fear trickled through me. Was he right? Would they think I had panicked and fled? I had tried to several times before, but . . .

"Sam knows you took me."

"Ah, the Mexican," he said on a sigh. "No great loss there. The man has the personality of a rock. Well . . . had." At my sharply indrawn breath, he added, "Oh, did I spoil the surprise? He's dead. He won't be telling anyone anything."

Grief flooded me. *God, why?* There were so few people in this world I counted as friends, and Sam was one of them. And Jace . . .

Oh, Jace. She loved Sam, and now he was gone because I hadn't left when I should have.

"I might have left him alone, but you made him an obstacle for me, one Drew was more than willing to remove. He just didn't have the spine to do it alone," Collin said. "Imagine my surprise when I realized the man being placed in the cell with me was Sam's disgruntled brother-in-law. And even more surprising was the reason he was there."

Me. Drew had been arrested because I pressed charges to protect Evey.

Collin stepped forward and then ducked back quickly when I swung the bat at him. "Strike one," he said with a grin.

I felt like a mouse trapped in the corner, waiting for the cat to pounce. He was toying with me.

266

"That pretty little crippled friend of yours, probably the only person who truly cared about you, will never forgive you. You're the reason the man she loved is dead."

Jace had opened her heart and her life to me when I desperately needed someone to care about me, and now she was devastated.

Collin took a small step forward, and I flinched back into the wall, my fingers tightening on the bat. "Don't . . . don't come any closer."

"Go ahead and swing."

He had said he would give me three strikes. Not that he was any more trustworthy than the devil himself, but maybe, for the sake of the game he was playing, he wouldn't attack me until I missed him three times.

"Jordan will look for me," I said.

"I hate to break it to you, but your precious sheriff is on the wrong side of the bars at the moment."

"Because you framed him."

He smiled and shrugged. "I did you a favor with that one. He's not the white knight he seems to be."

I didn't know what that was supposed to mean.

"If you think he'll come for you because he spent years looking for his childhood friend, you're overestimating your value," he said. "You're not her; you're just a hollow shell of the girl he remembers, and he knows that now. Do you really think he'll waste any more time looking for me now that he knows the truth?"

I wasn't that girl any more than Jordan was that little boy, innocent and untouched by loss and pain. Life had changed us, but that didn't mean he wouldn't look for me.

"He's my friend," I said.

"Friend?" Collin laughed. "You really are naïve. You think all the time he spends with you, studying you, and gaining your trust is because he wants to be BFFs? He's a man, Holly. All he wants from you is the same thing every other warm-blooded male wants." His gaze moved slowly over me, and my stomach pitched nauseously. "He's just biding his time until you give in."

"You're wrong," I told him, but my words lacked conviction. Jordan agreed to be just friends, but deep down I knew he hoped for more. I could see it in the way he looked at me.

"You might be able to confine him to the friend zone for a while, but the moment he touches you, he won't be able to stop himself from craving more."

My mind flashed back to the moment in Jordan's kitchen when he was brushing flour from my face—the intensity in his eyes, the urge to kiss me—and I realized touching me had only deepened his desire for a physical relationship.

"You're nothing but a conquest to him, Holly. He'll charm you into his bed and then move on to a real woman worth loving. Because let's be honest, no man will ever love a woman as broken and used as you."

I flinched at the brutal truth of those words. I never expected anyone to love me—to be able to see beyond the spiritual and physical scars and accept me for who I was, for what was . . . left of me—but I hoped desperately.

Collin gave me a sympathetic look. "Accept it. You're worthless and you don't *really* matter to anyone. Your value is only skin deep."

His words echoed my insecurities, as if he had pulled them from the darkest places in my mind and given them a voice. I blinked at the tears that misted my eyes. I wouldn't give him the satisfaction of seeing me cry.

"And before you desperately cling to the hope that Detective Marx will come to your rescue, he's not even in the same state," he continued. "He's with his family, and he certainly wouldn't leave them for you."

He prowled along the edges of my reach, and I shifted my sweaty grip on the bat as I followed him with my eyes.

"It was convenient—dear old dad's heart attack. After my first arrangement failed, I figured I would have to kill Marx myself. I even had a plan, but then I overheard the phone call with his mother."

"He'll come back when his dad's better," I said. "He'll know I didn't run away." I had promised him that I wouldn't try to run again, and he knew I kept my promises.

"Maybe. And maybe he will search for you because his conscience won't allow him to look the other way when there's a damsel in distress, but he'll search for you out of obligation, not because he cares about you."

"He cares," I shot back. He had told me he cares. He had yelled at me for not understanding how *much* he cares.

"Marx was raised with Southern Baptist hospitality, Holly. Do you know what that means? Being kind and generous toward people they may not like or know, treating women—even irritating ones—with respect, inviting complete strangers into their home. Does that sound familiar?"

Marx had always been unusually respectful toward me, and I'd asked him before if it was one of his perplexing male Southernisms. Because in my experience, men didn't open doors, pull out chairs, and offer women a hand to their feet. But when he invited me into his home because I needed a safe place to stay, I hadn't even considered that it might stem from the same roots as his manners. I had thought he invited me to stay because he cared for me.

He *does* care.

"You can decide for yourself if his feelings for you are genuine or just a part of his upbringing, but after everything you've cost him, I think it's a pretty simple conclusion," he said. "It wasn't bad enough that you got Jacob killed, but then you forced him to shoot his best friend to protect you. I bet he regrets his decision every time he thinks about it."

I was at least partially responsible for both of their deaths. Jacob had died trying to protect me, and McNera had died trying to kill me. Losing both had devastated Marx.

"And now he's lost Sam because of you. Why not just rip out his heart and stomp on it, Holly? Lucky for him his family doesn't live here. You might get them killed too. You're a walking curse."

I flinched inwardly. My family, Jacob, McNera, Danny, and now Sam. The bodies were piling up at my feet. So many lives. So many precious lives.

"If you really cared about these people, you would've left a long time ago. The best thing you could've done for them was disappear. And now you have."

He took a sharp step forward, and I swung at him on reflex, missing him by a hair.

"Strike two," he taunted.

If I could hit him hard enough in the head, maybe I could knock him out and search him for the key.

"What now, Holly?" he asked, spreading his arms wide. "One swing left. I somehow doubt you're the home-run surprise at the bottom of the ninth."

He took a relaxed step forward, and I shrank back in fear. He took another step, inching steadily closer until I had no choice but to swing and hope I hit him.

He caught the bat an inch from his face and shoved me into the wall. He wrenched it from my fingers and slammed the end of it into my stomach. My breath left me in a rush, and I folded over on the floor in agony.

"Looks like you struck out." He twirled the bat lazily through the air as he circled me. "That's pretty consistent with your life. One failure after another."

I struggled to breathe through the pain.

"Eventually you'll realize that none of these people you've attached yourself to care about you. You're like the kicked puppy that everyone feels sorry for but nobody really wants."

He kicked me just to drive the point home, and I curled into a ball on the floor with my eyes squeezed shut against a flood of tears.

I heard him crouch beside me, and the heavy bat thumped on the floor beside my head. "Let's have a little fun, shall we?"

28

I stared at the gray stone walls of my prison, illuminated only by the pale-yellow glow of a security light near the ceiling, and wondered if they might be the last thing I ever saw.

There was no way out of this room.

There were no windows I could break, and Collin had padlocked the door from the outside after he was finished with his *fun*.

I had drifted in and out of sleep after my body fought its way through the initial bouts of shock, and now I lay on the chilly cement floor, knees drawn to my chest, shivering.

He had taken my socks and shoes, leaving me with nothing but the thin layer of clothes I wore for warmth.

I didn't remember much from last night. Sometime during the torment, I had crawled inside myself, trying to hide from the unending agony.

There were fragments of memory floating around in my mind—things too painful to dwell on—but I had no desire to piece them back together. I wanted to forget.

For the first time in my life, I wished I could summon the amnesia that had stolen my childhood memories, that I could use it to wipe away the past twenty-four hours.

But that wouldn't save me from this place, and it wouldn't bring back my friend—my frustratingly logical friend who cared more deeply about people than he would ever allow anyone to see.

I had a sudden image of his too-serious expression as he walked in those wheezing Darth Vader slippers.

A bubble of grief swelled in my chest and popped, sending hot tears down my face. "Oh, Sam," I whispered into the silence.

I hadn't fired the bullet that killed him any more than I had set the fire that ended the lives of seven innocent people, but I was responsible just the same. I had chosen to stay even though I knew my past would catch up with me and destroy everyone and everything I cared about.

You're a walking curse. If you really cared about these people, you would've left a long time ago. The best thing you could've done for them was disappear.

I closed my eyes and released a choked breath that longed to be a sob. I mentally sifted through my vault of soothing Bible verses, seeking anything to fight off the hopelessness creeping into my soul.

There is nowhere I can go for refuge, and no one cares for me. So I cry out to you, Lord, "you are my refuge". Deliver me from my tormenters, for they are too strong for me. Break me out of this prison, so I can give thanks to your name.

I couldn't remember the book of the Bible or the chapter, but I clung to those words as I lay on the floor of that dark room, repeating them in my mind until I could no longer hear the echoes of Collin's taunting voice.

I counted the stone blocks on the wall in front of me to pass the time—seventy-six, the same amount as the last twenty or so times I had counted them—and created shapes out of the stains on the ceiling.

When I heard footsteps approaching, my heart skipped a terrified beat, and my eyes snapped to the door. I wasn't sure how much time had passed since Collin left, but it felt like forever and not long enough.

God, please don't leave me alone with him.

The light overhead flicked on, and the padlock clunked against the outside of the metal door.

I dragged myself up against the wall, desperate to put as much distance as possible between me and the man who stepped into the room.

Collin looked refreshed and rested, and delight sparkled in his eyes when he looked at me. "How's my favorite little bird?"

I tried not to let my fear show, but I was breathing too hard, and every breath felt like inhaling shards of glass.

He didn't bring the bat with him this time, but that was a small comfort. He had other methods. I wrapped an arm protectively around my ribs and cast his boots an anxious look.

He locked the door and dropped the key into his pants pocket. I considered how I might get it while I watched him set up the camera for his next twisted home movie.

He had recorded everything last night, and I didn't want to imagine what he might do with the video.

My heart punched against my aching ribs when he walked toward me. He crouched less than a foot from me, and I curled closer to the wall.

"I enjoyed last night," he said, brushing the backs of his fingers down my cheek.

I stared hard at the floor as I gripped the frayed edges of my torn sweater with trembling fingers, holding it together.

Collin's fingers grazed my throat, and I flinched, terrified that he was going to choke me again.

"Of course, last night was just the introduction. We'll get to the more exciting bits soon enough," he said, tracing the collar of my sweater in a way that was too familiar.

Fear burned the lining of my stomach.

He let his hand drop to my forearm, and I tried to resist as he pulled it away from my stomach, but it hurt too badly.

"How's the wrist?"

He pushed up the sleeve of my sweater to reveal the swollen, purple bruising. I wasn't sure if my wrist was broken; I could still use it, but putting weight on it sent bolts of pain up my arm.

"Looks like it hurts," he said, observing the injury with a small smile.

I prepared myself for more pain, but he released me. I wrapped my arm back around my stomach, tucking my injured wrist against my side.

He held out a bottle of water. "Thirsty?"

I eyed the offering warily. My throat was as dry as sandpaper, but he was never kind or generous without a motive. "Why?"

"Because I have plans for you, and I can't have you dying of something as mundane as dehydration."

If I was going to die here, I would rather die of dehydration than any of the other cruel methods he could think up. I leaned my head against the wall and looked away, ignoring the offering.

"Always so difficult," he said with a slight smile. "I could just fill a bucket with water and hold your head under until you drink. If you drown, I'll just resuscitate you and repeat. Or you could take the bottle. It's your choice."

One look into his eyes told me he wasn't bluffing. But it was the glimmer of interest that frightened me the most, like he was imagining the possibilities.

I took the bottle.

I felt dehydrated after the blow to the stomach that left me retching on and off throughout night, and the water felt blissful as it trickled down my aching, dry throat.

"Good girl," Collin said with a smirk.

I glowered at him and seriously considered spitting the water in his face.

His smirk broadened into a full grin. "I know what you're thinking. It's written all over your face. But if you do it, I promise you'll regret it."

I took another sip, glaring hatefully at him, and swallowed. My bruised stomach rebelled at having something in it, and I nearly choked trying to keep the few swallows of water down.

Collin took the bottle from me and screwed the cap back on. "I guess we'll be taking that slow."

He sat down across from me, legs folded, and pulled something from his pocket. It was a flip lighter. A fresh current of fear bolted through me. He had hurt me in many unthinkable ways before, but never fire.

"You're shaking," he observed.

I tightened my arms around myself, but I couldn't stop trembling. "It's . . . cold."

"I can warm you up." He flicked the lighter and a small flame ignited.

My heart rate picked up, and I tried not to focus on the flame flickering through the air. "This place . . . it's not . . . habitable for a year. I won't survive."

He gave me a patient look. "I'm not ignorant, Holly. I have everything we need stored in another room. Food, water, hygiene supplies. I also have bedding and clean clothes." He snapped the lid of the lighter shut and then open again, sparking another flame with his thumb. "You can earn them."

Like a treat for good behavior? I would settle for the cement floor and my current clothes. Maybe if I was filthy, he wouldn't touch me again.

"My parents, unintelligent as they were, did teach me to always have a plan," he said.

And he was masterful at plans. He had orchestrated everything just to get what he wanted, and somehow when things didn't go according to plan, he still succeeded.

"I brought you something." He pulled a folded newspaper from his pocket and tossed it on the floor in front of me. "This morning's paper. I think you'll find it enlightening."

I glanced at the paper with uncertainty, then stretched out a hand to pull it closer. I smoothed it out on the floor and skimmed the articles, my hope sinking with every turn of the page.

"Notice what isn't in there?" he asked.

Me. There was nothing, not even a hint that I might be missing, let alone abducted, and I double-checked to make sure all the pages were there.

"I've had you for seventeen hours, and no one's even looking."

My throat tightened with emotion. I wanted to crumple the cruel paper and throw it across the room, but I couldn't let him see how deeply the news hurt me.

I closed the paper as steadily as I could and said, "A lot of people go missing, and they don't put them in the paper. It doesn't mean anything."

The look he gave me as he took the newspaper back told me he recognized the lie in my words.

"I need to use the bathroom," I said.

My bladder felt like it might burst.

He snapped the lid of the lighter open and shut like a habitual smoker as he studied me. "Are you asking for privacy?"

I glanced at the black bucket and roll of toilet paper in the corner and grimaced. "I wanna use a real bathroom."

"No. Next request?"

Frustrated, I mentally struggled for a way to convince him to take me out of this room. I would never be able to wrestle the key away from him, which meant this was my only hope of escape.

Then I realized I had one advantage: he wanted me alive. "If you don't take me to a bathroom, I'm just gonna go right here and die of hypothermia."

A person could get hypothermia in 50-degree weather if they were damp long enough, and it was colder than that.

One black eyebrow lifted in consideration. "Wouldn't want that, now would we?" He tucked the lighter back into his pocket and stood. He grabbed my upper arm and pulled me to my feet.

The room spun around me and I swayed, trying to find my footing. My legs felt as limp as wet paper.

"If you're hoping to escape, it won't work," he said. He paused to grab his precious video camera, then hauled me toward the door.

My feet slid and stumbled across the floor as we left the room, and every movement sent an intense wave of nausea through me. If I hadn't already emptied my stomach five times over, I would've thrown up.

My eyes danced around the space outside the small, dark room, soaking up the details like a sponge. It was a warehouse—vast and empty—with checkerboards of plywood and glass for windows.

Every surface was painted with dust, and cobwebs swayed lazily from the ceiling and corners. This place had been abandoned for quite some time.

"So how does it feel knowing you're all alone and no one's coming to save you?" Collin asked as he pulled me along.

My gaze fixed on the staircase about a hundred yards behind us, a possible exit, as I muttered absently, "I'm never alone."

If I can just make it to the steps . . .

But I couldn't even seem to walk in a straight line. How was I ever going to run?

"Unless you have another personality keeping you company in that interesting head of yours, you're very much alone."

I spared him a glare. "I'm *never* alone."

He thought about that for a moment. "Ah, I forgot you *believers* think your Jesus is everywhere at all times. Must be a busy guy. I wonder, if He's so omnipresent, where was He the night your family was being murdered?"

The question struck a chord deep inside; it was one of many questions I had asked God: *Why my family? Why didn't You save them? Where were You?*

I didn't know if I would ever know the answers, but I did know that God didn't condone what happened that night. It was an act of evil, not of God.

"When you were kicked from foster home to foster home because no one wanted to keep you, was He with you then?"

He paused to let me answer, but I stayed silent.

"What was it, twelve foster homes? And not a single person thought you were worth keeping?"

Despite my efforts to be the perfect child, none of the foster parents had wanted me, and the repeated rejection left a wound that would never fully heal.

For years, I had wondered what I'd done wrong to make them reject me. I wondered if it was because of my unknown past or because I was too much of a burden. At the age of thirteen, I discovered the simple truth: I was unlovable.

"Where was your loving God all those nights I made you regret being alive?" he continued.

My tongue felt dry and heavy, but I forced myself to speak. "God never said life would be easy. He never promised we wouldn't suffer. Just that when we do, He'll be with us to help us through it."

"Seems to me He left you to suffer alone an awful lot. Just like now." He pushed open the door to the women's bathroom and flicked on the light before shoving me inside.

I stumbled up against the lone stall, and my head swam with dizziness.

Don't pass out. Don't . . . pass out.

I leaned hard against the stall for a few seconds, trying to stay on my feet. I had no idea what he would do to me if I passed out. Maybe I would be safer unconscious.

"Face it, Holly, your God doesn't love you any more than any of those families did. He doesn't want you."

"I know what you're trying to do," I said between shallow, rapid breaths. "You're trying to take away everyone and everything I care about so I have nothing left. But no matter what you do to me, you can't take my God from me."

"Really?" he said with interest.

I felt his body move behind me, and terror seized me. Too close. He was too close.

His stomach pressed against my back, and his fingers traced the length of my belt all the way around my waist, settling on the buckle. I realized two things in that moment: the warmth radiating from him felt like a furnace against my cold body, and he was going to hurt me . . . right here in the bathroom.

"Why don't you pray to Him now and see if He stops me from what I'm about to do," he suggested.

I bit down on my lip to keep from whimpering in fear and squeezed my eyes shut.

Lord, I can't go through this again. Please.

I felt Collin stiffen against my back, then withdraw his arms. "We'll finish this later." He walked back to the door to peer out, as if he had heard something.

I could've melted into a puddle of relief on the floor at the reprieve, but I moved on slow, shaky legs into the stall. I locked the door behind me and rested my forehead against it, trying not to think about the fact that he was just outside the door and this small lock wouldn't protect me.

"You'll recognize the truth eventually, Holly. Even the fact that this divine perfectionist of a God you so desperately and naïvely cling to doesn't care about you. You'll never be good enough," he called out.

I knew I would never be good enough for God; no one was good enough. But that was the glory of His love: we didn't need to be, because He loves us when we're hopelessly lost and broken.

He even loves Collin despite his cruelty. That thought sent anger scorching through me. I didn't want Him to love Collin. I wanted Him to hate him as much as I did. He deserved hatred. Hatred and pain and . . .

I clamped down on those thoughts. Those weren't me. Those were fear and anger talking, and they would destroy me faster than

Collin ever could. I pushed my anger aside and reached for God, my heart and soul scrabbling for a safe place in this Hell.

God, I'm so scared.

"Hurry up," Collin demanded, jarring me into motion. I scrambled to obey, afraid he would grow impatient and force his way into the stall. I heard the outer door tap shut as I sat down, and I would've leaned down to see if his feet were still there, but it hurt too much to bend forward.

My eyes took in every detail of the bathroom stall: the graffiti, names, and phone numbers marking the walls and door. I traced my finger over a message scratched into the blue paint: "Jenny was here."

Yeah, me too.

Someone had written "John 3:16" on the wall in black permanent marker. If this were any other situation, I might have laughed at the fact that someone had vandalized the stall to spread God's message.

I wondered about the light buzzing above me. Maybe the building was wired to leech electricity from another building, or the electric bill had been paid in advance before the business closed. Maybe Collin had rigged it somehow. If he intended to keep me here for a year, he no doubt wanted to be comfortable.

What part of town was the building in? Was I even in New York City anymore?

I finished, dressed quickly, and stepped out of the stall. To my surprise, Collin wasn't waiting impatiently by the wall. I looked around the bathroom, and my eyes locked on the small window near the ceiling.

I grabbed the metal trash can and overturned it. I stepped onto it and braced my left side when pain nearly took me to the floor. I breathed through it, then stretched onto my toes to peer out the grimy window.

There were other buildings, but none of them looked any more occupied than this one. I looked down at the paved alleyway. I was on the second, maybe even the third floor. Even if I could crawl out the window, how could I get down without splattering like a pumpkin on the pavement?

I searched the street for people, but there was no one. How was I supposed to get out of this mess?

The bathroom door opened, and I stiffened.

Collin's eyebrows lifted when he saw me standing by the window. "That escape attempt won't end well for you."

I pressed my back against the wall. I didn't want to go back into that dark room with no windows and a padlocked door.

Collin smirked as he strode toward me. "Thinking about resisting?"

Oh, I was thinking about it.

But realistically, I knew I didn't have a chance. Not right now. This space was too narrow, and he was between me and the door. If I tried to get past him, he would probably just beat me unconscious. All I would get for my efforts was a fresh headache.

I wasn't liking that plan.

I climbed down off the trash can, but I couldn't force my legs to move any closer to him.

Collin's perfect white teeth flashed in a grin. "So submissive."

He called it submission; I called it strategy. I lifted my chin and glared at him, which made him laugh. He snagged my arm in a tight grip and dragged me toward the door.

The moment we stepped out of the bathroom, I fixed my attention on the staircase. This would be my best opportunity to escape. Once he locked me in that room again, I would be trapped.

An irritatingly logical voice—like a tiny Sam—whispered through the back of my mind that I was outmatched: I was exhausted and in pain, and Collin outweighed me by fifty or sixty pounds, if not more, all of which was lean muscle and height.

I knew the odds weren't in my favor, but what could I possibly lose by trying? The consequences for failing would be the same as the consequences for not trying at all.

I decided to take my chances.

I wrenched my arm free of Collin's grip, toppling sideways off balance, then bolted for the steps.

Fire ignited in my chest, burning through my ribs into my lungs, and sending agony dripping like hot wax over my insides. Adrenaline and sheer desperation were all that kept me from doubling over.

There was a sliding door on the bottom floor, a way out, and I was so focused on it that I almost missed the suspicious shimmer on the floor in front of me.

I skidded to a stop mere centimeters from the sea of glittering shards that stood between me and the steps. I surveyed the expanse of glass—it was too far to jump over—and then looked down at my bare feet.

"Did you ever wonder what I did with the glass from your windows?" Collin asked, his approaching footsteps relaxed and confident behind me.

He had broken into my apartment in February, stolen all my clothes, and swept up the shattered glass to take with him. I had known he would do something cruel with it.

"There's something . . . poetic about you being trapped by your own windows," he said.

That was why he had taken my shoes. He knew I would try to escape, and he didn't think I would walk through the glass in my bare feet.

But the alternative was worse.

I yanked off my sweater and used it to clear a path, ignoring the tiny glass slivers that pricked the bottoms of my feet as I made my way to the steps.

I heard Collin pick up his pace, and I hurried down the staircase, clutching at the railing for steadiness. I was halfway down the steps when I was suddenly jerked backward by my tank top.

Collin had managed to snag a fistful of the material. He hooked an arm around my waist and started to pick me up, but I thrashed and twisted, knocking him off balance. We tumbled the rest

283

of the way down the steps and landed hard on the cement floor at the bottom.

I exhaled a pained breath, sending a plume of dust into the air, and looked at the door just feet away. It felt like every bone in my body was broken, and I couldn't seem to pull my sprawled limbs together.

I had to get up.

I heard Collin's breathless laughter behind me. "I forgot how dangerous you could be with a flight of steps."

I tried to push myself up, but my injured wrist gave out. I cradled it against my stomach and pushed myself up with just my left arm.

I stumbled to the door, desperate to escape, and tried to push it open. It jammed on something, but there was a narrow crack that I might be able to squeeze through. Before I could make it more than a few inches, Collin grabbed my arm and wrenched me back inside.

"Where do you think you're going?" He snatched me up by the waist, gripping tighter as I twisted and kicked at the metal door. "You're more slippery than I remember. I guess I'll have to be more careful."

He carried me up the steps and back to that room—that windowless cell—and flung me inside. I tried to reach the door before he could slam it shut, but I wasn't fast enough. I pounded my hands against it and screamed.

I heard the padlock snap into place, and my hope sank. I was trapped. The light overhead winked out, and the room plunged into blackness.

29

I lost all sense of time in that dark room, minutes seeming to stretch into hours and hours into days.

I spent most of my time curled up beneath the security light—a tiny beacon of hope in an ocean of blackness—wishing I could feel the warmth of it all the way to my frozen bones. I had shaken out my sweater and wrapped it around myself, but it wasn't enough.

I listened to the squeaks and groans of the old building as I tried to think of another way to escape. I had pounded on the door and screamed until my voice gave out, hoping someone might help me, but the only person who heard me laughed on the other side of the door.

He didn't give me another opportunity to escape. Sometimes he unlocked the door and cracked it open just enough to slide in a plate of food and water, and other times . . . he flipped on the overhead light, but he never let me out.

I quickly learned to dread when that light came on because it meant he would soon follow.

I wanted to scream at God and demand an explanation for why He was letting this happen to me, but I didn't have the strength. So I let the anger, pain, and bitterness escape in a flood of silent tears until exhaustion swept me under.

I drifted in and out of dreams, some so frightening that I woke in a panic, only to find myself in an even more terrifying reality, and others so comforting that I wanted to cling to them.

I was lost in one of those comforting dreams when something roused me. I peeled open my heavy eyelids and stared at the man crouched next to me.

My heart leaped with hope when I realized it was Marx, but then he evaporated like steam, replaced by bright walls and cracked cement floors.

Bright walls . . .

Every muscle in my body seized up with fear when I realized the overhead light was on. That must have been what had woken me. I heard the padlock release on the outside of the door a second before it opened, and I knew by the menacing smile on Collin's lips and the camera in his hand that he was going to stay a while.

I closed my eyes and folded into a ball on the floor after he left, too numb and exhausted to cry. I wished I could will my body to stop breathing, just to bring an end to this nightmare.

Jesus, I'm so tired of the pain. I just want it to stop. Please . . . make it stop.

Collin's irritated voice rose outside of my prison, loudly enough that I could hear every clipped word. "Because you brought the wrong one!"

Another voice, too muffled to understand, said something in response. It took my sluggish mind a few seconds to recognize the significance of that voice. Someone else was out there.

I tried to scream for help, but the strangled sound that escaped my lips was barely a whisper. My bruised vocal cords refused to obey me.

I fumbled for the bottle of water Collin had left and used what little strength I had to throw it. It hit the door with an echoing thud, and silence fell on the other side.

I waited with baited breath, praying that someone would find me.

The soft voice spoke again, their intonation implying a question, but I still couldn't make out the words.

"Holly's fine," Collin replied, his tone now perfectly relaxed, as if unconcerned that the person might discover he was holding a woman captive. "She's just throwing a tantrum."

The other voice spoke again, and Collin's answer sent a fresh ripple of fear through me. "I'll let you have some time with her after you finish cleaning things up."

I'll let you have some time with her. Did that mean whoever was out there knew I was being held against my will, and they were going to hurt me too?

Shoes tapped toward the room, and I recognized the rhythm of Collin's footsteps. I had hoped so many times to hear a different set—footsteps belonging to someone who might help me—but they were always his.

I stared up at the dark lightbulb, waiting for the inevitable. It flicked on, and the door opened with a creak of old hinges.

I watched Collin as he stepped into the room, all easy movements and relaxed posture. I envied that; I wished I could shut down my body's ability to feel pain, to feel nothing.

He picked up the bottle of water I had lobbed at the door. "If I didn't know better, I would think you were trying to get my attention. Miss me that much?"

I hated his voice. I wanted to wrap my hands around his throat and make it stop, like he had mine so many times before.

"Sorry for the interruption earlier," he said, a wicked smile teasing his lips. "I intended to spend a few more hours of quality time together. But as you heard, we have company."

I dragged myself up against the wall when I noticed the camera in his hand. He was here to continue where he left off. I pulled my torn sweater tight around me and hugged myself as he came to crouch in front of me.

"I told you I figured you out—the way you shut down and hide until the pain is over." He brushed the tangles of hair from my face, the gesture disturbingly gentle. "I can see it in your face right now. So I arranged a little incentive to encourage you to be more open about your feelings."

He turned on the camera and angled the display toward me. There was a woman frozen on the screen—tall and slim, with her wrists and ankles bound, and a black sack over her head—and I recognized her lanky frame even before he pressed play.

She was squirming in the trunk of a car, and I heard her desperate voice cry out, "Who are you? Why are you doing this?"

Collin paused the video. "I assume you recognize that grating voice."

I fought not to react as I stared at the image of Jace, but panic was fluttering under my rib cage like a crazed bird. She couldn't be here. He couldn't have her.

"I would've preferred Maya—I know how much you care about the little ones—but I think Jace will do nicely," he said.

I swallowed the words in my throat as I met his eyes. Begging him not to hurt her wouldn't keep her safe; it would only amuse him.

He clicked a button, turning the screen black, and I wanted to cry and plead with him to turn it back on, to let me see her again.

"She's still in one piece. How long that lasts is entirely up to you." He glanced at a plate of untouched apples he had left on one of his earlier visits. "Before we do anything else, you're going to eat."

I didn't think I *could* eat. I could barely keep water down. Something felt . . . wrong inside.

He dipped one of the browning apple slices in peanut butter and pressed it to my lips. I turned my face away.

"I won't let you starve yourself to death, Holly. I've waited far too long for this. So either you eat, or I go pay your friend a visit. She's not exactly my type, but I can work with it."

I shuddered inwardly at the thought of him touching her. Jace had her strengths, but enduring fear and physical pain weren't among them. I needed to protect her.

Begrudgingly, I opened my mouth and took a small bite of apple and peanut butter. Eating something he'd touched made me gag, but somehow I managed to swallow.

He fed me every single apple slice coated in sticky peanut butter, pulling the plate out of my reach each time I tried to do it myself. Tears of humiliation stung my eyes, but I blinked them back.

The food hurt going down, but it hurt even worse when it came back up a few minutes later because my stomach couldn't handle it.

Collin sighed. "I guess we'll have to clean you up before we continue our fun. And then there's someone who wants to see you." He pulled me to my feet.

Pain turned my body liquid, and my legs melted beneath me. He shifted his grip to my waist to hold me up, and little black dots danced in my vision.

I was sure I was going to pass out from the pain.

We were moving before I even realized what was happening. I hadn't been out of my cell since my first escape attempt, and the thin streams of sunlight filtering through the windows were almost too bright.

After being cooped up in that awful room for who knew how long, I craved the feeling of the sun on my skin, to cup it in my hands and watch it shine through my fingers.

My gaze swept blearily over the warehouse, searching for any sign of Jace. There were too many rooms. How would I ever find her? I didn't even know which direction to go.

We stopped at a storage closet before continuing to the restroom. Collin hadn't been exaggerating when he said he was prepared. The shelves were lined with toiletries, blankets, and food.

I recognized my clothes folded on one of the side shelves, as well as my travel bag that I had packed and taken to Sam's apartment. He grabbed a pack of moist towelettes from a shelf and my travel bag before closing the door.

He marched me to the bathroom and pushed me in. "Clean yourself up and change your clothes." He shoved the items at me. "You smell like vomit."

I had managed to throw up on my sweater and the ends of my hair.

I wanted to fling everything back at him, to tell him that I wouldn't clean myself up for him, but I was afraid he would take it out on Jace.

I hugged the items to my chest and staggered into the stall. I sagged back against the door and stared at the ceiling, weary to my soul, and far too weak to stand up straight.

I dropped the items to the floor and stripped slowly, wincing as pain knifed through me with even the smallest movements.

I sponged away the sweat and grime on my skin with the towelettes the best that I could and cleaned the ends of my hair. It made me feel marginally human again.

I pulled on fresh clothes, my fingers trembling so badly that I had difficulty sliding my belt through the loops of my jeans. As I tugged my purple sweater over my head, the lingering scent of Marx's cologne sent a pang of soul-deep longing through me.

It brought with it memories of warmth and safety, of late-night movies wrapped in a blanket, of laughter, and of the first man outside of my father that I ever truly trusted.

I missed him . . . which was foolish. I doubted he even cared that I was gone.

That single thought battered against every memory of Marx's arms around me, every kiss he placed in my hair, and I felt the precious memories cracking under the assault.

Had I been so desperate for someone to care about me that I fooled myself into believing it was possible?

I pressed the sweater to my nose, drawing in the scent one last time, before letting the memories go. That part of my life was over.

I sank onto the toilet seat and rested my forehead against the side of the stall.

I wondered what Collin would do with my body when he was through with me. Burn it? Bury it? Leave it lying here for someone else to find?

I hated the idea of someone stumbling across my broken, ravaged body. And I didn't want to be a victim on a coroner's table, a series of gruesome photographs in a file on some detective's desk. I hoped he buried me. At least that would be some semblance of a grave.

Only three-hundred-and-sixty-something more days of agony and degradation to go before it was over. Or was it three-hundred-and-fifty-something now?

Fear and despair mixed together to form a brief moment of hysteria, and I almost laughed, but it turned to a sob at the last second, and I choked it down.

God, I can't do this.

"Do I need to come in there?"

I flinched at Collin's voice just outside the door. It made me want to pull my feet up onto the toilet seat like a frightened child and pretend to be invisible.

He would just break down the door and drag me out, and I had a feeling he would enjoy that more. I gathered up my dirty clothes and stood, swaying dangerously before finding my balance.

I opened the door to find Collin directly on the other side, waiting. He caught a few strands of my hair and let it glide through his fingers. "Much better."

I swallowed and looked away.

"Put the clothes in the trash," he instructed.

I clutched the clothes tighter, reluctant to let the extra layers of warmth go, then forced myself to drop them into the trash can. I knew he wouldn't let me keep them, and I wouldn't beg.

"Brush your teeth."

He nudged me toward the sink, and I stumbled, barely catching myself on the edge of the counter.

My toothbrush and tube of toothpaste were already on the sink. I scrubbed my teeth obediently, grateful to be rid of the bitter bile coating my tongue, and rinsed my mouth.

I wiped my damp lips with the back of my hand and straightened, catching my reflection in the cracked mirror. I immediately looked away from the battered ghost staring back at me.

Collin lifted a hand to pull my hair over my shoulder and away from my neck, and I shuddered. His tender touches disturbed me more than violence. I understood violence.

"I enjoy seeing my fingerprints on your pale skin," he said, tracing the bruises on my throat.

I met his eyes in the mirror, unable to miss the desire burning in them. I thought about pounding my fists against the glass until it shattered, then picking up the sharpest piece and stabbing him with it.

Or myself.

A sense of relief flooded me at that last thought. Even if I couldn't reach that door on the bottom floor, even if no one came for me, I had a way out.

"There's someone here who wants to see you," he said, his fingers still lingering on my neck. "Let's go say hi." He pulled me toward the door.

The moment we stepped out of the bathroom, my gaze landed on a tall, hooded figure standing by the railing.

My pulse jumped as I took in the nearly six-foot figure in a black hooded sweatshirt and black pants. He was turned away, and I couldn't see his face, but I knew this must be Collin's accomplice— the man who wanted some time with me.

Fresh, acidic fear pooled in my stomach, and I tried to resist, but Collin dragged me forward with little effort.

"Well, say hello," he suggested.

Long fingers pushed back the hood as the figure turned toward us, revealing . . . a woman.

There was something familiar about her, and it took me a moment to see through the brown contacts and dyed blonde hair to the blue-eyed brunette I remembered.

I was staring at a dead woman.

30

"Rachel?" I asked, my voice thin with disbelief. When Marx found her blood and hair in the trunk of her husband's car, I thought Darin had killed her. But she looked perfectly healthy, if a little bruised.

"Hi, Holly," she said with a beaming smile that didn't fit this terrifying situation.

"Rachel's been eagerly waiting to see you," Collin explained. "But she had a few things to take care of first."

It took a moment for his words to settle, and then the scattered pieces slowly came together. I had been right about Collin having an accomplice, but I had been wrong in assuming it was a man.

The black platform boots Rachel wore put her somewhere just shy of six feet tall, and the loose dark clothes obscured her femininity. And the bruises on her face . . .

She was the attacker from the bathroom, the one I had punched and kicked into a stall when she tried to take Maya.

"It's so good to see you," she said.

I felt betrayed, and the only word I could seem to form was, "Why?"

"Because you were nice to me, maybe even my friend. I always enjoy seeing my friends."

I blinked in confusion. "You're helping him?" My voice was so hoarse and weak that it was unrecognizable.

"And you, silly," she said, still with that disconcerting smile. "I helped bring the two of you back together. He's been looking for you for years, and then suddenly there you are!"

"He abducted me, Rachel. He brought me to a warehouse. He's locking me in a room with nothing."

She shook her head. "This is just temporary. Until he finds the perfect home for the two of you."

I doubted he had any intention of moving me. But if he did, I would only be trading one prison for another.

"Please, Rachel," I pleaded. "Please . . . help us. Help Jace."

Confusion tugged her eyebrows together. "What do you mean? I brought her here so you're not lonely when Collin's away."

She had abducted Jace?

"I wanted to bring Maya, but you wouldn't let me. I thought maybe if I took her, you would follow. But . . . then that man came in." Her face pinched at the memory. "They were keeping you and Collin apart, and I knew I had to separate you from them. But that was harder than I thought it would be."

Separate me from—

"Who did you think was tailing your friends?" Collin whispered into my hair, bringing clarity to my jumbled thoughts.

"You were driving the red car?" I asked Rachel. She hadn't just tried to snatch Maya, she had tried to *kill* Jordan in that alley. And she'd followed Marx, probably with the same intention. "Why? Why would you try to hurt the people I care about?"

She licked her lips nervously. "Collin said he would protect me from my husband if I . . . if I helped him with this."

"And I have," Collin said.

"You didn't protect anyone," I snapped. "Her husband's in jail for killing seven people."

Darin Glass might have started the fire, but I didn't doubt for a second that Collin was the man behind it. He had probably manipulated Darin the same way he was manipulating Rachel now.

"Technically he's in jail for eight murders, since they think he murdered his wife too. I wonder if they'll ever figure out that he's innocent," he said. Then, in a voice that sent shivers crawling down the back of my neck, he said, "Well, innocent of murder."

He'd framed her husband? Was that how he was *protecting* her from him? "He didn't—"

"Kill anyone? No. And neither did I."

But if neither of them had started the fire, then . . .

A sick feeling pooled in my stomach as I looked back at Rachel. The idea was so horrifying that I could barely put it into words. "You . . . you started the fire?"

Rachel shifted her weight uneasily. "I had to. Collin said it was the only way to be free."

I thought about all those women and children who died, trapped in a building that was supposed to protect them. I thought about Maya, whose mother and home had been ripped away in a single night.

It was too much.

I closed my eyes against the tears, but I felt the heat of them as they burned down my cheeks.

"Betrayal hurts, doesn't it?" Collin whispered, and I realized too late that I had given him the tears he craved.

This was what he wanted. He could've chosen any thug to burn down the shelter—he had the money to pay them—but he had chosen Rachel because he knew it would make the wound that much deeper. This was all a part of his cruel game.

"Please, Holly, you have to understand," Rachel pleaded, and I opened my eyes. "Darin was . . . he was never gonna stop. Beth Anne told me I should do whatever I needed to do to get away from him. And I did."

I felt a flash of hatred for her. "Beth Anne took you in. She helped you and gave you a safe place to stay. And you *murdered* her. You killed five women and two children. *Children,* Rachel!"

She flinched at the venom in my voice and dug her fingers into her hair. "No, no, no. You're supposed to understand. He said you would understand."

Collin's silent laughter ruffled my hair, and my anger and hatred abruptly drained away, leaving nothing but pity and sadness behind.

Rachel had always been fragile, and Collin had taken those fractured pieces and twisted them into something he could use.

"Rachel."

She looked at me, black tears streaking down her face.

"Please. You have to tell someone where we are. You can't just leave us here."

Rachel wiped at her cheeks with the heels of her palms, smearing the black mascara across her face. "You'll be okay. He'll take care of you."

"He's . . . hurting me."

Collin rested his chin on my head and squeezed me tighter against him, sending sparkles of agony across my vision.

"A tumble down the steps," he was saying when my head cleared enough to track the conversation again. "You know how clumsy she can be."

Rachel bit her bottom lip and nodded, but I saw the uncertainty in her eyes as she studied me. "But her . . . her neck. It's—"

"A wonder she didn't break it in the fall, I know. She really does need to be more careful. But it looks worse than it is. She'll be fine."

I watched the internal battle play across Rachel's face as she looked between us, and then I saw the veil of rationalization, borne of years of abuse, fall over her eyes.

Any hope that she would help me vanished.

"Oh, Holly," she said, stepping forward and taking one of my hands in hers. "I know change is hard, but everything will be okay. Things are the way they're supposed to be now. I'm free now and safe, and you're with the man who loves you. Everything is perfect."

Perfect.

Jace and I were going to die in this place, but her world was perfect.

I pulled my hand from hers, and if not for Collin's arm locked around my waist, I would've stepped away from her. "None of us are safe, Rachel. If you won't help me, then you should leave while you can."

She blinked in confusion. "But I was hoping we could catch up. It's been over a year and—"

"Collin is a monster, and he will hurt you without a second thought."

"No, he wouldn't hurt me. He promised."

Collin grunted in amusement. "I lied." He shoved her so suddenly and forcefully that she didn't have a chance to react.

She shrieked as she toppled back over the low railing. I cringed and looked away when I heard the muffled slap of her body on the floor below.

Collin leaned over the railing, pulling me with him, and called out, "How did it feel?"

Silence met his question, and I reluctantly dragged my gaze back to the motionless body lying on the cement, a halo of red expanding around her head.

"Hm," he grunted. "I guess she's dead."

He had murdered her without a second of hesitation. It didn't surprise me—I had always known he was capable—but that made it no less disturbing.

I stared at her lifeless body, remembering the frightened woman I had broken plates with, the woman I had mourned for.

"Why?" I heard myself ask.

"She outlived her usefulness. To be fair, you did warn her, but she was too stupid to understand."

Outlived her usefulness . . .

We were all going to end up broken and bleeding on the floor, discarded when we were no longer *useful*. I imagined Jace's body lying next to Rachel's, her bubbly blue eyes hollowed out by death.

The mental image sent a shiver through me.

"Now, about the fun I had planned for us." Unexpectedly, Collin wrapped an arm around my throat and pulled me onto my toes.

I clutched at his arm and scrambled to find my footing on the cement floor. I couldn't breathe.

Marx's voice drifted up from my memory, cutting through the panic: *Grab his elbow, pivot, turn your head, and duck, Holly.* I had done this before. I had trained for this very moment.

Distantly, I heard Collin describing what he was going to do to me, but I was too busy mentally recounting the steps of the escape maneuver to truly hear him.

I grabbed his elbow, pivoted my right leg behind his, turned my head, and ducked out, leaving both of us off balance. I stumbled and fell, but I crawled across the floor until I could get my feet beneath me.

I was so light-headed.

My eyes grazed the various rooms, any one of which Jace could have been trapped in, and then landed on the steps.

If I could get out, I could get help.

I tried to cross the open expanse to reach the steps, but I could barely breathe, and the room started to dip and bend around me like a fun house.

The windows at the far end blurred into a kaleidoscope of light and dark, and I couldn't focus. I fell back to my hands and knees and crawled toward the steps.

I gulped in air, but I couldn't seem to get enough. It had to have something to do with the excruciating pain in my chest.

I collapsed to my stomach, too dizzy and disoriented to pull myself another inch. The steps were so far away. I saw Collin's warped figure approaching, and I told myself I had to get up, to get help . . . a moment before blackness descended.

31

*P*ain was the first sensation I became aware of as I woke. Everything from my ankles to the roots of my hair throbbed.

I opened my eyes and stared into the blackness that enveloped me. I blinked, waiting for my vision to adjust and pull shapes from the darkness, but there was nothing.

I tried to stretch out the ache in my joints, but I couldn't move my body. I was stuck, twisted into an impossible position that pushed my body to the breaking point.

No . . . no, no, no . . .

My hands were the only part of me with any degree of movement, and I frantically pressed at the walls on either side of me and then the lid that rested less than two inches above my head.

Fear fractured my thoughts, and I started to panic.

The box.

He had locked me in the box.

I pounded on the lid as hard as I could, mindless of the pain shooting through my injured wrist. I needed out. It was too small. The space was too small, and I couldn't breathe.

The air was too thin and getting thinner, and I couldn't—I couldn't breathe. I clawed at the lid of the box in desperation. I had to get out. I had to get . . .

Dizziness swept over me as I gasped for breath, trying to suck in air that wasn't there, and the last thing I heard before my mind slipped back under was the haunting sound of laughter.

When I came to, someone was rapping their knuckles on the outside of the box. "Knock, knock," Collin's voice teased. He paused and then added, "This is the part where you say, 'Who's there?'"

I stared at the blackness above me as I tried to take slow, shallow breaths. Panic clung to me like a second skin, but I couldn't give in. There was a hole in the box somewhere just big enough to let oxygen through slowly, but if I panicked, I would pass out again before the air replenished itself.

Collin knocked again. "I can hear your ragged breathing, Holly. I know you're awake. You have to remember to breathe nice and slow or you'll faint again, and that's no fun."

I closed my eyes and tried to imagine a wide-open space. I wanted to claw my way through the box, but I knew, logically, that I couldn't.

God, grant me your peace. Please.

A welcome calm took the edge off my panic, and I breathed easier. I wasn't alone in this, not this time. It might be a small box, but God had squeezed His way in here with me. Apparently He was a master contortionist. Of course, He did design the laws of physics, so it wouldn't be too hard for Him to break them.

"How does it feel in there, Holly?" Collin asked. "Your body must be screaming by now."

I hurt all over, and I wanted so badly for the pain to stop, but I knew the cost of begging to be released. Pain and pleading excited him, and I would take confinement over his touch any day. I so desperately didn't want him to touch me anymore.

He let out a disappointed sigh as he sat down on the box, but I had no doubt it was feigned. The boards dipped just a little beneath his weight, pressing closer to me. "I really had hoped to take this morning in a different direction, but you had to go and pass out like a drunken prom date."

Maybe his disappointment was genuine after all. He preferred his women conscious and terrified, and I had ruined his plans.

"There's always later," he said. "And we're going to have some interesting fun with the glass from your broken windows before the day is over."

A tremor of fear swept through me. I didn't want to imagine what kinds of ideas he found interesting.

"Are you giving me the silent treatment?" he asked when I didn't respond. "Well, that's okay. I have a cure for that." The boards groaned as he stood. The sound of his heavy footsteps echoed through the room and faded into the distance.

I wondered how long he would leave me in here. Hours? Days?

I listened when I heard his footsteps returning. A strange scraping sound followed his steps, and I heard a frightened whimper.

It had to be Jace.

I needed to help her. I couldn't let him hurt her. I pushed at the lid again, but it had no more give than before. A heavy weight dropped on top of the box, and I flinched.

"Stay," Collin said.

Jace let out another whimper and asked, "Where am I?" I could hear the sound of her frightened breaths as she shifted above me, no doubt straining for some detail to tell her where she was.

I wished I could tell her everything would be okay, but it would be a lie.

"Relax, Jace," Collin said in a soothing voice. "It is Jace, isn't it? Or do you prefer Jacelyn?"

"Where's Holly? You said I could see her. Take this blindfold off and let me see her."

"Not yet."

"Where is she, you sick, twisted freak? I know you took her!"

"Holly's in timeout." He knocked on the box. "Isn't that right, Holly?"

I heard Jace's sharp inhale. "What is that? Is that a box? You can't do that! You can't put her in a box! She'll suffocate. Holly? Holly, are you okay?" I could hear her fidgeting, like she was afraid she might suffocate me by sitting still.

My voice sounded hoarse as I said, "I'm okay."

Collin clucked his tongue in disapproval. "I don't think you're being truthful, Holly."

"What do you want?" Jace asked. She was trying to sound defiant and brave, but I could hear the fear in her voice, which meant Collin could hear it too. "Are you some sort of . . . of . . . sex offender? Because I keep tabs on the ones who move into my area, and you're not on my list."

She kept a list?

"You should ask Holly that question," he suggested, and I flinched inwardly.

I had never told her anything about what he had done to me. Best friends were supposed to confide in each other, but I had kept so much from her. He was just rubbing my nose in the fact that I was a lousy friend.

"Holly?" Jace questioned, her voice worried. "Is he . . . did he . . ."

I swallowed, and my throat burned as I repeated, "I'm okay, Jace."

Collin heaved a long-suffering sigh. "Always so difficult. Let me explain your purpose, Jacelyn. You're here because Holly has a problem with sharing. She likes to hide things. It's . . . difficult for our relationship."

"You're not in a relationship. You're just some creepy perv with an attachment disorder. She doesn't want anything to do with you!"

I heard a muffled slap, and Jace let out a small yelp of surprised pain. I gritted my teeth, furious that I couldn't shield her from this.

"Good, you do know how to be quiet," Collin said. "This is how things are going to work. Are you listening to me, Jacelyn? Just nod your head yes or no." A pause. "Good. I'm going to ask Holly some questions, and if she answers wrong or refuses to answer, I'm going to hurt you."

"Just ask me the questions. I'll answer them. You don't have to hurt me," Jace said quickly. "Just . . ." Her words trailed off with a gasp of pain.

"Hot, isn't it? Tell Holly what I'm going to hurt you with if she refuses to answer my questions honestly."

She didn't need to answer; I could hear the repetitive, familiar clicking of a metal lid—the flip lighter he had been playing with that second day. He was going to burn her.

I bit down on my lips to keep the protests from escaping. I needed to protect her, but I was helpless to do anything from inside this box.

"A l-lighter," she said.

"So, Holly," Collin began, "tell me how you're feeling."

"Angry," I spat, and he laughed.

"That's not what I meant and you know it."

He wanted to know the depth of my suffering so he could savor it. He had taken so much from me—my freedom, my hope, my dignity—and I didn't want to give him my pain too.

"How are you feeling?" he repeated, slowly as if I were just too dense to comprehend the question.

"I'm . . . in pain."

"You can do better than that."

I hesitated, and Jace screamed. I clenched my hands into fists as she sobbed above me.

"It hurts to breathe," I admitted, fighting down my own sobs. "My whole body hurts, and I just want the pain to stop."

There was a pause, and then I heard the pleasure in his voice when he spoke again. "Better. Tell me what you're scared of."

I stared at the lid of the box, listening to Jace's cries. I couldn't tell him that my deepest fear was for her; he would use it against me.

"I'm scared of you, of . . . what you're gonna do to me." I felt disgusting for giving him what he wanted, and I preferred the taste of vomit on my tongue to those words.

"Good. You *should* be scared of that," he said.

"Holly!" Jace shrieked, and the box creaked as her weight was lifted off.

"What are you doing?" I shouted. I slammed my hands against the lid. "Please. I told you what you wanted to hear. I told you the truth. Don't hurt her anymore! Please!"

"Oh, this is just the beginning, Holly," he replied, and I heard him dragging her from the room.

"Stop!" I screamed, ignoring the shattering pain in my chest as I breathed too hard. I pounded and screamed until I realized I was running out of air. I was using it up too quickly, and dizziness washed over me.

I couldn't pass out again.

My screams died in my throat, and I covered my face with my hands, forcing myself to take slow, shallow breaths. I tried not to think about what he was doing to Jace or the awful things he was going to do to me. Thinking about it only made it harder to breathe.

Instead, I thought about my family. Of Gin's bright, happy face as she twirled in her flowery dresses, her chirping voice and laugh that made me think of bubbles.

The way my father's eyes used to twinkle with delight when he read us a story. How he would lean in and meet both of our eyes as he whispered the best part, like it was an important secret meant just for us.

My mother's voice as she sang in the kitchen, windows open, her song drifting out on the air and into the trees where Gin and I played. The way she would take our hands and dance with us in the kitchen while we waited for the cupcakes to finish baking.

The scent of chocolate frosting being made. The sugary rich flavor of it as I licked it from my fingertips. Mom used to tap me on the nose with the spatula and say, "Use a spoon, Holly. No fingers in the icing."

So, naturally, I had picked the spoon that most resembled a shovel and scooped a heaping mound of frosting to lick.

I'd never once questioned that I was loved back then. For the first nine years of my life, I'd been a happy, vibrant child with a passion for people.

So much had changed.

Footsteps crossed the floor, and the sound of the lock shifting on the outside of the box had every muscle in my body tightening. The lid lifted, and I blinked at the flood of brightness before my eyes adjusted.

Collin leaned over me, cocked his head, and smiled. "You look really uncomfortable."

He tossed the hinged lid back until it smacked against the wall, and then reached down for me. I wished I could melt through the floor beyond his reach, but all I could do was cower in the bottom of the box.

He grabbed under my arms, dragged me out of the box, and released me. My legs—numb from being twisted into an unnatural position for so long—folded beneath my weight, and I hit the floor hard.

Knives of agony pierced my chest and slid into my lungs, the pain so shockingly intense that I must have blacked out. The next thing I became aware of, I was lying on my back with someone on top of me.

"No," I whimpered, trying to push him away. "Stop. Pl—" I swallowed my plea, remembering that it would only excite him more.

"Just like old times," Collin said.

His rough hands reminded me of the pain and indignity that would soon follow, and something inside of me switched off. My mind and body all but disconnected, with only the faintest thread of awareness tethering them together.

I didn't want to be here for what he would do next. I didn't want to be trapped in this body.

I had fought so hard to rebuild my life, to heal, and Collin was dragging me all the way back to the bottom. I couldn't go back there. I couldn't be that broken again.

I turned my face away and stared at the stones of the wall that I had counted so many times, letting my mind fall back into that familiar escape.

One, two, three, four, five . . .

Light glinted off something near the edge of the box, drawing my attention. It was transparent and reflective like . . .

Glass.

I stared at it, wondering if it was real. I stretched my fingers toward it slowly, afraid it would fade away just like Marx had, leaving me alone and helpless with a monster. My fingertips brushed the edge of it—sharp and solid.

Maybe it had snagged in the weave of my sweater when I used it to push aside the glass at the top of the steps.

I remembered my decision in the bathroom as I discreetly palmed the shard. I could end this with one precise cut. It would be over. No more pain and fear, no more cold and darkness.

A moment in the bedroom with Melanie flashed through my mind. She had been prepared to cut her wrists, and my own words echoed back to me: *He's taken so much from you; don't let him have your life too. He doesn't deserve it.*

Collin didn't deserve my life any more than he deserved my body, but if I didn't end this now, he would have both until he eventually grew bored with me.

I wondered how much of me would be left by then. Maybe nothing. I had a feeling I would die long before my heart stopped beating.

I would rather end it now.

Jordan's face drifted up from my memories, his eyes shimmering with tears as he said, *Please tell me you're never gonna try to hurt yourself again.*

I hadn't promised him, because I knew that given the choice between death and being at Collin's mercy again, I would choose death in a heartbeat.

I squeezed the glass in my hand, feeling the edges bite into my fingers, but another memory pushed its way through.

I was standing in the kitchen of Captain McNera's house, begging him not to end everything with a bullet: *If you kill yourself, you're murdering a little piece of everyone who has ever loved you, everyone who has ever cared about you. You're hurting them in a way they may never recover from.*

McNera had a wife and daughters who loved him, but my words hadn't stopped him from raising that gun. I had no family. I was an orphan who had survived by fading into the shadows, and I would die exactly the same way.

We care about you, Holly. No conditions. You understand me?

Marx's words rippled across the surface of my thoughts. He had told me he cared and that he would tell me every day for the rest of my life if that's what it took for me to understand.

But he had a career and a family—a mom, a dad, a sister—and he didn't need me. I offered him nothing but stress and complications.

Collin grabbed my face, forcing me to look at him. "If you keep trying to hide from me, I'll pay your friend a visit instead."

I hadn't thought I could feel any more fear, but then it crashed into me like a tidal wave. If I killed myself, he would go after Jace.

Jace was more than a friend; she was the first person I had managed to connect with after Collin upended my life. She was an amazing person who touched the lives of so many people, and I loved her.

People loved her. She had family and friends who would search for her, and I had to do everything I could to protect her until they found her.

The light above me blurred as I gave in to the tears, resigned to the fact that I had to let Collin have his *fun*. I hoped it would be over quickly.

"There's my little bird," Collin whispered. He wrapped his fingers around my throat, applying just enough pressure to make it hard to breathe.

Jordan's voice drifted up from a not-too-distant memory as I tried to loosen Collin's fingers: *Aim for the femoral artery that travels through the thigh and groin. He'll bleed out in minutes.*

I flexed my fingers on the piece of glass as Jordan's words ping-ponged around in my mind. Hitting a tiny artery was our only chance. If I missed . . .

I did the only thing I could; I prayed. I wasn't sure where the strength came from, but with all the energy I had left, I lifted my arm and stabbed the piece of glass into Collin's thigh.

I ripped it out and tried to stab him again, but he slammed my wrist to the floor and tightened his grip on my throat. The last thing I remembered was staring at the light above me before darkness folded around me.

32

Marx glided into the abandoned warehouse on light toes with his gun drawn, Jordan directly behind him. He'd tried to convince Jordan to stay behind and let the police handle the situation, but Jordan had snagged one of the bulletproof vests and said evenly, "Yeah, that's not happening."

The only way to keep him from coming was to lock him in a cell, but he'd just negotiated himself out of one of those.

Jordan couldn't stand aside any more than Marx could, not when they knew Holly was at the mercy of a man who terrified her more than anything else on this earth.

Marx had his doubts about the tip that had come in less than twenty minutes ago, but he couldn't suppress the desperate hope that it was genuine.

Someone claimed to have seen a girl matching Holly's description three days ago, screaming and trying to escape this building. He said he recognized her from her picture in the paper. It didn't set well with Marx that the man had witnessed a girl being held captive and had waited *three* days to come forward.

It made him want to ring the man's neck.

Three officers flanked him and Jordan as they entered the warehouse, and they dispersed through the building to search for Holly.

"I'll go right," Jordan said quietly.

Marx nodded and went left. A red-haired woman lay on the cement floor in the center of the main room, and Marx's heart staggered with dread when he first saw her.

Holly . . .

As he approached, he realized that the hair peeking out beneath her black beanie wasn't red; it was blonde stained with blood.

Crouching beside her, he noticed what his fear had initially blinded him to: she was much too tall to be Holly, at least seven or eight inches taller.

He exhaled in relief.

The woman's face registered in his mind as he pressed two fingers to her wrist. Rachel Glass. She'd been a brunette in the photo he'd seen of her. No pulse, but he'd gathered that from the coldness of her skin.

She'd been dead a while.

He looked up toward the second floor. It was designed like a loft that wrapped around a square hundred-foot opening, with a metal railing for security. Rachel had fallen or more than likely been pushed.

Marx stood and started for the stairs. There was nothing anyone could do for Rachel, and even if there was, he didn't care. As cold and heartless as that might seem, the only person he cared about right now was Holly.

He climbed the steps quicker than he probably should've, but he knew he was short on time. He slowed near the top to listen when he thought he heard a quiet, feminine grunt. It came again, along with the sound of glass scraping across cement.

He climbed the last few steps and scanned the visible space with his gun raised. If Collin stepped out, it would be the last step he ever took. Armed or not, Marx was putting him down, and he would deal with the consequences later.

Holly would never be safe so long as he was still breathing. Assuming *she* was still breathing. The thought shook him to his bones. She had to be alive.

There was no sign of Collin, but on the other side of the opening was another woman. He knew from her profile that it was Jace.

She was lying on the floor, grunting and wriggling like a worm. She cringed at the sound of his approach. There was a black sack over her head, with duct tape wrapped around her neck and mouth, and her wrists were bound behind her back. He crouched beside her, and a flash of anger swept through him at the sight of a noose around her neck.

"Are you okay?" he asked on a whisper as he pulled a pocket knife from his pants.

She stiffened and mumbled something through her gag that might have been, "Marx?"

"Hang on," he said. He carefully sliced through the duct tape and pulled the sack from her head.

She gasped and sobbed, the black makeup around her eyes running down her face. "He was gonna hang me. He said . . . it was a game."

Marx remembered the story about the little girl Collin had hung and the board of nails he'd forced Holly to walk across before letting her cut the girl down.

This time he intended to hang Jace and force Holly to walk across broken glass to reach her. The path of glass shards led from Jace to one of the closed doors like a trail of bread crumbs.

"Is Holly in there?" he asked quietly, pointing to the door.

"I don't know," Jace sniffled. "I didn't see her. He had her locked in a box."

Rage made his fingers tighten on his gun. *That twisted son of a . . .*

He needed to control his anger and focus on rescuing Holly. He could rage later.

"I heard her crying," Jace said. "He's hurting her."

Marx nodded to the officer who had just reached the top of the steps and then at Jace. "Help her."

He started toward the room. He tested the lever. Unlocked. He counted silently and then threw the door inward, expecting Collin to offer some kind of resistance. But there was none. His initial sweep of the room registered two bodies on the floor.

Collin was slumped over, unconscious or dead— Marx was hoping for dead— with blood pooled around his thigh. Marx's gaze skipped to the second body. He'd worked enough crime scenes that he could walk between bodies with practiced indifference, but now the air felt too thin, making it difficult to breathe, and for the first time since he was a rookie, he felt sick to his stomach.

"Get me an ambulance now!" he hollered.

He shoved his gun into its holster and stripped out of his jacket as he dropped to his knees beside Holly's limp form. Her red hair, pooled around her head like a crimson halo, was too bright against her ashen skin.

He only glanced at her injuries, but the dark purple spanning the length of her left side—ribs to hip bones—sent fresh fear pulsing through his veins. She was bleeding internally.

He swore in a way he hadn't since before he met her. He wanted to rip Collin into confetti with his bare hands and set the pieces on fire.

He draped his coat over her and cupped her face in both hands. "Holly, baby, can you hear me?"

Her skin was cold and clammy beneath his touch—like death—and it had him scrambling to find a pulse. It was weak, and as he leaned closer, he could hear the faint rasp of her breathing. Something was wrong with her lungs.

A quiet whimper drew his attention back to Holly's face. Her eyes were open, and silent tears trickled down her temples into her hair.

"Holly?"

Her breathing became even more ragged, and she let out another distressed whimper that made his heart break. She was terrified, and it took him a moment to realize that she probably thought the man looming over her was Collin.

"It's just me, sweetheart. It's Marx."

Her eyes blinked rapidly when he leaned over her, and he wondered if she could see anything more than a smudge of color through the geyser of tears.

"You're . . . not real," she choked out.

Did she think she was hallucinating?

"I'm very real," he said, wrapping his fingers around hers to let her know she wasn't alone.

She blinked up at him, her lips trying to form words as she struggled to breathe. "Ch-chest . . . hurts."

"I know, baby." He wanted to wrap her in his arms and hold her, but he was afraid to move her without knowing the extent of her injuries. "But the ambulance is on its way and you're gonna be just fine."

Rapid footsteps echoed through the warehouse, growing louder until Jordan stumbled to a stop in the doorway, winded. The expression of raw fear on his face mirrored the fear churning in Marx's gut.

"Is she—"

"She's alive," Marx told him.

Jordan stepped forward to kneel by her other side, but Marx shook his head, freezing him in place.

"Collin said some things. About you. Remember?" he said, recalling the conversation from the video. "The last thing we need is for her to get upset."

Begrudgingly, Jordan stayed in the doorway beyond Holly's line of sight. He wanted so badly to be with her, but he didn't want his nearness to send her into a panic.

"H . . . how bad?" he asked.

The pain in Marx's face gave him his answer.

Jordan's warm blue eyes turned glacial when he looked at Collin. "If he's not dead, I'm gonna kill him."

"I know the feelin', but you need to keep your anger locked down right now. It's not gonna help her. Give me your jacket. She's freezin'." He hoped it was just the coldness of the room turning her lips blue, but he doubted it.

Jordan shrugged out of it quickly and handed it over. Marx placed it over her legs and tucked it around her. "We'll get you warm soon, peanut."

She liked the nickname peanut even less than sweet pea, and her stammered objection brought a tight smile to his lips.

"N . . . not . . . a . . . p-peanut."

"You're about the size of one," Marx reminded her with a forced smile.

Her eyelids grew heavier, fluttering as she fought to stay awake. She tried to speak, but her eyes fell shut, and her fingers went limp in Marx's hand.

"Holly." He touched her face as dread cut through him, but she didn't respond. He twisted around and demanded, "Where is my ambulance!?"

The officer tending to Jace called back, "There was a really bad wreck on the way and they were closest to the scene. They were rerouted to help. Another squad is coming. Ten to fifteen minutes out."

"Ten minutes!?" Marx snapped back. "She doesn't have ten minutes. She can't breathe!"

The officer shrugged helplessly. "I'm sorry. There's nothing we can do."

If he waited for the ambulance to arrive, load her in, and then transport her to the hospital, he would lose her. He couldn't lose her.

"We can't wait," Jordan said.

"No."

Marx slid one arm under her knees and the other under her back, lifting her off the floor and cradling her against his chest.

"Detective, what are you doing?" the officer asked as he stepped into the doorway.

"Takin' her to the hospital myself. Get out of my way."

"But you can't just—"

314

"Move!" Jordan shouted, shoving him aside.

Marx shouldered past the stunned officer and rushed toward his car. Jace's screams for her friend followed him down the steps and out of the warehouse, but there wasn't time to reassure her that everything would be all right. As gently as he could, he laid Holly across the back seat of his car and tucked the coats around her.

He turned to Jordan and tossed him the keys. "You drive."

Jordan didn't question his decision; he dashed around the car and into the driver's seat. Marx climbed into the back and repositioned Holly so that her head was resting in his lap. "Hang on, baby."

Jordan turned on the flashing light and pulled onto the street. He weaved dangerously through the traffic in the direction of the hospital.

"God," Marx whispered as he smoothed hair back from Holly's face, "if You love this girl as much as she loves You, then fix her. Don't You dare let her die."

Within a block of the hospital, the traffic came to a dead stop. Jordan slammed on the horn and shouted out the window at people to get out of his way, but no one budged.

He could see a wreck up ahead—probably the one that had diverted the ambulance. It would be an hour before he could move an inch on this street. He glanced at the alleyway that served as a shortcut to the hospital.

It was too narrow for Marx's car.

He looked back at Holly and Marx. "What do we do?"

Marx opened the back door and got out. "We're gonna have to carry her. Run ahead and tell them we're comin'. Tell them she has internal bleedin'."

Jordan hesitated. "Maybe I should carry her. I'm faster. You call ahead."

Marx didn't want to entrust her well-being to anyone else, but he knew she would have a better chance with Jordan. "Okay."

Jordan was out of the car and at the rear door in an instant. Marx picked Holly up—she was barely breathing now—and shifted her into Jordan's arms. "Go."

Jordan darted through the alley like a marathon runner, Holly's weight barely seeming to slow him down.

33

*M*arx sat in the chair beside Holly's hospital bed, listening to the quiet sound of her breathing on the ventilator. His body ached from sleeping in a chair the past few days, but he refused to leave her.

Against his better judgment, he had left her to go home to Georgia and check on his father, and it had nearly cost Holly her life. She hadn't woken since that day in the warehouse, and the doctors couldn't explain why.

They could only offer theories: delayed complications from the blow to the head the night she was abducted, prolonged oxygen deprivation, psychological trauma.

Collin held her captive in a cold cement room for four days, tormenting her with lies and preying on her fears. He had beaten her so badly that he broke three of her ribs, one of which punctured a lung, allowing blood and air to fill her chest cavity and compress her lungs.

She had stopped breathing before Jordan reached the hospital.

Even after the doctors resuscitated her and stabilized her lungs, the surgery to repair the internal injuries had taken hours. No one had been willing to say whether or not she would survive.

She looked so lifeless lying in her hospital bed, pale and unmoving. Her right wrist was wrapped in a cast, and there were dark bruises all over her body. But it was the marks on her neck that sent a fresh tide of anger washing over Marx every time he looked at them.

He wanted to break every one of that man's fingers.

He leaned forward in the hospital chair and smoothed a hand over her tangled red hair. "I'm sorry, sweetheart," he whispered, trying to blink back tears. Despite everything he had done, he just hadn't been able to find her quickly enough. The four days it took to find her were the longest four days of his life.

Someone knocked on the door before cracking it open and sticking his head inside. It was Michael, one of the younger detectives from his precinct. He was just shy of six feet, with wavy chestnut hair and eyes the same shade.

"Mind if I come in?"

Marx straightened in his chair and gestured to the vacant one next to him.

Michael walked quietly and slowly—which was unusual for him since he usually moved like he was on a mission—to the chair and sat down. His gaze lingered on Holly, and there was a pinched look between his eyebrows.

"I uh . . . I meant to come sooner, but uh . . . my wife and kid's been sick. I've been juggling emptying puke buckets and working cases," he said, his eyes still on Holly. "How's she doing?"

"No better, no worse."

Michael looked at him. "Sorry, man."

Marx nodded automatically. "I owe you an apology."

Michael had been assigned to cover Marx's two open cases while he was on leave visiting his family. When an urgent package arrived at the precinct for Marx, Michael decided to see if it pertained to either of the cases. He popped the generic DVD into the player and quickly realized it was worse than what he had anticipated.

The video was of a young woman being brutally beaten. When Marx tracked him down to the conference room, Michael had looked pale and sick to his stomach.

Michael insisted on finishing the video and having it analyzed for anything they could use to find "the girl," but Marx turned it off and told him to get out. They argued until Marx lost his temper and all but threw him out of the room.

Michael shook his head. "No apology necessary. I didn't realize it was your girl in the video or I wouldn't have pushed."

Marx sighed. "We're not a couple."

"No, I got that. Anybody who's seen the way you look at her would get that." When Marx raised an eyebrow, Michael scoffed, "Hey, I know how it goes. My kid's adopted. Maybe he doesn't have my genes, and maybe we've had him for less than a year, but that's my boy. Anybody tries to tell me otherwise, they're gonna be looking out of one eye for the rest of the week."

Marx smiled a little for the first time in days. Michael was one of the most pacifistic cops he had ever met, and he couldn't imagine him punching anyone.

"It ain't blood that bonds people, man," Michael continued, sipping the coffee he'd brought with him. "It's love. And those bags under your eyes . . . that's love too. I got me some of them."

Marx had joked once that his mother would try to adopt Holly if she ever met her, and he realized that was exactly what he had done.

"I didn't recognize her in the video," Michael said. "But after I heard who she was, I remembered. Comes around the precinct with you sometimes. Always got her nose in the doughnut box. Cute kid."

"You're only seven years older than her."

Michael's eyebrows lifted. "For real? I figured her for like . . . twenty-two, maybe twenty-three. She's seriously twenty-eight?" He squinted at her, trying to see it.

"She has a baby face and she's tiny, so I can understand the confusion. Just don't ever call her tiny or a kid to her face," Marx said with a slight smile. Holly would hate to know that a man only seven years older than she was thought she was a kid. He could just hear her indignant huff.

Michael grunted. "Why do all women have a height, age, and weight complex? My wife is five-five and a weight I'm sworn never to speak of under pain of death, completely gorgeous, by the way, but according to her, she's too short and too fat."

"Holly doesn't have a weight complex that I'm aware of, but she certainly has a height complex."

"How tall is she?"

"She says she's five two. She's not."

Michael laughed and took another drink of his coffee. He stared at Holly for a long moment and then said with an edge of seriousness to his voice that hadn't been there a moment ago, "There's a few things we need to talk about, and maybe we probably shouldn't discuss them in front of her. You know, just in case she can hear us."

"We can talk in the hall." They left the hospital room, and Marx leaned back against the wall beside the door. "Let's make this quick. If she wakes, I don't want her wakin' up alone."

"Right. So, two things." Michael scratched the side of his head nervously. "The captain thought it would be best, since you're so close to Holly, that maybe I should work her case."

A muscle flexed in Marx's jaw.

Recognizing the impending explosion, Michael hastened to explain, "It wasn't my choice, man. I didn't ask to be put on this case any more than you asked to be taken off it, but she needs you here."

Marx wanted to handle Holly's case personally, but he wasn't willing to leave her side. He couldn't do both. "Fine," he gritted out. Michael was a good cop and an even better man, and he knew he would see things through. "But when she wakes up, I'll be the one takin' her statement."

"I already talked to the captain about that, and he's good with it. I told him she probably wouldn't talk to me anyway."

Even before her abduction, Holly would've been reluctant to talk with Michael; now, after everything she'd been through, Marx wouldn't be surprised if the sight of a man made her lock herself in the bathroom.

"Second thing." Michael hesitated. "Wells made two more videos."

Marx closed his eyes and rubbed his forehead. He had barely made it through the first video. But he had forced himself to watch

320

it, hoping it would provide some insight into where Holly was being held.

He wasn't sure he could handle more.

"The second one came in the mail addressed to you, and his face and voice are distorted just like the first one. Sully's not sure there's anything he can do to clear them up enough to make him identifiable, but it's obviously him," Michael explained.

Sully was one of their computer analysts, and the man was practically a genius. If he didn't think something was possible, it probably wasn't.

"What about the third video?"

"He didn't have time to burn it to a disc from the camera and distort his features, so we have his face."

"How bad are they?"

Michael hesitated before saying, "They're . . . intense. You probably don't want the boyfriend watching them."

Marx looked up at the ceiling as he wrestled with his guilt and grief. Something had told him not to leave Holly the night he got the phone call from his mother, and he wished he had listened.

"The first time I promised Holly that I would protect her from that man, you know what she told me?" he asked, anguish in his voice. "'You shouldn't make promises you can't keep.'"

"What happened to her isn't your fault, Marx."

"I left her."

"Your dad had a heart attack."

"That's not the point. I promised her that I would protect her, and when she needed me the most, I wasn't there. None of us were there. She was completely alone."

"She wasn't alone, and if she knows God, she knew that."

Marx scoffed. "A lot your God did to protect her."

Pain flickered across Michael's face. "He's your God too, and He didn't do this to her."

"He didn't help her either."

"Are you sure about that?"

Marx narrowed his eyes. "Meanin' what?"

"Meaning if you had been two minutes later finding her, she would never have made it to the hospital. She would be gone. And her injuries? Marx, it's a miracle that she's still alive."

"Yeah, I'll give you that."

"Try praying for her. God listens."

Marx remembered holding Holly's head in his lap in the backseat of his car and pleading, *God, if You love this girl as much as she loves You, then fix her. Don't You dare let her die.*

It had been a moment of desperation that caused him to call out to God. He wasn't even sure he believed. And yet Holly was alive despite the odds.

He shifted against the wall, uncomfortable with the direction this conversation had taken his thoughts. "How many people have seen the videos?"

Michael didn't call him out on the change of subject. "Just me, the lieutenant, and the crime lab."

"Keep it that way." Holly would hate that so many people had seen her so vulnerable, and she would feel humiliated enough without half the department seeing the videos. "I'll watch them later, but nobody else sees them. Understood?"

Michael nodded once. "I got one more thing."

"One more thing makes *three* things," Marx pointed out.

"Yeah, so sue me." Michael pulled a sheet of paper from his pocket and held it out to Marx. "This lady called for you. She said she tried your cell."

Marx was ignoring his cell, unless it was someone he really wanted to talk to.

"Holly's too. Couldn't reach either of you."

Marx took the sheet of paper and unfolded it. "We haven't found Holly's phone yet." He recognized the name on the paper instantly: Melanie Bordeaux—Collin's last victim—before Holly. "Did she say what she wanted?"

"She heard about Holly on the news."

Marx nodded and shoved the note into his pocket. He would have to call her and let her know how Holly was doing. "Thank you for the update."

"Sure thing. My wife and I'll keep Holly in our prayers. Let me know when she wakes up." He slapped Marx on the shoulder and walked away.

Marx pushed open the door to Holly's room and dropped back into his chair. He watched her slow, mechanical breathing as he thought about Michael's words: *Try praying for her. God listens.*

He dug his phone from his pocket. He felt like a child calling his mother because he felt lost and alone, but he didn't know what else to do.

"Ritchie, it's three in the mornin'," his mother grunted.

Tears burned his eyes, and he couldn't keep them from his voice as he said, "Did I wake you?"

"Not a'tall," she said. "I was just in the kitchen fixin' to have me some biscuits and jam."

He smiled at the familiarity of what she was doing. Somehow it helped to settle his distressed heart.

"What's the matter, baby?" she asked after a pause. "Somethin's the matter. I can hear it in your silence."

Hear it in his silence? "And it has nothin' to do with me callin' at three in the mornin'?"

"It might could have somethin' to do with that too, but a mama knows. What's troublin' my baby boy? If it's your dad, he's doin' fine. Grouchy, but that's nothin' new."

Marx released a trembling breath. "I need a favor. I need you to pray for somebody. For Holly."

His mother paused again and then said in a knowing voice, "That little red-haired girl you was tellin' us about. The one that keeps movin' your coffee cups and hidin' food behind the toilet paper?"

His throat tightened. He'd told his family about the girl living with him when he was home checking on his father. Baptist as they were, his father had disapproved of him living with a twenty-eight-

323

year-old woman he wasn't married to. His mother, on the other hand, had asked him a hundred questions and then decided he wasn't *living in sin.*

She understood his relationship with Holly in a way that his father hadn't, and she'd made him bend down so she could kiss his forehead and tell him she was proud of the heart God saw fit to give him.

"Somethin' happened to her and . . . she's in a coma, and I . . ." He exhaled and rubbed at his eyes. "I don't know what to do."

"I know when you was here, you got a call sayin' she was missin', but what happened?"

"A man took her." He heard his mother draw in a sharp breath, but she waited for him to continue. "He really hurt her, Mama, and she's not wakin' up."

"Oh baby," she said, her voice solemn. "You send me a picture of her for my prayer board."

His mother didn't keep a prayer list like most of the Baptists he grew up with; she had a picture of everyone she prayed for tacked to a bulletin board in the kitchen. She said it reminded her to pray for them three times a day: breakfast, lunch, and supper. And if she couldn't sleep, she prayed for them again while she was snacking on biscuits in the kitchen in the middle of the night.

That was his mother. Insomnia was just another opportunity to pray and eat biscuits.

"You know, God might not mind hearin' from you too," she said in that obvious tone she always used when she meant, "Get your behind to church."

He sighed, not wanting to be drawn into the age-old argument about his soul. "God doesn't wanna hear from me, Mama. I've rejected Him more times than I can count."

"That's the glorious thing about forgiveness, baby. God's gonna welcome you back with open arms, ain't no matter what you done."

"Mama—"

"Don't interrupt," she chided, and he clamped his mouth shut. "I'll pray for your girl, but it might not be my prayers God's waitin' for. He listens to your voice too."

Marx frowned. Why did he feel like he was being bashed over the head with that tonight?

"You wanna help that baby, you best get on them rusty knees," his mother suggested.

Irritation tightened his jaws. "I'm not gonna do that, Mama."

She heaved a theatrical sigh—the kind that always made his father roll his eyes. It had the same effect on her children too, now that they were grown. "You always was more stubborn than a mule," she said. "You need to decide what's more important to you: your pride or that baby's life. Now send me a picture."

"I will," he agreed.

They said good night and he ended the call. He opened the photo folder on his phone and skimmed through it to find what he was looking for.

He selected the single picture of Holly. Jace had captured her with one of her mischievous grins—her top teeth biting her lower lip as she smiled—and sent it to him.

He missed that smile and the mischievous little laugh that usually came with it. She might be sweet and adorable, but she was usually up to no good: bedazzling his wallet, tipping his pictures on the wall, butchering his morning coffee.

He hadn't imagined when he first met her that she would wrap herself around his heart without even trying.

He forwarded the picture to his mother and snapped his phone shut. He glanced at the monitor beeping steadily beside the bed and then back at the young woman clinging to life.

Pride or her life.

He pushed the chair back from the bed and got down on his knees to truly pray for the first time in almost thirty years. He clasped his hands together like a child in Sunday school and closed his eyes.

"God . . . if you have a minute," he began through gritted teeth. "I realize I have no right to ask you for favors, but I'm not exactly sure how else to do this. We disagree on a lot, but one thing we have in common . . ."—he drew in a steadying breath—"we both love Holly. There are very few people in this world I love, and even fewer I cherish. Don't take her from me. Whatever is wrong with her, whatever has her trapped in a coma, You fix it." He paused and then, remembering his mother's chastisements when he was a child, clarified, "By the way that's a request, not a command. Please and thank you. Amen."

34

*M*arx watched over the next few days for any signs of improvement, but the coma showed no signs of lifting. His mother had told him once, "If something grabs your heart, you don't pray about it once; you pray God's ear off." So he prayed every day, determined to make God see just how important Holly was to him.

The doctors decided it was safe to remove her from the ventilator once she was able to breathe on her own. That was the first good sign.

The media got wind of her condition, and there was an influx of journalists in the hall and outside the hospital.

One man tried to force his way into her room to photograph her. Marx broke his camera by slamming it against the floor repeatedly and then tossed the broken bits back into the hall.

"Next time I break you," he said before shoving him back out the door.

He didn't care if he had to buy the man a new camera. No one was taking advantage of Holly.

A story was published in a paper with an older photo of Holly set side by side with a picture of Edward Billings: *The Kansas Carver's Victim Attacked: Did He Have an Accomplice?*

Marx skimmed the article before tossing it aside. It was nothing but speculation, but he suspected it was only the first of many more to come. Holly would loathe all the attention.

Jace came every day and cried by Holly's bedside. She snuck her hippo of a cat into the hospital inside an oversized purse once, and he had flopped flush against Holly's side with a rumbling purr.

They had even brought Riley in under the guise of a therapy dog. He had whimpered and nudged her hand with his nose, apparently upset that she wasn't acknowledging him. Eventually he hopped onto the bed and stretched out next to her.

Jordan scarcely left Holly's side. He and Marx took rotations watching over her, but neither of them had left for longer than it took to go home and shower.

Jordan pushed into the room with two cups of coffee and dropped into the second chair by the bed. He offered one of the cups to Marx. "Black."

Marx took it with a nod of thanks. "How do you drink yours?"

"Three creams, two sugars."

Marx shook his head. Men did not drink their coffee with cream and sugar. "Well . . . at least it's not a vanilla mocha fropa cappuccino."

"That's not a thing," Jordan informed him before taking a gulp of his coffee.

"Probably comes with whipped cream and rainbow sprinkles."

"That's definitely not a thing, but Holly might try it. She likes sprinkles." Jordan nodded to the book in Marx's lap. "Are you reading to her?"

Marx rested a hand on the book. "The doctors said she might be able to hear us. Whether what she hears makes any sense to her or not, I don't know."

A shadow of a smile touched Jordan's lips. "Holly and Gin loved that book. Their favorite character was the Cowardly Lion. Gin liked the voice Holly used to read him aloud, but Holly said she loved him because he was always scared, but he was braver than he realized."

"Sounds a lot like somebody else we know." Marx leaned forward to tuck a piece of hair behind Holly's ear that had blown loose when Jordan came in. "Collin was her worst fear, and she didn't think she could ever face him again, but she fought back, and she did everythin' she could to protect Jace."

Jordan's fingers tightened on the Styrofoam cup, and he looked away. "She shouldn't have had to be brave."

Marx couldn't agree more. Holly had suffered enough for three lifetimes. He wanted to protect her from the world and help her build a fear-free, happy life.

"She knew Collin was setting me up that night outside the gym," Jordan said. "She begged me not to let him bait me, and if I had just listened . . . she wouldn't be here right now."

Several silent minutes passed between them as they both watched Holly's breathing. Marx shifted in his chair, crossing an ankle over his knee.

"You know your socks don't match," Jordan pointed out with a glance at the older man's feet.

Marx smiled. "Mmm hmm. Seems some mischievous little person went through my drawer and mismatched all my socks."

"You didn't notice when you pulled them out of the drawer that one was blue and one was black?"

"Sadly, no. I was in a hurry and got dressed in the dark and just assumed everythin' was as it was supposed to be. I didn't notice they were different until I got to the hospital. I should've known she'd mess with somethin' in my room. She just can't help herself."

Marx shook his head and smiled to himself. He could imagine how Holly would've cupped a hand over her mouth and giggled.

He glanced at Jordan and for the first time felt empathy for him. There were dark shadows under his eyes and grief lines etched across his forehead and around his pinched mouth.

It seemed he and God weren't the only two who loved Holly.

Marx stood and tried to stretch the tightness from his body. He felt like an eighty-year-old man. He handed the book to Jordan. "I'll give you two some time alone." He leaned down and pressed a light kiss to Holly's forehead before whispering, "Come on, baby, wake up."

Jordan sank lower in his chair and just gazed at Holly for a long time after Marx left. Fear, fury, and sadness warred for control inside him, and more often than not, the fury won. He didn't understand why God had let this happen to her.

His mind kept flashing back to the video that had been delivered to Marx, the one he'd demanded to see.

The precinct was going to have to renovate their conference room. He might have thrown some things into the wall and punched . . . things . . . or people.

It was hard to remember what exactly happened in his haze of fury, but he remembered collapsing against the wall and sliding to the floor with Marx crouched next to him. Marx had told the other officers to back off and give him space when they tried to restrain him.

Jordan wished he could attack the real target of his fury, but all he could do was sit here and wait, praying to a God he was angry with that Holly would wake up.

It pained him to think that she had finally begun to trust him, and now, because of Collin's abuse and lies, she might never trust him again.

He had cherished the moments of growth between them: the first time she agreed to go jogging with him, when she let him brush the flour from her face, and when she'd placed her hand in his in the back of the police car.

Her hands were so small and delicate, and he remembered the slight chill fear had left in her fingertips. But she had been determined. He'd enjoyed the feeling of her soft skin against his and the way their hands had fit together.

It had taken all of his self-restraint not to hug her in that car. She had no idea how absolutely adorable she was, and if he told her so, she would probably scrunch her nose at him, which would only prove his point.

He wanted to kiss her nose. He wanted to kiss her lips. He wanted to spend every free second with her. He didn't understand how anyone could ever want to hurt her.

He looked at her left hand lying on top of the blanket, hesitated for just a second, then wrapped his fingers around hers. "I know it's a violation of the border laws, but I hope you don't mind if I hold your hand."

He held onto her as he told her about some of his favorite childhood memories: Jolly sundaes, trick-or-treating as pirates, treasure hunting.

The heart monitor made an irregular blip when he was telling her about a time they had played in the woods, and he glanced at it. Holly's heart rate began to pick up, and concern flooded him when it doubled in a matter of seconds.

A nurse came into the room, and Jordan released Holly's hand as he backed away. "What's happening to her? Did I do something?"

Maybe he shouldn't have touched her. Maybe he'd said something he shouldn't have.

The nurse checked Holly's vitals and then checked her eyes. She brightened. "I think she might be dreaming. This is a good sign."

Marx hadn't gone far when he left the room, and he stepped back inside with his cup of coffee. "Why is this a good sign?"

"Well, there's some debate as to whether or not a coma patient can dream. It's difficult to know because they don't react like a person does when they're in REM sleep. The fact that we're seeing a physical and emotional reaction suggests she's coming out of the coma," the nurse explained.

"You mean she's gonna wake up?" Jordan asked, hope surging through him.

The nurse looked at him, considering her explanation. "Understand that if she does, she may be different. There may be unforeseen cognitive damage, but there may also be intense disorientation. I'm going to let the doctor know." She hurried out of the room.

Marx sat down on the edge of the bed with Holly. "It's okay, sweetheart. You're safe now. He can't hurt you anymore." He stroked her hair gently and continued to murmur soothing words to her.

He glanced at the monitor, watching as her heart rate gradually slowed, and her vitals returned to normal.

Jordan dropped back into his chair. "Did I upset her?"

"I doubt it. She was probably havin' a nightmare. Lord knows she has plenty to have nightmares about." He nodded to the book. "Let's read to her for a bit."

Jordan cracked open the book and started reading. He did the voices for the characters the way Holly did when they were kids. He read a chapter and then handed the book to Marx.

His voice seemed to soothe her the most. They took turns reading to her for the next few hours, and they both took pleasure in trusting that, while she wasn't awake, she could hear them and they were bringing her comfort.

The next several days had all of them on the edge of their seats as they waited for her to wake up. Her eyes fluttered open briefly, but she never seemed to be aware of anyone or anything around her.

"It might take her a few days to be able to cling to consciousness for longer than a few minutes at a time, and disorientation is normal," the nurse checking her vitals explained.

The third time Holly roused, her heartbeat started to climb rapidly and her breathing became frantic. Marx tried to soothe her, but she didn't respond to him.

The next few times she woke up, she started screaming, and the nurse had to sedate her. Marx hated the raw, terrified sound of her screams, and he tried to reassure her that she was safe.

He was holding Holly's hand and resting his head on the edge of the bed when a voice drew his attention to the doorway.

"That girl of yours has got her some lungs," Michael said, leaning against the door frame with his foot propping open the door. "I could hear her all the way at the reception desk half a mile that way." He threw a thumb to his left.

They had just sedated her again, and Marx felt helpless. He didn't know what to do for her. "What brings you by?"

"I was driving by and thought, *what a great place for coffee and some taffy*. And since I was in the neighborhood, I figured I would check in. See how she's doing." He took a bite of the taffy in his hand and then looked at Jordan, who was seated on the other side of Holly's bed.

Jordan acknowledged him with a subtle bob of his head. "She's out of the coma, but they keep sedating her because she wakes up screaming and we can't seem to calm her down."

Michael's expression turned thoughtful, and his gaze drifted up toward the overhead light. "So, I know I don't know her and I'm not a head doctor, but just a thought here. Wells kept her locked in a room with nothing, right? So he obviously wanted her to feel deprived. There was a light, but the switch was on the outside. In all the videos when he was with her, the light's on." He pointed at the lights above him. "Who here thinks the sadist left her in the dark until he was ready to hurt her?"

Marx and Jordan glanced at each other.

"It's just a left-field idea," Michael added with a shrug. "But if I knew the light coming on meant somebody was gonna hurt me, and the first thing I saw when I came to was a blinding light, I would scream bloody murder too."

The three of them stared up at the lights with a whole new perspective. The nurse had said Holly would be disoriented and possibly unaware of her surroundings, and the first thing she was seeing when she opened her eyes was the light above her.

If Michael was right, her instinctive reaction to that light was fear, because in the warehouse it meant inevitable pain.

"Turn them off," Marx said.

"Sure thing." Michael flipped the switch, and from that point on the lights stayed off.

35

A haze of pain washed over me as I strained toward consciousness, almost drowning out all other sensations. I couldn't seem to open my eyes; it felt like someone had glued them shut. The monumental effort left me feeling drained, but I was finally able to crack them open.

I stared at a dark ceiling above me. No light. Relief flooded me, and I let out a quiet breath. I searched the wall of the cell for the pale security light, but I didn't see it.

A deep sense of sadness and loss washed over me. That little light was all I had, and he had taken it from me.

I blinked in confusion at a pale outline on the wall—like light seeping in around curtains—positive the pain was causing me to hallucinate again. Once I had even thought I saw Marx leaning over me, telling me that everything would be okay. I had even dreamed that he found me, but then I always woke up alone in that cold room.

Why was there a window?

Was it a different room? Had Collin moved me because I kept throwing up and he couldn't stand the smell?

I wanted to see if it was real. I pushed myself up with difficulty and gritted my teeth against the pain in my chest. I realized suddenly that I was on a mattress, and I was covered with a blanket.

What had I done to earn a bed and blanket? He'd said I could earn things, but I didn't recall him giving me anything. The last thing I remembered was him on top of me, and . . .

I swallowed and stared at the window.

Pushing the blanket aside, I tried to scoot to the edge of the bed, but my left hand snagged on something. A restraint? I pulled harder, and a sharp pain pierced the back of my hand before it came free.

My body felt weak and sluggish as I tried to stand, and I wondered if he had drugged me. I made it to my feet, but my knees buckled, and I dropped to the floor hard enough to leave me dazed.

I blinked at the dark squares that were a hairsbreadth from the tip of my nose, trying to figure out what was wrong with them. Was it tile? The floor in my cell before this had been cement.

I heard footsteps outside of the room, and my heartbeat quickened. Was he coming back?

I pulled myself under the bed and curled up, making myself as small and unnoticeable as possible. I watched the unfamiliar door with fear, waiting for it to open. The footsteps continued on past the door, but they didn't sound like Collin's light, rhythmic steps.

Time crawled by as I waited for something to happen, and my head became heavier and heavier. I rested it on my arms but kept my eyes on the door. Before I even realized it, I was drifting to sleep on the warm tile floor.

Voices roused me.

"I came out of the bathroom and she was gone," a man said. *Marx*, my drowsy mind offered up. "About gave me a heart attack."

"Where did you find her?" another man asked, and his voice sounded familiar too.

"Curled up under the bed. She ripped the IV out of her hand and crawled under there. I tried to wake her, but she was out cold."

My eyelids peeled open slowly, and I blinked groggily up at the ceiling. I felt like I was wearing a pharmaceutical straitjacket. He had definitely drugged me.

Two shadowy figures leaned over me, and panic cut straight through the drug-induced haze and had me scrambling up against the headboard of the bed. I tried to move quickly, but my body felt clumsy and sluggish, and I fumbled over pillows.

"Easy, sweetheart, you're gonna hurt yourself," the one that sounded like Marx said, but it couldn't be him.

He was in Georgia with his family, and I was locked in a room in that warehouse. This had to be another dream. Or a hallucination from whatever drug Collin had given me.

I huddled against the headboard, unsure what to do, and watched the shadowy figures.

"You're safe here, Holly," the Marx-like voice said. "You're in the hospital."

He grabbed the blanket I'd lost when I moved, and held it out to me. When I just stared at his blurry face in frightened confusion, he moved toward me.

I cringed away. "Don't . . . don't touch me."

"Okay," he said calmly, placing the blanket just in front of my feet with exaggerated slowness. "Nobody's gonna touch you."

I realized I was wearing a scratchy dress that did little to cover me with the way I was sitting, and a fresh wave of panic washed over me. Where were my clothes? He took my clothes. I snatched the blanket with shaky fingers and pulled it up to my chin.

A single clear thought penetrated the panic and the foggy grip of the drugs: hospital. The man who sounded like Marx but couldn't be Marx had said I was in a hospital. This was a hospital gown.

"I'm gonna turn on a light," he said.

A small sound of fear escaped my throat before I could stop it, and the shadowy figure hesitated.

"Just so you can see me," he clarified. He walked to a door, leaned in, and flipped on a switch. A dim glow from what looked like a bathroom brightened the room and highlighted his features.

His hair was mussed, and a shadow of a beard covered his jaw, but he looked like Marx. I stared at him, half expecting him to dissolve before my eyes.

"If you're wonderin' if I'm real, I am," he assured me. "You're in a private room at the hospital."

My eyes darted around the dimly lit room I had fumbled through in the dark. The bed with knitted blankets, the monitor beeping the elevated rhythm of my heart, the wooden door without a padlock on it. The window.

My eyes landed on Jordan, who hung back silently beside the window, his glassy blue eyes watching me, and I couldn't help the anxiety that threaded through me.

Collin's words echoed in my mind: *You're nothing but a conquest to him. He'll charm you into his bed and then move on to a real woman worth loving.*

Pain flickered through his eyes when I pulled the blanket tighter around myself, like he knew what I was thinking.

"Jordan, why don't you go find Holly some pistachio puddin'. She needs to eat, and it's her favorite," Marx suggested.

It *was* my favorite, and I'd asked him for it the last time I was in the hospital. I was surprised he remembered.

"I'll be back in a few minutes," Jordan said as he pushed away from the wall. He looked like he didn't want to leave, but I wanted him gone.

When the door clicked shut, I said, "The hospital doesn't have pistachio pudding."

"I know that. He doesn't," Marx said with a thin smile. He sat down in the chair by the bed. "It'll take him a while to figure that out."

I studied him, taking in the details of his face, his eyes, his posture. "I'm not imagining you this time."

"No."

"I kept thinking that you found me, but it was always just a dream. I always woke up to that . . . place."

He let out a breath that sounded like pain, and I could see the shine in his eyes. "You're not dreamin' this time. You're safe." He cleared his throat and brushed the back of his hand across his face before asking, "How are you feelin'?"

I tried to find the right word to describe how I was feeling: afraid, violated, lost, thirsty . . . "Foggy," I decided on.

"That's probably from the morphine," he said. He poured a cup of water and offered it to me. "Or the sedative."

A little of the water sloshed over the brim as I accepted it with a shaking hand. I took a sip and then gripped it with both hands, trying to keep it steady.

Ordinarily, I would object to drugs, but considering my last memory of pain had been so blindingly intense, I had no objections. I hurt everywhere, but as long as I didn't move and I took small breaths, it was bearable.

I had so many questions, but I started with the one that was most important to me. "Where's Jace? Is she okay?"

"She's fine."

The relief was nearly overwhelming, and I sagged a little against the headboard. "How did I get here?" I looked at the beeping monitor beside the bed.

Marx explained about a tip that had led them to the warehouse where Jace and I were being kept, and that I'd been rushed to the hospital in critical condition. He told me I had been in a coma for eight days and had only begun to wake up three days ago.

I stared at him as I tried to process it all. I had stabbed Collin in the leg in the desperate hope that he would die and Jace would be safe, and only minutes later, Marx had led a team of officers into the building.

"Why did you come for me?"

"I drove back from Georgia the moment I got the call that you were missin', and I spent every minute lookin' for you."

Collin had told me Marx wouldn't leave his family to look for me. He'd also said that if he did, it wouldn't be because he cared, but because he felt obligated. I wanted to know if he was right. "But why?"

"Because I love you, Holly."

I flinched at the lie. "No, you don't. Don't say that."

"Yes, I do."

Moisture gathered in my eyes, blurring his face. "You can't love me."

"Why?" he asked as he leaned forward and rested his elbows on his knees. "Because some psychopath with no concept of love told you you're unlovable?"

Tears rolled down my cheeks, and I brushed them away with my fingertips. No one except my family had ever truly loved me. "Because the only people who ever loved me are dead." When he rolled up the sleeve of his black sweater and held out his arm, I drew back a fraction. "What are you doing?"

"Lettin' you check for a pulse. If I'm dead, I'd like to know."

I stared at him, uncertain. "They're just words. You don't actually mean it. It's like saying you love . . . Twinkies."

He arched an eyebrow at the analogy as he rolled his sleeve back down to cover his untouched wrist. "You're not a Twinkie, Holly. And words have power. I watched the videos, and I heard everythin' that man said to you. I know those words are bouncin' around inside your head, makin' you doubt that anybody can possibly care about you. But everythin' he told you was a lie."

I had wondered what Collin intended to do with the videos. Now I knew. He had sent them to Marx to torment him.

"Do you wanna know how I know that?" Marx asked. "Because I *did* leave my family to come find you. I broke just about every traffic law in existence to get here. I nearly put a witness through a window for waitin' three days to come forward about your location."

I felt a sudden flash of anger. "Someone knew where I was and still waited three days to tell the police?"

"He didn't come forward until I offered a reward for information." He let out a long breath that still held a bit of anger for the man who apparently valued money over a human life. "But my point is, I didn't do those things out of obligation. I did them because I will *not* lose you. That's not even an option. *I love you* and nothin' you or anybody else says is gonna change that."

I wiped at my nose and dropped my eyes to the blanket, trying not to let myself hope that he was telling the truth. He rose and sat down on the bed beside me. I stiffened at his nearness and fought the urge to retreat into the corner to keep him from touching me.

He seemed to sense my discomfort, because he kept his hands in his lap. "You know I've always wanted to have kids. A son to play sports with and a daughter to spoil. I would do anythin' for her, even attend invisible tea parties with imaginary people. I would hug her when she cried, and I would protect her with my life. But I'm forty-seven years old and divorced. I will never have a biological daughter."

My heart ached for him. "I'm sorry."

"I'm not. Not anymore."

That surprised me. Not being able to have kids had led to his divorce. He'd wanted them, but Shannon hadn't. For as long as I'd known him, it had been an open wound.

"I didn't get to raise any kids. I didn't get the sweet girl with fairy wings and princess dresses. I got an adorable young woman who puts her tiny shoes on my dashboard . . . and my leather couch, who mismatches my socks, who has a heart twice the size of her body, and whose face lights up at the sight of a bag of marshmallows."

"But . . ." I struggled for words and fell on the obvious. "I'm not your daughter."

I flinched when he leaned in and placed a featherlight kiss on top of my head before murmuring into my hair, "You're my daughter by love, and I cherish you."

Fresh tears gathered in my eyes as I looked up at him, at a loss for words.

The door opened and Jordan leaned inside tentatively. "They don't have any pistachio pudding."

"Then go find some," Marx said curtly. "Try the mini mart across the street."

Jordan's gaze lingered on me for a long moment before he said, "Yeah, um . . . okay," and ducked back out.

Marx waited for the door to shut before saying, "We need to talk about him."

I didn't want to talk about Jordan. My thoughts and feelings toward him were as twisted up as a Twizzler right now, and I had no idea how to sort them out.

"Collin told you that Jordan is only interested in you because he wants to sleep with you," Marx said.

I folded my arms over my stomach and stared at my feet beneath the blanket. "I don't want him to . . . to touch me."

Marx was quiet for a long moment. "Is it because you're afraid that if he does he won't stop?" *That he'll hurt you like Collin did* hung unspoken at the end of his question, but we both knew it was there.

"I know Jordan doesn't wanna hurt me, but . . ." I remembered the desire in his eyes when we stood in his kitchen, the space between our bodies uncomfortably narrow. "But when I let him touch me, it made him wanna kiss me."

"Did he?"

I shook my head. Jordan had chosen to leave the room rather than do something he knew I wouldn't want, but it had been hard for him.

"I held his hand in the back of the police car. What if he . . . wants something more now?" I swallowed, my throat dry. "What if I gave him permission to do more without meaning to?"

Marx sighed. "There are men in this world who *would* take that as an undeniable invitation for 'more.' There are men who would take a glance or a smile as an invitation. And those men fall into one of two categories—idiots or predators. I realize that you're used to bein' cautious around men because you don't wanna give them a reason to hurt you, but no matter what you do, there is never a good reason for a man to hurt you, Holly. You can hold his hand, invite him into your bed—you can even agree to sleep with him—and that still doesn't give him the rights to your body."

"But—"

"You always have the right to say no or stop, sweetheart. And Jordan might irritate me like a bad skin rash, but I believe he's a genuinely good person, and he would never push you into doin' more than you're comfortable with."

I knew Jordan would never attack me the way Collin had, but what if he was lost in the moment? What if he didn't have the strength to leave the room next time? What would happen then?

"You've made yourself quite clear on the subject of intimacy," Marx continued. "And after everythin' you've been through, I have no doubt Jordan understands that it could be years before you're comfortable with a sexual relationship."

"Never," I said resolutely. I would never let a man touch me that way again.

"That's okay too," he said, but there was a hint of sadness in his voice. "Nobody says you have to."

I stared hard at the hospital blanket, picking at a loose fiber until it started to unravel.

"I love you no matter what, and I think you know that," Marx said. "But Jordan cares about you too. He didn't decide to stay in New York because he views you as some kind of conquest. He stayed because he values you as a person, because he's drawn to your personality and your beautiful heart, and he enjoys spendin' time with you. Just . . . try talkin' to him, okay? When you're ready."

I nodded, but I still felt like there was a giant rift between me and Jordan that I didn't even know how to begin to repair. If it was possible to fix it, it was going to take time.

Marx drew in a breath and hesitated. "There's one more thing we need to discuss." He paused again, seeming to consider whether or not to continue. "It's about Collin." He glanced at the monitor when my heartbeat picked up. "You nicked the artery in his leg, but the paramedics reached him in time."

I stared at him, uncomprehending. "What are you saying?"

He studied my face as he said carefully, "He survived."

My breath left me in a rush, and I couldn't seem to get it back. Of course he survived. It would probably take a wooden stake or a silver bullet to kill that monster.

For one brief moment, one blip of a moment, I thought it was over. That maybe I would be safe. Marx was still talking, saying something about Collin being in custody, but I didn't really hear him. After everything he'd done to me, he was still breathing.

I curled over in the bed, ignoring the pain in my chest and stomach, and began to sob.

Marx gently pried me out of my curled position and pulled me against him. "I'm so sorry, baby." He wrapped his arms around me, and I sagged against his chest as I cried so hard my entire body shook.

36

I had cried myself to sleep in Marx's arms, but when I cracked my eyes open, I was lying down in the bed with the blankets tucked around my shoulders.

A gnawing ache sat in the center of my chest, but it was a pain much deeper than any bruise or broken bone. It made me want to curl back into a ball and shut out the world.

Unfortunately, my bladder reminded me that it would only stretch so far before popping like an overfilled water balloon.

I looked at the open door that led into the personal bathroom. It looked so far away, but I had to go, and I wasn't asking for help.

I bit down hard on my lip to hold in a grunt of pain as I pulled myself slowly up against the pillows. I dragged my legs over the edge of the bed and pressed my feet to the floor. I tested their strength before putting my full weight on them again. I didn't want to smack the tile a second time.

I slid off the bed onto wobbly legs. A searing pain cut through my ribs, and I dropped back onto the mattress. I gripped the blanket with both fists and sucked in a few steady, shallow breaths as I waited for the pain to subside.

When I tried again, I was prepared for my body's objection. I grabbed the pole with my IV bag, squeezing it in a death grip, and made my way to the bathroom one unsteady step at a time.

It wasn't until I was on my way out of the bathroom that I noticed what I'd missed in my single-minded determination to keep my bladder from exploding: stuffed animals, beautiful flowers in sparkling vases, and balloons of every color that read "Get Well Soon" were all over the room. It was like waking up in a flower shop.

I visually inspected the pretty things I would never in my wildest dreams have expected to find in *my* hospital room. So many flowers and teddy bears.

On the food tray next to the bed was a bouquet of freshly cut pink sweet peas, their sugary scent brightening the dark room.

Gee, I wonder who those could be from.

Then I noticed the stack of containers next to the flowers: individual pistachio pudding cups. Jordan had found them . . . twenty-four of them.

I had just picked one up to look at it when someone knocked on the door and opened it. My instinctive fear to hide evaporated when I saw his face, and the pudding dropped from my fingers and splattered open across the floor.

"Sam? But . . . but you're . . ."

Sam arched a black eyebrow and asked someone behind him, "Did no one tell her I'm not dead?"

"We may have overlooked that detail," Marx said from the hallway.

He wasn't dead. I hadn't gotten him killed. I was so overjoyed to see him alive that I cupped my hands over my face and started to cry again.

"Um . . . I think she's . . . crying," Sam said.

Someone sighed, and Marx asked, "What's the matter with you? One foot in the door and you've already made her cry?"

I wiped at my eyes to clear my vision and noticed Marx pushing his way past Sam into the room. He walked over and took me gently by the elbow.

"Come on, peanut. You shouldn't be out of bed." He guided me back to the bed.

Sam and Jordan lingered in the doorway, their attention on me, and I felt abruptly naked. The hospital gown left my legs exposed, and I wanted to put on as many layers as possible to hide in. Marx helped me back into the bed, and I covered myself up to my chest with the blanket.

"You know, seeing you beat up in the hospital once was bad enough," Sam said as he came into the room with a stuffed bear nearly as big as me. He plopped it into the vacant chair beside the bed. "Let's not make a habit of it."

"How are you okay?" I asked.

"I got lucky. There was an ambulance nearby."

"But . . . you . . . you were *just* shot. I don't understand how . . ." How he looked perfectly fine.

Sam glanced at Marx before clarifying, "That was fifteen days ago, Holly."

I blinked in confusion and then remembered what Marx had said: I'd been in a coma for eight days. To me, it felt like Sam had been shot only a couple of days ago, and my captivity with Collin . . . had only been yesterday.

"Oh," I said, because I wasn't sure what else to say.

Four days in captivity, eight days in a coma, and three days of intermittent consciousness that I couldn't remember. Collin had taken fifteen days of my life.

That surreal number tumbled around inside my head.

A hand touched my shoulder and I jumped. Marx pulled back and gave me an apologetic look before turning his attention on Sam and Jordan. "Maybe that's enough company for now."

Sam nodded in understanding before turning back to me. "Thank you for what you did. You risked a lot to keep Drew from killing me and taking Evey. And"—he tucked his hands into the pockets of his jacket—"I'm sorry I couldn't stop Collin from taking you."

There were too many emotions in his eyes for me to read, but I could see anger in the tightness of his lips and regret in the slump of his shoulders.

"Okay, everybody out. Holly needs rest," Marx said, ushering the two of them toward the door. Could he see the exhaustion and weariness weighing on me?

I would've expected to feel rested after eleven straight days of nearly uninterrupted sleep, but I just wanted to curl up and close my eyes.

Jordan glanced at me one last time before following Sam out the door. I shifted down in the bed and tried to find a comfortable position, but everything hurt. Finally, I settled on my left side because it didn't bother my ribs as much.

Marx sat down in the chair with a book. "You want me to read to you for a bit?" He showed me the book: *The Wizard of Oz*.

I had a vague recollection of him reading to me about a woman being smooshed by a house and midgets singing on a yellow brick road. I had thought I dreamed it, but maybe I hadn't.

"If you want," I said indifferently.

He opened the book and started to read, his gentle, Southern voice lulling me to sleep in minutes. I slept a lot over the next few days, and when I wasn't sleeping, I pretended to be. I didn't want to talk to anyone.

I noticed things when people thought I was sleeping. No one ever turned on the overhead light—not even the nurses—they spoke about me in whispers, and I was never alone.

Marx would step out for coffee or for a few hours to go home and shower, but Jordan was always just outside the door. I got the distinct impression they were worried something bad might happen if they left me alone.

Once, in a moment of anger, I told Marx to go away, but he just crossed his arms, leaned back in his chair, and said, "To borrow a phrase from a young lady I care about, you can't make me."

He slept in the room with me, and sometimes I watched him sleep when I couldn't. Other times I pulled open the curtains to peer out at the streetlights and the passing cars. They were beautiful—tiny beacons of light in an ocean of darkness.

Like my security light in the cell.

It was hard to believe I'd only been locked in that room for four days; it had felt like so much longer.

I leaned against the window and watched the lights of the passing cars until I was too tired to stay awake any longer.

I spent most of my days in a state of functional numbness, performing cognitive tests and answering the doctor's questions, but there were pockets of such hope-gulping despair that I would spend hours crying and not even really know why.

Marx tried to console me.

Occasionally he would hold me, and sometimes that was okay—as long as I could escape if I wanted to—but other times I couldn't stand to be touched, and it only made things worse.

I had a feeling not being able to help me was hurting him, but I didn't know how to fix that. I didn't know how to fix anything.

He kept trying to get me to eat, but I had no appetite, not even for pistachio pudding. I preferred to sleep than eat, which had Marx pulling the doctor aside for one of those whispered conversations more than once.

I wanted to go home to my apartment, shower until I'd scrubbed my skin raw, curl up in my bed with my cat and Riley, and hide from the world.

"How is she?" I heard Jordan ask when he thought I was asleep.

"She won't eat, she won't talk to anybody, even me," Marx replied, sounding worried. "She's shuttin' down and all she wants to do is sleep."

"What did the doctor say?"

"He's concerned her poor appetite and lack of responsiveness are due to the trauma she suffered, so he's gonna call in the Crisis Prevention and Response Team to assess her."

"You don't think she would hurt herself, do you?"

"I don't know. She's in a lot of pain right now, both physically and emotionally, and I think she's tryin' to hide from it. But she can't just pretend it didn't happen."

"Beth Anne said she didn't speak to anyone for more than a month after Collin attacked her before. Maybe she's just . . . trying to cope."

"Maybe, but I'm worried."

"I wish they would've just let me kill him," Jordan said, his voice low and hard with anger.

"And then you'd be in prison for murder. You're lucky they didn't arrest you for attempted murder. You nearly strangled him to death in his hospital bed. If Haber and Quinton hadn't pulled you off—"

"Then he'd be dead, and Holly would finally be safe. You can't tell me the thought never crossed your mind."

Marx was silent.

"That psychopath locked her in a dark room for four days, Marx. He beat her. He . . ." Jordan's tight voice trailed off, and he took a breath. "He doesn't deserve to breathe."

"I agree," Marx said. "And yes, in answer to your question, I would've shot him in the warehouse whether he was armed or not."

"He's gonna put her through a trial, isn't he? Just to make her relive it all."

"Probably. But we'll be with her this time."

There was a long silence before Jordan said, "I don't know what to do. Seeing her like this, it's . . ." His voice choked on emotion. "I need to help her, but I just . . . I don't know how."

"Neither do I."

Silent tears spilled onto the pillow as I listened to their conversation, and then I squeezed my eyes shut and tried to sleep again.

37

Snow crystals shimmered like glitter as they fluttered down in the lamplight outside the hospital window. I wished the pane of glass wasn't there; maybe I could reach out and catch them.

But it was a long fall to the pavement below if I lost my balance. I stared down at it, remembering the way Rachel had landed with a sickening thud and the way her life had flowed out of her.

"Holly," a deliberately calm voice called from behind me.

I looked back at the woman who had spoken my name. She sat in a chair beside the bed with a notepad and pen in her hand. She was a member of some crisis team sent here to assess my mental state. Dr. . . . something. Reynolds, maybe? You would think by her fourth visit, I would remember her name, but I didn't.

"What are you thinking about?" she asked.

I looked back down at the sidewalk. If I told her I'd been thinking about falling from a glassless window onto the pavement, she would probably have the doctors sedate me again . . . or lock me up like a crazy person. I'd had enough of being locked up.

"I hear you still haven't eaten," she said.

I didn't understand why everyone was so concerned with my eating habits. I wasn't interested in eating, and that was no one's business but mine.

I didn't respond to her question. I hadn't responded to any of her questions—did I feel safe, was I struggling to come to terms with what happened, did I have any unsettling thoughts or feelings—but she continued to try to pry information from me. Two days of relentless questions without answers should've clued her in that I wasn't going to "open up."

"The way you're feeling, the way you're reacting, is perfectly normal for someone who's been traumatized."

That made me angry. I wasn't some traumatized victim; I was . . . fine.

"People respond to trauma in different ways," she continued. "Some victims lash out or break down, while others close themselves off from the pain because it's the only way they know how to survive. But the thing is, Holly . . ."

I wished she would stop saying my name like she was my friend. I didn't know her and I didn't want to.

"You did survive. You made it through that awful situation and came out on the other side. You don't have to fight to survive anymore." She paused before adding, "Going through what you've been through can leave a person feeling devastated, vulnerable, ashamed, afraid . . ."

In those pockets of despair that overwhelmed me, I felt all those things, and I hated them. They made me feel weak and broken, and I preferred the numbness.

"It's okay to feel those things, Holly. It takes a lot of strength to wade through those emotions, and it doesn't make you weak to feel them. It makes you human."

I shifted my feet uneasily. How had she known what I was thinking?

"I understand that he controlled everything while you were held captive—when you could change your clothes, when and what you ate, when you had a light and when you had only darkness."

I stiffened at the mention of the light. It was a regular fixture in my nightmares, flicking on just before the door opens.

I squeezed my eyes shut against the images, wishing I could wipe them from my mind.

"He has no power over any of that now," she said. "I know you're probably struggling to regain control of your life any way you can, and I imagine being in the hospital doesn't strengthen your sense of control, but hurting yourself by refusing to eat won't help you."

I tugged at the sleeves of the sweater Marx had brought me from his apartment as I considered her words. I still felt nauseous, but maybe I could keep something down, if it meant everyone would leave me alone and I could go home.

"I'd like you to try to eat something—anything you want, whenever you want—before I come back and see you tomorrow," Dr. Reynolds said. "It's your choice, Holly. No one's going to force you, but please do this for yourself."

I wrapped my arms around my stomach and let my gaze drift out the window into the distance. I didn't respond to her suggestion, but I doubted she expected me to. I heard her gather up her belongings and leave the room.

Marx stepped out of the corner where he'd been silently observing the interview and came to stand beside me. "The city's beautiful at night."

I glanced up at him.

He was so exhausted. He hadn't gone home to sleep since I woke up, and I knew the hospital chairs had to be uncomfortable. He looked terrible. Not that I had much room to talk.

"I know it doesn't feel like it," he began. "But it will get better, sweetheart. It's just gonna take some time. The bruises will fade, and everythin' that happened in that place will become a less painful memory."

I blinked back tears, and my throat tightened against words. I wanted to tell him I would remember every detail of that awful experience for the rest of my life, and it would never stop hurting.

I remembered every moment that man had ever hurt me, and no amount of time or words could ever erase those scars.

But I was afraid if I opened my mouth to tell him that, all the pain would come spilling out, and I wouldn't be able to stop it. I closed my eyes and fought the emotions that threatened to send me spiraling into another trench of despair.

I leaned against Marx, craving the feeling of safety and security he offered.

He moved his arm slowly—as if afraid he might scare me away—and then wrapped it around my shoulders, tucking me against his side. "I'm gonna be with you every step of the way, sweetheart. You're not alone in this, okay?"

I stared out the window, his words resonating through me in the stretch of peaceful silence that followed. For a long while, he simply held me, and I listened to the soothing rhythm of his heart beating in his chest.

His voice was barely above a whisper when he spoke again. "Now that Collin's . . ." I tensed at the name as it sent an unexpected pang of fear through me. Marx's breath caught for a moment and then he began again. "Now that *he's* behind bars, I reckon you're gonna want to move back to your apartment, but I'd like you to stay with me, at least for a few weeks."

The invitation surprised me. Even though he said he loved me like a daughter, I never expected him to want me to stay. I'd been nothing but trouble for him. But when I tipped my head back to search his face, I saw only desperate hope and worry.

"Please," he said. "I know you've been through a lot these past few months, and you just wanna get back on your feet, but . . . please stay and let me help you."

His apartment had begun to feel like a second home to me, and truthfully I would feel safer there. I nodded, and he let out a relieved breath that ruffled my hair.

"Okay, I'm gonna talk to the doctors and see when we can get you out of here." He kissed the top of my head before pulling away, and I didn't flinch this time.

I watched from the window as he opened the door to leave, and a large German shepherd nearly plowed him over trying to make it past him.

"Riley," he scolded.

Riley barreled across the room toward me, his tongue flopping happily and his leash—well, half of it—trailing across the floor between his feet.

He stopped inches short of taking my legs out from under me and whined as he pranced in place with excitement. I lowered myself gingerly to the floor and hugged his head.

It was good to see him.

He licked me like he was trying to memorize my face with his tongue. For the first time in weeks, I felt myself smiling. I loved this dog.

"Stupid dog," Jace exclaimed as she wheeled into the room. I looked up to see her throw her broken half of the leash on the floor.

The first night I met Riley, he'd broken his leash to come rescue me. He was up to his old habits again.

Jace stopped at the foot of the bed, and I could see the tears welling in her eyes from across the room. This was the first time I'd seen her since waking from the coma. I'd heard her voice in the hall a couple of times, but Marx and Jordan had told her I needed to rest, and hadn't let her in.

"Oh, Holly." She wheeled over to hug me—her embrace oddly gentle, like I was an egg that might crack under the slightest pressure—and cried into my hair. "I was so scared."

Guilt twisted my heart. I was the reason her life had been in danger to begin with, and she'd experienced something no one should ever have to.

She pulled back and looked me over, her face shining with tears. "Don't ever do that to me again. Don't you ever almost die and end up in a coma. That's what happened to Scott, but he never woke up, and I thought . . . I can't lose you too, Holly. I can't."

I hadn't even thought about how my coma might have affected her. With everything that happened to Scott, it must have been terrifying for her.

"From now on, you're not allowed to get anything worse than a hangnail," she informed me. "Not even a paper cut." Riley tried to lick the tears from her face, and she swatted at him. "Stop that."

He snorted at her rejection and leaned against me, his weight nearly knocking me over.

"I brought some movies and popcorn, and some packets of hot chocolate with extra marshmallows, you know, in case you feel like eating something."

My stomach turned at the mere thought of food.

"I know you don't eat anything when you're stressed, but Holly, you have to . . . you have to try. You're . . ." She sucked her bottom lip into her mouth as her eyes welled with fresh tears. She tucked her dark locks behind her ears and dried her face. "I promised Sam I wouldn't lecture you, so . . . let's just watch the movie, okay?"

Sam had made her promise that? Sam the lecturer? Well, there was a prime example of the time-honored adage "Do as I say, not as I do."

I climbed back into my bed and curled up on my left side again, while Jace parked her chair beside me. She stayed for most of the night, and we watched movies on the DVD player Sam had hooked up.

We didn't talk; I think she realized I didn't want to, but she held my hand the entire time. Riley stretched out at my feet and lifted his head every hour or so to make sure I was still there.

Dr. Reynolds came back to see me in the morning, and I overheard her discussion with Marx in the hallway after our session. Apparently, she was concerned about my emotional state and didn't think I should be discharged just yet. She recommended a psychiatric facility.

Marx assured her he would watch over me, and if I was still refusing to eat in the next three days, he would bring me back. I didn't want to have to come back here. She begrudgingly agreed to his terms and gave him her business card to pass along to me.

38

The car ride home with Marx was comfortably quiet. He didn't glance my way every thirty seconds to make sure I was okay, and he didn't pepper me with questions.

When we finally walked into his apartment and I looked around the familiar space, a small sliver of tension fell away from me.

Safe, my mind whispered.

I heard Marx's quiet exhale as I retreated into the bathroom and locked the door, but he didn't say anything. I turned on the water before stripping out of my clothes.

A pale, starving wraith stared back at me from the mirror above the bathroom sink, her skeletal frame painted in dark purple bruises and fading scars. But the mirror couldn't reflect the deepest wounds, the ones that marked her spirit.

The woman looked . . . haunted and defeated, and my mind struggled to come to terms with the fact that she was me.

It's gonna be okay, I told my reflection. *We'll survive this. We always survive.*

I turned away from the mirror and stepped into the steaming hot shower. I let the scalding water melt away his fingerprints, cleansing every inch of skin he had touched.

I used every last drop of soap to scrub myself until my skin felt raw, but I still didn't feel clean. When I climbed back into the shower two hours later to try again, there was a fresh bottle of soap in the shower.

Marx.

I wrote a little note and left two dollars, thanking him, before sneaking back into my room and curling up in bed with Riley. I didn't sleep, but I had no desire to do anything other than lie there.

A paper slid under my door, and, curious, I got up to see what it was. It was a folded note with my two dollars inside that read "I don't want your money. Stop it. And I'd like it if you joined me for dinner. P.S. there are . . ."

What did that say?

I squinted at the word. *Mashmollws?* Oh. Marshmallows.

He had horrendous handwriting.

I sat back on my legs as I considered the invitation. I didn't feel like eating. I scribbled a reply with my left hand, since my right wrist was still in a cast—it looked nearly as bad as his writing—and nudged it back under the door.

I hadn't realized he was sitting in the hallway until the paper reappeared in front of me a second later. Beneath my response of "No thanks, not hungry," he'd written, "Yes you are. Just because we're having a conversation through a door doesn't mean I can't tell when you're trying to lie."

I wrote back "not lying."

"Mmm hmm. I'd at least like to see your fa[squiggle]."

I frowned as I tried to figure out the last word. Finally, I wrote back "See my what?"

The paper shot back under the door. At the bottom in huge, exaggerated letters was the word "FACE."

Oh. I smiled a little.

I pushed the pen and paper aside and opened the door. Marx was seated on the floor, his back propped against the bathroom door, with a plate of French fries, a Swiss roll, and a bowl of chocolate marshmallows on a plate in his lap.

So much for the well-rounded meals he was always trying to make me eat. I scooted to the edge of the doorway, and he stayed where he was.

The worry clouding his green eyes belied the casual nature of his voice as he said, "It's about time. I thought I was gonna have to write a book to get you to open the door."

I folded my arms over my stomach when he tried to offer me the plate of food.

He lowered it back to his lap. "Sweetheart, please." He looked desperate. "If you don't eat, you're gonna keep losin' weight, and you're gonna need to be hospitalized again."

None of my clothes fit anymore; they were all too big, but I didn't mind. That just made them easier to hide in.

"If you won't eat somethin' for yourself, please do it for me," he pleaded, and I thought I saw a faint sheen of tears in his eyes. "Even if it's just a little bit. Please."

I didn't want to cause him any more pain than I already had. I was just going to have to force the food down. I scooted across the hall floor and sat against the wall beside him.

He didn't try to touch me, and he was careful to move slowly when he offered me the plate. I knew he wouldn't hurt me, but sometimes my mind was trapped in that warehouse, and I flinched instinctively if he moved too quickly.

I picked up a marshmallow and stared at it in my palm. Ordinarily, I would've been excited by marshmallows, but no appetite stirred at the sight of it. I popped it into my mouth and swallowed.

I ate the marshmallows mechanically, but they made my stomach hurt. Every last one of them came back up. Maybe solid food was a bad idea.

A couple of hours later, Marx knocked on my door and waited in the hallway with a bowl of chicken broth and a few crackers.

Riley sat perfectly still beside me as he eyed the bowl of broth. I sipped it down with a spoon until I could see the bottom of the bowl, and then set the rest on the floor for him. He greedily attacked the bowl, knocking it into the hallway walls with his snout.

Marx woke me up every couple of hours, even in the middle of the night, with something else he wanted me to eat. I wished he would stop, but I doubted he would even if I asked. The more I ate,

359

the more the stress lines around his eyes softened, so I ate whatever soup he prepared.

One day quickly became indistinguishable from the next: I showered, slept, and ate every few hours for what felt like an endless stretch of time.

Eventually Marx decided it was safe for me to try solid food again. "The protein will do you good."

He offered me the plate with a peanut butter and jelly sandwich on it, and my stomach lurched. The smell brought back memories of stale peanut butter sandwiches and of the apple slices dipped in peanut butter that Collin had forced me to eat despite the pain in my stomach.

I barely made it to the toilet before I vomited, and that was the last time Marx offered me peanut butter anything.

The next time I woke up, it wasn't because he was nagging me to eat. I jerked upright in bed with cold sweat beaded across my body, and I knew by the raw, scratchy feeling in my throat that I had been screaming in my sleep.

Sometimes, after one of those particularly intense nightmares, I could hear Marx pacing restlessly in the hallway. Most of the dreams faded away upon waking, but some left me shaking and sobbing into Riley's fur for nearly an hour afterward. It was in one of those moments that my last real conversation with Beth Anne resurfaced in my mind:

Holly, I don't know why I feel like I should tell you this, but . . . sometimes life catches us by surprise and bad things, sometimes heart-crushing things, happen, and it's hard to get back up after that. But just remember that God is in the darkness with you, waiting to lead you out of it if only you take His hand. Know that you're loved and you're never alone.

She'd known. Somehow, even then, before everything had fallen apart, Beth Anne had known I would need those words. God had known. I couldn't get back up on my own this time, but I didn't have to, because I wasn't alone.

I didn't really know what day it was when I finally wandered out of my room into the kitchen. I slid silently onto one of the peninsula stools while Marx prepared breakfast. It smelled like pancakes with . . . blueberries.

My stomach gave its first rumble of hunger in quite some time. I had been able to keep soups and crackers down for . . . however long it had been. But this was the first real sign of my appetite returning.

Marx flipped a little pancake onto one plate and then a stack of larger ones onto another plate. He turned around with the plates in his hands and blinked in surprise when he found me sitting at the counter.

"Hey, peanut." He glanced back down the hall like he expected me to bolt back into my room at any second.

I didn't move.

He set the plates on the counter and asked, "Mind if I sit beside you?"

I shrugged, and he took the stool next to me. He seemed both relieved and pleased to see me out of my room, and I was glad I could do something to ease his worry.

Apart from insisting I eat regularly, he hadn't pushed me to heal faster; he'd given me space and time, but he was always there when I needed him. That meant more to me than I could ever express.

"These aren't exactly my mama's pancakes, but I did try," he said.

Mama . . .

Memories so thin and foggy that they might have been pieces of a fading dream rather than a memory drifted through my mind: *God doesn't wanna hear from me, Mama. I've rejected Him more times than I can count.*

Marx had turned away from God after all the darkness he'd seen in his line of work. I stared hard at my pancake as I tried to remember the rest of his words, but they were so slippery.

God . . . if you have a minute . . . I realize I have no right to ask you for favors . . .

I looked up at Marx, who was watching me with concern. "You prayed." My voice sounded rusty from lack of use.

Marx's eyebrows inched upward. I wasn't sure what surprised him more: that I had finally spoken or that I had heard him pray while I was in a coma. "Heard that, did you?"

I nodded.

He poured syrup onto my pancake and then poured some onto his. "I did pray. I prayed every day for God to heal you, and I'm still prayin'."

"But . . . you don't even like God."

"But I *love* you," he said without hesitation. "And I would do anythin' to keep you safe, Holly, includin' settin' aside my differences with God. We will never agree on everythin', but nobody ever does."

He'd reconnected with God . . . for me. I didn't even know how to express how that made me feel.

"Eat your breakfast before it gets cold," he said.

At a loss for words, I picked up my fork and cut into my pancake. I paused with the bite halfway to my mouth when I heard a floorboard creak. My heart thumped harder as my eyes darted to the front door.

The sound of footsteps coming closer sent panic burning across the edges of my nerves. A series of thumps on the outside of the door had me dropping my fork and backing against the wall.

"It's okay," Marx said, and I saw him stand slowly in my peripheral vision, but I couldn't pull my eyes away from the door. "It's just somebody knockin'."

What if he was out there? What if . . . if he came back to break in again? I didn't know whether to run for my life or hide. All I could seem to do was tremble.

"It's not him on the other side of the door, sweetheart. He's still in jail."

"How do you know he's still in jail? What if he got out? He got out before, and he—"

"He didn't get out."

"You don't know that. You can't know that!"

"Holly, I promise you it's not him. You're safe here with me. Okay? You're safe." He wrapped his arms around me, drawing me into a hug, and I could feel the rumble of his voice against my cheek as he said, "I won't let anybody hurt you ever again."

The pounding on the door stopped abruptly, and I could hear the rapid thud of my heart in the silence. I buried my face in Marx's chest to hide my tears and let the familiar scent of his cologne wash over me and calm my shaking nerves.

"Even if he had gotten out, this is the last place he would come," Marx assured me. "That would be a good way to get a bullet in the head, and he doesn't have a death wish."

I didn't think he was bluffing about shooting him, not after the conversation I heard between him and Jordan at the hospital. I drew in another long, shaky breath and let the remnants of my fear drift away.

Whoever was at the door had either left or was patiently waiting for someone to answer, something Marx seemed to be in no hurry to do.

"You okay?" he asked.

I nodded as best as I could while he had me wrapped up like a present. "You can let go now."

He released me with obvious reluctance, and I fumbled back onto my stool, feeling humiliated and foolish for my reaction. "I'm sorry. I didn't mean to . . ."

"You have nothin' to apologize for," he said gently. "Okay?" He waited for my nod before saying, "I'm gonna see who's at the door."

I watched stiffly as he walked to the door. He peered through the peephole and then unbolted the door, pulling it inward a few inches.

A quiet male voice from the hallway asked, "Did I scare her?"

"Yes. I told you to give her a few weeks," Marx replied tightly.

"It's been two. I just wanted to see how she's doing."

Marx sighed and stepped aside with a halfhearted wave of his hand. "Well, come on in then."

Jordan stepped through the doorway, and the muscles in my body tightened. I didn't want to see him. Despite everything Marx had tried to explain, I didn't want him here right now.

He paused just inside the door, and his blue eyes looked sad as he fixed them on me. "Hi, Holly."

I glanced at my room, contemplating a quick escape.

"I'm not here to make you uncomfortable," he said, stepping in to let Marx close the door. "I just wanted to see how you're doing. You look . . . good."

I folded my arms over myself and shifted uneasily on my stool. I didn't want him looking at me. I didn't want anyone looking at me.

Marx leaned into him and whispered something too softly for me to hear. Jordan listened and then cleared his throat. "I mean you look healthier. You, um . . . have some of your color back."

I watched him as he walked slowly to the couch and sat down on the arm of it to face me. An uneasy silence hung between us.

"How have you been?" he asked.

I pressed my lips together, holding in the words that wanted to escape.

He glanced at Marx when I said nothing, and then tried again. "I know you're upset and you're hurting, and—"

"I'm angry," I clarified, and he fell quiet. The pain and anger I had tried to keep tightly tucked away spilled free. "I'm angry with myself for staying when I knew I should leave. I'm angry that I listened to you, to any of you, when you told me I would be safe. I knew better, but I hoped . . ." I wrestled back my tears and looked at the window. "I wanted to believe things would be different this time."

364

No one spoke as I gathered my breath to continue.

"I told Sam that none of you would be here to protect me when he finally came for me, and you weren't. He and Marx had a good reason, but where were you?"

I caught Jordan's barely perceptible flinch out of the corner of my eye. He'd been sitting in a jail cell because he let himself be baited, because he lost his temper.

The emotions were so thick in my throat that I could barely speak. "I . . . needed you."

He squeezed his eyes shut, pain etched into every line of his face. "I'm so sorry, Holly."

I looked back at the window as a trembling breath escaped my lungs. "Why are you here, Jordan?"

"Because you're my friend, and I care about you."

All he wants from you is the same thing every other warm-blooded male wants. He's just biding his time until you give in.

"I know he said some things about me that make you doubt that," Jordan said, his fingers tightening into fists in his lap. "I can see it on your face when you look at me. But I'm not that person, Holly. I would never do those things. Do I think you're beautiful? Absolutely. But that's not why I'm here, and that's not why I care."

I wanted to believe him, but I didn't know what to believe anymore.

"You remember when Marx told me about your past?" he asked.

My gaze flitted to the hole in the wall that Jordan had made when he threw a table into it out of anger.

"I asked you that day to let me be your friend, and if that's all that ever develops between us, then I'm happy."

"So you don't want . . . more?"

He sighed and rubbed the back of his hair. "If there ever comes a day when you wanna explore that, I certainly won't say no. I can't deny that. But if that day *never* comes, I'm more than okay with that. I have the friendship I've wanted for eighteen years, and I

365

wouldn't give that up for anything. Certainly not for one night of lust. I told you before that I don't ever wanna hurt you, and that's all that one night would accomplish. But more than that, I don't ever wanna lose you, Holly."

I didn't know what to say to that.

I twisted and stretched the sleeves of my sweater as I stared down at my legs, trying to work it all out in my mind. I was tired and confused, and I didn't want to think about it anymore. I hopped off the stool and went into the bathroom to take another shower.

Jordan was gone when I came out, but he came back every day for a Marx-supervised visit. Sometimes we didn't speak, and he just sat in the room with me. Other times we watched a movie or he read to me. He had a nice reading voice.

He brought me chocolates and doughnuts to fatten me up, and sometimes he brought groceries. Marx didn't want to leave me alone to go grocery shopping, and even thinking about leaving the apartment sent my anxiety spiking to dangerous levels.

I was safer inside.

Everything bad had happened outside.

I knew it would probably take a long time to mend my friendship with Jordan, but slowly I began to enjoy his company again. And even more slowly, the wounds inside and out began to heal.

Maybe things would be okay after all.

Epilogue

*T*here were butterflies tap-dancing on my nerve endings as Jordan pulled his car into the unfamiliar parking lot.

After a month of refusing to set foot outside of Marx's apartment, I had finally managed to leave the property without being leveled by a panic attack.

The first three attempts had been a disaster. I hadn't even made it out of the apartment the first time before everything blurred into a haze of terror and confusion. The next thing I knew, my head was resting on a pillow in Marx's lap, and he was whispering soothing words to me while stroking my hair.

The second one had left me curled up in the shower for hours, and the third . . . well, Mrs. Neberkins, Marx's elderly neighbor across the hall, had called the police again when I started screaming.

This abandoned-looking building, which was about four blocks from Marx's place, was the furthest I'd ventured since conquering some of my anxiety, which . . . made me anxious. Being alone with Jordan didn't help matters either.

Our relationship was healing, but I still felt uncomfortable around him. He seemed conscious of my need for space, though, because he gave me five feet of it whenever possible. I knew it must hurt him to take that step back, but he concealed it well.

He came around the car to open my door. "M'lady," he said with a gallant wave of his arm.

I stepped out into the cool spring morning and looked around the parking lot before fixing my attention on the building I was pretty sure used to be an old medical clinic.

"Where are we?" I asked.

"It doesn't actually have a name yet." He closed the passenger door and then walked ahead of me to the building. He unlocked a metal grate and slid it up, revealing a flimsy front door and two windows. He opened the door, flipped a switch, and stepped back. "After you."

Hesitant, I stepped into the building. I looked around at the hideous yellow walls streaked with water stains and the florescent strip lights on the tiled ceiling. There were chairs and end tables that reminded me of a doctor's waiting room, and several closed doors that might have been exam rooms at one time.

"What is this place?" I flinched when I heard the door close behind us.

Jordan left it unlocked, reminding me I was free to leave if I wanted to. "It's my place. I'm leasing it."

"Why . . . would you wanna live here?"

He smiled. "I don't. I'm gonna work here."

I frowned in confusion. "But it's a medical clinic, and you're not a doctor."

"Hey, I can take a temperature as good as the next male nurse, but I was planning on solving crimes and finding missing people rather than asking people to say *ah*."

"Finding missing people?"

"Yeah." He perched on the edge of one of the chairs. "When you were . . . taken, I thought we would never find you."

I swallowed the emotions tightening my throat. I hadn't thought they would find me either.

"People disappear every day," he continued. "But there just aren't enough resources to find them. Cops have too many cases, and people stop caring when the media moves on. Some people disappear and aren't even reported missing."

I sank onto a chair on the opposite side of the room as I listened.

"Every single person matters, and no one should simply disappear. No one should ever have to think, *no one's looking for me*."

I had thought that, but I couldn't have been more wrong. I knew now that Marx and Jordan had spent every possible moment of those four days searching for me.

"No one should have to feel that gut-clenching fear and uncertainty when someone they care about vanishes. So I wanna do what I can to help find those people."

"What if they don't wanna be found?" For years, I had survived by disappearing, and I hadn't wanted to be found.

"People don't typically *want* to disappear unless they're hiding. If they're hiding from themselves, there's nothing we can do for them, but if they're hiding from an abusive spouse or lover, or from a bad situation they've gotten into, we can help."

Puzzled, I asked, "We?"

"Yeah, that's one of the reasons I brought you here. I resigned my position as sheriff in Stony Brooke and—"

That news shocked me so much I interrupted him. "Resigned? Why?"

He smiled mysteriously. "I have my reasons. Anyway, I got my private investigator's license, so legally I can investigate. But I could use some help." He stood and gestured for me to follow him. "Let me show you something."

He led me to the furthest door, opened it, and flipped the light switch. A strand of lights ignited on the ceiling, and they twinkled like fireflies in the night. They were enchanting.

I stared up at them—tiny beacons in the darkness—and tears pooled in my eyes. "How did you know?"

"Sometimes I cracked the hospital door at night to check on you, and you were almost always staring out the window at the lights of the passing cars. I took a guess that you might like these."

"I love them."

My gaze wandered around the rest of the room, taking in the eggplant-purple walls, the white desk with a purple laptop, a photo printer, a shelf lined with books, and a fluffy chair that looked like it might swallow me whole. It was a warm, inviting space, and I wanted to curl up in the chair with a book.

"Why are you showing me this?" I asked.

He leaned a shoulder against the wall and said, "Well you see, the thing is, I can't run the business on my own. I need a partner. I'm pretty particular about who I work with though. I'm hoping for a female partner, red hair, soulful brown eyes, about . . . yea high." He put out a hand to measure the supposed woman's height, and she looked about five feet tall.

"You might have a hard time finding a redhead that short," I said, tapping my lips with a finger.

He grinned, and it brought out his dimples. It had been a while since I saw that smile. "I think I might know where to find one."

I folded my arms. "Don't look at me. I'm five foot two."

"Yeah, I thought we might hit this little snag." He grabbed a long stick I hadn't noticed resting against the wall and set it in front of him. "I brought a measuring stick, so let's see if you measure up for the job."

I smirked and shook my head. "I'm not letting you measure me with a stick."

"That's okay. I already know you're five one."

I pressed my shoulders back and corrected, "Five one and a quarter."

"Oh, so you admit you're not five two."

I scrunched my nose at him, and he grinned. I looked back into the office at all the nice things and the beautiful lights. "So, is this a bribe?"

"No, this is your office if you say yes, or just a cozy place for you to come hang out and read if you say no."

I couldn't believe he was offering me a job at his detective agency. I couldn't believe he *had* a detective agency.

"Where did all the stuff come from?" Surely, he didn't have that kind of money lying around.

"Well, aside from all the money I've saved up for the past ten years in Stony Brooke, my parents—mainly my mom since my dad and I aren't on speaking terms at the moment—wanted to help out. I also got a start-up business loan."

Wow.

"What does Marx think?"

"That it's a bad idea," a Southern voice said, and I turned to see Marx coming through the door. "I don't relish the thought of you bein' involved with missin' persons cases or people in trouble."

"It's not like I'm gonna send her to go question a pimp or drug dealer by herself, Marx. When we do investigative work, the plan is for me to be with her."

"Right, because things always go accordin' to plan when little Ms. Independent's involved," Marx grumbled sarcastically. He pulled a small, sparkly box from his pocket and handed it to me. "I had somethin' made for you."

Ooh, presents. I liked presents. I opened the package slowly and gasped at the beautiful silver bracelet. It had little charms on it: a cat, a dog, a camera, a rainbow, and a little pair of running shoes.

It was the prettiest thing anyone had ever given me, and I didn't know what to say. I lifted it from the box and realized it was huge. "I'm not sure this will fit my wrist."

Well, maybe with the cast on. I was supposed to have gotten it off two days ago, but I also wasn't supposed to get it wet . . . which was like some kind of contortionist exercise when I took five showers a day. Some days, the better days, I only took two. This was a better day.

Marx smiled. "It's for your ankle. Let me help you with it."

I handed it to him, and he crouched down in front of me. I stood stiffly as he nudged up my pant leg and wrapped the cool bracelet around my left ankle.

"There." He lowered my pant leg back down. "There's a charm on here that has a small GPS tracker in it, but it's not activated. Whether or not you activate it is entirely your decision, but if you decide to and somethin' happens, we'll be able to find you."

By *something*, he meant if I was abducted again. I had a feeling the tracker was as much for his comfort as it was for mine. The trial was coming up, and if . . . *he*—I couldn't even bring myself to think his name—was found not guilty, he would come after me again.

I tried not to think about that as I asked, "It would only be for emergencies?" Because I didn't like the idea of people always being able to find me.

"I promise," he said. "None of us would ever use it to infringe on your privacy."

I would have to give it some thought.

"So, about the job," Jordan said, bringing the conversation back around.

I looked at Marx for advice.

"Whatever you decide, I'll do my best to support it," he said.

"Are you gonna want me to make you coffee?" I asked Jordan.

"Um, assuming the rumors I hear are true, why don't you leave the coffee making to me?"

"Wise decision," Marx commented.

I did tend to murder the coffee.

I chewed on my lip as I considered the offer. The weather was warming up, and I would be able to take portraits in the parks again, but that took up very little time. I could get paid to snoop and take pictures of things besides people. It was awfully tempting . . .

"I can't work in a place with pee-yellow walls," I decided.

Jordan held up a finger as he walked away and then came back with a tub of slate-blue paint, a paint tray, and three rollers. "I wasn't planning on keeping them yellow." He offered a paint roller to each of us.

Marx sighed, stripped out of his jacket, and rolled up his sleeves. "Well, let's get started."

I grinned and tossed my jacket aside. It was a good thing I had opted to wear my paint-splattered overalls when I rolled out of bed this morning . . .

Author's Note

We all have a past—mistakes, trauma, loss, failures—that sometimes comes back to haunt us. It can blindside us, leaving us overwhelmed and reeling from the impact.

Collin is the personification of that past for Holly. He is the inner voice that whispers her insecurities: you're not good enough, you're unlovable, you're a failure, you're broken. He is the force that tries to tear her down—physically, spiritually, and emotionally.

That force isn't always a physical one for everyone. Sometimes it's a regret, a bad circumstance or habit, an illness, or the voices of cruelty echoing through your mind long after the sources are gone.

In our lowest moments, it seems impossible to fight that force. It feels bigger and stronger than we could ever be, and it feels like a hopeless battle. But you know what? God's bigger.

You put God in a ring with whatever pain or trouble you're battling, and He will win that fight every time. God is bigger than anything this world can throw at you (and it *will* throw some punches in your direction), and when our God is with us, who or what can possibly stand against us?

You may not always see God or know how He's working, but no matter what you're going through, He's always with you. He's the light in the darkness, the hope reaching out a hand and waiting for you to take it.

God will place people in your life who will love you and lift you up—a friend, a church family, a relative, sometimes even a stranger.

Holly comes to this realization at the end of this book. She learns that no matter how her past tries to bind and define her, no matter how many times it rises up and tries to bring her down, she is never alone, and she is loved.

My hope for you is that if you're battling some kind of darkness right now (a physical, spiritual, or emotional Collin), you know that you're not alone. And you don't have to let that darkness define you. Jesus makes all things new; let Him redefine you.

You are beautifully and wonderfully made.

How to Connect

Facebook: https://www.facebook.com/ccwarrens
Website: https://www.ccwarrensbooks.com/
Email: ccwarrens@yahoo.com

Stay tuned for C. C. Warrens's next book, *Injustice for All*, featuring
Detective Marx.

CPSIA information can be obtained
at www.ICGtesting.com
Printed in the USA
LVHW041952061120
670968LV00004B/721